Written to Toil

Musab Momany

Edited by Muna Hamza

ISBN: 0692347860
ISBN-13: 978-0692347867 (M.M Ltd.)

Library of Congress Control Number: 2014921873

Acknowledgement...

Special thanks to the editor who paid a great deal of effort on revising and editing this work.

Musab Momany

*Edited and revised by
Muna T. Hamza*

DEDICATION

TO WHOM WHOSE EXISTANCE WAS A WIND STORMING MY LIFES' STEADY LEAVES...

TO WHOM WHO FLIPPED MY LITTLE HEART WITH HER FINGERS BETWEEN GUIDANCE AND LOSS; APPEALING ALWAYS TO KEEP HERSELF IN DISGUISE...

TO YOU, MY LOVE,
I PRESENT MY EARLY THROE OF WORK...

MUSAB MOMANY

CONTENTS

"YOU SPOILED ME WITH LOVE.. THAT I AM NO LONGER GOOD FOR A THING ELSE.."

ZEYAD AL JUNEIDY

"YOU SHOULDN'T HAVE COME OVER!!
YOU SHOULDN'T HAVE RE-AWAKENED THAT FEMALE INSIDE ME AGAIN; HOWEVER YOU DID, AND RELEASED YOUR BRIDLED LOVER, THEN RELISH THE FLAVOR OF THE WOMAN YOU LOVED, AND WOE TO BOTH OF US FROM AN EVIL THAT IS SURELY COMING CLOSE."

SUZAN AL AHMAD

"It's not death that a man should fear, but he should fear never beginning to live".

Marcus Aurelius

~ 1 ~

I had this stinging thought in my mind that if I visit him at an early morning hour, he and I will be in seclusion together, with uninterrupted talk. It was very early, with the dormant death mastering the moment in that place. Odorous embalm and camphor is smelled everywhere with the flimsy blown breath of air, adding to a tightened heart a sense of missing. One's unconscious is being slapped to get awakened to the now certain moment. Moving by the tombs along the cemetery's doorway, praying for peace on souls of the dead, suddenly a kneeling woman dressed in black loomed not too far pouring tears on a tomb. A few steps were sufficient to recognize her. I didn't mistake her. She was not but his wife *Sura*, sadly weeping, sobbing, and rolling in the dust around the tomb. When she finally felt my existence within her space, she gazed at me with her red-eyed, pale, and ghost-looking face. The closer I got to her, the more doubted she became. She was as if questioning who I was to cry so badly and sadly and be such a jealous from her tears while glancing to his tomb near her. Even in such a place a woman cannot be less than a fiercely jealous female once another woman competes on her missing love. Forgive me darling, for her and your sons' sake I shall erase you of her memory, even if that was killing for her now.

- A second wife?

She asked in a wounded voice, as if now dying.

- Wasn't such a lucky.

I answered.

She stared at my pregnancy boom as if asking "That.. Son of whom!"; an instant reply flew from my mouth to comfort her doubts and suspicions.

- None he had except from you. I replied.

For a while, she seemed wrathful and befuddled as if hardly attempting to inquire who I am. I wanted to mercy-kill her and relieve her painful hardship:

- That grave belongs to me. And that mourning, which will prolong, is mine.

I moved a step towards her to kneel beside the tomb, and gently touched the tombstones and pebbles.

- Wasn't it enough pleasure for you that you snatched the dearest moments of his life time?!

She asked while embracing a handful of tomb dust in her hand, and clenching her teeth.

- It is a promise that I shall never break. I will keep his memory alive forever.

- Go away! Don't commit a double sin of taking him away from his children and wife!! In his life and death, for God's sake?!

She asked in shock.

- "Be the last ever whom I see with my eyes, the last ever who forgets me, and the one who meets me there first." he once whispered to me.

Instantly, she quivered with her dusty dress staring at me for a while, and then ran hastily crying.

My fingers were penetrating deep into the dust. My body was trembling timidly with silence, sadness, and cry. It is my turn now to experience the life of missing, darling, to get used to the thrill of your evocation as you used to do, until days conjoin us together again. I don't know whether I could be good enough in writing and telling stories just like you were. But those events are still memorable and vividly living in my mind as if they happened yesterday. Whatever ideas born in your mind that are unknown to me I know they were elaborately created in your writings and diaries, thereby with them I shall begin.

*****

"I was never really insane except upon occasions when my heart was touched"

Edgar Allen Poe

~2~

"Sweet Suzan..

How would you like my first letter to be? Would you like it written with drips of ink? Or tears? Or an album of photos and kisses? You might think it didn't take that long since your absence, knowing not how torturous is the emptiness and wailing I live with every day and night. One day you will realize that my unsalable longings have nothing to do with time. Darling, my meter is an inscribed memory, foretelling, astrological insights, certainty, and metaphysical knowing of dates that "have been coming soon"!! Yes, not to say "are coming"; we were taught in language that the absolute belief of future could always be evoked as past... and I have a date with you. It is not your farness which kills me the most.., neither those distances which stand between you and me. It is indeed the loving and longing to be the Kohl on your eyelids.., the fragrance of your chest.., the tender breaths of air playing with the hair wisps of yours.., as once you described me.

How can I forget your delicate touches, the looks replete with warm love.., your genuine tears and unbelievable whispers, those seducing acts, those rebellious dances and moments of feebleness, the fever of intermixed breathes, thirsty kisses, and being dwelled in each other? That madness of you..!!

Who else loved and caressed the soft, barely visible hair on your right cheek? Who else other than me touched the lovely scar on your left eyelid? Who else had been ever excitedly thrilled with the lovely mole at the far corner of your right eye? Who else counted the moles and birthmarks in you, and pleasantly inhaled and tasted everything in you other than I?

Your hair, your fingertips, palms, arms, forehead, eyes, tears, nose, cheeks, lips.., your delicious saliva, your chin, neck, ears, chest, breasts, buttocks, legs, toes, and everything in you I am obsessed with, caused me this madness. The handsome costume, magical perfume, the glorious halo, your confident steps, majestic presence, the courteous talk as delicate as a kiss.., that remarkable maneuvering in argument, converse, and referring to a broad knowledge-base of wisdom, Quran, Hadith, Sunna, retrospective *Ijtihad*, your receptiveness to opinions of others, equity and advocacy of others, your sociability, and having all anecdotes wrapped in those ironically biting folk proverbs, all of that and more, my sweetheart, is the springing fountain wherefrom I've sucked my madness in you.

Who else knows you more than I do? This is not a six-year love story, not the count of restaurants we had been to together, nor it is the number of cafés that witnessed our promises. It's rather a tale of frenzied love, and a blind trust that nothing could change you. I trust you. One like you could only be a lover or nothing at all. I will never only mean to you that phone caller coming over the air.., or just a pleasant past moment remembered when life exhausts you with its plights. I am instead, your dreamed wish of me being there on your couch, playing with your tufts, and whispering in your ear my song of love. I might be one of the passers by your neighborhood. You will see me in every face. I will always be there around you. When you dress up I will be there. When you put on your jewelry, style your hair, I will be there to mirror in words how beautiful you are, even more than a colorful butterfly. I will stay silent at make-up time, as you dislike the presence of others at that moment, and we will have coffee together in the evening; "Abu Soboh's" coffee, which you prefer most.

I am here to be yours, owned by you, closer than you would imagine. Search for me underneath your white dress, over your roseate cushion, on your left ring finger, behind your papers, among your bottles of the *"Euphoria"* and *"Ja'dore"*, at your balcony, on your tanned body, whereat traces of my kisses are still visibly hanged on memory; seen, smelled, tasted, and touched by you. The resounding echo is heard in your ear that makes you about to say my name whenever you want to call your "soul mate"; as once said Ahlam Mestghanmi: "your five senses are readily harnessed day and night to defend him, calling you to bring him from the sky, or from underneath ground".

Dormant inside you wherever and whenever you are; in your clear or gloomy mood, in storm and in quietness, and in your ins and outs of rationality. In your yesterday I was, and started our tale together, in your present I am with you, by retrospection of our past days and the hope in our promising tomorrow, and in your tomorrow I will be, waiting to renew a love story that took us away from predestinations, but still alive in us. Nothing is more lasting than an inscription made in memory, and a dream wherein we live or die for until it comes true and elaborately retrieved. You and I, Honey, are residents of each other, no matter how unwelcoming harbors and airports are. I am a toddling love story. My love is blossoming inside you every day. My love, sweetheart, is our baby in you, that will see the light whenever you want. I am forcibly displaced away from you, and will come back to you against the current, defeating the in-between distances, and closing the port of travel behind us. I will be back to my snatched homeland inside you, to my heart that is implanted under your ribs. I am writing to you to liberate you, to bring you back again, to recover a homeland. For whom my life shall be if not for you? Oh, daughter of Java and its coasts..! Oh, glorious history of Sham and its jasmine! My home, my freedom, your knight is still horsing his destiny so far; taking in one hand a strong held shield of memory, and unsheathing a sword of determination in the other. It's one of two bests; either victory and triumph in regaining you, or martyrdom with honor in attempting doing so."

How to spell out spirit in these words? What talisman or sacred spell should I cast to have them enchanted? Which of the names of saints should I evoke? I will bring the Blackstone and Cambodian incense, I will invite people of miracles to spell sacred words, and I will make charity. I want my early message to resist the elusive virus which penetrated every corner of her today. I want her to reread the letter twice or thrice as a lifelong antidote, until she remembers her words to me that I am an "unforgettable man" and her marriage is only a common event that deserves no or little mention, just as secondary as any ordinary occasion. I want to immunize her with a spell casted on her, adorn her with amulets. I want to relieve the mania she feels and dispel the manes that occupied her with our love placebo. I want to repress her demon into a safe flask, and create for her a guardian; averting every man or jenny.

Since her travel five days passed so far, and I am still in the darkness of my cave; conversing with doubts, suspicions, and destinies that wrecked my patience down, exhausted my strength, and left me defeated to the ground of hopelessness. What keeps her busy? Is it him, the *"Mr. Master"*? No. Even mocking him with a title like this would fail to fit with its masculinity. She can maneuver and evade him for a while of privacy for herself. Is she still stunned with the beauty of Dubai and its lofty buildings? I don't think she is one of those who would be captured with such scenery views, even though she wished to clear her memory from backwardness, filth, mustiness and tried out norm of idle talks of Irbid. Most often, she has been criticizing deteriorated buildings and worn-out roads of our city, and wishing to cast away and get rid of those memories even before reaching the airport. She would make comparisons between the two cultures, but she is not of that kind of people who would glorify modernity to classics. Does she maintain passionate longing to friends and relatives? No. I don't think so, either. She has been struggling bitterness to evade the intrusion and tyranny of her brothers, sons of oriental masculine community, rustic in nature, that defines manhood only as taking double-standard authority on women. Still, she is also of Levantine mood, and would not mind to follow a wiser man who with a courteous and tactful character would embrace her. So, what happened? Why is she late? I don't know. She loves surprises and would make it one, perhaps today, tomorrow, or maybe the day after tomorrow. What concerns me the most is that she finds me in that letter the way she's used to. I need something to pacify my worries and show me that she is still keeping the promise. Her feelings are still mine, and that bloody delay will finish soon. She resembles no other woman in the world. I don't say this is out of my love for her, I just tell the truth, no more, no less. It is not extravagance to tell that she is literally an unrepeatable miracle, and for her lovely eyes heroic wars could be waged. "Helen", supposedly the cause of Trojan War depending on epic narratives, could barely be compared to her beauty, elegance, and smartness. Everyone who happened to acquaint *Suzan* is surely a Spartan, Trojan, and a true Arab; whose sense of honor and manliness would not accept less than launching a battle to defend her, and lay down his gown under her feet.

I still remember her first breeze, as warm and soft breaths leaked into my heart in winter of 2005, when I caught a glimpse of her at AL Bayrooni precinct while I was heading to my office. She was with her girl companions, sent me a glance, then left her friends and walked towards me, surfing a tidal wave of student body. She was dressed in brown corduroy "Jilbab", holding a purse in her arm in a showy style imitating that of the early women of Sham. Not so tall, her steps were confident, with a graceful stature as elegant as a filly; attentive to every stimuli, putting on a head cover that elicits curiosity and adds on more lure and temptation. The rain drips were still there hardly trying to catch her Jilbab. She stood before me as a conquering queen, with keen looks of an occupier who estimates accurately the influence of his halo on the occupied. She was beautiful more than any depiction, Spanish with her bold eyes and tanned skin, with a small nose of Caucasians, a gushy body effusive with femininity, her desirable lips hid pearl-like teeth, and infused with scents of Coco Channel, life, springtime, love stories, and history.

- Good evening, Doctor.

- Good evening.

- Can I have a minute of your time?

- Sure.

- Well, I think no matter how confident or famed one is, and no matter what words of praise and laudation said to him, he remains a human being who likes hearing words of commendation and admiration even from the most humble, right? When someone abuses us by a word or act we usually react by taking every opportunity to attack him in almost every occasion or meeting his name is mentioned. How about a professor, who would be a cultural model of an entire generation! Of course, when he delivers ineffective teaching, or otherwise happens to be poorly prepared in classroom, students will compete each other who to criticize him the most. But rightly, when someone performs a job perfectly, he should be thanked and praised by others, and the best deeds should last in memory rather than to wait one to die so as to remember his deeds. A gentleman, a professor who is talented, is supposed to be praised and thanked by all students, not to see him every morning with no one single student to salute him!! Today I attended your 09:00 a.m. lecture before my eventual registration to the course, and I would like to share some thoughts that in a way or another agree with yours, depending on what I've apprehended from your way of speaking English, seemingly British. I agree that the Arab society is somewhat seen as an immobile one that abides to a certain place. However, this matter cannot be simply generalized, particularly in the present days. We still live under a sort of family cohesiveness supported by heritage and religion factors. Meanwhile, we started the first steps towards a mobile society. So, one can see in this a turning-point on the short run, meaning that we are in a position better than that of Western societies either way. What do you think?

Was she really expecting a response, or was she of that kind of students who would bomb their instructor with arrogant comments or ideas to attract their classmates, and capture the instructor's attention, of course, with a message that they are also smart? Is she different from other students, and really feels grateful that she praises my lecture and asks questions to learn more? Whatever her intentions were, I can't ignore how she alluded to a point that I've never gotten-to previously in this issue in specific. Typically, I would make general comparisons between the Arabic and European societies, but honestly, this is the first time I become aware of the point she mentioned, though significant.

- You know, you're definitely right. You have a point in this interposition! I would also like to thank your praises of my efforts. This is the first time in my life a student makes me feel modest to his/her generous appreciation of my effortful teaching. Thank you.

She smiled with no other word on the subject, as a token that the message is delivered, nodded slightly asking to leave, then walked a few steps back, turned around and joined her friends again. Along my way to the office, she was the only thing my head could ever think about.

How didn't I ask about her name? Why did she say that she did not register to the course yet? And why for three years of teaching this content I did not have such insights as she did? How could not I realize the positive aspect of being relatively immobile society, while we still have intimate belonging to place and family ties? She's right. We are lucky to be in this time, on one hand we still feel the warmth of family relations and support despite many inconveniences, and on the other hand some of us would find excuses for others if they did not visit them for a long time. Finally, I reached the office and started jotting the note on the book as a reminder for the next lecture. Meanwhile a call interrupted my note, and at the same time my colleague Naser walked into my office. I hinted for Naser to have a seat and went on with the phone call.

- Good morning, Zeyad.

It was Murad, one of the few friends with whom I usually talk in this university, and one of the persons who were doomed by the destinies and sent to the profession of teaching, in a time of humiliation for knowledge and literacy of this nation.

- Murad! It's been a long time, brother! How are you.. Where have you been all this long?

- You blessed…too early to say that. The semester is still fresh, and you know the schedule is still not so final. Once the courses go in order I will take some time to have a cup of coffee with you. Zeyad, would you do me a favor?

- Sure, what is it?

- A student wants to get enrolled in a class of yours, and as you know, classes are almost full. Would you please tell a friend registrar to help her enroll in your class? Well, she matters to me. She is a sister of an old friend of mine.., and I want to do him a favor, if that's possible.

- That's it?! No problem. I need some details to do that. Give me her name, student number, and class code in which she'd like to enroll.

- "Suzan Al Ahmad" is her name. I told her to see you at your office and tell you the matter. She will introduce herself to you.

- Suzan Al Ahmad. Ok sir, don't worry.. be sure it is done. But don't forget to wind up at my office when you have free time. We did not talk since a long time.

- Sure Zeyad. I don't want to bother you now.. thanks in advance. Salam.

- Don't mention it. At your service any time. Salam.

I finished the call and went on checking my e-mail inbox while talking with Naser.

- How are you, Naser?

- Thanks to God, I'm ok.. Content. Who was it on the phone?

- It was Murad. Didn't you hear me calling his name? He recommends a student who wants to register in my class this semester.

- Suzan Al Ahmad?

- Yes.. do you know her?

- Yes. She enrolled to my class before.. but dropped it. The girl is more than pretty.. and smart, too.

- Ahaa.. it seems that you have been underrated, friend, hahahaha!

Then we talked about some issues.. and left to classrooms as usual. After lecturing time I drove out with my car back to the dumped "Bride of the North", the retired city of Irbid.

*****

Love is predestined, deprived of choice we act it,
otherwise Romeo& Juliet would've
been just fools!

~**3**~

Next day morning I went to the office to bring student name listing and textbooks. There were three lectures on my schedule that day for the same level, the first to start at 09:00 am, and the last comes later on, at 03:00 pm. I delivered my lectures as usual, bounded to office to put my textbooks there, and was about to leave when I heard a soft knock on the door:

- Come in.

Carried my looks slowly to the door quietly opening.. It was the same girl who I was talking to at Albayrooni precinct.

- May I, Doctor?

What a girl!! She asks for permission to come in knowing that she almost has taken over my will, occupied my world, and penetrated my office. She is really smart and knows that polite cliché words and protocols give enough time to reassess ideas, aim at a target, and shoot most suitable words.

- Of course.., come in.

For a while, she tried to take a breath, and in a flashy look she could probe the office's contents, then she spoke:

- I am Suzan Al Ahmad; Political Science student. Your friend Mr. Murad told me to come and see you for help to enroll for "English-2" course.
 - Ahaa.. then, that is who you are!! Murad phoned me yesterday about your matter. Don't you worry, that's nothing. Consider it done.

- That's very kind of you sir, but frankly.. I want to make it clear from the beginning that I have some inconveniences; I might come late to some lectures and would miss some others altogether. As Shakespeare once said: "Before we blame we should first see whether we cannot excuse".

Though I was taken by her Shakespeare in the Syrian accent, still I knew that she wasn't playing on me, nor would she exploit me. One like her knows not but to be sincere. When one peaks the age years hunchbacked with hopelessness and frustration, when ones' dreams dry out in the bloodstream, and when the desert reality creeps down to ones' roots while earning a living in serving the public face to face, then expertise become the precious gain to acquire, and the genuine parameter to find out whether one is honest or hoax. Phonology also plays a very significant role in the analysis of one's personality. Accuracy in points of articulation, choice of precise words in specific tones, and steadiness while breathing, in addition to fluency and quality of voice; all indicate confidence, strong personality, and honesty. Not to speak of body language; the way she sits with open hands even when lifting them up, implies sincerity and integrates my intuition. Moreover, the relationship between pragmatics and pitch of utterances, consequently "love" word of a tenderhearted means entirely the opposite of "love" word spoken by a frowned face, bad tempered, and displeased husband; who lost passion distant ages ago. This girl is honest and sincere.. I can tell.

I imitated her Syrian accent:

- "Before we blame we should first see whether we cannot excuse"? Hahaha.. Syrian accent obviously runs in the blood, verily not pure but grafted by Palestinian. Am I right or..?

With royal confidence and full trust she leaned a bit, accommodated an elbow on the desk, smiled and said:

- What horoscope sign are you, Doctor?

What is it with women and fortunetelling fever? Most of our satellite channels are overrun by such uncounted programs. I attribute women's curiosity and tendency to meddle in the unseen more than men, to time affluence on one hand, and their fear of biological clock ticking on the other. They are more worried for lots of reasons. I've read a research once written by students of Aleppo University, who attempted to find out whether the reason behind the whim of women with fortunetelling, is a kind of breaking routine or vending hopes. It turned out that helpless women find it a lifebuoy and a resort for their hopes and wishes, of getting married, or knowing the fate of love, or a chance of bearing a child, or even a want of agreement with their husbands. Though the world is crowded with people who lay their hands seeking the unseen and concealed, I find it useless even if calculated on concrete feeble knowledge. Everyone who was urged by curiosity and wanted to know the unknown was punished by knowledge, deprived of blessing, and answered by the curse of God since Adam and Eve. Since the dawn of time and the existence of matrimony, and even before legitimatizing intermarriages, both genders have endeavored to understand the tactics of each other in a try of understanding counterpart objectives and purposes. Unfortunately all these attempts were futile and undervalued. Thus, each helpless one latches on any tinge of hope or glimmer as a last chance for reviving the heart of love before announcing its death. Could it be possible that horoscopes generalize our attributes in one periodic table without the need of sampling? This girl looks different. I wonder if she asks for the same purpose, or if she has something else in her mind.

- Aries.

- Aries? Oh God!!

She asked surprisingly, as if I was accused of being an Aries or if I had just exposed myself by mistake. Ignorance in the attributes of Aries made me feel beneath her for a while. I tried to hide being in hot blood by weaseling as if I am aware exactly of the attributes.

- Yes, Aries. What's funny about that?

- Nothing at all. I just have foreseen it.

- Yeah right!! How have you? Is it written on my face?

Her smile was a despisal. I felt as if I lost control and not the one who runs the converse anymore.

- Almost.

- How?

- Your awe was bluntly apparent when we met in the precinct. Your reaction now is also glaring and can't be veiled. Talented, as it shows in your photo playing lute, a survivor that doesn't give up easily, caring, venturesome, occupied with worry just like now moment; clicking fingers' joints. If I wasn't mistaken, Hitler, Casanova, and Nizar Qubani are eminent figures of the same horoscope sign.

- You deduced and figured out all this in a glance? Is it a generalizing model tuned by such features and attributes?

Absurdly I tried to mask my fuddle and confusion, and asked myself if I am this much uncovered and without a roof? Do other people see me in the same way this augur did? She rocked my confidence like a sudden fate and left me deranged.. without a life boat.., helpless before her like an open book she reads however she wants.

- Your fatal mistake lies in telling the truth.. so, be careful, be diplomatic.

Finally, she misses a hit, and the turn is mine. I will fire back at her and hold the rein again.

- Yeah sure, no doubt Hitler was sensitive, unmasked, reconsidered his decisions, and cared great deal of his nation, that's why he caused them defeat and destruction! I might accept Nizar as a figure belongs to Aries according to the attributes you've just mentioned, but how do these attributes match with Hitler as well, for God's sake?

- Why? What is the contradiction here? Just because he was a militant? When you know that people born under Aries sign are naturally leaders, hasty, easily irritated, you won't find it contradicting. Military has nothing to do with this. Have you ever read the love letters of Napoleon to Josephine who was six years older than him, and he knew that she betrayed him? Though Napoleon was a Virgo, still it proves that romance doesn't contradict with being churlish. If Hitler's love was not deeply rooted in Eva Brown's heart then how do you justify her committing suicide by swallowing a cyanide pill and die at the age of thirty three? Aries people are extremely tough in love, Doctor. A woman who falls in love with one of such clan must be patient. Love is an invasion. Believe me, Doctor, Nizar is not different from Hitler, both of them could invade you if they wished.. kill you if decided, with a bullet, a sword, or with a word. Don't you notice the hauteur of Nizar in his god-like tone, obliging the thoughts of his, running the concrete and the abstract to wash your brain of your thoughts and adopt his, convincing you of an ability of performing miracles, till you become a prisoner in his cell of words and rhymes and comply to his teachings? Speech is indeed a weapon. The power of a word depends on its connotation. Would people uprise to wage wars or to liberate their country if there wasn't an inspired leader who throws a speech with heartiness, quoting verses of Qur'an, poetry, and rhetoric? A demagog like Antonio, Hitler, and others know their influence on people. How about a nation sensitive to language pawned to its intimacy and principles like Arab nations; those who have over three different satellite channels dedicated to poetry competence, in time of calculations and globalization? People who still boast among their ruins and announce state of emergency when "Bab El-Harah" and "Ahal El-Raya" series start? They made us believe in valor, which I doubt if ever existed, trying to convince us that we are the ones who exiled invaders, not the invaders who chose to retreat tactically. Here we are again, invaded, why can't we call back chivalry and valor? They say "Never believe a person who went abroad, nor one whose all companions are dead". Certainly, Nizar alone can invade us, even without a weapon. "Que sera sera ".. Well.., are you going to help me, Sir?

I was about to say an expression heard it once by my grandmother, "Blimey!", she used to say it when she got shocked with bad news. Where did she get all this information from? I thought generations are getting more illiterate by the course of time because of focusing on technology and neglecting reading! The age gap between me and them is thought to stand as an obstacle in any probability of understanding each other, by analogy with the Americans for example, who mostly are unaware and unconcerned with what happens in the nearest state to their place of residence. This girl doesn't only talk of past days as if she spent part of her life back then, but she also analysis figures on personal judgment!! Is this augur only acquainted with horoscopes issue or is she an exceptional case in other issues as well?

I've always been waiting for a girl like her coming from the unknown, to turn my life upside down like a tsunami, make me forget this boredom and dullness, so pretty, highly educated, with a charisma that would break the record on the scale of surprise, attract my senses, enchant me by her beauty, her language is silence and aroma, and narrates with her body what spares a thousand of words. Now, and after being enthralled this much by this augur I don't care anymore who runs the other and who steers the wheel. I will not waste this treasure in greed for another. She's but a roseate dream that will not be enjoyed twice. I'll close my eyes and live it among medieval harp and Andalusian terza rima, over there, on clouds, in the castle of domes and wide precincts with dangling branches and leaves. I'll live it for a few months, at least till this semester is up. Who knows where would we port?! I'll live this dream no matter what it takes; she deserves one who dies for her, with a wide smile.

Perhaps I should hold my horses a bit and not let my childish dreams cross the bridge yet.

- So, what do you say, doctor? Will you help me?

- Absolutely, and regarding missing some lectures or being late to some others, you shouldn't be worried about that at all. In fact, it doesn't make any difference, the door is open to whomever who wants to attend my classes, but I am not going to oblige anyone to attend.

- Really?

She toned disappointed, probably thought it a despisal to her pride that I don't care this much if she attends or not; which flew in the face of her expectations.

- I beg your pardon, didn't mean what you understood. Simply, I guess if I was a jolly good fellow, students will attend my classes without invitation, but if was wearisome and unbearable, they will pile me with excuses.

- You are right, Doctor. Ok then.

She took a paper out from the calendar of the office and said:

- Here you are, Doctor, here is my mobile number, and my student number. I depend on you sir. Forgive me if I nag, but would you reply to me when you get it done so that I start attending officially?

I wasn't hastening my dreams and wishes. My feelings carried out their promise, otherwise why would she entrust me her mobile number if she doesn't want me to make advances to her. She could have come back again to check out her registration officially, but she tended granting this in a personal and private way. She sensed the effect of her halo on me.
That's how things usually start; so easy and simple at first, but soon complexity and hardships bloom, just like the fall down of Isaac

Newton's apple, or any simple line in a painting which hides lots of interpretations, easy but rather difficult. Suzan is elegantly simple and difficult. One believes that she is easy to maneuver with, and rather easy to master, but no sooner you start dealing with her than you realize how hard she is, and how useless all your used weapons are. In round one with her you start getting yourself used to all the buttons on your joystick, but suddenly she shocks you with "Game over" announcing your defeat.

- I hear.. I obey. At your service.

I noticed that it was getting almost 4:00 p.m., in such a time in winter it benights soon. I looked around, took my chapeau, put on my raincoat and carried the umbrella. She kept looking at me observing every move. I closed the door behind us, and we walked out together in silence for a few steps.., then I asked her:

- And you..?

- What about me?

- What horoscope sign are you?

- "They asked the rooster to crow, but it said only when it's time!".. Do you want me to crow or you would prefer to wait till it's time?

- How would I know if you are going to come late to some lectures, and miss some others too!

- Why? Are you wearisome and unbearable?!

We laughed loudly like.. lovers under the same umbrella, sharing sullen cloudy sky, curious and jealous looks of teachers and students, and shrunk listening fates. Suddenly, she stood in my way to stop me.. looked at me with promising eyes and said:

- It's getting late..

- Yeah.., it could have been earlier!

- Bye, Doctor.

She walked a few steps, as if not touching the ground, but rather tickling it with her feet, dancing in her avoid of rain drips.., looking upward to the sky invoking it for springs, roses, and meetings to fall. I wanted to get her back to me, to hug her, to run with her, to clench with her astral body. I was in a bad need for her aroma to be tied around my neck after all this dust and waste.. I don't know how my voice surprised me and sneaked after conspiring with my lips and called her name..

- Suzan!!

She stood still like a guilty one called by the police at the last moment. She knows that she was the one behind this conspiracy.. all my senses were conscripted.. even my will was allied with her.. as if I was hypnotized, falling for her charm unconsciously. I looked for excuses of calling her name but found none except saying:

- Take my umbrella.. I don't need it.. I am going by car.

She turned around smiling as if the goal was attained.., took a few steps towards me, held the umbrella and said:

- "If you want to keep a friend forever, you should neither borrow nor lend him a thing".

- That's not a big deal, "They asked Joha if he could count the waves, he replied: those of coming flow are more of those of ebb", I am also acquainted with those proverbs.. ha ha ha

She smiled, took a few steps backward looking at me, then turned around and walked away. I kept following her with my eyes till she disappeared like sunset.

*****

"One word frees us of all weight and pain of life; that word is love".

Sophocles

~4~

"Sweet Suzan..

For I don't depart from you whilst you did, thus I decided to die for you twice, and be tortured for you twice. Once, for leaving me behind, though temporarily, facing the blaze of longing and parting; once more by flashbacking all the moments we spent together, thereby blinding my future for an indefinite period of time. Such sublimation in the superego presented in the art of evocation of a woman I loved, spares no missing and feeds no hunger. My table will never be clear of the daily dish of pain, benumbed now moment, burning embittered waiting, and the pleasure of clinging with the....

I wonder if there is a word in the language that describes times occurred other than "past"? Every user of such a word spices it with negative connotation of missing, loss, and the inability of restore. I will change the destinations of words and make them port in the connotations I decide. The anchor of a word will be thrown in the context that suits the meaning of mine. "Past" from now on will stand for repetition, restoration, and resurrection like "Phoenix". Words ameliorate and pejorate by the course of time. I will repeat this story of grief and sorrow till my spirit is high.

Spirits and souls are not made masochists by nature. Delicious pain isn't fast food that can be easily found in common restaurants with lots of customers. In fact, delicious pain is served as a meal in restaurants with rare and selected customers. It's the only meal offered in such little demand places, for the rare and special ingredients it has; strong memory, care to details, and well-founded satisfaction. If memory is warmed up at the heat of details, and replete with analysis, melted, and finally a lump of high level of satisfaction is dropped to this mixture, we'll get a delicious and irresistible meal of pain that is liable for sufficiency of seclusion, masochistic ecstasy, and lack of appetite for the future. Masochism is not deliberately patterned after, but my ecstasy is exclusively clicked by you. Therefore, if you had to go, then my fate of dying for you twice is a must. I don't know why masochism is always related to sexual deviation. Do the feelings of pain, abuse, and oppression deliver a kind of self-relief and pleasure? Is pleasure exclusive to sexual orgasm? Wasn't physical suffering as ever a way of sanctifying the spirit? Isn't all the hardship and discomfort of body during acts of worship in pilgrimage a way of sanctifying the spirit? Doesn't fasting go in the same manner as well? What is sauce for the goose is sauce for the gander. Does this mean that my pain and suffering in evoking you sanctifies me and makes me sublimed? Has your evocation become worship? The meanings are nuanced. I seek art of worship in evoking you, but I desire not to repent of being dormant in you.

I am to get insane, only thinking of you is an invitation of shedding tears over your leaving, and a smile drawn over your attendance. Permanence of pleasure and pain.. pleasure and pain.. "

I arrived back home; everything was regular as usual, Mom was sitting on her couch in the living room listening helplessly in silence to the same complaints and demands of my sisters all over again; party aggrieved and unjustly treated by life as they claim. They are all "Venusians" exchanging views to ease down plights of life through their broken waves without the need of real outlet, as Dr. John Gray explains. This is one disadvantage of being particularist in an immobile society. I wish you were here Suzan.. to find out that the rehearsal of all details of the people whom you are living with, by virtue of customs and traditions, without being able to adapt oneself with, is real troublesome.

- Good evening, how are you?

- Hi son, God bless you.

Checking up my "Martian" father in his cave was also one of my daily acts of worship. The quadriplegia was a trophy and a Medal for Merit and Honor of life for all the services he rendered. He was the last decent warrior of the time for me. I expected his death in no time by the sneaky malignant emaciation. He was a great, sarcastic man. My Bernard Shaw was of high prestige, who accepted Allah's fate in firm and prophet-like patience. I used to dress all his ulcers, clean him up and talk to him for hours. It wasn't easy for me to stand and walk whilst understanding the feelings of a disabled.

- Good evening Sir. How are you doing today?

- Hi son, come over, Give me a hug.

I hugged him and helplessly looked at all his ulcers and emaciation incapable of resurrecting him. Dear God..!! What do days hide for us? How did death creep up his highness spraying and spreading decay all over? Looking at him helplessly, wondering if the death of his body spares him all kinds of agony. He is a stubborn, arrogant and a real man, who would persist on his sanity and firmness of faith till the last moment. We talked for a while, then farewelled him for that night, and went upstairs to my last area of refuge.

My wife and the two kids received me regularly with the same ballad; "dad..! He hit me.. No, he hit me first!". My mate on the other hand, the "Saturnine" Sura, who doesn't belong to any of the planets suggested by Dr. John Gray; stands as a weird category. She is Martian in her cave, Venusian in her broken waves but seeks no passion or sympathy of Martian, or Venusian at the same time! I completely gave up trying to understand her; an abhorred category from both sexes, and a real challenge to Dr. Gray. A woman who hates talking or dealing with others, apathetic towards everybody, and stubborn, but decent, and good to her kids. She will remain a puzzle that I am used to avoid solving. I went to bed early that night. It wasn't like the rest of the nights.. I recalled Suzan's converse again for a couple of minutes, and retrieved her image before my dream loosened its anchor, freed its sail and announced departure.

*****

The stronger the "repulsive force" between love and sanity, the further you are taken by one of the extremes

~5~

I woke up early in the morning the very next day.., delighted with the sunshine after a boring rainy day. It wasn't the same sun that dried out the face of an Arab since so long, cracked up his skin.., and decreased the number of his seasons into one that made work at Al al-Bayt University a rehearsal of hell blaze. That day it was rather a London-like sun, hiding a bit behind the clouds, posting its rays like intimate virtuous letters, before being slain and deflowered by technology.

After arriving at the campus, I headed directly to the Admission and Registration department.., met the registrar Imad and got Suzan enrolled in my class within a few minutes. While leading my way towards Quraish complex, I wondered what would look more appropriate; sending her a message to inform her with the latest news of enlisting, or calling her? "She could be busy, or maybe it's still early, I don't want her to get a bad impression of this haste", I said to myself. Ascending the flight of stairs to the second floor, I decided to write her a message:

"Good morning. I bumped into your registrar this morning.., asked him to enroll you in my 9.00 a.m. class, and gave him your student's number. He promised to process it within an hour and told me to consider it done. Zeyad".

I started my lecture with a quick revision of "Tenses", umbrageous at the illiterate regiments of students who kept their mouths open, as if decoding puzzles. I spent fifteen minutes writing examples on the chalkboard knowing for sure that they were out of repair, when suddenly the door was knocked and all students turned around to see who. An angel dawned in grey majestic Jilbab..as if designed precisely for her, moved her languishing glances graciously, sublime in her catwalk, like a pomp of love, confident, tailed by her perfume as a Cleopatra, looking for a seat, or rather two; for her, and for her scent, lavish with beauty and elegance. She sat without looking at anyone, a leading lady on stage, spotlighted, the one and only.. It was Suzan. She caused me confusion.. didn't look at me, as if the converse yesterday never was. I started turning over some pages to get myself together and hide my obvious distraction. Insisting on deranging me astray she sent me a message saying:

"No one would understand and justify an Aries's confusion and spontaneity but me. Please carry on.."

I switched on auto-run lecture to give myself enough time to think of her unexpected talks and responses, and predict what she might say in words and in silence when we meet again. Finished the lecture, headed towards my office, being tailed by her splendor. No sooner I entered my office than she knocked the door and entered. She put her purse and sat without talking; I thought she was going to blame me for embarrassing her before the rest of the students, so I decided to talk first:

- Look.., I am terribly s..orr..

- You're amazing..!

I was about to apologize to her when she shut my gob like an electric shock, didn't know what to say, and couldn't hide my thrill with her reply. I thought that I got myself well prepared for anything she could say, but there she is, anesthetizing me, and leaving me no time to respond even. She wants me dead to the world. I like her style. She is a disobedient and agitated state. Henceforth, I will ride this madness regardless of all bruises; my will is up to such disobedient, untamed, and never touched mare.

- You are out of your mind!
    I said.

- It's called marvel, Doctor. Any mysterious person who has a special character, capable of introspecting issues to come, who does not admit impossibility, and who's self-absorbed to play his mental energy on inventing abstracts and concretes in secret, is referred to as a marvel. Such a person, on his/her turn, justifies madness of similar sorts and calls this process inspiration, or Satanic fancy of poetry, or music, or even love. It's weird how people attribute this sublimation of invoking metaphysical inspiration to Satan, as if mind and certainty are boring programs! Flights of fantasy are truly slips of mind. I heard that you composed a melody once; can you tell me how dared you throw aside what such a conservative society would name a teacher like you doing such a thing? And where did you get this melody from? Theories and calculations of mind, or Satanic fancy of music? You justify my open-heart in talking to you and I did the same when you got drifted before the students. The difference between us is that I always keep my mind switched on though.

I pointed at her, and as if anesthetized or got facial nerve palsy, said:

- Y..ou are.. in..sa..ne!

- You didn't pay attention to the reaction of the students around on your confusion. I was thrilled with your madness and daring of revealing your emotion, though I blushed for a while. Tell me, what were you thinking?!

- I was unaware of their attendance, some of them are proponents begging to pass this course only, and some are opponents I comply with till this semester is up, and some others are unbelonging, don't know what they are doing. I was only aware of your attendance, of your halo, as if you were a melody off- the-cuff invoked by the fancy to carry on before mind and reality hinder this current inspiration as usual. I was in solo like high.

At that time she stood, got herself ready to go, preferring to withdraw:

- I need to go... pass by the department of finance first and get all procedures done for this semester, then drop by the book store and get the course book of the material, would you allow me to?

- Certainly..

She looked so happy as if she likes such contests and debates. She went out of the office knowing for sure that a Cupid arrow is deeply inserted in my heart.

Lots of weeks passed, and lots of contests took place too. Hours were spent on phone calls. We talked about so many things, undressing the worlds of each other, dwelling and profaning the precincts of privacy, tuning our responses and feelings, and harmonizing our differences, till one day I couldn't resist an overdose any more. In her last visit to my office, I surprised her with a request, ignoring how she would respond:

- Suzan, please forgive my madness, my desire, and my haste in request, but I want to see you out of campus.., set with you without being interrupted, go on a trip with you, I am so curious to know you better; your art of seduction just ruined me.

- Would you believe me if I told you that this girl ,you are talking to, never talked to a stranger before, or sat privately with someone, ever in her life?

- I believe you.

- What if I told you that I am engaged to someone?

I was shocked!! My eyes and mouth were left open. I didn't know what to say! She looked at the desk, held a photo frame of my two little kids and pondered over for a while, then said:

- Your kids are so cute, may God bless them.

She slowly put the frame back in its place.. didn't know why she sounded apostrophic. Was it a response to my request? Or was it to slow down the pace? Or may be to stop it altogether? Whatever her reason was, I couldn't deny being umbrageous, I didn't repeat my request. She took her bag and said:

- It's about time for my next lecture.. I'll hardly be able to make it.

She took a step or two towards the door, but then stopped and looked back at me, as if she got my goat to check up my reaction, then said:

- Are we still on a date?

- Oh, sure!

- Then, let it be tomorrow morning, nine o'clock, next to Manqal restaurant. Till then, take care.

She was all ears; she wasn't neglecting my request, nor singing a seduction lullaby. She was rather pretty as she was meant to be, without affectation. What about her fiancé? Why didn't she mention him before? Why did she choose that moment intentionally to speak about him? Why did she accept my invitation then? We must talk about that tomorrow.

At that night, while being through thoughts labor in my mind, birth of hope, and longings for confronting dates of mystery, I received a mobile message that agitated my appetite after fasting for a long time, and withholding myself of temptations and maneuvers:

- What is your favorite poetic line?

- Each line tastes differently; has its function, specificity, and wisdom. How do you want me to prefer one line over another when they convey different subjects?

- I mean, in general.. a line that you feel it represents a belief of yours.

- "*Fate met thy wishes, putty in thy hand, applies whatever thou may, Disobedient age is thou slave, yields to thee whenever thou say*".

- Tendencies of madness of Aries are tempting.. You are really wild and people should be aware of you! Good night.

I wanted to send her a message back to tell her that she is the one with surprises and the one people should be aware of, fearing her wildness, but I preferred to say this in details later when I meet her face to face.

"...it was written I should be loyal to the
nightmare of my choice"

Joseph Conrad

~**6**~

"Sweet Suzan,

Sometimes people are imposed upon us despite of our counter choice and opponent will. You know, we did not choose our fathers, nor mothers, neither our neighbors, nor friends, not even our mates as some might believe. It's rather an ambiguous thing that provides the circumstances and paves the way for such a bond, for someone to be a friend of yours, or a wife even, and then it simply disappears at once leaving you alone facing your kismet, and your "choice", asking yourself how did all this relation or bond start? Some of us face this fate the way we face hemiplegia after a brain stroke; at first, you deny it, insulting the paralyzed part, rejecting its existence, its eternal abhorred adherence to you, its smell of decay, and its mouth's musty smell. But then, after you get over the shock and become calm and desperate of denial and disapproval, you start learning the art of drowning, living with this inefficiency, accepting it, getting satisfied with it, confirming its recognition, and finally dying with it. Some others remain opponents to such a fate, rejecting this impotence even if in secret, insisting with a strong determination on changing their fate no matter what it takes. You and I , sweet Suzan, are a mixture of this and that; we are trying to live with mates brought to us from underneath the ground by fate, and announcing at the same time our fierce fight against wishes and desires that were written putting us apart on records of Heaven.., seeking this disunity on virtue of fate, religion, ethics ,morals, and law, when our love stands in a survival.

I've heard once that nothing can stop fate and destiny from being applied except praying. "Oh, Allah.. thou consorted our hearts, accustomed our spirits, and guided us by thy will into hardships, she complains to thee her agony, and I complain to thee mine too, if half of thou will is accomplished and we were set apart therefore, then let it be thy merciful remainder of thou will, to unite us again..."

How can we stop wills when they are out of our hands? It is fate that consorted us, and the one behind putting us apart. Shall we believe and comply to some will and deny others? I loved you since the first time I saw you, and I knew you loved me too. Nothing will put us apart, no country for love, nor a legitimate certificate. Our legitimacy stands between the tangible and the intangible. Our prosperity has ebbs and flows between ports of peace and fright. Our love is truly legitimate, requires no number in civil records or a photo. A month has passed since your leave, and I am the one who knows how much you detest the time being, and invoke our coming time."

I stood in the balcony the next morning, having my coffee. It was rainy. I pondered over old Irbid, the flimsy Irbid, the one that grew old before time, the one that politicians deliberately kept it lagging behind Amman for long. God, how much I love this city, and how much I am hurt for its death struggle. In the old glorious days, it gave much of aid and assist of power hand to the rest of governorates, those ingratitude power hands who were never loyal to it after being polarized. Even those who returned back in wealth hybridized it into an abhorrent beast, neither classic nor modern. Nothing in my lovely country stands as an ancient monument to our own immemorial culture, or presents purity of origin, the great LEGO-like Amman left no nobility of descent after being Americanized. When I observe how the domes of Baghdad, the district of Egypt, the lanes and the thermal baths or spa pool of Sham tattoo memories to times of culture birth, I feel sorry for the melt of identity in my country. I feel no intimacy towards the sculptured city or towards its tiles. This native land is simply not of home or family. I thank God for the remains of Islamic shrines and castles that at least refer to Islamic culture and identity. How weird! Enlisting Irbid in Guinness Book of World Records for having the greatest number of Internet Cafés in one street, when all its streets are ruined with sumps, sewers, drains, and peddlers stuff. The people here are pitiful and stupid, just like their city, seeking decent death for a survivor, but the smooth-tongued officials ninety kilometers away insist on pilling them with taxes. The people here fool themselves in occasions like Valentine's Day, or on days of Barca and Real football matches, and generously spend lots of money surfing the tides and worldwide fever to feel equal to other nations, but in fact they fear striking against soaring prices of materials, the unjustified annual increase of tuitions in private schools like other nations. Other governorates, at their best, are not better off than Irbid. Jerash governorate for example used to flourish during its annual festival, which lots of gentlemen spent all means of effort to promote it worldwide, before being extinguished by the breathing fire of the new reign for no reason. Each era has its festivals and its Marie Antoinette!!

I got dressed slowly and headed towards the University Street, passed swamps of rain with a great difficulty, and stopped near Al-Manqal restaurant. The voice and the unjustified laughs of the host on the radio irritated me a lot, and stormed questions in my mind. How did this opportunist manage surfing two waves at a time; the wave of the radio in which he praises patriotic songs and boasts as if he's the only one who loves Jordan, and the wave that gives him immunity to bridge the gap between people and officials and give real dressing down in public to some ministers, too? He pointed out himself a reference as if this country isn't based on institutions. You have to call him to get your regulations handled and processed. He turned from being a correspondent into a real rich man overnight. He is great, Jordan is great too, and weird is history, because it celebrates the great only. It's not necessarily that great people must always be intellectualists, or leaders, or scientists, they could be tyrants, cited in international conferences, or accused but not proven pilferer, or war mongers, or even pimps. Ghada El-Saman had to write fifteen novels about our politicians, who declared heaping up billions when living in a country that depends mainly on foreign cash assistance in consideration of loyalty to Uncle Sam. Who dares accusing anyone of impeachment of waste when knowing that immunities shield them and keep us from doing so? Seventy percent of the seven million inhabitants from mixed bag are employees for fifty families; none of them ascends from pure Jordanian families. This is probably the common factor between Jordan and America; every recruit holds Obama's banner "Yes, We Can", but our own banner is "Dreams come true". If you ever had a dream of becoming a millionaire you only need to adjust the two banners and head directly to Jordan. Merchants of thyme, sons of gas oven fixers and shoe repairers had the opportunity of gaining both authority and money claiming being self-made men. My uncle had worn out his life serving in almost all governorates as an agricultural engineer for more than thirty years. He was accused of "res angustae domi", for not being pilferer. My uncle's utmost wish nowadays is rendering the five prayers at the mosque. I wonder if history will ever record people like him!! The world is falling apart..

There she is, I saw her in the side mirror, coming and holding two umbrellas, how lovely she is. I opened the door of the car for her... she was laughing of rain drops held at her face when she got inside.

- Good morning. Did I keep you wait for long?

I knew that she would keep her promise.

- Aren't you the one meant by Mahmoud Darweesh:
"Wait for her..
And haste not
If she looms after time,
Wait for her,
If she emerges before time,
Wait for her,
And if she comes on time,
Wait for her".

She was thrilled with a majestic smile, and then said:

- How nice!! I've always admired his writings, then "beware of startling the bird from above my queues", did I really make you wait for long?

- Eight years..!!

- Wow.. What an answer, almost a finishing stroke too, I am only responsible for a couple of minutes delay, other than that, ask the fate for timing. Where are we going?

- How about if we go eight hundred and twenty six years back in time, and ride a cloud over one thousand three hundred and twenty meters high, leaving the now moment to its concerned, and this land to those who are satisfied with it?

- And where is that time gate?

- "Only when it's time!"

We laughed at recalling such sentences and everlasting contests. I took my mobile and called my friend Naser, asking him to cover up my absence for that day. I was so curious to start a conversation with her that would lead to her fiancé, but I preferred to wait till she finds the right time to do so. I changed the radio station to suddenly hear Fairouz singing "When on the door way.. oh, my love… we farewell..", I couldn't resist that angelic voice in such a romantic mood and attendance of "the most beautiful of women kind". We set off under rain fall heading towards the south destined for Ajloun Castle. She didn't ask me about our destination, as if she was enchanted and taken by the voice of Fiarouz to different worlds. I could hear her crooning and been enraptured due, without drawing her attention, to let her carry on. I swear hear beautiful voice was beyond expression. Some might think that hoarseness voice is due to repeated sore throat or pharyngitis, but when it is deliberately meant to be and used professionally, it becomes like an ornamental nicety; out of context tone, looming deliciously, sudden and sad. We drove that highness towards the sky under the patronage of her angelic voice till we arrived at *Auf* Mountain. We stood there for a while with a profound look at the dignified castle touching the clouds by its summits, and surviving the hardships of fate. Looks and smiles were exchanged between us before the castle. She was pleased with my choice.

We bought two tickets, ascended the steps, hand in hand, when the castle emerged the octopus wooden bridge and the four towers. I dropped my sight down as a sign of respect to the survival of holding together stones and the fabulous arches. Suzan passed her brunette's two little hands on the wooden bridge and stones as if she is wiping tears off a child's face. If visitors and tourists listened carefully they would have heard groans of the stones when touched. Arches and stones were breathing, and narrating tales that passed long time ago. No sooner had we started walking the aisles among other tourists than Suzan held both sides of her Jilbab with her two hands, as if she was the true born and the inheritor queen of this castle, and took me upstairs where the sky and towers were the roof. Under light rain shower, she looked at the skyline and set free her wings, this scene urged me and caused ticklish feeling over my body. I left her there and went up creeping to the highest stone of the summit, raised my hands upward calling her while looking at the sky.

- Suzan.. look! I am touching the clouds!! Would you like me to write our fates or modify undesirable ones and leave our autographs, or would you like flags on desirable ones?

- Oh.., no..!! Get down. Don't you ever say that again!

- Let me pick you a big cloud first, do you like cotton candy, Suzan?

Nizar crossed my mind at that time, "*I love you, on clouds I write it*", and I wrote it in the air.

- For God's sake, get down..!

I felt fear in her trembling voice, went down hurriedly towards her, held her hand and looked at her, she was terrified. Her eyes were baptized by her tears consorted with drops of rain. I wondered who invoked the other!! I hugged her and revolved carrying her many times before we got interrupted by the applause of tourists who came near and started taking photos for us. Her tears were struggling with her defeated laughs. It started to rain heavily later on, so we ran into the castle and sat near bowshot spots watching the sudden convulsion of nature... then she said:

- So, you want to write your fate by your hand, ha? Did you see the reply of heaven on those who revolt against it, being ungrateful, belittled its seriousness? Who the hell do you think you are? Some kind of mythical hero brought up in side of Gods and sucked Milky Way? Do you want to fight the windmills? I care about you.., and I can almost see your doomed future! I don't know how did all this happen this fast, but.. but I don't want anything to take you away from me, I want to spend my whole life with you. You are playing with fire, you will get burnt and you will cause burn and destruction to everyone who happens to be around you. You are kind hearted and loveable.. don't scare me.. God! Climbing up the summit, announcing revolt against heaven, paying no attention to the risk of us being photographed together, don't you care about me? Don't bring us troubles!

She was like a frightened child stuttering and incapable of forming a complete sentence.

- This is who I am Suzan. A man who fears fate and destiny will be afraid of telling the truth in front of a boss, a governor, a minister, or even an invader. He who cares much of fate will lose the dignity of risk, the right of dreaming, and will have no chance of living big. I've been looking for you since so long!!You told me before that telling the truth is an Aries sign defect. I am telling you the truth, I am crazy about you. I am not of the wise men, but rather of the fools who rush in. Do you want me to sing it for you? "*But I can't help, falling in love with you*". What do you want me to do Suzan? This is who I am, and by the way, I've found out that you are an Aquarius, am I right? You are honest, and much of prevaricate before telling how you feel, because your brain arbitrates your decisions, but when your mind approves the decision of your feelings, you become insane and behave irrationally, and you get crazy, too, with your lover, just like me. I know I can trust you, and depend on you. Your love is so violent and your thoughts are still virgin. Most of Aquarius sign women are either divorced or seek living in freedom, your personality is too strong to be a follower. There is no difference between us, we are both crazy, and we will have our crazy moments. I, who never believed in horoscopes and fortunetelling, started surfing the internet and read books to know more about you and find out shortcuts to you!

I got closer to her, wiped her tears, kissed her hand, and said in slow pace of tone:

- Would you accept my invitation for a cup of coffee in the family farm? It's very close from here. Consider it a compromise, and I promise you in my turn to slow the pace, and to slow down my madness too, if you are still afraid of me.. deal? I am honest, and I'll keep my promise. Will you forgive me?

- I am so scared of this rash with you. I don't know what to name it, but we are not giving enough time to consider and process all these events.

She looked afflicted with undesirable will, scared of introspected mystery, and expert of both hardships; she wanted to avoid me all the awes and troubles by her wakefulness. Her sudden feebleness and tears were unjustified for me, neither infidelity nor apostasy were announced against heaven. She hid a delicious frailty behind this strong personality and contests in her stands. This very frailty makes her more beautiful and tempting. A pile of contradictions and extremes like my country; stabs me and deeply roots its love in my heart. Our mutual feelings, this fast, laid a hanged bridge that wrote, in short hand, years of courtship, yet the bridge is high and dangerous. Probably that's what scared her the most.

I stood in front of her trying to absorb her sudden wreak of wrath, but she went on saying:

- We dashed with admiration and unusual mutual love towards each other in a very short period of time. You didn't give yourself enough time to know your beloved better, and I was taken by to such an extent that I deliberately didn't mention being engaged. I don't take the consequences of being with you into consideration, and you don't also pay attention to how or what people might think of us. You state openly your feelings before teachers and students. You're married, and you have kids too, but you didn't think of how this relation would ruin them. You don't care if this breaks the heart of your wife, who desperately burns the candle at both ends to please you. You didn't think about how an engaged woman would be affected and would feel when she's in affair with another married man. I ain't two timing, Zeyad. Look at you; don't you care if you miss your classes? Don't you fear punishment? Don't you care if such photos were handed to, or seen by somebody? When you chose a place for a picnic you chose a castle on a mountain! When you decided to challenge you challenged heavens' will? Don't you give a fig for anything? You will never be satisfied, and you blame Hitler for causing destruction of his army in the snows of Russia just to make his dreams and wills come true! You, men, have no satisfaction even if invaded the sky, Nizar was right about you when he said:

"I am a man, same as others,
Bearing God-fearing virtues and dissolute of immoral, meekness of
children.., and cruelty of savages",

He also addressed your virtues..! Didn't he also say,

"I am a child, I love with all my nerves, I love with my paintbrush, I love
with my whole, with no moderation, nor sanity!"

He was talking about you!! You, Aries sign group, are all insane!! Do you want to know if I love you or not? I do.., yes, I do! Since the first moment I saw you I knew that you were the crazy one I've been dreaming of. I wanted to endear myself to you from the beginning, and now, after being in love with you, I don't want to live without you. I want to live all my life with you. How do you challenge the heavens' will with the fact that I am engaged and you are married? Tell me!

She suddenly hushed up, all the heavy rain and the flare-up of nature calmed after her silence. I approached near, bowed a bit, and whispered in her ear:

- Jupiter and Neptune lost their minds for your fury; please, I don't want to be responsible of Hades' and Pluto's rage as well!

She smiled, with tears standing in her eyes, condemning my reply and said:

- You've not been listening either! Do I look that stupid to you?

- May God forbid, no darling, but I will not give up my love no matter what it takes. I don't have voodoo spells to answer your questions, but I know I will live with you no matter what the circumstances are. I've been looking for you since so long Suzan, as if I knew you since the creation of the world, that's why I didn't need for introductory courtship and words of love. Whether your family approved it or not, whether you broke up with your fiancé or you didn't, I don't care. *"He who widely opened the doors shall close them, and he who sat the fire shall put it out"*, but if fate decided to resist me and put me apart from you, then I am not the one to be blamed, because I will leave no stone unturned to change this opponent written fate and rewrite it the way that I desire. After hearing your answer and your announcement of my love, I will sarcastically front my chest to its stabs whatever it may cost...

"Live in barricade or die noble-minded among stabs of spears and flags flutter,
Hence spears tips; most removal of fury and do quench spite of ill-wisher,
Unlike living detested and when dying never being cried upon,
Seek glory and honor in hell and leave lowness even if in paradise it exists".

The old question that has been asked so often by people, whether to live like a dog or to die like a lion. As you said before, heavens' will can't be opposed.., meaning I will be defeated anyhow. Do you want me to lose you and die in lowness? Handing you over without resisting? Who knows, fate might stand by me one day. If I told you that I loved you from the beginning, you would have said, "how did you love me over night?", that's why I preferred not to say it, to let you feel it first, but you have to understand that you are my dream and I am crazy about you and I don't intend to give up loving you, so do you want to stay beside me whatever it takes and never give me up, too?

My thinking compulsion ceased, and my nerves drowsed away afterwards watching her looking at me, then she drew near surrendering herself and laid her palm of hand in mine. I wiped her tears again. She said:

- Don't leave me. Don't you ever give up on me. Stay with me, do you promise?

- I do.., till the end of my life.

As long as I remember and since forever, vows, promises and pledges of love were main pillars in all love stories I read, and mostly written in a dramatic and legendry form to leave an effect on lovers, a thing I used to make fun of because of manipulating with readers' emotions with clichés like "forever". When Suzan said to me "don't leave me.., do you promise?" I hugged her, then snapshots flashed and appeared before me, as if doors of heaven were open. I lost my breath, and sensed the fright and superb.

We ran out of the castle when sky summoned up its wrath again spelling heavy rain fall in roar and in lights of Zeus' arrows. We headed towards the farm in a hurry. It was a couple of miles away. I parked near the gate, and we went running under rainfall into the house.

Suzan took of her Jilbab and head veil while I put firewood into the fire place, set the fire and waited till the wood started to crack. Reddening fire blaze lightened Suzan's body.., her hair was black and long, she kept drying it, shaking it off, and swaying it like a mare. She was wearing a pair of jeans, a wool jersey, and a chamois boot. She brought a chair and sat in front of the fireplace looking at the wood cracking with a smile. I said:

- I'll make two cups of coffee and get back to you.

She didn't say a word; she became completely obsessed by the fire. I went to the kitchen and turned the stove on. No sooner had I started making the coffee than I heard Suzan's footsteps behind me, she took the pot from my hand and said:

- Go and have a seat, I'll make it myself.

I went back to the living room and pulled the bed's mattress towards the fireplace, lied on and pondered over the reddish firebrand. Suzan was crooning in a charming and warm voice like the fire before me, I heard it like leaves' murmur, as if she was singing a lullaby to a sleeping baby:

- *"The night has rested,*
And in the rest gown dreams do hide,
Full moon has widely extended,
Verily full moon upon days is open-eyed,

Come near you daughter of fields to visit the lovers' grapevine,
We can quench by that juice your thirst of longings and of mine...".

If death was a punishment or a price of this integrity; of romance, charming voice, warmth, and beauty, I accept this swap. I have no idea why death obsessed my thinking at that time!! Probably because we were not used to be treated with this kindness and with this optimism by life, even the "optipessi" of the Jordanians seek Allah's protection if laughed so much, and when we see a cute baby or a smart one who attracts us by a gift or a talent we say: "won't live long or prosper", as if this is a praise!! Here I am regarding this dream, which I longed to live, as too much. We are a melancholic nation!! This depression is clearly reflected on our way of thinking and our state of mind. We look at things from a melancholic temperament side, despair, and failure. Everything in our life, due to this whim, has been related to either despair and failure, or to optimism and happiness. A turtle, a sheep, crescent or new moon and some faces bring goodness and blessings forward, whereas a goat, a pair of scissors left open, and counting money bring unfortunates and bad luck forward. Nearly all houses of fatalists are piled with dreams interpretation books; we all became people of prophecies, visions, and miracles, and we consider every portent as a sign! "Whom did I bump into first this morning?", "my eyelid trembles", "my hand palm itches". Almost all nations have such portents but we overreact and exaggerate believing in them.

She came holding two cups of coffee in her hands trying to hide her confusion of pulling the mattress towards the fire place. I didn't say a word, instead I took my cup of coffee and she kept standing for a while, then she took off her boots and said:

- Make room for me, I want to lie down close to you.

She dropped herself close enough. Methought her body a writhing serpent, I didn't feel fear of, instead I wanted to obtain an ember of, I hugged her.., wanted her whole body to be embraced and sheltered by my impair, groped for her tender face by my right hand fingers, and ran my left ones over her twisted and bent legs, pondered over, then kissed her. She took her course biting my fingers. I unleashed snaps of kisses all over her body.., played tunes on her flute and listened to Marsyas wailing sent out from a bottomless well. Her hidden busty chest curdled the blood in my veins. I hugged her firmly.., all her fears ebbed and all her flow of libido ran high and rough for a minute and then.., suddenly she was taken aback by the sound of thunder and gave up surfing the unconscious. Her ember was set out by reality gust, awakening tremble and demanding looks. I kept strumming her tufts, and then whispered in her ear:

- I didn't know that you hide a young crying baby girl behind this courageous personality!

- If I were with someone else, you would have seen me other than this, but as long as I am with you I don't care. I weaken, frighten, shed tears, drop myself in your lap, shield myself by your chest, tell you all my secrets, and I know you will love me, pamper me, be loyal to me, carry out your promises to me, trust me, stay by my side, and never break up with me, thus all this will be shown clearly on me.. I will never feel the same with anyone else. In other words; you will ruin me Zeyad!!

She wasn't entrapping me into a thing, or aiming at a document by someone legitimizing our love story, she is above that. She didn't want to repeat the experiences of those who wanted marriage and ended up cursing its commitments. Suzan was seeking a special and a unique love that is away from marriage. She wanted this very ember of love to last in youth forever the way it sparked in the first sight. Hundreds of books were written as first aid for marriage burns, thousands of ointments were invented to hide such marks and scars, apart from new hopes implantation after the amputation of old love's broken parts. Unfortunately, the body often refuses new parts after a later time. The function of such first aid, ointments, and implementation or mediators exists in repairing those parts and making life last longer, exactly like lifting up the spirit of a cancer patient!! Just like what the Kuwaiti singer Abdullah Ruweished says:
"A matter of time"!!

- I am already in love with you, and I am crazy about you. If needed, I will sacrifice my life for you, but if I indulge myself into a lost battle, I promise you.., this will be held away from you and I will not pull down the temple on you, too. Now tell me the story of this charming voice..!

I kissed her lips, being dragged by her *"Hot Couture"*, she didn't want me to free her, her saliva oozed a mix of honey and coffee. She looked at me deeply then turned around towards the fire place and started pondering over the ember as if looking at a crystal ball, whetting the appetite, the augur started telling fortunes:

- I am the youngest of my brothers and sisters Zeyad, my family wants me to join in marriage to have their mission accomplished in life. My mother, who got divorced in the peak of her youth, and dedicated her life raising us up, also exerts pressure on me and wants me to get married before she dies. All my brothers and sisters also want to get rid of this responsibility and burden of worrying about me. They make my mother hear the clichés, "she is late", "came under danger", "talk of the town", "got old", "becoming a spinster", "what reasons behind refusing proposals", "in love with someone ", "disreputable flaw"…, at the end a girl gets married because of being nagged upon not because of being offered a decent proposal. After earthquake shock of marriage, of course, there are earthquake swarms which are of the same level of danger. In such paternal paricularist societies females are always recalcitrant, mistaken, mentally defective with lower IQ, and of second rank "religiously" speaking, as they claim. She has to deal with the man as a privileged master who is given the immunities by his paternal society and the arrogant oriental Sharyar of manhood to flirt and do all mischievous things without being questioned, just because he holds the license that dangles between his legs. She might also pay for its defuse by his lack of reaction towards her without giving her any right to complain even, because no woman dares complaining of such a thing in a paternal society on virtues of religion, customs and traditions as they claim. Not to mention the differences between two environments in education, and in customs which the girl will never find out before marriage. Even if she does find out such differences and real attributes of his after marriage, it will be too late, and she ought to find a way of dealing with her mate. If she has a flaw like a bad breath because of a bad tooth, the whole world will give him a permission to get married to another, and he will bluntly announce it. But if the other way around happened and a fault is found in him beginning with a bad breath and ending up with his impotency, she ought to remain silent and never tell or expose the secrets of her marriage. Just give me one convincing reason for marriage to get out of this whirlpool, Zeyad! To what extent must religion be flexible to allow a girl to set with a man privately so that she gets to know him better? Even If a girl met someone and knew him for a couple of months, she will recognize later, after marriage I mean, that he was pretending all the time. Name me one approach by which I can explore the personality of someone away from "horoscopes", and one convincing reason for getting married! Do we really get married for the sake of cultivation and establishing firmly connected families? We, the girls, grew up with inherited guilt from the beginning that we were born girls. Had it been not a sin with later punishment they wouldn't have hesitated burying us alive like old times. How on earth should we establish families when we are unsteady? I saw how my mother was left alone to raise us. I accepted the proposal of an entirely opposite counterpart under my family's pressure and nagging. Here I am breaking up with him next Thursday after betrothal that didn't last for more than a year. Didn't they think of the consequences and how much I am hurt because of their pre-judgmental decision? Didn't they realize that this hell I am living should have been the best days of my life? Women should also keep their eternal youth after marriage, by the course of time, and during and after their pregnancy, I don't know how, but they should. In such a society, aging is a privilege for men. Solemnity, maturity, glory, and potency are exclusively attributed to men. Women must do miracles to keep in shape to please their husbands, knowing for sure they will never be pleased or satisfied. Why does a girl have to love someone and get married to another "good offer", from her family's perspective, to suffer later for the rest of her life? You know what! It should be written in the marriage contract that first party (man) has the right to abandon and exonerate second party (woman) without declaration of reasons at any time, and second party is thus not entitled to plea for accidents of labor and remuneration, which entitles first party to pay deferred sum the way first party sees appropriate and suitable!!

I was engaged in the art of listening to what she says, shifting into the levels of importance from the less concentration to the strongest sublimation beginning with hearing, paying attention, listening, hearken, analyzing, reacting, raising eye brows, opening mouth, sitting instead of leaning!! She was right about what she said. I sighed, and then lied on my back thinking of the same comments heard before by my sisters and the rest of the girls in the family as well. My mother returned home one day from school, and found my father accompanied with his parents at their house sitting with her parents proposing and asking for her hand. She was only sixteen years old. She kept saying to me if that "I had not married at that time, I would have been a doctor by now". I wonder what is she sorry for, missing her childhood, or not being a doctor.

- "She lives.. by her own.., without your love, you clown
   Stop talking about your love, you became the talk of the town..
   You love her.. yes you do.. but with, or without you, she survives"

I sang in a sarcastic tone, when Suzan burst into laughter. She turned around towards me with tears in her eyes and burst out laughing again, and said:

- You hit the needle on the head and made me laugh; I don't like being drifted in talking about troubles for more than five minutes. I want to get into sleep, cuddle me..

The warm cat closed her eyes with left over smiles on her lips and went into deep sleep. I thought she was kidding first, but when I realized that she was seriously fallen into sleep, I hugged her, kept looking at her in scrutiny, and dallied with her tufts.

The princess slept for two hours before she woke up to leave. As usual, life passes out before our dreams and wishes come true. We got ready to get back to Irbid when the scream of the sky became louder. Under the heavy rain, we got into the car. A strange feeling of happiness streamed into our bodies, and life ripped open ran inside us like water in plants in outset of April. Suzan opened her purse and got a cassette out of it and slipped it into the recorder. I kept looking at her, observing her smile, and smelling *Hot Couture* mixed with burnt wood tailing her, then suddenly an orchestra music burst from heaven, and an angelic voice shuddered my whole body in a beautiful foreign language. Suzan carried on reiterating..,

"Questa Mia Canzone
Inno Dell' Amore
Te La canto Adesso
Conil mio Dolor
Cose Forte, Cose Grand..... "

I didn't want to stop her, I fully surrendered my body to this shudder and numbing, and then I asked her:

- What was that? Who was that? What was he saying? Why didn't you tell me that you know other languages?

-That was the *Melodrama* by Andrea Bocelli, and I don't speak other languages rather than Arabic and English, but I was so curious to learn the lyrics by heart, sing it, and know its meaning as well. Feelings and beauty are just like music; a universal language. Isn't it, doctor? I can translate it to you with managing..

- Please do..!!

- "This song of mine
hymn of love
I sing to you now
with my pain
so strong so great
it stabs my heart

But the morning is clear
among the fields the scent of wine
I dreamt of you and now
I see you still there
Ah, what memories
fresco of hills
I cry what madness
it was to leave and go

This melody
hymn of love
I sing to you and feel
all my pain
so strong, so great
it stabs my heart.

But the morning is clear
among the fields a windmill rises
there my destiny was born
Bitter without you...
bitter without you

And this heart sings
a sweet melodrama
it's the hymn of love
I'll sing for you
It's a melodrama
I sing without you"

The words stabbed my heart, just like she said in the lyrics, her elocution was outstanding; she conveyed hidden meanings and preponderated Yazeed El-Hadeed's elocution of Nizar's poetry. Of course, she is concerned with its meaning, but no.., I will not sing the *Melodrama* over her leave, I will rather sing a love hymn with her. I took her in arm and said:

- Nothing will put us apart. I will not ascend a platform of heaven nor its altar to deplore our love story.. but, we will rather live it together.

She looked at me, tears, wailings, and begging stood in her eyes!! Then she turned away and pondered over drops of rain fall on the window. After a long silence interrupted by rhythm of rain we arrived in Irbid. Suzan asked me to drop her in Naseem area, so I stopped aside, and we looked at each other, exchanging determination and begging.

- I love you.
    She said in a crying voice.

- I love you too. I am crazy about you.. See you tomorrow.

I said decisively, and then she went away under rain fall and darkness of winter imposing authority on the twilight. I myself went back home again moving about its alienation, loneliness, and chill.

*****

It's when your mind's grip loosens and dreams are of no good to conceal things, a world of lapses is created, where secrets are revealed and the mere YOU emerges.

~7~

"Sweet Suzan..

Usually the adhesion and blending of things bring about new combination into existence, and such new outcomes might please our lives and bring variation that would break the routine in our world, exactly like mating which is similar to the intertwine of watercolors. This pollination, as it were, manifests brand-new autonomous elements with separated attributes. Mating a red father with a yellow mother definitely declares a delivery of an orange son, who is neither red nor yellow. When a vigorous, courageous, and excited father mates a smart, realistic, objective, free running, and a cheerful mother, who is also distinguished of being wise, intellectual, and of expectations, they are expected to have a tender, peaceful, and a proud son, but unfortunately sad, feeble, and weak-hearted. Even in music, when two *Maqams* are twisted and played in melodies you feel as if taken to an entirely different world, compared to the feelings when hearing them played separately. What confuses me, darling, is that kind of interlace; a weird mesh between fire and wood, a pleasant weave that raises questions and wonderment at the same time. How come that a man who has been married for fifteen years and called his wife thousands of times by her name, slips and calls her by the name of a different girl whom he is in an affair with for only a couple of months? What kind of overlapping between consciousness and unconsciousness that conducts to half-breed area which we always try to hide, and fear its emergence; during our sleep, when being anesthetic, or even when being blind drunk? Why do such treasure troves pass through centrifuge? If this unconscious takes place during our sleep and when being anesthetic, then why don't we show some sort of control upon it when we are awake? Darting glimpses of hallucination and gear of draw forth, awakening in us as a backfire so quickly, and leaving us trying hardly to be in charge again afterwards. This intertwine, my dear, and these quantum leaps turn my whole world upside down, but I am fond of them and so grateful as well, because they stand as signs of how much I am taken by you. Could it be possible for a man to keep whatever he wishes of pleasant memories in his short run memory for ever, to enjoy restoration of all details, and never send them to the long run memory where they become loom and unclear by the course of time? A mingle of what we hide and what we expose that causes loss of control and drives us into an inevitable accident. It could be possible to tame the body and unleash the unconscious, just like a yoga trainer, but can we make the opposite; immunize the mind with a secure shield that prevents memories from osmotic passing through? Could an assassin admit his crime with a slip of the tongue? For once I beg your pardon, dear Nizar, verily there is a land between hell and paradise, life lies in this "in between land", love is a hallucination that inhabits there too, misery of marriage is also a dweller there, intellectuality is insanity that shacks there, and calling you openly by your name, my dear Suzan, is a mad wave residing the in between land. All people around me started confirming my insanity. I frequently go for a walk by my own, finding myself visiting the same places where we used to visit. Even the waiter at "El- Rabiah Café" brings me two cups of coffee upon my request, knowing that you won't come anymore. He makes a sign to his friend that I am a bereaved, or unbelonging stupid lover in times of being good hearted is considered a flaw".

After one month of Suzan's going to The Emirates, and precisely on August 22nd, Sunday morning, nine o'clock according to Jordan timing, while I was holding my mobile, inspecting its breaths and pulses to make sure that it's not announcing crib death due to any technical thrombus, it was suddenly revived by a message alert after this long coma. I was quite sure that it was from Suzan. A strange long phone number..

"His honeymoon leave ended this morning, he is at work now. The country here is beautiful, and it affords lots of job opportunities. I started penetrating in his connections to get a decent job for me and you. If I succeed, I will come to Jordan to work things out with you. Regarding......, you were right!! It is only a job that has to be done, a duty, no more!! Miss you my love."

I wish I was mean enough to enjoy the wane of any possibility of happy marriage after her message, which conveys the ravage of any threat that would endanger her devotion. Being in the habit of sailing between the lines, I sensed disappointment and deterioration in her message. No doubt she is more than happy of a real civilized and developed environment, becoming responsible of her own decisions, and gaining full independence, when on the other hand her words imitates someone who had a "limited promises" bank account for a long time. Suzan sounds like a founder member in a bid bargain and already uncorked the genie. There she is rehearsing her expertise, obtained in a very short period of time, to whoever wants to enroll in this institution. Am I going to hear proverbs of defeatists from the wild Suzan, not before long? "Walk beside the walls and pray for your safety", "Whoever marries my mother I shall call him my uncle", "Place your head among the other heads that are about to be cut, and then invite the executioner to proceed". Nay, Suzan has no likes among womanhood; she will rather flick such frustrations and fiasco to fly back again. A lioness like her shall never be tamed no matter how smart Petruchio becomes, because Suzan's wildness is not like Kathrin's fabricated groundless outburst. Suzan is highly educated and very intellectual and doesn't allow herself to be easily driven by her outburst. Yes, I said this once to her brother Sa'ed when I first met him.. This takes me three years back in time.., when Suzan once entered my office while I was busy gathering up my papers.

- Good morning love. What are you busy with? What are all these papers? Look, if you are that busy I'll come back later..

- You must be kidding, I put everything aside for the sake of your eyes.. God how beautiful you are!! So.., what happened between you and your fiancé?

She started helping me, collecting the papers and classifying them according to page number.

-Yes.., it's all over now. I don't want to talk about it. Really, what is this mess all about?

- It's a novel I wrote one day and tried to publish it, but the censorship committee of publications refused to publish it according to printed matter of publication sources ordinance. They attributed their refusal to a hundred reasons such as; conspiracy of undermining the monarchical regime, aggression stirring up, sparking civil commotions, spreading racial discrimination, insulting influential and political quarters, causing misunderstanding between the kingdom and other countries in the region..

- Oh my God! Why? What does it say?

- Not much.. The novel simply recites a loin's revelation of a dream in a jungle to the rest of the animals, you know, anthropomorphism like "Kalila & Dimna".

- Tell me about the dream..

- Well, one day the lion dreams that he abdicates the throne, and he wishes to make the rest of the animals participate in fair election and run for it. Every species finds itself up to this position, therefore they start allying according to tribal species against offspring of other species. Bribery spreads over to make some abandon the idea of running for the throne, consequently a chaos takes place because of believing that even the most stupid member with the greatest number of fans and supporters could be the king, the thing that makes other jungle's animals greedy and grasping to take over their kingdom and jungle. Finally, the lion awakes and finds the wisdom of the dream interpretation and comes to the fact that his coming to the power is the rescue and salvation of his jungle!

Suzan burst out laughing while classifying the papers, looked at me with tears in her eyes and said:

- And you expect them to publish it! Were you insane to hand it over to them? You definitely lost your mind.

- I will publish it even if I had to do it abroad. You will see. I've been arraigned by security quarters many times before, their tone was strongly- worded rather than just a warning. Forget it..

- Really! Well.., I came to tell you that I mentioned you before my eldest brother Sa'ed.., you know, that you were of a good help for me, therefore he asked for your mobile number to call you and invite you for a cup of coffee to meet you in person and thank you properly.

Though I was so curious to be acquainted with everything related to Suzan, eager to meet her family, familiarize myself with her referential which splendid me, turned my whole life upside-down, and became a turning point in my life, still, I find meeting her brother who considers himself her father as well, and who will be curious to probe the nature of our relation in an oriental society, strange and unusual.

- I am honored. I will take the opportunity to know those men who participated in bringing you up this way.., and learn from them what to do and what not to do in bringing up my children too.

She looked as if she despised a saying she never expected from me.

- Right..! But it was me who brought me up.., autonomously. All the favors, merits and credits are attributed to me not to anybody else. It's not necessary that all brothers are alike! Why do you always ascribe the favors to men? I don't deny the fact that they supported me financially, but according to oriental Islamic society it's their job to do so, they didn't create Suzan whom you are in love with!!

It was my first lapse with the one I am crazy about. I missed the right words and used the wrong ones that brought me embarrassment. Confusion was drawn all over my face, and I couldn't put myself together. How did she misunderstand me like this? Why didn't she overlook my unintentional mistake? She went too far in blaming me to the extent that she made me feel as if I am meeting her for the very first time and I master no manners in starting a conversation even! Am I hypersensitive as she says about me, or does she despise being hurt even if unintentionally, thus she shows me her red card not to hurt her again? Does this mean that I have to start again making advances to gain her trust? Does this destroy the hanging bridge between us? I'll never forgive myself! Shall I apologize and tell her that I didn't mean to hurt her, or would that add insult to injury and make me beneath her after she admired me for being picky in hunting words? Oh God Suzan, I wish you understand that I would rather kill myself before hurting you. I didn't mean to confiscate you from efforts you spent in bringing yourself up. Forgive me if my voice is not high enough announcing my apology. Silence of men when criticized and condemned is a sign of accepting severe punishment. My eyes didn't stop tearing, and my heart break didn't absorb the woes I made. I caused her hurt.., the die is cast.

- What is it? Why do you remain silent? God! I didn't mean to hurt you. No reason to be annoyed so much.., forget it.

What does she mean by "No reason to be annoyed so much"? Does she persist on the fact that I am guilty.., and that's why I deserve such a reply? Or does she mean she forgives me? The assumption of the first meaning caused me more hurt.

- Look at me Zeyad..

I was inclining my head, didn't want her to see the confusion and mess drawn on my face, she drew near, squatted and looked into my eyes. Her eyes were glittering with tears, she didn't talk to me but she hugged me for a while, then sighed and said:

- I don't believe it!! God how beautiful the sensitivity and weakness of men is! You fool, you challenge fate, security quarters and governments when a girl like me cries you?

- If I were with someone else, you would have seen me other than this, but as long as I am with you I don't care. I weaken, frighten, shed tears, drop myself in your lap, shield myself by your chest, tell you all my secrets, and I know you will love me, pamper me, be loyal to me, carry out your promises to me, trust me, stay by my side, and never break up with me, thus all this will be shown clearly on me.. I will never feel the same with anyone else. In other words; you will ruin me Suzan!!

Till this moment I still remember her facial expressions when I said that. She was shocked when I repeated her words literally with a broken heart, the reason why she believed me and forgave me. I was dragged out of the mire by my sincerity not by my smartness.

Suzan later told me not to worry about meeting her eldest brother Sa'ed, and then she went out to attend a lecture. I was terrified by the worries of irritating her or even losing her at worst, I didn't think about the consequences of the meeting with Sa'ed at all.

- Hello Zeyad? Absentminded?

- I beg your pardon.. Oh, hi Naser.

- What's wrong with you? Where have you been all this long? I didn't see you since this semester started!

Naser is the only one who will understand my crash. Fate has diversified in crushing him and blowing his haze and dust in the air. He is a God-fearing person who believes in his message as a teacher, never forgives himself if ever he lags behind or misses a class. He burns the midnight oil preparing for his lectures, asks for opinions if he doubts his reaction or any of his performances, doesn't believe in bias or treating students with double standards, in brief, he was how the rest of teachers are supposed to be. The reason behind his crush was due to a car accident which he had while he was taking his wife to a hospital to deliver when her labor began. It was raining heavily that day and a car slipped from God knows where, fronting Naser's car. His wife and infant died immediately out of the blue. Fate didn't get satisfied with this much of crush, it went too far damaging his left leg and drawing scars on his face, as if he had to remember it with every limping step he makes or with every reflection of his in the mirror. He is the leftovers of the man he used to be.., trying hardly to hold on to his faith and his belief in fate and destiny to hide what can't be hidden.

- Naser.., it's the first time I experience the fear of losing somebody. I feel so weak, terrified, and out of control. I can't help tearing.. Is it natural to feel so weak? I was brought up in an environment where men are not supposed to expose their emotions of love and sadness in public. Is it justifiable to fear the least of hurting or missing someone whom you love?

He looked at me trying to guess whom I was talking about and doubting himself that he was the one.., held the *Gitanes* box of cigarettes and lit one with a long drag that his cheeks dived within, then erupted his boiling memories out to answer my question with clouds and fog of sighs and groans.., and then smiled. What a smile it was!! He stood up and stepped outwards limping like Captain *Ahab* after losing his leg in a round with Moby Dick. I thought he would understand me and answer all my questions but he rather took it personally, flashed back all his sorrows again. He probably answered me indirectly! What's wrong with me today, incapable of having a conversation without hurting my beloved ones?!

I returned back home that evening. Back to my "cave".., after an awful day in which my novel was disapproved, irritated my beloved, and hurt my close friend. I reconsidered all my flaws of that day, that day that I wasn't myself, but instead, weak, surprised of myself, and out of control. I kept me in solitude trying to gather my confidence again, justifying all my flaws with good intentions, but I didn't stay long in my cave, the telephone rang and interrupted my self-judgment. An unknown number..

- Hello.

- Hello, Salam Aleikum, is this Dr. Zeyad?

- In propria persona, who is it?

- My name is Sa'ed el-Ahmad, "Abu Ghazi", I am Suzan's brother. Sorry for disturbing you, but in fact she told me much about you and I would like to meet you and thank you in person if you don't mind!

His voice sounded confident, gentle, not dispersed, picky in choosing words, triggers one's curiosity to meet him, speaking in a masculine tone that obsesses ears. Even his silence, waiting for my answer, was elegant and didn't last longer than a puff of his cigarette.

- It honors me, of course. Why would I mind? Would you like to visit me at my home?

- No.. no. Let's meet elsewhere outside at seven o'clock.

- Alright. How about *Hakoura* café in University Street, near the mosque?

- That would be great. See you then.

I wasn't surprised. Though it was a mistake to attribute Suzan's grandeur to references that I sensed their influence on her, still, I am quite sure that if she was influenced by any of her brothers, that means all of them are distinguished with obvious smartness, physiognomy, good knowledge base, picking intentional functional words, fluency, elocution, and charisma. Since Suzan told me that her mother was left alone to raise her children, then that means this mother has no likes. I didn't meet her and I might not, but if I had the opportunity to meet her, I would have kissed her hands, pondered over them, reading the nights she spent alone suffering the unfair confrontation with fate; either she sacrifices her youth for the sake of her sons and daughters, or she becomes more cunning and she barters leaving her children to seize her youth.

At half past six I sent Suzan a message before going to meet Sa'ed:

- *"Essence tongue is one's own behalf, and his heart is the integrity, nothing beyond is left except flesh and blood"*.

- He is the most kind hearted, and the wisest among them all. I know you will like him.

I arrived at the café a few minutes before him. I wanted to know him before he introduces himself to me with another phone call. He himself didn't mistake me. He advanced forward towards me the minute he arrived, as if we usually meet in the same place, on the same table.

- Good evening. Sa'ed El-Ahmad, "Abu Ghazi".

- Nice to meet you. I am honored.

His clear eyes confused me, and probably he realized this within a look. He pored over the place to give me time to revive from confusion. His eyes were strong and ready to leap upon in no time, but his silence which was sealed with a smile made me get over the tension. He let his box of cigarette and his lighter out of pocket and placed them on the table. I noticed his slanting neck which was a distinguishing mark for those who dedicated themselves to reading and office work.

- Nice place. May I smoke or does it bother you?

Have we still got such noble men, speaking in courtesy? Every time I take precautions in order not to be surprised by anything associated with Suzan, I get shocked with something I didn't take into consideration. There she is, the girl of wonders, impresses me again through Sa'ed. I smiled and looked at him then said:

- A man of courtesy and a confident personality is an endangered species. I am a man like you but can't deny that I was impressed by your question! I wonder how a woman would feel with the perfection of the prince of her dreams!

He smiled and looked away behind me then lit his first cigarette.

- May I call you Zeyad?

- Sure.

- "Prince Charming" is no more than an inherited wish that would lighten the fears of the future, and ensure protection for emotions during mystery. It remains a dream because no one is perfect. Who would dream of a prince with a cigarette between his lips? The prince of dreams ought to be a romantic figure, but smoking is a decayed reality. Nevertheless, this could be the modest disappointment for girls and women. How about if this "prince" had other defects too? By the way, time has changed and the scale is different now. This generation prefers the rotten smell and the dirty look if all such disgust parallel with stupid materiality, like place of residence, type of car, brand names of clothes, salaries, and quality of cigarettes! On the other hand we have "Cinderella", as long as she imitates the beauty of all celebrities, accepts you with all your flaws, and forgives you when you cheat on her. We also assume that she has got to be a loyal wife, a good mother, and a keeper. Romantic, and from a family with good reputation, healthy, wealthy, and revived, it all comes into the bargain. Where can you find such one? It remains a wish and a dream, that shouldn't come true in such double standards. We have got to learn how to live with our realities and accept each other with all the goods and bads of us, no one is perfect.

"Dear people, how many statues and figures have you glorified that carry no chastity and purity of statues".

Forget it. I don't want to be occupied with other issues rather than the reason of our meeting. Please allow me to express my gratitude for helping Suzan, and supporting her. I am in the place of our father, I took care of her since she was a baby, but due to living conditions I had to leave and work abroad and not be by her side during the most critical years of her life. She is somehow different from her brothers and sisters. She is of a strong personality, smart, and joyful. She rarely admires a person, that's why when she told me about you I decided to meet you, first of all to thank you and secondly to please the curious cat in me after hearing about you.

- Mr. Sa'ed, I am not going to tell you that Suzan is not an exceptional case, and that I help all other students as well, just to keep away your expected and justified fears since you're considered her father. Helping Suzan exclusively and supporting her is a de facto and a must for me. Alas, in our oriental societies brothers are brought up away from their sisters on virtue of religion and traditions because of their different gender. By the course of time the gap between them widens, and brothers become completely unaware of their sister's fears and concerns. Girls, naturally, learn how to keep their secrets to themselves, solve all their problems without resorting to their brothers. How about when eldest brothers play the part of fathers! The problem certainly would be bigger because of having respect, fear, veneration imposed instead of endearment. Long ago mothers used to know all the secrets of their daughters, unfortunately such a phenomenon disappeared. Suzan is an independent young lady, with a strong personality, just like you said, capable of judging and estimating things objectively according to her intellectuality, religion, and principles. She is also capable of resurrecting without the help of anybody. She can find substitutions for limited choices. Suzan surprises the wisest men by her education and gained experience. She usually opens new horizons, mentions missed out ideas, and never gives in except to what she strongly believes in. Suzan taught me the virtue of reading *Al Kahf Surat* on Fridays, and *Al Kursi Ayat* after prayers. I learnt lots of other things from her that I wouldn't learn from anyone else. Your gratitude and thankfulness are highly appreciated, but I am not double-faced, and I will not lie to you. You shouldn't be worried about me, though Suzan is a sister of yours, but honestly you will not worry about her more than I do. You wanted to see me because you are her brother and it's your job to make sure that she is untroubled, but I will always be there for her without social dictations or blood ties. Trust me, I will not be a stumbling block or a barrier in her way, and I want you to trust her, too.

I often wondered who controls the other and imposes its tyranny on the other part, is it the body or the mind? It's said that the mind doesn't only dictate its laws and logic on the account of the physical desires and demands, but it also goes too far, freezing and confiscating the authority of the body and switching off its biological functions. The state of coma, for example, is a malignant grip of mind over the body that spares the mind any emotional plights or crises. Not to speak of mind authority over complete biological shutdown, like in those little miracles when one postpones death willfully till something is achieved regardless of somatic death; as those who are in await of somebody, or the beginning of Ramadan, or even the opposite, hastening death as when exceeding the limits of proper longing to meet God, or martyrdom for the sake of Allah.

On the other hand, we have the strong desires and instincts of the body over the mind and its logic, such as those who are addicted to drugs, alcohol, watching T.V, eating, and other kinds of addiction which the mind is fully aware of the importance of limiting their threats, and completely speculates their consequences. Which controls which? Why do we have to pay the price of such unconcerned conflicts? We are victims of the body that lazes about prayers though the mind recognizes the consequent punishment of this laziness. We are victims of the mind that recognizes the threat of driving fast but loosens its firm grip over the instinct and recklessness of the body. I started talking to Sa'ed with hidden desires that my mind couldn't keep hidden for long. My talk sounded as if made by a mastermind, but in fact, it was of an irrational drifted love. How didn't I recognize that my talk was a direct declaration of my affair with Suzan? She told me many times before that my honesty is a threatening defect in my character. What response was I expecting from Sa'ed when I let the cat out of the bag, and drift all the precautions without taking Suzan's position into consideration? What stupidity!! Was it my strong belief in loving her that made me remove all veils? I'll sacrifice my life for remaining with her no matter what it takes. This frequent absence of mind and logic in my love story became a nonstop addiction that requires an overdose each and every time, to make me become more and more isolated. The awakenings of mind were warning me of the outcomes of the one last overdose of carelessness, demands of body and spirit, and wanting her. The strong addiction spread over me for Suzan, brushed aside any sound of mind and logic. I didn't care much of my fate and destiny, but talking with her brother about the legitimacy of our affair was a big mistake that might hurt her. I will not blame her if she got mad at me, "*excused, if aborted my hopes, it wasn't your mistake, but my idiocy!!*"

Sa'ed remained silent for a while, then smiled and asked:

- Coffee?

His offer was a relief. I saw him comprehending the logic of love by the tongue of Satan, understanding the honesty of my relation with Suzan, which was nonnegotiable. Sa'ed didn't want to know more, so he decided to talk about other things. We had coffee and talked long like friends till midnight and left the place on the hope of meeting again. He was a great man, he didn't tell Suzan anything about our meeting, nor did I, except it was a friendly talk.

I didn't know how to make her forget her exile and loneliness after reading her text message.., and how to make myself forget my estrangement in my exile too. Which of us departed and left the other behind? Which of us stayed to cry over the remains of days of honey-like relish, and suffer the bitter of parting? I will write her till days bring us together in the following and lasting days to come. A weird love story will not live in peace for long, but rather it will be blown by all kinds of wills to port on lands of glory and valor under fates' guillotine.

We remained satisfied with such correspondence for almost a year and a half, till one day patience flooded with longings and I sent her a letter that she didn't realize its seriousness among other letters..

"Dear Suzan,

Do you remember when you sat in my lap while I was on the swing? You hugged me then as if we were breathing our last of love, your tears kept me from telling you that in every time you said good- bye to me, getting back home or getting out of the car, I felt that choke and lump in my throat as if giving up the ghost. Your pure tears back then ablated me and baptized me from impurity of fake reality, undressed me, rained heavily on me, to let fall mulberry leaves and reveal my feebleness, and the frailty of the mask that covered me. At that day sweet heart, we practiced the art of spirits melting into one, thus we dwelled in each other closing behind all doors in the face of others.

Don't you ever think that I underestimate your suffering at the now moment, I, the one who knows how all those towers, markets, parks, and beaches stand helpless in making you happy. Your smile will never be drawn on your map unless the absentee is there with you. You are my speech organ, for you speak on my behalf uttering my sorrows. Your grief is my tragedy, and my joy is your pleasure that tickles your imagination and creeps up to your crying rapture. We were treated unfairly from the beginning, and now we can't take it anymore. From now on, I'll announce my love to you publically in the face of fate. We were created normal human beings not prophets, we'll change the direction of our history that was manipulated and willed by fate, even though "*the pens have been lifted and the ink has dried*".

I know I will not overstep God's wish because God will leave me no choice but to carry out his fate and destiny. I also know that it was written on me whether to joy or to toil since eternity, but this of course will not contradict with my right of choosing, my right in adopting one of the two high ways for my final destination even if I chose the wrong passage. I am neither of *Al Mu'tazila*; believing that our deeds are attributed to our choices, nor of *Al Jabariah*; believing that we are not choosers and our deeds are decided and dictated by God. I am simply a man who is inflamed with your love. All my mental, physical, and spiritual energies are merged and integrated to utilize and accommodate the surroundings to port in your eyes…

Dear Suzan, I am coming to you soon, I will not stand the unbearable anymore. We are being manipulated by fate. Fatalists have always been victims of their own oppression and unawareness of their abilities of adopting means to reach an end.

On March 10th TESOL Arabia Conference will be held in Dubai to offer comprehensive job fair, where job seekers will be brought together from different parts of the world. I'll do my best to be there one or two days ahead. I'll inform the administration board with my decision before that of course. We'll keep in touch till we meet".

I don't know to whom I should attribute the saying, "*So it has been written, so shall it be done*". Some say that Pharaoh of Egypt, Thutmose II is the one who said it; others attribute it to Moses the prophet when God inscribed the Ten Commandments on two stone tablets given to Moses. It's incumbent upon us to take a decisive standpoint towards the coming days. She is incapable of changing her fait accompli, and I will not wait the wind of change to decide my destination and my port. This is how it is going to be. I will start from this moment preparing all my papers and documents, translating all my certificates, informing the administrative board of my intention of having sabbatical leave, and rewriting my résumé in a proper way. I'll also burn the midnight oil writing a research paper. My novels and my writings can also have a chance of being published there. I'll start my life again.., not allowing the pickax of fate to ruin my dreams. Everything here is becoming so abhorrent and increases my isolation and my depression. The smell of despair strangles me, the bitterness of subdual rises and sets in my food and my drink, my ambitions are becoming crippled, and the arid of opportunities is rooting out the nectar of my dreams. Yes, I'll leave; Gods' land is spacious to dwell on the quiet, rather than settling down on stake pile banged into us. It's time now to make my eyes get used to blueness of sea beyond the dusty colors. It's time to smell iodine and taste phosphorous in the creatures of God after having ulcers of Falafel frying oil, and after being a regular customer at the pharmacies of Irbid buying Famodar, Nidazole, Librax, and Deflat.

*****

Some spirits remain disturbed in their orbits of fate,
seeking stability and steadiness in other ports.
During transfer, storms wind up their
expectations and cause them
gross change of state

~8~

Lean years loomed and predominated in the end of the first decade of the second millennium, dubious phenomenon in the country followed in succession, like the falling down of the so called bourse in Jordan in general, and in Irbid governorate in particular. Actual international crises in economy made sufferance a common humane subject in all parts of the world. I wasn't specialized to understand the economic situation analysis; actually I hardly understood the differences between synonymous words like deflation, inflation, recession, and depression at the time. All what I understood was that such terms were behind marking up the tariff and the price of a salad pot. Cucumber became tight commodity, and listed on parliament agenda sessions. Tomato also became exclusively reachable by people who earn a little more than the have-nots, and whose incomes were blessed as much as four hundred JDs, as they claim. Those in fact shape only twenty eight percent of the population, when on the other hand the pigs of the farm possessed alone ninety five percent of the country's macro economies. Irbid was not the city I knew. People there were depressed by then and had one hell of a time to keep soul and body together. Their psychological suppression was threatening to flare-up. Catching sight of people shouting and fighting over trivial things became an ordinary scene. Unusual records of death states among ages of thirties were alarming. Heart attacks, diabetes, blood pressure, and thrombosis extended beyond normality too.

At the latest of those years, and before her graduation, Suzan had already mounted the throne of my heart and willingly took over my mind, my soul, and my desires. She was the one who kept me on hope; put forth leaves in my spring, and pumped profluent life in my tomorrow. She had an outstanding sense of humor, wit, and a charming singing voice. She was the knowledge base I take from, my dearly loved whom I consult with all my affairs, and my only refuge for crying. She diversified in mastering my happiness with her modest tricks and potentials. Suzan could switch me from depression into rapture and carelessness by singing "*Soiree of Love*" mimicking all personae in the musical play, she could also imitate Abu Bakr Salim in his marvelous way of singing, and recall dialogues of "*Tash Ma Tash*" while crossing her eyes like Sheikh Fuad. It was an alarming time of my dreams deflation, my passions' inflation, my ambitions depression, and recessions for any hopes of ease or relief. We spent most of our times together by then, seizing every opportunity or any excuse to meet. Those were the best days of my entire life, though they were like meetings on travelling ports. From my own view, Suzan became the scale and the reference of Eve's perfection; intellectuality, knowledge, beauty, and innovation. She was the one I trusted, and the one to seek for consultancy. Suzan was unique in drawing her demands, needs, and answers after refining and filtration. She was also confident enough to express her opinions on personal levels no matter how the issues in questions were compromised, agreed upon, or even sacred. Her beauty was so perfect that she left no space for the use of "except" or "but" for a person when describing her, the thing that made one in her halo become tearful, complying, heartfelt, supplicant, safe, and peaceful. Yes.., she was my love, my mother, my refuge, and my country which I sacrifice my life for. Five years of daily meetings for long hours have flashed, through which I never felt boredom listening to her, or got accustomed looking at her, or even tepid sitting with her. Could it be possible that each person has an invisible spacing distance of his own that bans others from enter passing, which makes one a separate individual? Could it be possible that I enter passed this spacing distance of privacy and merged mystically in her halo? Is the death wish obsessing me this much, pushing me willy-nilly to slip away from my fatal orbits to unite with hers? Is there anybody else befallen by curiosity to rehearse Suzan's body map, her treasure of memories, and precious gems of her knowledge and wisdom? Is there any competitor to me in knowing the rhythm of her breath, and roll of her mood? Would Suzan, one day, bring forward her password to anyone else? I am the only one who knows her.., the only one who knows how to access her, how to explore her, how to liberate her, and how to run up flags of victory upon her fort.... but her black magic lies in the curse of coming out of her, in the maze of her direction, in the loss of Roadmap around and about, and in an endless Odysseus voyage after mad love in a forgotten island.

*****

"Love ends with marriage, marriage is an entirely different institution with different thoughts and demands, but love stands for the feelings lived by two forever, if not married"

Osamah Anwar Okashah

~9~

On June 25th of 2009, and shortly after the final exams of the second semester and the declaration of the graduates listing, Suzan called to tell me that her name was listed with the rest of the graduates. I was the first to receive the good news and the first to congratulate her. I advised her not to tarry, and acquire more expertise by enrolling in TOEFL, IELTS, and ICDL. Suzan took her course on certificates clearance and quittance to start a new life heading for knowledge acquisition, expertise, and labor market. I was so happy watching her taking the first steps towards her future in steadiness, but so sad on the other hand for missing her presence for our usual early morning coffee before starting the day. Suzan strained every nerve to make up for the empty space she left behind, she even offered to visit me several times at work, but I found it much of a trouble for her and preferred to meet her in Irbid. We used to sit in restaurants and cafés for long hours to discuss the courses she enrolled in at private cultural and educational centers, and to talk about the increasing number of marriage proposals after her graduation. Now, from an oriental paternal point of view, Suzan has all the potentials of being a good catch; she is pretty, educated, and a graduate, meaning if the bridegroom had stress in low water one day, he can rely on her income after she is employed. Her family kept nagging on her, doubting the reason behind her refusal of marriage, till one day Suzan asked me to meet her in Al Rabiah café for some important reason.

I sensed the warning bell-ring of an outbreak approaching. Suzan's brothers were not convinced by her excuses of the courses she was taking. They started forbidding her from going out, and kept her from being associated with new courses. Then they made her feel guilty for standing in the way of improving their financial situation. I was certain that it won't be long before Suzan inclines to their request, not because she is convinced of marriage need, but rather for face-saving. If they had known her the way I had, they wouldn't have dared asking for her sympathy to incline, nor insisted on hearing her approval in stalemate like. I've heard much sayings and comments on this regard; some of my close friends, who realized my relationship with Suzan, told me that no woman gets married unwillingly even if she had to go through the worst of her brothers. They were trying to imply that if she approves any of the proposals, then that means she is totally convinced and isn't yielding by force. I was always on a disagreement with this opinion, not because I was the person concerned, nor because I didn't want to believe her marriage to someone else, but because I know her better than anyone else, and I know how much her pride means to her. She would prefer to sacrifice her life than to feel herself a heavy burden on her brothers' shoulders. How is she going to tell me this? I arrived at the restaurant fifteen minutes earlier, occupied a table near the corner affording a view of *Al Naseem* precinct, and waited for her to show up. No sooner had the waiter brought me a cup of coffee than she arrived, heading towards me in tatters.. She dropped her purse and sat inclining her head between her trembling arms, crying her eyes out. Tears were running on the glass of the table. I preferred not to start the converse, but rather ran the tip of my finger over her tears on the glass, when she looked at me, summoned up her courage, put herself together and said:

- Look, even if you were the last of mankind I wouldn't think of you as a husband..! Do you hear me?? It seems that there is a difference between love and marriage! Love is just like what's between us of feelings, affection, warm-heartedness, and obsession of each other. Marriage is a business; an opportunity of sealing a deal or a good buy through which a girl makes all her dreams and ambitions come true with a shortcut that spares her years of hardships, and keeps away all kinds of embarrassment her family had to deal with because of people's interference and suspicions. A deal and a valid profession to practice licensed adultery in which a girl sells herself like Dr. Faustus to the devil in return for tangible property and wishes, but I will sell my body and abhor my soul forever, not only for twenty four years. You won't be able to tell me "Homo, Fuge.. Flee"..!! It's over. You have never been a deal or a business to me. You are my only love in this world, and I will love you for all my life even if I get married. You know how crazy I am! But I mean what I say. I'll do what they want, other than that, it's no one's business whom I am in love with, and whom I am thinking of. Marriage is love's loathsome thing, and I will not venture losing the only man I love in such a loathsome assembly. We'll stay together forever.., isn't it so Zeyad? Tell me that you'll love me, stay beside me, never desert me or let me down, and never change your attitude. I'll prove it to you, marriage will mean nothing to me except imposition, you have got to believe me. The family believes that girls are immature and naïve, therefore they step over us and authorize themselves to decide and determine what's good for us, confiscating the most personal of human rights, thus some of Arab girls are circumcised, others are made celibates by resorting to metaphysical powers in the purpose of sex abstinence, and the luckiest ones are only tongue-lashed if their hips gain weight and breast get big during puberty. There is no space for love in their beliefs; they suppose that love comes after marriage!! These ideas are of course strongly supported by their understandings of religion, which blows the idea of love before marriage as a whole. They cite lots of examples, if needed, of unlucky people who fell in love before marriage but couldn't keep their marriage firm after getting married. Thus, according to their deduction, we need to try another technique when thinking about marriage; it's the irreplaceable good deal. Regarding love, some girls get themselves convinced of their love to their husbands later on.., tricking themselves, blinding themselves, and deliberately misleading themselves, which backfires later after giving birth. Mothers of this kind, persuade themselves that taking care of their kids is their utmost job in life. No sooner the young birds start abandoning their nests, and start spending most of their times with other people, than mothers realize their waste of life and the wrong choice they had made. Man, in our culture, switches his brain off and his instincts on before marriage. After marriage, and after having all his instincts quenched, man's brain starts to awake and he bluntly starts exposing his complaints and his discomfort. The likes of him drag him to their union of despair marriages, informing him with his rights as an oriental polygamy man, or as being licensed to two-timing in shade if not being capable in shine. This is the mode of life according to their beliefs. There is a difference between getting used to something and loving it. Man feels the pain of others even if wasn't much concerned. We can get ourselves used to live with people whom we are obliged to deal with, but certainly that is not love.

Not to mention the curse of comparisons..! God.., Zeyad.., name a man in this time who created a language for love, understood adoration and its secrets, and touched my soul, like you. Who can understand the language spoken by us other than you and me? Do you think it will cross the mind of anyone else to hit the veins of the left arm with the tips of two fingers of the right hand to invoke a dose of love? Do you think that someone else will invent a daily love report and mention the expected love temperature of the day and night and forecasts of days to come, other than you? Who else other than you can break all his commitments and slip away of his gravity to be by my side at times of need? Who would care if I had eaten or not, if I got sick, or even if I got bored other than you? Who would feel embarrassed if he had to meet me for an urgent matter with his beard unshaved? Who else other than you, would stay after making love to whisper in my ear songs of love? In spite of all the worries I see in your eyes, believe me; what's between us prohibits any intruder. We will remain dwelling in each other with the curse of comparisons, each with different mate. We'll invoke each other for ever. Zeyad, I am capable of walking through this minefield of fate, expecting an explosion in every step I take, but I don't care. Please, let me feel that you are backing me up and not deserting me. My pride is above all considerations. My mother asked for divorce even when she was a mother of five boys and four girls, for the sake of her pride. I'll do what they say.., but if they ever induced to allow themselves to step over my pride, I will not hesitate to do what my mother did long ago. I used to blame you in the past when you got busy with something, because a lover is selfish. Nevertheless, you tried hard to prove to me that you were capable of leaving everything behind to be with me. I can't accept half of your attendance, half of your love, and live with half of your commitments. At the same time I can't oppress you if my love asks for your love and your attendance at the same time. Thus, the balancing of the situation will be like the following..: I'll get married to get rid of my family nags.., I'll sell my body, imprisoning it in marriage to liberate and let free my soul, but I'll demand you all the love without sharing it with any partner, keeping your marriage stable, and winning my love. Though this balancing contradicts with reason, customs and religion, but this is all what I can do. What do you say?

It seems that things were more complicated than I expected. No doubt all maneuvers were put to an end after hearing this commentary, and she definitely inclined to a marriage proposal. Suzan is sobbing her heart out, speaking desperately as if she lost control. She speaks of herself as though she was put up for auction. No matter how a man is considerate, broad-minded, and rational, he will never understand the soreness of bridle, the subdual of hand cuffs, the humiliation of slavery and subordination which a woman feels when she gets married to a man she is not in love with. How could this stupid man, who proposed to her in a traditional way, not feel the abhorrence of the bride towards him and towards herself even, whenever he makes advances to her? How doesn't his sense come to the point that his beloved one is emotionally occupied by someone else? Aren't there warning signs? If he was that stupid, then it's his tragedy, but if he sensed it and deliberately disregarded it in hope of quenching his pleasure and desires, expecting to make changes in accomplished facts, then he will push her to hate him and hate herself as much, because this will literally stand for legal rape stripped of any approval or feelings. What kind of man on earth was the one who sat with her for ten minutes and couldn't realize or observe all the warning slipping signs before falling into this abyss? What do fates want from us? Who of us will be happy? It's a trinity; each pole will bring misery and destruction to the other two poles. I promised Suzan that I will not bring her any ravage, and if I had to go through hell that will be away from her. I didn't expect such things to take such a course or have such an end. At that rate, commanding me to stay with her, believing in the love between us, asking me not to let her down regardless of all new conditions, I consider all this a call for help from Suzan, whom my heart and my mind always complied with. I am crazy about her, and I will not allow anything to stand between us, even if it was the fate and will of Zeus himself. Suzan is the one calling for help, and commanding me to stay with her.

I wasn't the one who chose to start the fight with fates, it was written on me, the son of mankind, in spite of debility and being at loss and fail before the wish of Zeus which desired splitting the integrity of me and Suzan. I will keep looking for my integral part, healing the stroma again, not to ascend the sky targeting to fight back, but to return the situations back to normal. It's a hazardous love travel for search of origins. It's a love travel before being split of each other, and during looking for each other, and staying of love after reunification. Darning, dressing, and doing up the reality to accept the wills of Zeus on the hands of Apollon, is a deformity rejected by love that enhances us to search for origins. I will sit out my journey to search for her even if reaching her was a delusion. My hunger pushes me to adhere to her and never satisfy my appetite. How does Jameel claim love to Butheinah when he says "*The love in me dies out when I be gathered with her, but revives when we depart and verily is restored back again*"? Why do I revive and become fortunate when I be gathered with her and all my body blossoms and brightens by her everlasting spirit when we depart? She dwells in me, and regardless of body split, still the saws of Zeus haven't affected our spirits yet. Suzan.., I took a vow to dedicate my mind, body, and spirit to this love. Do whatever you please.., you will always find me by your side, dwelling in you. The tragedy of losing a dear is always received by denial and a fierce rejection of this loss, the thing that creates worlds of delusions lived by the bereaved lover and makes them fantasize conversations, and visualize complete representation. An entire secession from reality; proving love, devotion, hallucination, and disability of carrying on alone in life. How about when you, my adored one, are beside me, touching my soul, able of bridging spaces between us, and dwell in me every night? Death couldn't stand between lovers, whose credits were expired. In a world of fantasy where gatherings and resurrection become possible, just imagine how much the jaws of spaces between us are weaker than death! I don't see any competitor other than me in winning your heart, that's what your love made me feel for the last five years, and you still ask and wonder if I am going to stay in love with you? Do I have any other choice than determining to break through terrors and suffer the consequences? Only the unfortunate doesn't care two hoots about having more sufferings.. You spoiled me with love, that I am no longer good for a thing else..

- Oh, Suzan.., I disliked equations and mathematics all my life. How about when variables contradict with being beside you and don't lead to balance the situations or make all dreams come true! I've heard lately that one plus ones equals two is reconsidered, and some say three, as an answer, was proven! If these were the constants on which science and technology is based on, then the abstracts which leave the door open to possible interpretations shouldn't be found strange nor causing wonder. I'll put the ball in your court, though I know your answer, but I am not the one to be asked such a question. Are you ready to take the risk of walking in a minefield of fate, as you said, expecting unpleasant surprises without regretting my companionship, and without blaming me or make me feel your blame to yourself even? Are you capable of being with him when you are with me without ruining your life? Are you satisfied with the idea of surrendering yourself to him to expropriate or profane you every time he pleases without deserting me when I need you?

- Enough..!!
- No.., not yet! Are you competent of invoking me and setting his breaths aside whenever you like? Are you in a position to make your tongue get used to his name without calling mine by mistake? Are you willing to let a stranger share with you your privacy, your breaths, and profane your…

- Stop it..! Stop it.., please!!

She started slapping her face and swaying to-and-fro, biting her cry silently in order not to draw the attention to us, the thing that made her cry without an outlet ready to explode. I didn't want to tease her, I just wanted her to be aware of what's going to happen by uncovering facts before her, and wanted her to know that fate will make her pay the price for treading no-man's-land. It's unfair to claim the sacrifice when she is the one who has to be torn in between, to satisfy two parties, to be in two places, to live two lives, and adopt two principles. Suzan is the weakest link in the chain, not to speak of her internal conflict..; she sanctifies abstinence and virtue, and wishes to gratify God and dedicate herself to study religion thoroughly. Either she loses control, when I am the one concerned, thus I become the devil who knows her ins and outs and she hates me accordingly, despite my beautiful insinuation and temptation, or she adopts a new moderate medial principle which she creates to allow this split between body and spirit, and tries to make peace between fire and water. The three of us have to live with this chaos and this temerity. Regarding me, I can't live without her. I'll satisfy her in my platonic love, living beside her forever, so that not to cause her any misery or internal conflict. I was, and I am still ready to accept the least of what she can offer me on condition of staying beside her, and that's my utmost of what I can take, but if he wishes more than that, I will not hesitate to burn him, send him out of sight, and make him forgotten. How doesn't a man feel the bitterness his wife feels, when getting married to another woman while keeping the bonds of his first marriage, and not even try to imagine the other way around situation; if women had the same right, regardless of religion and the confusion of children uncertainty as to the father of child? Am I being stimulated to justify and rationalize the existence of the other in my relationship with Suzan? Am I going to occupy the second place from now on, as long as Sharia's wand and custom's mace are in his hand? If man was to choose between intermarriages of bodies or matrimony of spirits, what would he choose? Does the beauty of a flower lie only in the four days it brightens, or in its origin and true nature? Is the pleasure of love lie in the "Eleven Minutes" only, or in the rest of the love travel except those "Eleven Minutes"? What would Suzan say if I told her that I intend to stay with her till we grow old, and would miss her for "Eleven Minutes" once or twice a week? Who knows.., I might have a share of those "Eleven Minutes" too, if she invokes me by then.

- Enough Suzan. We'll stay together and bear the consequences of our choices. I had to say what I said.., stop crying my love.. Calm down, and tell me.., what is his name? What does he do for living? How does he look like? Where does he live? What background does he come from? Is he broadminded? Is he conservative? I need to know everything about him before I meet him and befriend him to stay beside you.

- He came accompanied by his family last night to meet mine, they asked to see me.., a brother of his happens to be Sa'ed's friend. They said they heard that I am a pretty girl, holding a bachelor's degree in Political Science, and I will meet their demands as required. He works in Dubai as an accountant in a construction company, his financial condition is good. Now he is on a leave for engagement but has to get back to Dubai within a week. He will come back two months later to get married. His name is Waleed Radi, he holds a master's degree in management. He asked to see me in private and talked to me for almost an hour. I met lots of suitors before, and I don't know if you will understand what I am saying, he looked kindhearted and easygoing, if I had to get married anyway I don't have to die each and every day. One time is enough.

- Kindhearted and easygoing, or weak-willed and can be taken care of? There is a difference Suzan, such attributes are easier to get along with, but would you feel safe with a person like him? You will have to cancel half of your strong personality to make him feel his manhood before others, even in your sociality.

- Do you doubt my abilities on working out things the way I like? Fate is unjust sometimes Zeyad, but in other times it's extremely fair; if Waleed doesn't deserve such a stand, fate wouldn't have willed him such a destiny. Believe me, God knows him better. Greed is one of the seven deadly sins. As long as his greed pushed him to get engaged to me, he has to pay the price and get punished too. Why does a woman have to accept earlier experiences of a man, as a part of forming his masculine maturity in oriental societies, whereas if she had an innocent expertise, such as if she had been engaged but not married, everybody takes an attitude against her, and she remains unforgiven? If she kisses right, she becomes a suspect immediately! Why does the expertise of a woman even if it was through reading or surfing the net become undesirable and ill-boding? Men are obsessed with comparison complex, that's why they fear any openness of media and intermixing of women and men, but of course if their women are not involved, they don't mind being intermixed with women at all. I don't pity him Zeyad, he deserves it, he is just like the rest of the sinner men and he was sent for a purpose, "*And in no way did We do injustice to them, but it is they who were the unjust*". Certainly we get punished differently.

Suzan might be surprised if I told her that I don't take an attitude against the so called Waleed, she might even doubt my love to her if she heard me saying that. Actually, I don't find him a competitor after hearing her talking about him in this manner, I don't feel sorry for him for being in a situation which he chose in the first place, but for a while I saw him a scapegoat led to a slaughterhouse, and inattentive person thrown in crematory. I wished if he was a mean, fox like, and deceiving person equivalent to any coming confrontations. I need to concentrate on my following step to stay beside Suzan, but rather to dwell in her, not look in the eyes of a lamb and create an internal conflict of hesitation stronger than confronting with a "kindhearted" man. My immortal victory of Suzan's heart and spirit bears no internal conflict between good and bad, or reason and unreason, or legal and illegal. Pricking of the conscience and pangs of remorse should cease forever. It's a war by all means, to retake what has been snatched from me. All kinds of weapons are allowed, even deception. Means justify the ends, my response will be a smart determination and faster than my conscience's hesitation. Defeating such hesitation is possible by shooting the targets before recognizing its nature and its motivations. Even if targets were recognized, not being taken by tricks makes such a haste and rashness justifiable. It's a struggle of existence. That's how we were occupied, and that's how they killed our children and innocent ones in cold blood. That's how killing the old woman by Raskolnikov was justifiable. Dostoyvesky was not sick as he claimed, but he was moved by the reason of crime. Let evil be spread all over, if fate has no reason then reason and logic do have power and violence.

- If someone heard you saying this, he would think that I pity him and that I am hesitant to stay close! Come on Suzan, you will not be surprised when you know that you are a firm belief and a steady faith that is deeply rooted in my heart, because you know me better. I will dedicate my life for you, in the madness of a lover by which he touches the intangibles.. I do understand you, hear your language of silence, and reply to you in my way. Believe me, you don't have to make me feel a thing, because I can sense you and read you well, regardless of all distortion that will take place in our ways of communications. I'll buy you the wedding ring, and I will put it on your finger, you will never take it off… we will prepare the ceremonies of your wedding party together.

If your family and fate want to manipulate us, we will manipulate them back in our way, in our madness, by our rules. We will be the ones to choose our ends, let evil fall upon us all..!

Finally, we became aware of what awaits each one of us, and we also became acquainted with our postulates that will govern our handlings of recent developments. Our tablets of deeds and agendas of fate for years to come are in shine by now. We will not tease each other anymore, but instead we will ease the stress on each other. Suzan will get married to Waleed and she will suffer great deal due to her love to me. I, on my turn, will see her accompanied by someone else, and be aware of exposing what's between us publically. I must get used to it as long as she loves me this much, regardless of my heartbreaking and blood boil when imagining this scene. Madness imposed by fate upon us, madness that has no reason, madness of waging a war against a nation that is left with no choice but to fight back. I looked at Suzan's eyes and saw the heartbreak, the fear, and the call for help in them, as if she was saying, what if the situations were different, wouldn't we live like lovers? Wouldn't each Narcissus of us love the other, thinking of the other as his reflection? Why do affairs in secret, illegal love, and deep penetration of physical desires impose themselves upon us? Why are the more sublime feelings of humanity being led to fierce settlement? Does heaven enjoy the sorrows of humanity? Is there wisdom behind the suffering of man? Oh, Suzan.., I wish I can answer all your questions. Do I have to believe in what Anthony Hopkins said in "Shadow Lands", that "*We're like blocks of stone, out of which the sculptor carves the forms of men. The blows of his chisel, which hurt us so much, are what make us perfect*"? Is it possible that we may admire fear, get used to it, and draw from it the midnight oil to keep the burn of our immortal love? There were lots of questions in her eyes, but my only answer was so short, represented in cuddling her palms in mine and kissing them.

*****

I wonder what we miss more, the beloved ones or the times of joy we had once with them. Could the regret of missing times we could have been happy and could have made them happier be behind my thought?

~10~

"Dear Suzan,

I don't know how the connotation of deprivation and loss has been acquired in your mind, as long as each one of us has his/her own expertise, different images, and a unique conception that keep us aloof from one another. He/she, who dwells in deserts, doesn't have lots of images of a sea, or waves, or beaches, or even of boats, but no doubt he/she is considered a reference of dunes of sand, desert, wilderness, dormancy, sun heat, bitter coldness, and moony nights. That's how connotations are created due to experiences and environment around us. Void.., an abstract word which I thought stands for loss.. But loss can be repaired and compensated whatever painful the miss was. But rootage of void, metaphorically speaking, after your leave, my love, didn't keep me alive. Void; that growing pain by the course of time, instead of fading to become of memories, does invoke bursting the memories of the agonized heart. Death without prior notice, amputation of living and vivacious parts of us opposed by denial and inspiriting previous enliven moments. Resurrection from the dead of images, converses, deeds, and meetings and having them paused in time. Void in my conception, is a bitter thing in my chest that makes me feel the frailty and weakness internally, as if being a helpless feather in the wind. I inhale all the air of the world and hold it to burst out crying this void, but the severe pain disappoints me and my cry doesn't blow up, it rather fades and goes out to make me go through the worst. All that makes us cry doesn't necessarily hurt us by far; real pain roles over when you lose your ability of crying, and even when you cry, you cry the void in the wrong time due to motivations, and strange related links. The more developed the brain is, with increased experiences and awareness of good and bad; the faster it loses the pleasure which it used to have in the past. I wish I could live the pleasure of your attendance again in my life and have no knowledge of what fate hides for me of void's bitterness."

That was a new phase in our story. Suzan worked hard to tune and organize the meetings. Once she meets Waleed and arranges all the ceremonies of engagement party, and once more, we meet and rearrange things in the way we see right and appropriate. I accompanied her while she was looking for a gorgeous dress for the party, I replied to the etiquettes of the shop assistants and the contractors of wedding halls with thanks and appreciation as if I was the bridegroom. I can't deny my happiness for being with her in those moments, I was so grateful for her for offering me this role. From one side, she set my mind at rest, showing me her firm feelings towards me and allowing me to share those details with her; and from the other side, she made me feel as if I was the one who is marrying her. Apart from those funny situations; Suzan used to introduce me to the contractors as her fiancé, and if the man slips by mistake before Waleed, Suzan sets right the misunderstanding explaining that she came before accompanied with one of her brothers and met the contractor. She didn't make me feel any changes in our relationship whatsoever. She spent most of her time with me, and even more than before, because she had an excuse of planning the wedding thus needs to go shopping every now and then. Was she really expecting this relaxation and ease after being engaged? I don't know.., I started to believe that smartness of oriental men is possible to be contained by the foxiness of oriental women, they are capable of employing their potentials to achieve their ends, whereas the intelligence of men is presented in planning for achieving their desires and instincts of winning, losing, and competitions depending on paternal oriental support and the wrong biased justification due to the double standards.

Suzan.., this girl whom I have never dreamt of meeting before, and never read of her likes in books or novels, is real, and she loves me, and is asking me to stay with her forever. Are we a cute case of illness or an uncommon temerity in the eyes of others? It seems to me that the extreme behavior of us, overstepping the sacred human relations as seen by some people, is entirely rejected starting by the least civilized and conservative tribes in the world to the most bohemians, luxurious, and rebellious over customary. What rank of weird practices, on the scale of human extreme approaches for happiness do we occupy? If we surveyed the approaches applied by man since the dawn of time, that increased his thirst for more pleasure, satisfied his/her appetite towards the other sex, and pursued him/her to dwell with the beloved, then we could justify the legality of this relation. What's a bit stranger is that man always tries to justify the existence of temerity logically speaking, and when being incapable, he/she attributes this temerity to abulia of psychological needs and cases of illness.

Thereby, nymphomania; which stands for excessive sexual drive of females, corresponding to satyriasis; referring to that lustful horse-like creature as a sign of excessive sexual drive of men, came out to light as cases of illness. Incest; sexual attraction to unmarriageable persons followed, then SSAD referring to same sex attraction disorder. Gradually, masochism; deriving sexual gratification from being physically or emotionally abused, and sadism; derivation of pleasure as a result of inflicting pain, humiliation, and cruelty on others, became popular and justified raping. Cuckolding also is referred to as a psychological state, even Freud and Roy Baumeister explained the resort to such a practice in a way that pleases a curious to relieve him/ herself of the stress of the burden of their social role. The suckling baby girl/boy in certain schools and ideology didn't escape danger of being sexually abused by adolescent for sexual stimulation. Man also went beyond reason by Necrophilia; the disgusting sexual attraction to corpses, profaning their sanctity by mentally sick people. Yes, man went too far approaching pleasure by all means; he/she has also been sexually attracted to animals, and once again is given a name that marked it as a psychological state of mind, out of Beastiality. Finally, insanity of mankind led to being attracted to objects manifested in Objectophilia. Every day we hear demands for legalizing homosexual marriages, reasons and excuses for polygamy, common-law marriage, precise marriages; where women abandon some of their basic rights, and marriage for pleasure which is allotted to a limited time and with the abandonment of women to their rights too. My equation in which I guarantee no harm to the bonds of marriage, and a commitment to Suzan's stable social and marital life will be considered a taboo and atrocity. I am not looking for a new world where such relations are allowed, neither looking for a religion that permits and justifies sexual intercourse with a boyfriend or a lover, nor a space for my attendance under that legal umbrella, but Suzan always surprises me with the coming out of the unobserved choice that crossed no minds before. She obliges me to respect her abstinence and virtue, and approves what's beyond endurance as same as feelings and delirium of spirits to dwell in each other. I certified this offer and choice, and I will not go back in my word. Obviously, the assumption of my love to her as a platonic love away from any physical approach is next to a lie. Utopia doesn't exist, and the assumed city where Plato enforced the physical desires to the superiority of spirit is some kind of fantasy, that's because spirit itself constantly urges doing mischievous things, otherwise, what's the benefit of all these religions? Aren't they for behaving the spirit, and subduing it? The utmost of what I can abide by towards Suzan is never to cross the red lines that would ruin her marriage, but that of course will not cancel the spaces of ebbs and flows in our middle land. I have always admired the greatness of William Golding's "The Lord of The Flies", in which he revealed the nature of human spirit, where he explained that we were not made and created well-doers, as assumed Plato before. Joseph Conrad's "Heart of Darkness", emphasized the same idea too. Who would, then, blame me if I love a girl and sacrifice my life to her, justifying all means to this end? Who would blame me if I stay close to her and listen to her complaints? Who permits this to a psychiatrist and confiscates me this right? Our belief of the possibility of this adoration brought us out of the hell of forbidden and welcomed us to the heaven of possibility.

*****

*"Our dead are never dead to us, until
we have forgotten them"*

George Eliot

~11~

After days of preparations for the engagement party, red letter day has come. Suzan called me early that day and asked me to give her a ride to buy some stuff, and then drive her to *Suha*'s saloon. I dropped her at the saloon exactly at twelve o'clock, and went hurriedly back home due to a phone call from my mother, informing me that my father's health state wasn't good at all. After one hour, Suzan sent me a message saying: "He went crazy for not being the one taking me to the saloon, I told him that I had to do some other women stuff before, and you didn't have to be with me". I sent her back a message explaining why I won't be able to send her any more messages or make any phone calls on account of not embarrassing her if Waleed was around, and I also mentioned the deterioration of my father's health state, indicating why I have to stay at home. My father's health was indeed relapsing so fast, I tried to stay by his side most of the time in the past, and Suzan excused and understood my absence due to this reason more than anyone else. She was totally aware of my solicitude towards my father, and most of the times she felt sorry for herself for not experiencing the same feelings towards her father. I used to tell her about the influence of my father on me, and the part he played in bringing me up. She loved him through me, and wished to meet him too.

I stayed helpless there, doing nothing except surrendering to God's will, and wait… I sat in the living room, and could hear the crying voice of my mother trying to talk and get my father to reply to her and "bear witness to the oneness of Allah, and Mohammad as God's prophet", to try to stay awake. My sisters were crying in separation of each other, then they all came into the living room and entreated me to call the ambulance and to take him to the hospital. I did that several times before, and doctors were helpless by then, in the last time they were bluntly clear and said to me that he is dying and it's just a matter of time. Under their insistence, I inclined and called the ambulance, and went back to sit beside my father, I was taken by the view of his oculogyric crisis, till he emitted the last breath and passed away before my eyes!! I froze.. Is this death? Is this "*The*" death? Is this the almighty vanquisher of mankind? Where is its veneration? Why does it keep itself out of sight? Why does it unsheathe spirits stealthily and in quietness? Why wasn't I scared as I am supposed to be? The screams and crying of my mother and my sisters disturbed the clarity of my mind. Does this mean that my father is dead? This man whom I lived with for thirty six years acknowledging all his sayings and deeds, dies... just like that? Why don't I feel a thing in such a situation? Did my feelings die? Was my spirit pulled out from me? Who is the one who died? I didn't conceive the shock, didn't cry, didn't even shed a tear..

I was driven unconsciously acting autonomously till we arrived at the hospital in the ambulance, and the doctors notified his death. I sat in the entrance of the emergency hall taking my breath, when the members of my family started arriving to the hospital. They started hugging, delivering clichés of condolences, "*hit your stride*", "*who left a successor behind, verily didn't die*", "*to God we belong and to him is our return*".... I was awakened from the confusion and the maze by a call alert. It was Suzan. I didn't know what to say to her, if I didn't answer she will figure out what happened, and if I answer her call she might notice the shock and confusion in my voice, I don't want to spoil her special night..

- Hello.

- Hello, Zeyad. Where are you? Did anything wrong happen? Tell me.. I've just read your message.

- No.. nothing happened, darling. Calm down. He had difficulty in breathing for a while that's why I brought him to the hospital, he is much better now.

- Tell me the truth! Is this what really happened?

- Definitely, he is fine now.

- May God bless him with good health, alright then, I want you to reassure me of his health condition within a couple of hours.

- Don't you worry, he'll be fine. I'll call you back later, bye.

- Take care. Bye.

I didn't call her back that night, because I was so busy with the preparations of burial and funeral ceremonies with some of my friends who kept me accompanied all the time. I called my two brothers Yusuf in America and Ibrahim in Italy and informed them of what happened. Because they hadn't enough time to attend before burial time next day, I kept all preparations the same. At three o'clock in the morning, Suzan sent me a message on the phone saying that Waleed stayed at her family's home to have dinner with her and her brothers, and passed the night awake talking, she asked again about my father's health condition. I didn't reply to her message, knowing for sure that she will figure out what happened next morning.

At eight o'clock in the morning, people started knocking at our door to help us preparing for the arrival of consolers and to be there as usual for the bereaved to help them overcome the brunt. This is one of the habitual customs, where first-degree relatives work on supervising things out, but second-degree relatives and the rest of the consolers are the ones who go into action. At eleven o'clock, Suzan sent me a message saying that she made an excuse to leave the house and come by our house in a taxi to know the reason behind not sending her messages or making phone calls. When she saw the crowds by the house she figured out what happened and blamed me for not telling her the truth. I told her that it wasn't appropriate to disturb her and cause any kind of unease in such a night for her. She sent me back a message saying:

- I will leave you now, because I know how busy you must be, but that doesn't mean I am letting this pass easily. May Allah be merciful to him and rest his soul in peace.

- Thank you Suzan. Forgive me, I thought it was the right thing to do.., didn't want to trouble you. I'll call you later if I have a chance.

After the funeral ceremony, we went back home and found the big tent erected in the middle of the street. Such tents are erected for several social occasions, and most of the times those tents come with supplements to accommodate a big number of people. Second-degree relatives and relatives by marriage start the series of banquets as alms handout for the dead's spirit as a special favor to please the consolers.

The bereaved must recall, on the other hand, everyone who gave a banquet so that if same kind of brunt happens to them then the bereaved of today will be their consolers by then and give back banquets; a blow for a blow. The bereaved must also listen to the pieces of advice as part of receiving the condolences, preachers seize the opportunities of being in such places to throw preaches, to show off, and to pray for the spirit of the dead. Such preachers make one feel as if he/she was away from the right practice of religion in a way that pleases God. Such gathering is taken advantage of for more important issues; as politics, cursing and insulting the governments for the purpose exhibitionism and back-biting each other for four days. I wished that Suzan could attend such occasions to see and hear what really happens in such situations.

The four days came to a close so slowly; we were so tired as a result of receiving and meeting consolers till midnight. My mother and my sisters went through the worst surely, a woman who has no other place to lash or to backbite or even to indulge in converses, finds such a gathering an outlet for her hidden and suppressed defamation. Rights of accommodation represented in banquets, Arabic coffee, and prime dates, that suit the dead and inheritors financial condition and class, last for four days. Meals for consolers who happen to be at lunch time, and they are so many, must also be offered, too. Not to speak of the silly repeated questions that you have to answer and which distress you all over again and again such as repeating and describing the last moments of the deceased. In the morning of the fifth day, and after the tent was removed, I called Suzan and told her that I needed to see her. We decided to meet at four o'clock in the evening. Meanwhile, my mother asked me to help her in some stuff, which was behind the blow up of my safety valve of bearing the void my father left behind five days ago. I still remember standing before her; she was wearing a black long cloak, standing before my father's opened closet's doors. She asked me to bring the clothes down so that she hands them as alms for poor people, saying:

- The reward of alms is better than the keep of abandoned stuff!

No sooner I drew near the hanged shirts than I burst out crying. He was so handsome, and highly appreciated his elegant appearance. He had the solemnity of prophets. How can we erase a man from existence, and burn his history as if he never was before? What sinful and evil hand that would bury the memories of a man who lived for sixty three years, without leaving any of his ruins and remains for memories? I revered him when he was in good health, and I loved him during his sickness as if I was his father and he was my son, and now I can sense his appearance watching me erasing him, cancelling him, and allowing life to fold his derelict property. Will my son stand to bring down my stuff too? Will he claim that he is doing it for the sake of reward? Nay.., my father's stuff will not be brought down. These are his property which I dare not touch.

I left the house terrified of my father's chase to me. I wanted to deny his death for the second time. I wandered about in the streets till it was time to meet Suzan, I passed by *Al Husn* street, where she was shopping, and picked her up. She was confused and not as usual, but she looked so pretty in her nun-like white and black dress; virtuous, and chaste. She sat in silence, had a quick look at me, and turned away her face without talking. I felt the swelling of my eyes' bags due to crying. Headed towards the hills of *Samad* where pine and cypress trees bent due to western wind, turned the front of the car towards *Sahl Horan*, stood still for a minute, then went out of the car and took a few steps forward, then sat watching the faraway lands. I heard her getting out of the car and walking towards me, then she kneeled and hugged me with her both arms. She cried and made me cry for a long time, later on she looked into my eyes with her crying eyes and said:

- I'll not console you; I want your grief to last forever. Consolation and solace for the dead lies in having a sighing and crying bereaved behind, who would wail and moan over the dead. The dead might not be pleased with your agony, but knowing how much is missed, and how life becomes boring and unbearable after him/her in the eyes of a bereaved, could be the only solace and consolation to the spirit. Regardless of the grief and pain seen on you, still I consider it my consolation. Would you miss me this much and cry over me forever?

I was analyzing each and every word spoken by her. Suzan was the only one who offered me an invitation to sadness without meaningless filler clichés. God, how much I needed her! She was the one who could understand my constraint from crying for days.

- My father died Suzan.., and you got engaged… Void took hold of my heart. Do I have to cast my beloved into the river and wait till they are restored by the just of heaven back to me? You are right. I want this pain to last forever, I want to remain sighing and crying till God restores you all back to me. I will not be delighted or be in peace before I get you back. I seek no words that would beg mercy of fate to spare my killing and my defeat. Let fate make me go through hell, my father will not die, and you will not love someone else other than me. I will knock all doors and leave no stone unturned looking for you, till I die embraced by your arms, do you understand what I am saying?

I shed tears while telling her this. She wiped away all my tears with her brunette's fingers and embraced me again and whispered in my ear:
- I do, that's what I wanted to know. I can't live without you.., and you will not die my love.

I hugged her firmly and heard her groaning. I felt as if she was my lifeboat in despair sea. This girl, who writes shorthand my language into looks and glances, knows how to bridle my anger and when to let the rein free for my outbreak. She was the one who could make me cry and laugh the way she likes, as if she was a legion of women. She was everything I wanted in a woman. Each one of us lives in a strange sadness and everlasting tragedy, each one of us persists on his/her right in love regardless of misfortunes acupuncture and thorns of wills.

We pledged a vow to spend the rest of the time with each other. Our moments became overloaded with feelings of love and full of details, codes, and signs that were exclusively known and understood by us. We used to go shopping to buy her needs, and then stop at restaurants to have lunch, drink coffee, and spend the rest of the day together. She initiated talking to Waleed daily through the internet after he returned back to Dubai to get to know him better. Unfortunately, she got caught in comparison traps. Though I was happy to know that I became her reference point, still I have tried to be evenhanded, explaining to her that we are different and she must stop comparing us, I tried to convince her that there are men who are even better than me and she must accept him with all his goods and bads. I made it clear for her that she needs time to get to know his way of thinking and his way of dealing with people and things around him. She complained that when she talks about literature, art, language and history, he becomes bored and tries to change the subject. I explained to her that he might be of those who are not good in speech and elocution, and she steals the limelight from man stage in a paternal society which is "wrong". I advised her to pretend stupidity and ignorance sometimes and bump deliberately into things so that he teaches her the dramatically manly leading, the way he sees it right!

Two months slipped by. We didn't realize by then that the sun rises and sets while talking to each other. We talked about everything, took all probabilities into consideration, and studied all future arrangements and consequences. We explored the phases of Waleed development from the outset so that we understand this cancer which occupied present. We went tens of times to the farm and spent long hours dwelling in each other. Suzan wasn't a feminine body only, otherwise I would have become bored of, though it was perfect. She was the maturity of mind, spirit, and body, changeable and novel all the time, she never made me feel the dullness and the routine when being with her at all. She was a twinkling diamond spirit in the darkness of nights. She taught me that the times of romantic love didn't run out yet, and we can still recall and invoke the love of *Abd El Haleem* to *Shadia*, and sense the madness of romance of *Amitabh Bachchan* to the gorgeous *Parveen Babi* when riding a cart on the beach, declaring his love to her in an ageless song that is still known and remembered by millions of people. She also taught me that love is the eagerness of being close to the beloved like his/her vein. She told me once that love is the adoration of the beloved's details and the curiosity of knowing what is he/she doing now, wishing if you were a camcorder to record even his/her breath. Yes.., innocent and naïve love can exist regardless of corruption dunghill, the world economic deterioration, the increase of responsibilities, unemployment, and poverty. Suzan taught me that love is a liquid material state which waves in the heart of a lover, quenching the deep thirst in the roots of persistence so that fruits of devotion grow on branches of eternity.

Why do we love? Do we look for a missing thing when we love? Why don't we sometimes love those who adore us, but rather love others? Poets were our representatives since the dawn of poetry. They competed with each other trying to come up with more descriptions of their beloved, but as far as I know, they didn't answer the questions of love's essential nature. Can anyone live without love, for example? Since I met Suzan and fell in love with her, I used to strict myself and split it into two, no other self can answer my questions but a self driven from mine. I want to investigate about that love which overawed and ruined me.

- How were you before my love to Suzan? Don't evade, I know you better.

- Since you know me better, why do you ask?

- I want to undress love and know and see its defects and points of power, and... I am the one who asks here, you don't ask, you just answer.

- Let's see, I was unaware of my frailty and my human attributes.., I think I was stronger.., or may be unkind and ruthless.., no, less sensitive towards others. I was the center of the universe, and I used to sense the around by my instincts and my senses only.

- Were you happy by then?

- I can't call it happiness, may be less loaded, but more impatient, void, and bored.

- Isn't that a relief?

- Not a relief for sure. When you feed the animal desires inside you, you fidget looking for something else... probably that's what makes us different from animals.

- Who said that animals don't love and feed their desires?

- No, animals feed their desires in all situations, even in their feelings towards their babies.

- Are you trying to say that we look for that thing when we get our instincts and desires satisfied?

- May be... it's because we are quite sure of the importance of that missing thing, we come to the conclusion that we can live without having all these desires satisfied. But on the other hand, you keep looking for that missing thing which you can't overlook or live without, because it removes boredom and defuses your animalistic motivation.

- This is philosophy and bullshit. Try to be clearer.

- Simply, when you compare yourself before and after love, you realize that someone else becomes the center of your universe, while you are considered as his/her center of universe. Your happiness turns to be conditioned by the happiness of the other.

- So.., love is a need for the other, right?

- It's a journey and trials which you take to please the other, though your happiness is conditioned by his/her happiness, still it comes in second rank. Love is unmasking your sight to let you feel the joy of perfection and happiness of your beloved. The more you bestow liberally upon your beloved, the happier you become. Everyone of us has his/her codes, exactly like the ones of the genetic codes, that make you dedicated to please and love one person only. If you get polarized by others for some kind of reason, your happiness will not be integrated, and you will breed a beast that will ruin your world. That's why a person who depends on feeding his desires only is capable of ravish, rape, and violation of those who share with him/her no cordiality and clemency. Love means not to wish for a red apple with a taste of a green one, but to live in comfort and luxury of a red apple, of its taste, its touch, its blessing, its kismet, and trying by all means to eat it, enjoy it, and accept its seeds, and never let it down wishing the green one before it.

- That's why I am miserable and my life is abhorrent… my code was not made or created for a green one; simply we won't click with our mates. I will not concede to my misery, nor approve of her distress. It's a matter of adoration, cordiality, and compassion that we will not take pleasure in with our mates, but instead we will bask in with each other in shade.

On July 10th Waleed made his arrival to Suzan's family house a surprise, at that time Suzan called me. I was at the office by then. She spoke to me while she was on the verge of tears:

- He arrived..!

Silence occupied our conversation for a short period of time, we exchanged sighs of despair, and our voices stood still in our throats.., then I said to her:

- Dear Suzan, we both knew that the date of his arrival was drawing near and was already determined. Be patient and sustained, and be confident that the promises and vows we have made will be kept and never be broken. You have to be on the level of this madness. Show the fate that our love is a survivor, so that fate inclines to us willingly or unwillingly. Recite me day and night like your prayers, put me on like your elegant shawl, embrace me like your favorite perfume, or as your childish memories and properties under your pillow. I will always be there for you; you will see me in sunshine guts…, in moonlight grief, in adoration popple, and in slight breeze of love around you. I am the summer in your awakening and the winter in your sleep. Vivacious April runs in my blood, Oh Suzan, my soul flies all around you, I can see you, hear you, and speak to you if you listen carefully. Call me anytime you wish, I don't become weary of you, or bored of listening to you, or even tired of talking to you. I promised you to be conjured up before you till we meet again. I promised you Suzan, and my promise is a decision that will be carried out.

I heard a nearby voice on the phone calling for Suzan, saying:

- What are you waiting for? Come on!!

I said to her:

- Go on Suzan… I am with you baby.

- Don't leave me!

- I am not going to leave you. Come on my love, be courageous. It's fate's alarm sound, we have to start playing.

- Alright, I promise you.

She said it with a stronger and more stressed tone this time as if she decided to initiate..

- I love you.

- I love you too, Bye.

- Bye.

As soon as she closed the phone I felt how the in between bridges were lifted, and how the desert stretched its spaces and distances between us. Our hopes yawned in the nightfall of meetings. The shortness in spaces we accomplished once is taking its revenge now by the flowing waves between us, by knocking down the mast of hopes, and by tearing the sails of our gathering; beginning with slaying us by sowing the seeds of devastation on bedewed lips. This is the backfire of fate on the uprize of lovers, overstatement in obstruction and effluent fountain of expatriation. Chapeau to you fate.., well done, and bravo this victory.. Enjoy your irony making fun of us, and imposing your upper hand on us. Is this all what you are capable of doing? Cheer over this round.., but you should have crushed us first before having this smile of victory drawn on your lips. You should have got confirmed first that we were left as a thing forgotten, dust in a jar, before filling the sky with joy and triumph. You become high when you blast this almighty power of yours and hide behind the shield of disappearance… What are you afraid of? That I stop you from carrying out your cosmogony, death, love, resurrection, blessings and boons, or torture? What are you afraid of? Everything is in your hand… What pride and dignity do you seek by your victory when I am barehanded and have none of your weapons? How can I confront the unseen? Nay… I'll follow your traces, your wills, and corrupt them by mine, by my persistence.., by my commitment.., and by my vows and promises. I love her, and you will not prevent me from being with her but through death. As long as death is one of your weapons, I beg you by the pride and honor of brave worriers to make me your opponent, and to spare Suzan and never touch her by any of your grudges.. I beg you to show me any sign of approval for this sacrifice.. I indeed seek chivalric death, but grovel before you to spare the life of Suzan.

I broke into tears in the office till I shuddered, yielded to a strange tremor that occupied my whole body, but then calmed down and felt a sudden drowsiness creeping into my flesh and spirit, leaving behind leftovers of crying hanged on my chest.

I didn't finish my lectures that day, instead I went back home, that home which is not the same home that used to be in the past. I stood before the window that affords a view of my father's room the minute I arrived as usual. I used to talk at him through that window if I happened to be on the balcony. His bed was void, tidy, cold, and lifeless. I held the window's safekeeping bars like a prisoner, and became distracted with talks that once took place between us.

- What is it dad, why don't you talk?

- I am thinking..

- Pardon my curiosity, but what are you thinking of? What thoughts that disturb you this much and make you worried?

His eyes were wide opened, staring upwards… He looked scary..

- What thoughts would occupy a mind of a bedridden but death? How many years are left? How many breaths do I still have? What is death like? Ahh.. I am scared.

- Scared? But you believe in God, you keep on praying, you read Qur'an and most of your time you are busy in extolment and asking God's forgiveness!!

- I could have seized every opportunity while I was in good health to be righteous, but I've wasted many times. I fear death..., I fear its agony and struggle, I fear the separation, and destiny.

Where are you dad? Come back for a minute and tell me what separation is like? Is it the same as death? Why do I cry over her separation but don't cry over your death? I didn't admit your death yet, nor got used to your absence, I don't even feel satisfied for what I did for you. I feel negligent. I could have hugged her more.., kissed her more.., and told her that I love her more and more. Why were you oriental, dad, and taught me that men don't cry, and should never expose their feelings and emotions before anyone? I could have seized the opportunity to tell you how much I love you, but feared that you don't die and abhor the frailty of your son. I will not spare a trick up my sleeve but benefit from to be with Suzan. I will not postpone a chance to meet her or kiss her from now on. I will tell her every morning when the sun rises that I love her.., with every sunset.., and in every destined meeting. I will let her know how much my feebleness is delicious when I am with her. Oh, Suzan, I wish that you know what your love made of me, I know how things will end up like, I wish that Waleed knows what your love made of me! Would he by then see you like any other woman whom he finds no sanctity in? Would he look at another woman when he is accompanied by you? You won't be able to tell him that you have an adorer, too. You will take all the stabs in silence and you won't dare confront him with the hidden secrets, a thing which is below decent women. Suzan, I will not allow fate to crush you, nor times to masticate you. I will stay with you, and inform the world that you are the first woman of mankind and the most beautiful. Your firebrand exclusively will not be put out. You are more sublime and unique of what is of the common and frequent... God, how much I long for penetrating my fingers among your tufts! How much I want to hug you.., kiss you.., and sip your saliva off your lips. I feel that you are not safe unless you are with me. I don't even trust putting you in the hands of your husband. I wonder what you are doing now, Suzan!

*****

When my shrink asked about the symptoms, I told him that I lost the appetite of being awakened and sought refuge in sleeping. He recommended writing my dreams, so I began bleeding my agonies

~12~

On Wednesday morning of July 21ˢᵗ, Sa'ed; the eldest brother of Suzan's, dropped me a line to invite me to his sister's wedding and apologized for not being able to deliver the invitation card by hand. I invoked a blessing on, and made him feel the probability of not being able to attend the wedding, I also asked him to pass my blessings to Suzan and her husband. It seemed normal, but I probed a scenario written by Suzan herself, signifying inviting me to the wedding. I wonder if Sa'ed remembered me as he claimed, or if it was Suzan who hinted at inviting me as a step forward towards introducing me to her husband! Suzan.., who else other than me knows what crosses your mind? God, how much I love your lunacy!!

In the evening, I took a shower and shaved my beard, keeping my goatee which Suzan never allowed me to shave it. I don't know how women get enchanted by the simplest of men, when men dedicate themselves to the most complicated to please and seduce women. I preferred to wear a black suit and a black blouse; I wasn't in the mood to put on a shirt and a tie. I headed to *Tulip* flower shop in *Al Hashimi* street, I picked up many white, red, yellow, and violet flowers, then picked a pen to write a dedication when I suddenly asked myself; what am I doing? Have I lost my mind? Am I this much convinced of this confrontation that I didn't collapse, and about to attend her wedding party? Lots of questions stung my sanity, made me miss my steadiness, and were about to make me go crazy. I left the flower shop, laid the bouquet on the car seat and drove to *Al Sharq* wedding hall. The motor convoy consisted of a few cars filling the air with honked horns, the bride and bridegroom's car led this clumsy parade. I couldn't get out of the car!! All my joints froze, broke into sweat. A sudden stroke of silence damaged my hearing, and I felt palpitation in my chest as if my heart was about to breakthrough my ribs. No it's not time to faint; I won't let my body overcome this moment with a faint that would spare its agony. Suzan wants me there for her now, and I'll answer her call even if it costs me my life. I am not going to let her down. I stepped out of the car and went forward, headed to the hall entry, watched the crowd of people clapping, yelling, and dancing.., all this in deep silence. I saw the veins stiffed in the necks of some who were shouting.., but in silence. Among the crowd, Suzan emerged in her white dress; her brothers carried her on their shoulders. The scene killed me in grief, and drew an ominous scene in my mind, very much contradicting with a wedding! I couldn't make any more advances, I felt that I was collapsing and would attract everybody's attention. I turned around and went hurriedly to the car, throwing myself inside, resting my determination with closed eyes.

I woke up later on the knocking of someone on the windshield, shouting:

- Are you alright, Sir?

- Yeah.. Yeah, I am alright, who are you?

The strong headache was hitting like lightning, I was still sweating.

- I am the hall guard.

- Oh, I see.. What time is it?

- Half past one after midnight, everybody is gone.

- What? Half past one? Oh.. Alright.. I'll leave now.. sorry..!

I went back home swaying, as if I was walking on robes. I sat on the balcony surrendering to my fatigue and my crash. I could hear *Sura* moving around in the kitchen. She brought me a cup of coffee and asked me if I was alright.

- Don't worry. I am OK.

- For how long?
- Hmmm? What did you say?

- For how long? Since your father died you've been getting deranged.

- Am I supposed to be alright? Forget it.. Leave me alone.

I gestured to her to go away. We were both tired of our surroundings and of our short conversations. I stayed late that night on the balcony. Suzan was looking at me behind the night darkness with her gorgeous eyes, I hugged her and laid her head on my chest and didn't make a move so not to disturb her. I felt her hand on my shoulder patting to wake me up saying:

- Go to sleep in your room.. It's morning.

- Ah *Su..ra..*!

I went to my bedroom half dead. I slept in my clothes for more than a whole day. I didn't know what happened to me that night, I just wanted Suzan to know that I was there attending her wedding party, and nothing will stop me from answering her calls as I promised her.

"Suzan, my joy, my sweetheart, my pleasure, the delight of my eye and the home of my soul.., I've been dying by with sunrise and sunset for the past seventeen months since your leave. Writing to you has become my escape and my outlet; still I didn't finish the least of what I want to say to you…"

That period of time and those days were real successive breakdowns and a whirlpool of sadness that pulled me to the depth. Suzan, that angel who took over all my senses and connection with the world around me, left me this void, deprivation, and slow killing overnight which didn't lead to any kind of peaceful death. I could hear her around, where ever I go, talking to me, and I talk to her, too. People around didn't leave me alone, they insisted on disturbing our converses. I could see her among the students in my lectures, coming late as usual, sitting, looking at me with sad glances, till one day I went too far imagining her sitting in front of me…

- Dr. Zeyad.. Dr. Zeyad..!!

No sooner had I heard Dr. Omar's voice; the manager of Language Center than Suzan faded away inclining her head.

- Yes.. Yes Dr. Omar, what's up?

- Would you please come with me to my office?
    I didn't notice him entering the classroom..

- Sure.., sure.

I stood behind the desk, gathered my stuff while observing the suspicious looks of the students, then walked away with Dr. Omar heading towards his office. He asked everybody inside to leave us alone for a while, and then he asked me to sit and started talking.

- Dr. Zeyad, one of your students came to my office complaining about your behavior; saying that you act in an eerie way inside the class room, and this is not the first time, by the way. What is it? Tell me, if you are facing a real hard time, I can be of a good help for you and we can work things out. Talk to me, I am speaking to you unofficially.

I didn't utter a word, and didn't understand what was going on! What problem was he talking about? And why did the students look at me in that suspicious way?

- If you don't want to speak to me, I am sorry to tell you that I have to recommend a medical board consultation check up to assess your state before you get back to work again.

- What? Medical board consultation!! What for? What did I do?

- That's exactly the problem! You are entirely unconscious and don't know what you are doing or saying. You are losing control over your senses and over your behavior. I am sorry, you are the most intelligent of the teachers, and you're highly qualified, but this will not make me reconsider my decision of having a final medical consultation that would decide your mental state. I will write to them right now.

- What are the indications for care seeking? For God's sake, what did I do?

- Would you please wait in the secretary's lounge till I finish?
    I was shocked, but feared any clash between me and Dr. Omar that would lead him to call a spade a spade in the eye, and tell me what I did.

I stepped outside and waited, but couldn't resist the idea of asking the secretary of what was going on..

- Suzan, what's going on? Why does Dr. Omar look so upset and nervous? Why does he want me to get a medical consultation?

I still remember the way she looked at me by which she answered all my questions, that sympathetic look in her eyes and the fear of being near me. She was holding the phone, her voice was clearly shaking:

- Samar.., my name is Samar Dr. Zeyad, not Suzan..!!

The presence at the health center which is appended to the college and the mere showing up at the clinic of psychology was a catastrophe for most people. Oriental societies are still divided on regard of considering psychological treatment into two groups; civilization-pretenders who don't mind seeing a shrink, and might even boast among others about the unbearable pressure of work and social life as they claim, or even using the excuse of boredom and free time. This category is exclusive to the rich of them. The people of the other category still reject this kind of medicine and don't acknowledge it, due to the fear of society and the shame that might come over if people started doubting their sanity, mental state, emotions, or even behaviors. Those themselves wouldn't hesitate much seeing a juggler or a quack to let grow the hair again, or take a prescribed spell that would replace the performance and magic of *Viagra,* or even to let somebody fall in love with somebody else by using black magic. I was neither of this category nor of that. In fact I wasn't worried of being at psychological clinic; I instead considered it a governmental institution which I had to go to like the rest of the citizens to finish up paper work. Unintentional movements came out of the patients in waiting lounge; one was biting the inside of his cheeks, and one was biting her nails. A girl was crying accompanied with another girl, her friend was the custodian and the wise of course; she heaped her up with commandments and preaches of what to tell the doctor. I guess she was heartbroken, a victim of love. Her state didn't need psychological treatment, that's why appointments with shrinks are usually scheduled at wide intervals; time heals such wounds, except mine. Time for me functions as a vaccine; it increases my immunity against the germs of forgetfulness. I waited there for an hour when at last my name was called..
- Mr. Zeyad Al Juneidy.. Zeyad Al Juneidy..

The nurse enjoyed to shame the patients' names in public, her voice was so masculine like that which had never been tuned before. She tried that morning to mask the pimples that filled her face with makeup, but it was of no use, thus she decided to place her anger on those poor patients.

- I am Zeyad Al Juneidy!

I shouted.

- I am a teacher of English language in the Language Center, my national number is 97010066625, and I am seeing a psychiatrist; I am getting insane..!!

At that time, the doctor dashed out of his office and started to pat on my shoulder in a friendly way to make me calm down trying to make me enter the examination room, but I proceeded screaming:

- And by the way, pimples and acnes of menopause can still be seen on...

- Hahaha.. Come in man!! That's enough. I don't want to know what happened outside, but I can guess.

The doctor sat behind his desk trying to cover his laughs by his fist, he was fifty something, and he looked respectful. His laughs started to fade away little by little, then he put on his eye glasses and started reading a file.

- Hmmm.. Mr. Zeyad, what is the problem? Have you got any idea why you are here?

- No.

- Your manager says, according to complaints of your students, that you were talking during the lecture to a woman or a girl called Suzan who didn't exist, and that it wasn't the first time. Is that true?

- I was talking to Suzan!!

- Yes. Who is Suzan, Zeyad?

I didn't answer him. I didn't know what to say! Was I really talking to Suzan during the lecture? I can't deny that I invoke her presence and bring about dialogues and stories between us all the time, but to speak in a loud voice to the extent that students witnessed this derange is a sign of deterioration!

- Is she your beloved girl?

- She is more than that.

- I understand of course the levels and degrees of love which vary from one person to another, every lover thinks that his love is exceptional and has no likes.

- What do you want to say doctor?

- You are married, you have kids, and you are a prestigious teacher, one of the best, as stated. Tell me, why would a smart man like you expose in public the well-kept and hidden secretes of his?

- Either his inner vessel is overfilled with the hidden secret thus flowed against his will, or he is infatuated and obsessed with this strong belief that he doesn't want to abandon it, and feels no harm in stating it openly.

- Great, now answer my question in specific, was "stating openly" this secret made intentionally or unintentionally? Were you aware of what you were doing?

- Do you attend live musical concerts, Doctor?

- I beg your pardon!

- Answer me. Do you attend live musical concerts?

- Yes, I do.

- Do you attend those concerts because you are fond of music or you just incline to the demands of your companions?

- As a matter of fact...

- So, you only go to please your companions and meet their demands. Do you like dancing, Doctor?

- I don't get it, what's the relation here? These are irrelevant questions.

- You are wrong, Doctor. These are very relevant questions.

   The tone of my voice started rising.

- If you were of those who attend such concerts for their own pleasure, then you would have tolerated the fans who lose their minds and start singing, clapping, and dancing. You fear exposing your feelings and reactions publically when the fans don't care if they lost control on their behaviors willy-nilly. The state of being enraptured doesn't harm anyone. Love is what freezes you enraptured, but adoration is the motion of life inside your body. It is glee and insanity. I have carried out an ulterior soliloquy or monologue like any artist who is driven by ardor a little; I have probably hummed and chanted like a composer or a melodist who feared losing a tune. Critics often considered the soliloquy and madness of *Hamlet* as genius of *Shakespeare*. Didn't prophets have soliloquies and confidential talks invoking God? Didn't *Caliph Omar* shout once, "*Sariyah! Watch out the mountain!*" in front of people while he was standing on the platform, and when asked about it he said he didn't know, something was carried out on his tongue? Why do you consider it a big fuss? Students come late, talk during the lecture, cheat in exams, write indecent comments about their teachers, answer their phone calls and reply to messages, hug and cuddle in public and we do nothing to stop these ridiculous behaviors. On the other hand when I hum or expose or carry out sheltered thoughts I become an outlaw and exiled from your paradise! Don't you think that you are confiscating my right of expressing my thoughts and prejudging me for a crime that I didn't commit even? Are you going to accuse me of crimethink like the one stated by *George Orwell* in his novel *1948*? Listen to me carefully, my thoughts are relevant and coherent. Look at me, I still care about my appearance, and I keep on taking care of the cleanness of my body. I didn't lose my mind yet!!

- Calm down, Mr. Zeyad. Listen to me, I didn't say that this accidental symptom is considered a state if illness. You just speak aloud instead of keeping those secrets hidden to reconsider what happened; trying to organize the scenario and the scenes in a more comfortable and desirable way. Probably, those events ended up in a way that didn't please you, therefore you keep trying to change them, or you might indulge yourself after getting prepared for situations created by you, to carry out what you wanted to say or do the way you want. Those scenes are scripted, directed, and acted by you, unlike fate which is written on you. How about if we come to a compromise between us? You know that regardless of your convincing hearing, nobody likes to see people speaking to themselves in public. How about if you make an outlet to your agonies and dedicate a specific time to this release? Try writing what you want to say on paper, on one condition, that you don't talk to anyone about this paper?

- You, doctors, think that all your patients are lunatic. A painter, a poet, or a melodist doesn't know when inspiration comes to spare it or postpone it for other times, in spite of that, your idea sounds like a good one. Alright then, I will write everything that crosses my mind and I will not tell anyone about it.

I had already started writing since Suzan's leave, but I didn't mention this to the doctor because I wanted to safeguard the relationship between us, which is hanging by a thin thread by now.

- Great! We are on agreement then, I will inform your director that you are fine, and you can go back to work, and there is no need to over-egg the pudding.

- I didn't come here for any medical report, Doctor; I have already applied for a sabbatical year which will start on March, within two weeks. I just wanted to know why Dr. Omar was so upset and insisted on coming to your clinic.

- I will make you an appointment for next week. Can you make it before you leave?

- Sure, why not.

- Good, see you then. And remember that your thoughts will decide your destiny.

- Good bye.

I went out of the clinic so confused. I may have succeeded in deceiving the doctor for one more week, pretending that I intentionally talked to myself in a loud voice in front of the students, anyhow I am leaving this college soon, and I don't care about what they say or what they think of me, enough for me that I become acquainted with my deteriorated state.

My major concern by then was to start the conversation of my intention of leaving the college and going to Dubai, with my mother, wife and sons. In almost every family of the oriental conservative particularist immobile societies like ours, there is someone who is scapegoated and should pay the price of being responsible and in charge of the family concerns, when the lucky selfish ones turn their backs abandoning their responsibilities, depending on the scapegoats. My mother, for example, didn't find a problem when my brothers *Ibrahim* and *Yousef* decided to leave the country and live in America and Italy; she claimed that God allotted their lucks and fortunes to live in the other part of the world. I was quite sure that she hid her grief by then for their leave, however, she hid what was much more important from my own perspective, which is her gratitude towards the scapegoat, me! My father once told me a story of a woman who had two sons, *Ibrahim* and *Yahiya*. The mother lived in the house of *Yahiya*, but after every prayer she used to pray to God to protect *Ibrahim* and bestow upon him his great blessings. *Yahiya* decided once to take his mother to perform Hajj, and because she was old and couldn't perform *Tawaaf* circumambulation of *Ka'bah* seven times, he had to carry her on his back. No sooner had he carried her and started going around *Ka'bah* than she began to pray for *Ibrahim*! At that moment *Yahiya* lost his mind, he put her down and said:

- Let *Ibrahim* come and take you back home!!

Personally, I don't understand how parents discriminate and treat their sons and daughters differently. At the end it's a fact that no one can deny, parents do distinguish between their kids for undeclared hidden reasons. The family and the whole society will not forgive the last son available if he leaves, leaving behind old parents and frail daughters. This will make me look like an ingrate and disobedient in the eyes of the people around me here. So be it, let the chips fall where they may, I will not go back on my word and decision. In *Arthur Miller's "Death of a Salesman"* the irony was in knowing that the disappearance or death of someone could be more beneficial to others around than his existing or staying alive. I will make my leave of a great benefit to my kids, I will not claim that it's the main reason why I am leaving so that "*they may witness the benefits provided for them*"! I will not be emotional pretending that being among my kids is what my kids really want, because at the end there are calculations that need to be taken into consideration away from emotions. We became a torn nation that roves far away countries to meet the demands of their kids, who count on their parents to carry out miracles to please them.

It won't be easy, and I won't hurt my mother and my family and run away in peace. This will tear me apart and ignite an internal conflict for me, but I am totally convinced that it won't be harder than the void of death. Everybody is busy working out for his/her better life, my father is the one who died alone, and life goes on as they say. It's the mode of life God created, he placed them the bliss of forgetting to make them survive, but punished me with a strong memory that recalls all the details that would make me suffer the void of death and the void of leave. My father dies before me in every minute, and Suzan talks to me, cancelling the fact of her leave. Mother, Sura, kids, you will break my heart in every moment, but I will tolerate this pain and be patient so that I seize every opportunity of my life to take away your worries and grief. I don't expect you to understand, but at least I expect you to pretend of understanding so that you make it easy on all of us.

"If you are brave enough to say goodbye, life will reward you with a new hello"

Ella Wheeler Wilcox

~13~

I entered the house and found my sisters sitting in the living room; each one busy with her matter and concern. I saluted them and talked to them for a while then asked:

-Where is Mom?

They pointed at her bedroom, I went there to find her busy as usual, cleaning and setting things in order. I saluted her, kissed her and sat talking to her. No sooner had I started speaking than she stood still, stopped working and became absentminded, distracted to nowhere, then she shed tears in silence, but didn't interrupt me. She waited till I finished talking, then she looked at me with tired, full of tears eyes, and said:

- I wish you the best of both worlds, son. May God keep you safe.

So are the women, they say something and mean another. If she wants me to go, then why does she prevent me by her tears which weaken my intention? It's time for the Arabs to stop being sentimental. Such emotions need to be replaced by reason that would be good for everybody. Why do we consider travelling a difficult matter? Is it because we didn't get used to nomadic life, and we drew back like conservative societies; stuck to closeness and neighborhood to keep the strong bonds between the members of the family? Once, you talked about the privilege of being of such societies, Suzan, but now mom states the other side of this society. We can get used to things by the course of time, it doesn't take us more than a day to get back home from the furthest lands, but if the fear of death is what makes this fuss, then such misfortunes could happen even if we stayed in bedrooms.

I went upstairs to talk to *Sura* and my two little kids about the same matter. *Sura* responded differently. She asked me if I am going to marry another woman, and whether the whole issue of travelling is no more than an excuse. My relationship with *Sura* might have been troubled with sludge of ambiguity, confusion, and cold war, but we know each other well. Trust, honesty, and respect were our marriage banners that we have never doubted once, or disagreed on. I assured her that her matter of question will never happen, and I made it clear for her that I am just leaving for search of daily bread, and mood change. She knew how much I was fed up with the routine of the tribe which governed the institutions, and ruled my country; she knew that I will never surrender to such facts.

After that I took my kids to *I'amar Irbid Park*, which I thought it a place that would please them, but it wasn't a good idea! I found tens of other kids overcrowding and crushing into one swing, and there was no place to set; all benches were broken. Some of the people spread out lying down, making a real chaos of food leftovers, cans of soda, and juice cartons. Each group's chief tried to impose his domination on occupied territories, compelled his custodianship on the land, and drove away greedy ones by his ready flaming masculine glances to prove his jealousy and sense of honor before the women accompanying him. Let alone the bequeathing of the swing from one brother to another, as if it was a family property, disregarding the rights of the others to play and take part too. I didn't find a federal territory in the whole park to sit in peace with my kids. I preferred to retreat and withdraw due to the incapability of peace-keeping forces of doing their job and imposing their prestige on territories of tribes and clans. I bought ice-cream and talked to them in the car, making them understand that I am going to work away so that I earn more money and make their dreams come true. I also told them that I'll keep in touch with them daily and come by whenever it is possible. Yes, that's what I am going to do; I will not cook stones and pebbles till they fall asleep.

I had enough time to gather up all my research papers, wait the admission on approving my leave after the final exams, to bid farewell to *Naser* and *Murad*, and also to confirm booking a room in *JW Marriott* in Dubai, then to pack my suitcases, and take my two best friends with me; the laptop and the lute.

I wanted to spend what's left out of the days with my kids, *Sura*, my mother and sisters. I might manage mending their broken hearts with tender loving words and honest promises. I didn't mention my arrival time to *Suzan* but once, either she forgot the date or she didn't take me seriously. We talked lots of times over the internet, but she didn't even accidently mention the oncoming of the date. That's better. I don't want her to do anything that would confuse her or confuse me till I figure all the preparations of the conference upon my arriving, two days ahead of the conference premier.

On Sunday morning, March 8th, I took a shower, put my clothes on, kissed my kids, wife, mother and sisters, without exaggerating the burst of passions, then stopped a cab, put on my luggage, and without looking at them I said:

- I'll drop you a line upon my arrival and let you know my phone number and my address, don't you worry.. Take care.., bye.

I didn't want to see them crying or shocked by my insensitivity. It's the first time I leave them, it's really hard for all of us. I had to act the triviality of my leave till they get used to it. This is the first-time shock and they will surely get over it.

On my way to the airport, my eyes voraciously swallowed up all sites and scenes. I wanted to pause everything and ponder about its details… This morning my country looks purer, clearer, and much more beautiful. My heart became congested with hatred, detestation, despair, and routine for many years. This morning is different, the daylight baptized me with *Zamzam* that removed all stains of disgust which piled up by patience.

I arrived at the airport one hour ahead of the departure time, finished all the procedures and sat in the departure lounge to have a cup of coffee in peace. I got distracted by the scenes of the passengers among the screams of the kids here and there, till I heard the final call announcement. I passed the tube and got into the plane, handed the boarding pass to the stewardess, she pointed at a window seat where I sat and waited till the captain introduced himself and informed us of arrival time. After fifteen minutes of taking off, I put the headset on to listen to some music and not to think of any depressing pesky, but as usual fate doesn't leave me in peace. No sooner had I heard *Dalida* singing *Hilwa ya Baladi* than I burst into tears. Why don't we appreciate the things, the places, and the people till we miss them? Why do they force us to go abroad in order to love and respect our countries more? They should have chosen songs that would be more helpful for bearing loss and void, by analogy to the way they run the influence of slow music in malls to increase the mode of buying. I took off the headset and started humming:

"So it was....So it came to be..
You have no right to blame on me..
Why to blame on me, or to rebuke!
They plundered the sources, and left us the puke,
State the goods they left for us,
Then blame me and spell your cuss"

How great you were Sayed Darweesh!

*****

Oh, yes, I was right… When I met her again after all this time, I felt the same, like eternal first sight love. The firebrand rekindles forever and ever.

~14~

The captain announced the arrival after two hours and a half, declaring that we became in the skies of The United Arab Emirates and about to land at Dubai International Airport. I looked through the window, for the first while I thought that my compass got confused and lost direction including the ups and downs. I am neither accustomed to blue color beneath me, nor to the intertwinement of colors with green. The airport looked well organized from the sky, and so beautiful like a stretched out metallic serpent. Planes were on both sides like joints of Regatta boat oars. I looked at the skyline and saw spectacular scenes.., an outreach of concrete arms imitating palm leaves and branches in the sea, and vertical creeping invasion to its skies by skyscrapers, towers, and high buildings in a very organized way. The smile imposed itself on my face, and I got myself prepared for more fabulous comparative issues. The plane landed in peace and within minutes we entered the captivating Dubai Airport. The golden lights and the movable stairways among palm trees and magnificence of decorations made the scene a kind of fantasy. Everything was organized, and all procedures went so smoothly. I was really taken by the open shopping centers, the several restaurants, the internet availability, and the hotels.., even the floor tiles looked like glittering water on corals.

I was a clerk at Queen Alia International Airport in 1996, I worked in Baggage Department for almost a year and a half, during that given period of time I managed to know many defects and flaws in the kingdom's formal airways institution. The income from cargo alone was enough to make this institution a profit tributary for the kingdom, let alone save it from sinking under hundreds of millions indebtedness. Foreign area managers used to practice jobbery and became apple polishers for the executive manager of the institution, who happened to be a son of a minister. Those area managers used to spoil the executive manager to the limit of bringing *Pampers* for his newborn baby from other countries! My job was to enter and store the coming stuff and tag them with numbers till their owners or concerned come by and receive them by hand or by correspondents. I used to register everything that lands at the airport, and wonder about the Mafia there. I swear to God that some ministers disdained local boons and blessings, and ordered all their clothes, furniture, food, and seasonal fruits to be brought from abroad. Some of the people from the up used to send their friends overseas lots of antiques found in archeological sites in the country. I was in a very critical position that made me aware of the plundering taking place to and from the kingdom. There was no institutional system, and no standardized applied rules on officials, all procedures were made in savagery and whimsical way by the board of directors. Nobody knows, for example, why a Rumanian stewardess earns one thousand and five hundred JDs, while a Jordanian hostess earns four hundred JDs!

I went out of the arrivals terminal, the weather was good and the humidity was bearable. I took a taxi to *JW Marriott* hotel which was fifteen minutes away from the airport. The driver was Syrian, and like the rest of the drivers in the world, he kept me busy with his questions and talks. He started complaining about the hardships of life away from home. I was about to remind him of a Syrian adage that conveys the message of those who like to have everything on their pizza and wish to eat the cake and have it at the same time, but I preferred to replace my responses with fillers instead of starting my life here with short-temper. So, I kept saying; "this is life, what can we do about it! ... patience is a virtue...., all things are difficult before they are easy..., we are in the same boat...". After his ongoing nagging and grouch for the whole way we arrived at the hotel's gateway. The porter took down the luggage, and I paid the taxi driver while looking at the gorgeous facade of the hotel which was made of glass engrafted with marble. I entered the reception hall, the hall of myth and fantasy. I checked in and assured my staying for four days till I find a place to stay. I got upstairs to the suite and started unpacking my bags, then I enjoyed having a hot shower without the fear of water break or exhaustion of gas cylinder. After that I called my mother and my wife and informed them of my arrival. I also assured them that I will stay in touch. Later on, Suzan's turn followed, it was about six o'clock in Dubai timing.

- Hello.., good evening.

- Good evening.

- Is this Mrs. Suzan El-Ahmad?

- Yes, who is talking, please?

- I am Elias Baroudi, the director of Elite Center for Teaching English. A friend of your husband's whose name is Ali Khidr handed me your papers and told me that you are looking for a job. I have your résumé before me and I would like to interview you for a couple of minutes on purpose of employing you as a secretary, if you don't mind of course.

- Ali Khidr! Never heard this name before.. Where is this center? When do interviews start?

- Well, interviews will start within half an hour in JW Marriott hotel. If you start putting on your black Turkish *Jilbab* and the grey veil engrafted with the silver thread, and wear your J'adore without wasting time, you will be able to make it on time.

- You.. mean evil!! You swindler…!!

She yelled cursing and swearing at me.

- When did you arrive? Why didn't you tell me that you're coming? God! I've just been looking in your stuff, thinking about you.

She burst out laughing.

- I guess you are not interested in the job, then?

- Hush hush.. shut up..! I am coming right away. Waleed won't be back before nine. God! I want to see you..bye.. bye.

- Wait..! Hello..?

She didn't let me finish, she was shocked and went crazy. I just wanted her to wait till I find a place to stay in, and figure out what I will do and how she will introduce me to Waleed!

I called the reception to get the suite well prepared in the way I see appropriate, asked for bunches of water lilies, daisies, tulips, lavenders, and some candles. I also informed them of the arrival of a visitor and cleared up the necessity of delaying dinner a bit. After that I dimmed the lights and played a record of slow music that fits for the occasion. Finally, I sprinkled Loris Azzaro perfume on my suit. I would not forget Suzan's gift of course, after all this time, the gold brooch. It's time for my risks to shudder; it's time to throw away my fears in the sea of fate to make the tides drift them where they may.

Forty-five minutes passed while I was busy trying to finish all preparations as fast as possible. At last, the receptionist called and informed me of the arrival of Suzan. I went out of the suite heading towards the elevator, I wanted to meet her there, but at the last minute I changed my mind and went back towards the suite door. Would she unconsciously throw herself on me in front of residents? Or would she meet me with a less rash manner? I don't know, but..

- Zeyad..!

I looked behind, and there she was wearing her black *Jilbab* and hastening her walk, her grey veil itself the one engrafted with the silver thread, and head cover cap which crowned her. She threw herself on me hugging me, I embraced her with my arms till I felt her tears on my neck.. God! How I missed her perfume, how much my eyes looked up towards her sky invoking her attendance and fall, to revive this crying heart in my chest. I looked at her, wiped her tears away stuttering and choking with her name.

- Su..zan.. I love you..

I lifted her, closed the door with my foot behind us, and laid her down like a baby girl on the bed. I lied on my side close to her, she hugged me again. She was still confused and torn between crying and smiles, fear and unbelieving. I kissed her many times, the nectar of her breath was still delicious. I whispered saying:

- I promised you to live for you, and never to leave you, and here I am keeping my promise.

- I don't believe it!! Is this you? When did the past ever come back? How come lovely moments start rekindling? Are we returning back to the past? You are my stay supporter in this life, Zeyad. Every time I convince myself of being broken and alone so that I learn to survive by my own in life, you emerge before me with a message, or with a recollection to prove to me the impossibility of life resumption without you. And now here you are.., in flesh and blood again embraced by my arms! But no.., I won't let you go away from now on, do you understand? I am tired... I can't take it anymore... Please.., promise me to stay.

- I promise.

We talked a lot about the days we spent away from each other; she told me much about the life in Dubai, and how UAE is a nice organized and a clean country. She started to walk in the suite while talking and looking at me every now and then, touching everything that comes across her, pondering at the bunches of flowers and the perfume bottles near the bed. She sprinkled some perfume and smelled it, passing from one topic to another talking about the high costs of living in Dubai in return for the services and public utilities available. She also talked about the advantages of dealing with the various colonies and communities in Dubai. In few sentences she decoded the puzzle of life away from home and the new city for me; she offered me the access and the password to *Ali Baba*'s cave.

- You will see darling how many job opportunities a man like you, smart and hardworking, will be offered, and how much appreciation from the ones who will judge you by your efforts, not by your tribe. Cheer up, our coming days will be splendid.

I called the receptionist and ordered dinner. We began talking about our plans for the days to come. A few minutes later, we were sitting at the table having our meal and resuming our talk. I made it clear for Suzan that the most important thing at the moment for me was to present my research paper in the conference, and after that I will see what will happen and start looking for a place to stay in. Later, we sat on the sofa having tea with ginger and honey, and we started planning for a proper way of introducing me to Waleed.

- Tell him that I informed you by an e-mail about my intention of attending the conference. I already sent you one after I called you. Tell him that I am staying in this hotel, and we'll see how he would respond.

- Consider it done. Regarding a place to stay in, don't you worry, you can depend on me. I'll take care of it.

She took a glance to her watch, it was about half past eight.

- Oh, I need to go now.

She stood by the mirror to get herself ready and freshen up her look.

- Just a second.

I opened the brooch box and pinned it on the turn up of her *Jilbab*, and then I kissed her and said:

- I didn't come with the grudges of Heathcliff to take revenge on Catherine, and I am not as innocent and impotent as Great Gatsby, I love you and I want to spend the rest of my life with you as I promised you before.

- I will not be satisfied with less than that. Obsessed by your tact as usual. I love you.

She kissed me and headed towards the door, I walked with her till she got into the elevator, and before the door closed she gestured a good bye kiss. I went back in heavy steps, picked up the file of the research paper to read it again in bed. The perfume of Suzan clinched on the bed sheet and became dominant on other fragrances. I threw away the papers and pulled together the bed sheet where she lied and voraciously sniffed her scent like cocaine.

*****

When life is too good to be real and your passage is paved with luck and opportunities, you have to realize that fate is sniggering in secret for what will come

~15~

The very next day I woke up on Suzan's phone call. Her voice was a scenario that was rehearsed in my dream, making of its huskiness a rapture that ran in my body, as if my soul has been just awakened from a love night with her. I tried to stand up but my body was unsteady, like a newborn baby learning the principles of kinetics. Chaos was all over the place, papers on the floor, food leftovers on the table, cups of tea, and messy bed.

I took a quick shower to begin a real busy day. First of all, I have to call the general office supervisor of the conference, and then I must check my e-mail to know all the procedures that need to be followed, later, have my breakfast and start preparing my research paper. When I finish all this, I have to buy a suit that is appropriate for meeting the sponsors and patrons of the conference represented in *Princes*, *Shyoukh*, and English teaching experts from all over the world, who came to participate and to attend the presentations.

My father taught me, since I was a kid, how to address and deal with English language audience, he guided me to the strategies which they follow to convince the addressee and the recipients, not only by reason, logic, and strong defense, but also by as much important issues; like appearance, body language, sense of humor, and exposure of personal humane expertise to gain the audience's support and trust, all this lead to the credibility of the presenter. The knowledge of a man and the capability of mastering the issue in question, go in parallel as such. The gangs which work out knocking the whole world dead with the American President emergence in written or in oral speeches on T.V, are organized guerilla gangs that identically work like star makers. Some lines in their speeches are written in red, so that the president raises the tone of his voice when reading them and lowers his tone in other parts, he is also asked to wave a hand here, draw a smile there, and pause in silence in specified parts too. Such procedures are probably instructed through a small receiver fixed in his ear, if not written. At the end, the world's knock-dead is not more than a puppet moved by shrinks and experts, who know exactly how to gain the trust and support of the nation by deception and misleading. I also owe Hollywood films, which explored and criticized the most personal and embarrassing details and crossed all red lines of high rank politicians and exposed them to the public, when our leaders and kings in the Arab world speak a third language, that is neither theirs nor their nation's. Such a third language is quoted, when spoken, by their star makers the very next day to occupy all newspapers' headlines and invade schoolbooks for years to come, as if they were verses of his "Almighty" that prophesies ages to come. We have found ourselves in the fire many times before, after having our "Almighty" interviewed by a foreign correspondence. Such misunderstanding has always been attributed to translation, but in fact the reason was a completely different speech targeting a different audience which we shouldn't have known about it, so that we believe the "Almighty's" intentions and his love towards the nation. An extremely unveiled stupidity imposed by the lion when the foxy smooth-tongued become helpless.

It took me about three hours to rehears the research paper, during which I marked all the notes and marginal comments that I will play as if they were on the spur of the moment. I mocked myself for doing this, but famous people, leaders, presidents, and kings should have rejected such cheap performances with all the more reason. However such fillers and tricks became standards of fame, reputation, and stealing the hearts of the stupid. I'll follow their steps and play their wiles.

My research paper's topic which I wanted to deliver in the conference was "The Translation of Concentration and Shorthand in Quran Dictions In *Kahf Surat*"; a problematic issue which a translator to English language faces due to his/her weakness in the mother tongue. Suzan told me once about the favor and good turn of reading *Al-Kahf Surat* on Fridays. I've never doubted any of Suzan's recommendations; therefore I dedicated myself on reading it. Every time I read it I found some eye-catching words which I felt embarrassed of not understanding their meanings, which conveyed concentration of implied meanings that are not taken care of when being translated; such as "so his fruits (and enjoyment) were encompassed (with ruin)" which is supposed to stand as the translation of two words; *oheetah bethamareh*, and many other examples too.

Suzan dropped me a line at five o'clock in the evening to check on me and to see if I needed anything. I told her that I intend to go to a shopping center to buy a suit. She asked me to wait till she arrives and associate me with her to the well-known places.

I got dressed and went downstairs to wait for her in the entrance hall. She phoned me again within a half an hour to tell me that she was outside waiting in a taxi. I went out and got in and sat near here. She asked the driver to head for Burjuman center. I kept looking at her the whole way, holding her hand. I still couldn't believe my eyes! My heart was still athirst for her..., her beauty was glossed like gold, her scent gust swayed by her movements, elegant like a queen, her smiles were noble deeds, her glances were confident, neither hesitant nor dispersed, and her tender looks embraced me as if they were two expanded arms. I wished that the driver would range around the world nonstop. We arrived at Burjuman mall and entered its hall and portico. The roof with the painted glass ornaments imitated Sistine Chapel. Regardless of its small size compared to other shopping centers, still it stood as an eminent edifice of lavishness, luxury, and opulence like the rest of the places in the legend of Dubai. Long time ago people used to consider arrivals from America as lucky ones for having the opportunity of living the American dream in the country of bridges, trains, fascinating entertainment centers, and the hugeness of its construction. We used to burn the midnight oil listening to those people's fairy tales performing comparisons between America and our country to make us, the agonized, feel torment of living on the fringe of life. I might agree with them that we are the agonized for being under the severity of two burdens; the burden of wars which is imposed on our region every decade, to snatch safety and bliss from us; thus we grow old before time on the plea of disarmament, and the burden of our leaders and retinue, who plunder the boons and blessings and vend the sources leaving nothing but heartbreak to the fellow citizens. Today, one fact of heartbreak, disgrace and shame has changed, we don't envy those who come from America anymore, in fact we started to see them pathetic for running after a mirage. Comparisons are tuned nowadays with those who work in Dubai; the pearl of the Gulf.

I bought a nice suit and tried it on before Suzan, and then we sat in a café to have coffee. She told me that she has found me a bachelor apartment in *Al-Rashidiyah* district, near the metro railway station and neighboring Burjuman mall. I asked her to confirm the reservation of the apartment and told her that there was no need to wait for my opinion because I trust her taste. I made her feel that my optimum concern was staying close to her. I told her how her leave slew me and caused my heart to bleed, and that I only get revived the minute I see her. She recited some thirst and desire which brought about a shudder in my whole body and tears in our eyes. I felt calm and tranquil after her exposed torrid love. She told me that she informed Waleed about the must of inviting me on dinner after the conference closure. By his turn, Waleed told her that he will call me, and asked her to organize with me what she sees proper, so that he comes on time to pick me up from the hotel. Of course she didn't tell him about the bachelor apartment she rented for me, and she left me the floor to tell Waleed about the place of my residence. Two hours later, Suzan took leave of going home, so we got on a taxi, drove her home to know where she lives, then I went back to the hotel.

I've tried to imagine the occurrences of this global assemblage to which people from different parts of the world will perform pilgrimage, invoking pities and approval from the charged with authority and benefactor to offer them jobs. I've never been an opportunist and I've never went after being one. My father told me that the dominion of a free man dwells in standing on his own feet, not being a sycophant in royal court. He was right, I have the benefit of saying whatever I want, and I also have the use of good potentials and qualifications that keep me from calling for concessions. I was as good in English language as in Arabic; my mother tongue. Intensified courses in computer software programs were also my greater interest through the last few years, in addition to my long experience in teaching. I got myself well prepared for this real challenge, if I couldn't succeed in promoting myself properly tomorrow as expected, I will move to the apartment and start looking for jobs on my own.

At nine o'clock next morning, I headed towards the conference hall at the hotel. The gathering of people from everywhere was extraordinary; a mixture of different nationalities and races, and of different ages, I even met one of my teachers and some of my old students too. The preparations were at utmost punctuality, accuracy, and arrangement. The staff were prepared to receive the more so of participants, and achieve advancement in securing services and meeting participants' demands. The competition started the minute the protocols and ceremonies were carried out and the welcoming speeches were delivered. The contest of delivering research papers and brains' show by English speakers was a real challenge. I had to wait two hours for my turn. Although the subjects presented were different a bit and probably of recent date, and the least of the participants was a pioneer in English teaching who is celebrated in this domain, still the style of performances were all the same like catwalk on the runways by the models. All of them pretended the fluency in speaking English regardless of the falling down and flaws of some, they kept looking and checking their paper notes from time to time, took off their glasses and threw jokes here and there, emphasized the importance of their topic, and walked unjustified steps during their performance, claimed missing some of their publications names and references to promote them indirectly, aside from not taking care of the arise of their tone while trying to emphasize their confidence regardless of voice tremor of some of them. It looked like a play before me.

- Dr. Zeyad al Juneidy.

I don't think I'll achieve anything from this grinding contest, but I'll do my best to leave a good impression. I stood up and headed towards the dais holding my papers with me. I observed how the audience followed my steps while walking to the stage. When I arrived at the stairs, and exactly before I reached the dais, I deliberately let fall my papers as if it happened accidently. One of the ushers trotted towards me and started picking up the papers, but I with a hearable voice asked him not to bother and leave the papers on the floor. I stood behind the dais and fixed the microphone, looked at the papers on the floor, then glanced at the audience saying:

- Some of you might say "Poor man! He left a bad impression even before he started", but the fact is I am trying to draw your attention in an unconventional or typical way, since I got bored of the timed taking off glasses and throwing books, rapping and knocking the tables, referring to some incidental jokes, and walking the number of steps recommended by experts for those who complain of overstress when performing before audience. If any of you got ahead of me with the trick of calling your attention by the dropping of the papers, I can think of a more terrifying trick like acting a heart attack, or a more joking one like slipping my pants for example! Enough of such cheap performances and let's try to concentrate.

I still remember how some of the participants acclaimed and laughed, and some others kept their mouths open. My interjection was a bit rude especially from Arab participants' perspective, but they were not my target anyway, it was enough for me to make a foreigner participant laugh to make the rest of the parrots laugh accordingly.

- Great. Whereas I drew your attention, I can begin.

I presented everything I wanted to say with all my proficiency in lecturing and capability in convincing within fifteen minutes, I brought my performance to an end with recommendations that were warmly welcomed by the attendants. I went out to the hall to have a cup of tea and rest for a while. I talked with some of the participants, but those talks were unproductive. I felt like a prostitute on the game, thus spared what was left out of my pride and sent Suzan a message informing her that I finished my presentation of the research paper, and I am on my way back to the hotel to take the rest of the day off before I start looking for a job in one of the private institutions or educational centers.

My disappointment was due to my relying on this conference, in which no one bothered asking me about the country I came from or the college I work in. All participants had to fill forms mentioning their places of residence and phone numbers only. I didn't know how to start all over again. I went to my suite and sat to summon up my thoughts for a minute, and took a glance at the lute. It was the only thing that made me feel at ease in my seclusion. I started playing, and for a while I forgot and missed the set of time and place. The lute was my "she" companion that didn't speak unless I ordered her to speak, and even when speaking she only said what pleased me, she cried my sorrows and delighted my joys.. My fingers ran smoothly combing and styling her strings, braiding her *Maqamat* till my ascetic and mystic absence was interrupted by a phone ringing.

It was Suzan of course; she tried to lift up my spirit, and asked me to get prepared at six o'clock to have lunch with her in a place she chooses. While talking to her, the phone of the suite rang. It was the receptionist informing me that a visitor was waiting for me in the hall! I took leave of Suzan, assuring meeting her at six o'clock, then I went downstairs to the entry hall, asking the receptionist where the visitor was, he pointed at man. I walked towards him and saluted him.

- Good evening, Dr. Zeyad.

He was sixty something years old, looked prestigious and dignified, in ease and comfort.

- Good evening sir, how can I help you?

- Albert Assaf... May I have a cup of tea with you?

- Sure, allow me.

I ordered two cups of tea, and started detecting the man, I figured out that he was Lebanese, but like the rest of the emigrant Lebanese whose purity of original accent got distorted due to mixing with other nationalities through the years. His emaciation was not attributed to his old age, but to the apparent several diseases shown in the color of his skin which was bluish, the intermittent coughs disturbing his breaths order, the dental plate, and the remains of nicotine tan on his index and middle fingers. We started the conversation by implying his attendance of the conference sessions in the morning, describing the conference's break out as if it was a war between the best brains of the educated. Then he changed the subject and talked about the gap between the highly educated people and the dealers of education; the planners and promoters who codify laws of profit and loss. He talked a lot about those people who don't get the benefit of their certificates and don't get bored of repeating themselves over and over again. I didn't understand why he chose to say this in such an occasion.

- I beg your pardon, but.., are you trying to say something through all these introductions?

- Yes, the one who exposed the shame of participants and gave them a real dressing down in public, and was this close to slip his pants too, is the one whom I am looking for, indeed.

- Looking for? For employment somewhere, you mean?

- Yes, but it is not what you think. It's a free enterprise which the participants wouldn't spare; in fact they would gasp to obtain such a job regardless of their high standing certificates and fame. To make a long story short.., if they knew how much they would earn, and what advantages they would have, they would have given up their jobs to seek shade under the *Sheikh*'s cloak.

- What did you say? Cloak? And Sheikh?

- Wait, again it's not what you think... This Sheikh is not like the rest of the Sheyoukh you are acquainted with. *Sheikh Mite'b*, may God grant him with long life, is an educated man, who is concerned with all the updates, and highly appreciates the opinions of his assistants. He is a generous man, a very smart one, and a successful businessman who has a good reputation among other lords, priority, and icons of businessmen. God wished him to be barren, and be in want of a son who would inherit his enormous wealth, may God grant him with long life. Thus, work is everything he has, and he is very serious at. *Sheikh Mit'eb* runs his business intelligently, and he doesn't forgive the neglectful, slothful, greedy or traitorous.

He pulled a Dunhill box of cigarettes and a golden lighter, and he lit a cigarette with a deep drag and started to cough.

- Sorry.., you might say, why was I exclusively chosen? The fact is, *Sheikh Mite'b* has entrusted me, after begging him many times to discharge me for my bad health condition, to look for a suitable man to recruit, and prepare him to take the charge of this trust and responsibility, and will hold me responsible in case of wrong choice. I can't travel around anymore as you see, nor find pleasure in arguing with area managers and officials. Once again you might ask, why you in precise. Honestly, life taught me that starting all over with the novel revives a new spirit and pumps a fresh blood, whereas repairing is just a waste of time and money. I don't want a man with an experience in commerce and management, because I want to teach him what I find right to keep the success of business, in addition to that, no one knows you in business field, therefore your competitors will fear you. I might disagree with Sheikh *Mit'eb* on regard of this point, but I guess I am more than a school or a college in running such enormous business like this, and I believe that Sheikh *Mit'eb* trusts my potentials, and that's why he entrusted me with this mission.

- Great, but why didn't you choose someone you know, or of your nationality?

- We have spent our lives together, and I owe him gratitude and thanks. He is my brother and supporter. When you are entrusted with such a mission by someone of his rank and dignity, there mustn't be a miss choice due to tribalism or clannishness. In addition to that, I am a fastidious man when it comes to picking and choosing. I watched you carefully while you were listening to the presentations and mocking those whom you couldn't rib a shoulder with. Even when defeated you tried to convince the others of your victory and of your privilege, and these are components of a good negotiator and wily deceitful. You remain calm regardless of the boiling blood in your veins; which hints a seed of mystery that grows respect and tameness in the hearts of others. Your ambitions carried you all this way, regardless of the raptors you have been among; and this makes you an ambitious and an adventurous. "Slipping the pants"! Hahaha.. That was your last shot. Regardless of your defeat you won some of the attendance with this joke, and you also made others lose their grounds and reputations by unmasking them. Even those who came afterwards were apparently confused, fearing that the attendance would follow their flaws, because they had no other plans. Be sure, Zeyad that I'll stay beside you and back you up and support you with everything you need to make you up to this responsibility.

I looked at the man's eyes; he was honest and confident.

- Are you ready?

- What? Are we going to start now?

- No, tomorrow.., if contract is executed, but first I have to introduce you to Sheikh *Mit'eb*, may God grant him with long life. Before we go, tell me.., does anyone know you in Dubai? I mean have you met anyone you know?

I didn't know what to say. Is Suzan meant by this question? Or is he only referring to businessmen?

- Are you referring to women too, Mr. Assaf?

- Call me Albert.

He looked into my eyes introspectively, and smiled understanding what I was referring to, and then he went out. I walked with him out of the hotel. The driver drew near welcoming Mr. Assaf opening the door of the car for him. Mr. Assaf asked me to set in the backseat with him and ordered the driver to set off to Marina Resort to meet the "granted with long life" *Sheikh Mit'eb*.

*****

"All things truly wicked start from innocence."

Ernest Hemingway

~16~

We arrived at the Palm Island Resort. The view was fascinating, but the many dictations of Mr.Assaf and his recommendations on how to converse with Sheikh *Mit'eb* kept me from enjoying the gentle wind of the sea, which was filled with iodine and whish of palm fronds.

- Don't forget.., keep calm however Sheikh *Mit'eb* tries to annoy you with his questions and comments. Keep your voice low, your answers short, and your self-confidence apparent.

- Alright.

We went into the resort and passed the bodyguards base. There were lots of busy men and women of different nationalities, the jumble made them look like a beehive, but the short skirts and the bluntly open shirts of blond Russian and brunette Spanish waitresses bestowed pleasure upon business. Mr. Assaf saluted everybody with an audible voice that made them turn around and split into two groups on both sides, Sheikh *Mit'eb* came to light sitting with papers in his hands. He was an old man who insisted on reviving his youth again and again, well built with dark black hair that didn't fit in color with his pale skin. At first sight you think him arrogant with his detective glances accompanied with grimace and shrunken lips emerging of a dyed goatee. There were several files before him on the table, and a half filled glass of scotch. He casted the papers away, then took the cup and gulped the scotch altogether, but kept rinsing his mouth with while staring at me, after that he rested backwards and swallowed the whisky down.

- Sheikh *Mit'eb*.., you authorized me to pick a man who would do, on my behalf, all the work I am entrusted with. I just wanted to present him to you before I recruit him for this mission.

Mr. Assaf applied all the recommendations he taught me of speaking to Sheikh *Mit'eb* within seconds. His voice was calm and low and he apparently sounded confident. No sooner had Mr. Assaf spoken those words than all the responses of the attendants came to view. Some of them brought out good impression and admiration, some others exposed their rancor and grudge, but the foxy ones waited for Sheikh *Mit'eb*'s response who put the cup of scotch on the table and said in a husky voice to those around him:

- We'll continue later.., now leave us alone.

The gathering disbanded in seconds. The expression on Sheikh *Mit'eb*'s face confused me more than when I stood behind the dais in the conference.

- Sit. What's your name? Where are you from?

I sat and tried adopting Mr. Asaaf style in talking.

- May God grant you with long life, my name is Zeyad al-Juneidy. I am Jordanian.

At that moment Sheikh *Mit'eb* tangled the fingers of both hands, inclined his head guffawing, then looked at Mr.Assaf and said:

- You must be kidding me Assaf! A Jordanian?

I felt an insult that was about to unleash my anger and throw aside all my reason and patience. I wanted to respond but Mr. Assaf interrupted me saying:

- You taught me, may God bless you, not to prejudge people at first sight or deal with them in advance, you also taught me to make just estimate of people. I've never met Zeyad before, but I went to TESOL conference at Marriott hotel, and Zeyad was one of the participants there. You know how I pick proper people for our missions. If I haven't seen potentials in his character I wouldn't have risked your trust in me, Sheikh *Mit'eb*. He has all the qualities and attributes we need; he is smart, ambitious, and cunning. The rest of the things needed come with experiences which he will gain when I start training him. I promise you, he will be your man in a short period of time.

- You.., the Jordanians…, are one coin of two identical faces!

He addressed me pointing his finger at me.

- No one denies your sense of honor, your education, your moral and religious obligation, your generosity and hardworking, your ardor and knightly conduct.., but those very attributes are the ones that made you a nervous and a stubborn nation, a satisfied and a compliant one, an emotional society; that left a spacious ground for tribal minds and emotions to decide for you. You accept the least and never grand any concessions what so ever, you don't flatter slavishly, that's why you stand still to mark time. You are kindhearted and you don't step over others by laying ambushes and conspiracies to show up and obtain gifts, presents and bonus, and that makes you determinists and fatalists living in the wrong time and in the wrong place. Life ….. What did you tell me his name is?

- Zeyad, may God bless you.

- Yeah.., yeah, life is not on the edge of the extremes like truth and lie, Zeyad, but it rather depends on when is lying praised and commended and when is truth dispraised and slandered. You deal with things in seriousness but I want elastic minds in my business. Minds that know how to win all the time, not lose because of sense of honor or a moment of obstinacy. Minds that know how to pamper themselves after hard work, not minds that prefer others to themselves and treasure up for coming generations. Why don't determinists depend on God, on regard of saving needs for their kids? It's an equation that no one is capable of understanding or dealing with but Jordanians! You don't love or appreciate life Zeyad, and you don't enjoy it, that's why you got used to loss, which I abhor most. You attribute your failures and lack of happiness to economic situations and religious banners all the time…, but in fact, those remain excuses only and you know that.

It was wise not to deny an archetype or a popular generalization to make Sheikh *Mit'eb* trust me in what I was about to say.

- You hit the nail on the head, may God grant you with long life, that's why I couldn't stay anymore in my country, and the likes of me are so many. It was written on us to have wild ambitions and restive dreams that refuse to be tamed, that's why lots of us travel over the lands seeking opportunities to make dreams come true. Some of us are capable of bringing about miracles, but we are in need of what you said, the approaches and tactics which Mr. Assaf mentioned too. Some of us stand as exceptional cases that discord with such archetypes and popular generalization.

He looked at me and smiled as if he approved and admired my reply. He stood up and walked towards me, put his hands on my shoulders, and asked:

- What's your major study?

- Translation, your Excellency.

- Are you eager of standing-in as a substitute of Assaf, taking the charge of our restaurants' group in London?

- Your Excellency, if you find me up to your trust and speculation, and qualified enough to do so, be sure I'll devote myself wholeheartedly, like you just described Jordanians at work, to measure up to your standards. You will notice that I am creative, ambitious, and descend from a family that pledges the word and trust. Still, as Mr. Assaf mentioned I still need lots of teachings and guidance to master the skills of management and trade so that I don't risk my decisions which would backfire negatively. You said that there is no space for emotions and mistakes at work, thus you won't hesitate firing me if I happened to be beneath this job.

He stroked my shoulder gently, then went back to his place, held the cup and filled it up and sat in front of me, then said:

- I would like to start a new business, a new group of restaurants and halls, but I am a bit hesitant between choosing the target place; countries of far east, or countries of the middle east, what do you think?

I think it was a question in culture and knowledge more than in commerce and management, Sheikh *Mit'eb* wanted to explore my opinion and anticipation for the coming period.

- May God bless you.., "*The eye does not get over the eyebrow*", as long as you achieve such success and prosperity in business, you are capable of investigating the future with all its ups and downs. As to my own inspection, which I wouldn't withhold from you, I really hope you don't do this. Countries of Far East are industrial countries, and the people there are aware of the value of supporting their local industry. They are conservative prejudiced and illiberal. I don't think it wise to "sell coal to Newcastle", but on regard of the Middle East.., forget it. A way from all the riot, disorder, revolution, uprising, call this chaos in the middle eastern countries and northern African countries whatever you want.., this region is a very hot spot, and any kind of investment is considered a real risk and a sort of insanity. You know that the whole region is considered a consuming market of weaponry and armament; it takes in sixty percent of worldly imports of weapons' industry. All these weapons are out of order and broken and not made for a real confrontation with an enemy, in fact they are made to market deals and transactions for a great amount of money to deplete and exhaust the fortunes of these countries. When weapons are kept up with tribal minds, it is easy to establish wars due to sectarian reasons; such as religious clashes, cultural and historical grudges, borders disarray, and ideological contradictions. Exporter countries on the other hand grip firm the sinews of survival represented in oil, nourishment, and weapon, conspiring with leaders of those countries in return for their stay in position and plundering as much as possible. Such countries, may God bless you, are targeted with investment projects, as called, that are imposed on them to make them sink in debts for the International and Development Bank and be in the red to incline for their dictations. We have a war every decade and that makes investments so risky. Expanding business in Europe, America and countries at rest relatively speaking, is the best policy in my opinion, and the choice is yours.

Sheikh *Mit'eb* kept listening and nodding his head approving while I was talking, when I finished he put the glass of scotch aside then looked at me admiringly and said:

- What kind of wind and fate that carried you to me Zeyad!

Then, with his husky voice he called Mr. Assaf who was a few meters away near the bar.

-Assaf!

Mr. Assaf came swiftly; he was still coughing and hardly breathing.

- Two weeks. You have only two weeks to get him prepared as he must be.

Then he looked at me again and said:

- Let this sly fox teach you everything. You will have a very significant stand and a promising future in our group one day.

We went out of the resort and I was still under the influence of the shock that made my hair stand on ends. After a couple of suffocating coughs the "sly fox" gathered himself again and said:

- The driver will take you back to the hotel. Get good sleep now, I'll be in your suite at nine o'clock in the morning. We will get you a place for your staying and prepare you with everything needed.

I looked at Mr. Assaf, wanted to hug him and tell him that he offered me a job that I've never dreamt of in my entire life, but I said to myself that serious and full-fledged people like him are content with thanking and shaking hands, they keep saying that emotions need to be bridled at work and such feelings can be translated practically by doubling the efforts at work and to live up to well-thought-of.

He laid his hand to me to shake it as a sign of accepting his offer, I shook his hand and said:

- I depend on you Sir in teaching me all the ins and outs of such a domain which I am completely ignorant in, I want to rib the shoulder with your great expectations and never let you down.

- Zeyad, I've never regretted a decision in my life.

- Thank you, Mr. Assaf. I'll be waiting for you in the morning, and I will not let you down.

I wonder what Mr. Assaf would say if he knew that two weeks ago I was talking to a psychotherapist about my state of mind!

I went back to the hotel powerless and starving, I called Suzan and told her that we will have lunch at the hotel and that I will explain to her the reason for changing the plan when she arrives. I asked the receptionist to get two meals of sea food prepared, and then I went up to the suite and had a nap without even changing my clothes. I woke up later at the knocks on the door, I thought that I slept for hours, but in fact only forty five minutes passed since I fell asleep. I got up and went exhaustedly to open the door.., to see that a no mortal goddess has occupied the doorway, femme fatale, sedition of women, not only man has a great regard for, but also his mind surrenders and inclines in obedience before spirits of such aura of glory. She was dressed in Indian Sari as if brought to life from *One Thousand and One Nights* folk tales. She got in, greeted me, and then took off the head veil. I pondered at her from the twisted tufts which looked like a night bundle of darkness, to her classical strappy interlaced sandals. I was speechless. She drew near me and hugged me. I kissed her for a long time, till I helplessly shed tears and hardly inhaled my breath. I tried to suppress the shake which took all over me, but I couldn't. She sensed what her figuration did to me, she patted on my back and repeated saying:

- Hush.. hush.. hush..

My voice rattled in my throat.

- I thought that I'll surprise you with marvelous news that even I couldn't believe, but you turned out to be a world wonder.

She looked at me and kept her body stuck to mine, then she asked:

- What news?

- Come and have a seat, I'll tell you the whole story.

I told her everything, beginning with my presentation at the conference till meeting Assaf and Sheikh *Mit'eb*.

- I can't believe it Suzan! All this happened to me today as if it's my day of fortune, reality could be stranger than fiction sometimes!

- I've never doubted your potentials, your qualifications, and the possibility of gaining good opportunities, my love. I told you before that you are highly qualified and up to good chances of finding decent jobs. It's true that I didn't expect you to be that lucky and start with big game hunting, but here is Mr. Assaf assuring my certainty in you. Why wonder Zeyad? Didn't drummers become the presidents of national parties overnight in our Arab countries and ravaged for years? At least you are educated, kindhearted, affectionate and amiable. It's time to have luck and fate on your side, even if it was beginners luck. Strike while the iron is hot, dear. Waleed will pick you up at nine o'clock and bring you to our house, we have invited some of our friends on dinner, too, to introduce you to them.

- What? It's half past six already, and I am exhausted! What am I supposed to tell him? Why did you invite your friends? How do you want me to behave..? What if he was stalking you? Could it be…

- Relax. It's just an invitation on dinner with some friends. I'll tell you how things will go on while having lunch.

I ordered lunch to be brought to the suite, Suzan asked me not to fill my stomach because she prepared dinner herself. She started telling me about her guests, and informed me with all the details needed to be taken care of when dealing with Waleed. After we finished dinner she told me that she had to go home because the women will arrive earlier to give her a hand in having everything set on time, so she kissed me goodbye and went out. I took a shower and got prepared at eight o'clock, I didn't find anything to do except playing music on my lute. The sad *Hejaz Kar Kurd Maqam* moaned over the revelation of Suzan, the maple wood smell of the lute's deep round back shell transcended me to an ambiance of sublimation, asceticism, and piety for almost an hour. The knocks on the door later intensified slowly as if creeping up from a deep well to pull me down to reality, distorting the ardor of my heart, the passions of my conscience, and the inside thoughts purification. I stopped playing music and went to check the door, holding the lute in my hand, when a bantam figure with disharmonious features that didn't fit with his shrinkage was standing at the door. He had big eyes, flabby embossed mouth with thick lips, and a burly nose. He tried hardly adding a few centimeters of length to his stumpy shape by raising his shoulders. The sarcasm and dispraise of *Al-Jahidth* to *Ahmad Bin Abd Al-Wahab* in his message *"Tarbee'a & Tadweer"* was brought to my mind. He smiled to me and said:

- Dr. Zeyad? I'm Waleed, Suzan's husband.

So it's you..!! Ahhh.., I wish that you know what you did to me, and how you brought forth my devastation! Is it really you? How did this shrinkage cause me all this pain and grief? Is this the one whom fate preferred over me and made my adored woman at his back and call? What kind of wisdom fate is after by destroying me at his hands? God, how much I want to kill him! Burn him! Crush him under the feet of my anger and jealousy... I wish I can destroy him and shoot him like an arrow to the sky!

- Oh.., Waleed! Call me Zeyad. Welcome.., please, come in.

- No, you are the one who will come with me, people are waiting for us and we shouldn't be late. Would you please bring your lute with you?

- Oh.., the lute.. Let us have a cup of coffee first.

- We don't have time for that. I heard you playing music before I knocked the door, please bring the lute with you.

- Sure, let's go.

He spent the time greeting me till we reached his car, then he started the conversation with what is much important.

- Suzan told me a lot about you, and how you helped her for years.

- I did my job. She is a good girl.., sorry.., a good woman I mean, that descends from an educated and kindhearted family. I met her brother Sa'ed many times and we became friends. So, tell me about you.

He talked at great length about his earliest years in Dubai and how he went through the worst till he landed on his feet. After that he winded up at his marriage to Suzan. He talked about her in brief as if she was like the rest of mortal women. Every time he named her *"Mastoura"*; the veiled or bashful, I wanted to slap him. It took us only ten minutes to arrive, then we went into the lift to the sixth floor, while exchanging the views. He knocked on the door, then asked me to come in. Everybody stood up when they saw us to greet me. Waleed started introducing the guests by their names and titles. There were three couples and a woman, I introduced myself to them all:

- Zeyad Al-Juneidy. A teacher in languages and literature at Al al-Bayt University, I came to Dubai for the purpose of participating in TESOL Conference, but it seems that I will stay to work as a translator for a Sheikh.
Everybody murmured in admiration.

- Which of the *Shyoukh* are you working for?

Someone asked.

- Sheikh *Mit'eb*.

They started looking at each other wondering if any of them heard the name before. It seems that Sheikh *Mit'eb* doesn't like the show-off and pomposity at all. No one of the eight attendants including Waleed heard his name before.

Suzan entered the hall and greeted me:

- Welcome to Dubai Doctor. It's nice to see you around.

I stood up as a sign of respect.

- Hi Suzan, how are you? I am not your teacher anymore, that was a leaf which is turned over so stop calling me Doctor, call me Zeyad. How is the family, and Sa'ed?

- Everybody is fine. Thanks for coming.

- I am the one who should thank you, I am so glad to meet you all, and I hope I become a friend of yours..

Later, dual talks started and lasted for almost fifteen minutes, during which some of them tried to talk to me from time to time. Among the women there was a single one who, descended from Persian roots, her name was Dilber. Suzan mentioned her to me and said that she is beautiful and she works as a teller in one of the banks. She was a crush for all the men attending, and an ambush to me! Dilber also probed and maneuvered a little.

- *Shma..ah..* You play music Zeyad?

- Yup, since long.

- *Khoushkel.* Would you please show me how?

Waleed found it a good chance to talk to Dilber.

- I heard him playing music when I was standing on the door of the suite, he was playing proficiently, come on Doctor, sorry.. Zeyad, let us hear you playing.

- Yeah.., come on..

- Come on.

At that moment Suzan whispered to another woman and they started setting up the table. I didn't know who laid this ambush! Was it Waleed? Could it be Suzan?

- Alright. I will play the second couplet of *Abd Al-Wahab* masterpiece *"Min Gheir Leigh"*.

I started playing *Hejaz Kar Kurd Maqam* seeking to please Waleed first, and then I played and sang *"Min Gheir Liegh"*. I don't know if it is true or not, but all those who hear me playing music and singing tell me that my voice is beautifully sad. I've never performed before such a number of people, still I guess I did well. Every time I said *"Aarif leigh"* all of them replied *"Min Gheir Leigh"*. Suzan stood still faking interplay as if she heard me singing and playing for the first time in her life, but I know her better than anyone, she didn't like what I did, she waited till I finished and then she acclaimed with the rest and called:

- Come on to the table, help yourself. Waleed, would you?

- *Kheily Qshanq..*, very beautiful!

Dilber said.

Then Waleed invited all to the table, they were still flattering me. We sat on the table and started eating and talking, Suzan wasn't herself, she put food before me without looking at me. We finished eating and had tea in the living room. Men started boasting as usual; each one of them tried to analyze the rage and revolts in the streets of Arab countries according to different perspective. One of them, whose name was *Na'eem Seelawy* tried to ask me about my opinion of the Arab Spring, but I washed my hands of being indulged by making them believe that it won't be nice and wise to make some of them take attitudes either with or against me according to my stands, when I meet them for the first time, but I promised to share and participate in this talk in other times. Suzan's silence and withdrawal enraged me, thus I didn't want to stay any longer. I took leave of the hostess making clear that I expect an important man in the morning to arrive and start work with. Waleed offered to take me back to the hotel, but I refused saying that it won't look good to leave his guests twice for that night. Dilber also asked for permission to leave, I was sure that a misunderstanding will take place by then. I shook hands with everyone and promised to meet them again soon. Suzan came to say good bye to me in the greatest affectation expected. She asked me in front of everybody to keep in touch with them. I entered the elevator with Dilber who started talking to me while she was checking on her mobile phone. After walking her to the parking she offered to give me a ride to my place of residence. I agreed to resume the play, but wasn't quite aware or sure of the incidents in the next act. I wonder who fabricated all these details so accurately. Could it be Waleed to check on what it is going to be like between me and Dilber and shame me before Suzan? He didn't insist on giving me a ride back to the hotel, he got convinced by my excuse so fast. Dilber on the other hand got busy with her mobile phone all the six floors down, is she recording what we are saying, or is Suzan listening to our live conversation at the now moment, to check on me? I kept careful during my talk with Dilber and told her that I am staying in *Al-Nahdah* district, we didn't come across my place of residence during the night gathering. No sooner had we arrived to the district, than I asked her to stop and thanked her for the ride. Before I got out of the car she asked me if I am going to invite her for a cup of coffee, at that moment I smiled and told her maybe next time, and then I rose up my voice saying:

- Good night Waleed.., or Suzan.. Whoever!

I chuckled and got out of the car, Dilber broke out causing uproar behind.

I woke up early next morning and I was well prepared to meet Mr. Assaf. At eight o'clock Suzan dropped me a line.

- Good morning. I hope I did well in accommodating you in my house last night, Doctor. Or probably Dilber welcomed you better and treated you hospitably! I hope that she wasn't negligent?

- Good morning angel, good morning you lunatic… Come on, you will not fool me with your tricks. I didn't come here seeking a job and you know that, I also wasn't deprived of sleep before thinking of other women but you. I have burnt all my ships behind and landed on your shores, stop this art of deception, honey. By the way the okra stew was delicious.

- What art of deception are you talking about? I can't read you!

- You don't want to confess, ha? Alright then, I am not going to talk about it again.

- Why? What happened? Didn't you leave with her? Didn't she give you a ride to the hotel?

- You wouldn't have called me again if anything had happened. This ambush is either laid by you or by Waleed.

- You are skeptical and distrustful honey... *"Kheily Qshanq..,* very beautiful"! She was *"Kheily"* touched by your music, and I was sure that she will seduce you and lead you astray. Though I trust you more than you can imagine you distrustful, still I don't deny my annoyance and my ardency, I am a woman, like the rest of my kind. So, you preserved yourself from sinning! Do you love me so much that you turn down Sassanian Palace and the charm of Assarian *Shahrazad*?

- Quoting Nizar *"When will you know how much I love thee, thou hope which I barter the world, the top, and the bottom of it for"*.

- This is the point; I don't want to know... I want you to pursue, to search, to rove and to cruise for all means possible to make me feel and to make me know how much you love me.

- How long this grief is going to last, Suzan?

- Good luck with Mr. Assaf, I'll call you later.

Like the usual course of Arab businessmen who highly appreciate punctuality and commitment due to the influence left upon them because of dealing with foreigners, Mr. Assaf knocked on my door at nine o'clock sharp, accompanied with two others. He looked pale and exhausted, Mr. Assaf kept a facial tissue on his mouth and couldn't help coughing, he pointed to his assistants to put the file on the table and leave us. When his coughs ceased fire, he asked me to order two cups of tea, to sit before him, and listen carefully to what he is going to say...

- Our restaurants are spread out in the most important suburbs and boroughs of London; in Westminster, in Kensington, in Chelsea, Camden, Oxford, Piccadilly, Notting Hill, and Golders Green. It's the capital city of money and business with a population of more than seven million, Zeyad. Hundreds of five-star competitive restaurants of different origins dwell there; those restaurants are of good reputation and rib the shoulder in quality with ours. More than twenty percent of those restaurants, which vary between three-star and five-star restaurants, serve Arabic food. We started our business there in the early eighties and accomplished our latest spread out in addition to reforms with the beginning of the new millennium. There are about a thousand employees in those restaurants who work as area managers, chefs, waiters, accountants, supervisors, and guards. This file includes all the names of the employees and their salaries. That one is concerned with perpetual lease, payments, receipts, inward outward transfers, inventory, gaining, and bank account number of each branch. The one over there contains all taxes and governmental papers. This is the data and information given to you Zeyad, challenges are so many and so risky at the same time. I will start talking in details now, then I will supply you with my prospect of how to come and overstep such obstacles.

Six hours passed since Mr. Assaf arrived, during which I didn't have time to catch my breath. I was busy reading files, taking notes, listening to details about events of such competitions and where it winded up at. After that he said to me:

- It's almost three o'clock, enough for today. I have to attend an important meeting, try to relax, have lunch, go to the markets, but also try to run over these files and review all the jots. Zeyad, I expect you to shorten as much time of the given to us as possible, and be acquainted with all the ins and outs of the business in order to be behind the wheel.

- Don't worry, Mr. Assaf. I will.

- By the way.., we have prepared a place for you to stay in, and a car. Try to pack your stuff, you will move the day after tomorrow.

- Thank you Mr. Assaf. It's very kind of you.., you really don't forget anything.

- I'll leave now. We are going to meet tomorrow morning, same time. Bye.

When Mr. Assaf left the suite, I had a quick lunch and slummed towards the folkloric and popular markets, though Dubai had no poor districts, still it reserved the oriental old-fashioned and antiquated places. I wasn't one of those who admire shopping places of western fashions and huge malls. I read about the old market on the banks of *Khor* through the internet, I will start by visiting it and if I had enough time I will go to Cosmos line consumer goods. . I took a taxi to the old Dubai market, and when I arrived there, I started walking through its narrow lanes, I was shocked by the intermingling of modernity in Dubai (the city) and the originality represented in restoring the walls, the roofs, the ancient wooden doors of its market. Some people might think, on first consideration, that all Arab popular and folkloric markets are the same because their exterior designs are alike. They all have narrow lanes, wooden arches that shape the roof, and small shops on both sides that are separated with three or four meters most likely. But in this market one can find antiquity firmly fixed by the concrete of modernity, to bring you in homelands of oriental tales, manifested in dim lights and arabesque wooden inscription which is painted in a color that fits the aging color of the walls. That's what I call the genius and artistic touch in oriental architecture. *Hasan Arabesque*; the protagonist of *Osama Anwar Okashah*'s masterpiece "*Arabesque*", had to bring the palace down and start all over to create the oriental spirit and the genuine originality of the east. Metaphorically speaking he denied the idea of the intermingling of cultures that gives rise to a beast of none. This market made me reconsider *Hasan's* belief all over. While pottering around Suzan called me and asked if I finished the meeting with Mr. Assaf.

- Yes, we finished for today. I am in Dubai's ancient market now.

- Where? Oh, dear..! This tendency of yours will never be changed. Have you touched the walls and the woods as usual? Has your neck got stiff for looking upwards at the arches, and you looked like a stupid tourist in the eyes of others, or not yet?

- Hahaha this is exactly what happened, love… Why don't you join me in this tour?
- No, enjoy it yourself; I have lots of things to do. Don't go out tomorrow when you finish with your Assaf. I'll come to you and spend some time together.

- Whatever you say… "*Kheily Qshanq*".

- Don't you ever refer to this again, even if you were kidding! Got it?!

- On one condition, you give me a kiss that is much more important for me to stay alive than a breath.

- Keep dreaming of it the whole night. I want your lips to fall asleep repeating my name.

- "*Mighty is your snare*"!
- This *Ayah* referred exclusively to *Zuleikhah* and her companions; the one who tried seducing Prophet Joseph.

- You said: "I don't deny my annoyance and my ordency, I am a woman like the rest of my kind".

- Love you.

- I said a kiss..!

- See you tomorrow, bye.

I didn't complete my tour to the old market of Dubai, I had to go back and get ready to excogitate and study carefully the file again. I put Mr.Assaf's trust and confidence before my eyes, not for any reason rather than proving to both Mr. Assaf and Sheikh *Mit'eb* that I am solid and up to their expectations. I burnt the midnight oil reading, rehearsing, and going in depth to have all details at my fingertips. I wondered how on earth Mr. Assaf could run the group of dining restaurants in London by his own. For me, I was like a tightrope walker who was trying hard not to drop any of the circles and keep his steps balanced and steady. I noticed later that it was three o'clock in the morning, and I was completely fatigued, so I went to bed and fell asleep.

Next day, Suzan tweeted like early morning birds at eight o'clock, emphasizing her arrival after Mr. Assaf's leave. I called the reception and asked for coffee, and then I started reviewing some details, checking the files from time to time. Mr. Assaf arrived at sharp nine and started asking me about certain issues. He was so pleased to find me acquainted with all information needed to answer his questions. At that time he began illustrating the essence of management to me and how the new world order goes on. He stopped before the window and got distracted, holding the cup of coffee in his hands, he recited.

- In this world, one has to decide at an early stage to which category he or she belongs, or wants to belong to, Zeyad. One becomes of the common people category, or of the government category, or of great companies and factories category, which the previous two categories kneel down before. I heard what you said to *Sheikh Mit'eb* about the armament in the Middle East, but you forgot to mention the other beasts; drugs factories, insurance companies, nourishment monopoly, electronics industry, tobacco productions and many others. We are at their command and service, I am afraid. Anyone who denies the conspiracy theory is a fool, simply because we have winners and losers. Such factories and companies need legal cover that supports them with credibility which constitutes their irregularities, for this reason we have governments. Governments practice abusing the common people by the name of the law; which is constituted of course by the paralegal, undisciplined and above law companies and factories. Rules are made for the commons and mobs only. That's why some companies support campaigns here and there; they know exactly who would serve them and make all their deals get through. Wars are started to carry on transactions and deals. Such governments are brought to office by what the commons like to call "elections". People of the nation, as described in the film *Matrix*, work day and night as electrochemical cells which convert chemical energy into electrical energy to run the government's battery, which such great companies will confiscate at the end. In brief, it's our job to serve the paranoid master who doesn't like seeing us or hearing from us, but no doubt needs us bad for his survival. Such people, Zeyad don't understand passions and emotions, that's why they simply don't care if they discharge thousands of employees at any time. They believe of themselves as gods that need to be worshipped, and order to be treated as such in all domains, that's why they seek authority, money, and rule of their servants forever. They believe that they have the right to be distinguished by granting indulgences, even where all people are supposed to be equal, like religious places, you find them under "golden" or "excellent" pilgrimage. You must think according to this system, Zeyad. Your goals must be precise and your devices ought to be secure and certain. You must hold all cards in your hand and run your business, take use of materialistic Micaville, be as smart as a fox, and as ruthless as a lion to meet all your demands.

I don't deny the loath I felt after Mr. Assaf's talk, but unfortunately such people are rarely wrong. He was convincing and rational in his embodied talk which carried and conveyed more interpretations than what words could say. *Sheikh Mit'eb* was right; I have to learn much of this resourceful fox. His broken coughs, gentle walk, and choice of words obsessed my attention. Yes, I was before incomparable expertise manifested from outside and inside. I don't know how six hours pass when I am accompanied with this Lucipher. I was like a fertilized land that waited his seeding and cultivation. He guided me directly to the goals through the worst facts in politics and secrets of existence. Mr. Assaf made it clear to me that if we continued this perseverance at work, I'll be a playmaker in a short time.

- The driver will pick you up to your place of residence which we prepared for you in the morning. You will find everything you need there, so don't buy anything. The car will also be ready there for you. Bring me your passport; I need it for visas, sponsorship, and immigration papers. By the way, we have paid your bill for the two days at the hotel, so don't bother. Please! Give Suzan my best regards!

Though I knew that I was dealing with a fox, and all my responses should have been studied carefully, and that I should expect everything from him; still I was shocked when he mentioned Suzan to me.

- Don't be surprised. I have to know everything about my successor. This is a trust grounded on mere devotion and loyalty not on blood relationship; we are all knights of King Arthur. See you.

No sooner had Mr. Assaf left, and I had jotted down all memos which I will sleep on for tonight, than Suzan dropped me a line saying that she was on her way to me. She asked me to get ready for shopping some important stuff for the bachelor apartment she rented for me. I didn't tell Suzan that Mr. Assaf will provide me with a place to stay in. I wonder if Mr.Assaf knows about this bachelor apartment too! This man scares me.

Suzan arrived at half past three, and as usual she kept me in confusion, in rapture, and in stupor for some minutes. Knowing and seeing her for seven years, still I get the feelings of the first time I saw her. We talked about the dinner I had in her apartment a night before, and the impression I left on her guests. I didn't talk about Dilber of course and I didn't try to draw her attention to the eagerness of Waleed for talking to Dilber and the crush bluntly appeared on him while talking to that Assyrian. I told her about the place Mr. Assaf offered me which she regarded as proper saying:

- Great. Then the apartment will be exclusively ours, let's get it ready as we always wished.

We went down to the market to buy some stuff, Suzan performed singlehandedly and decided what is necessary to be bought, because she was the one who rented the place and she knows what is missing. Indirectly Suzan redressed moments we should have had together like a married couple.

- Suzan.., you are setting up our home.
- Yes, I know. I have dreamt of such moments.

- Aren't you afraid of being seen by any of your acquaintances or of your husband's?

- This is not Irbid, Zeyad. This city is of two millions and a half of population. Ninety percent of them are of migrant labor. Since when did you start caring about the consequences of being seen together? Risks in Irbid were of much more madness.

We walked hand in hand from one shop to the other, among the shelves and goods, filling the baskets with food, detergents, kitchenware, and a bunch of flowers. When we finished shopping we carried all the stuff to "*Les Fleur Du Tulipe*", as Suzan named it. I had to take safety precautions into consideration to secure the place of assembly, therefore I generously tipped *Abu Mahmoud*; the residential building keeper to play the role of the three wise monkeys. The place was great, looking down upon strategic projects like Metro, Burjuman mall, and the stretched beach in the skyline. Suzan lied on the sofa and closed her eyes smiling.

- I still don't believe that you are here, would you stay when I open my eyes, or would you fade away like a dream?

I sat close to her and set her head in my lab, dallying with her hair tufts in silence, when she let herself go on saying:

- Even in dreams a human can sense standing, walking, flying, trembling when falling. I was possessed by you even when you were not here, my dreams were haunted by you. Some nights I shuddered; feeling your touches, and hardly shut my mouth from calling your name.

- I am the one who wants to touch you, to know that I am still alive. I love you darling.

- Don't move for a while. I want to nap like this.

Sleeping Beauty didn't take a long siesta, she was annoyed by the ringing of my mobile.

- Your Assaf is a real troublesome.

- That's really strange!! He never called me before; he finishes everything he wants to say before he leaves.
She leaned back on the sofa, making me have one hell of a time with her moans and sighs.

- Go on, answer that tedious.

When I saw the name on the mobile screen, I couldn't help laughing.

- You are right; he is tedious! Hi, Waleed, how are you doing? Sorry I got busy today but I wanted to call you to thank you for your invitation and accommodation last night, and for introducing me to your friends, too.

- Don't mention it, I just wanted to tell you that they were glad to meet you, and they insisted on keeping in touch with you. Are you alright?

- Absolutely. I'll keep in touch, please thank Suzan for me, and I'll call you back the minute they decide a place of residence for me.

- Sure. I'll wait for your call.

- It won't be long. See you.

- See you. Bye.

Suzan kept her eyes widely open in surprise, then she started unpacking the baskets. She looked confused, distracted, and subject to pangs of remorse due to Waleed's phone call. Things began falling down from her hands, my attendance and my voice were both undesirable at that time. I remained silent, looked at her, she tried hardly to hide her tears and irritation. I waited for a mutation in her mood, but she needed help.

- Suzan, I didn't come here to disturb you, Waleed is your husband and this is a fact that both of us have to deal with. I will not turn my back and leave you, and this struggle will last forever. I am really sorry to say this, but it's you who must adapt yourself to this situation. Do you think that meeting Waleed didn't enrage me last night? In spite of this, I pretended to be happy to meet him, I faked being cool to earn his trust, and I assumed warmth and friendship with my most offensive extorter for the legitimacy he has of you in his hand.

- Enough. I am not hesitant as you think I am. This love which is deeply rooted in my heart is nonnegotiable. Such pangs are out of my hand, and you are not the one to be blamed for. Come on, you will help me preparing my first meal in *Les Fleur de Tulipe*.

I opened my arms and waited to embrace her as a sign from her that she truly stepped over this trouble, she ran into my arms to be sheltered from any remorse. She hugged me strongly for a couple of minutes before she calmed down again, her breath got regulated, and her tears were withheld. Her touches afterwards were like baby girl lulls that seek awaking some warmth which would embrace her.

- You know what love?

- What?

- Every time I see you running towards me like a filly after being troubled by fate, I call to mind the story of the five horses. There is some kind of a basic instinct imposed on you by reality, which needs to be fulfilled; still you leave out all such calls of benefits to answer the call of loyalty and devotion. Look at me.

She looked at me from behind the drapery tufts on her forehead.
- I'll never forget this. You have bestowed upon me a crazy sort of love and a legendary devotion. A man who says that all women are the same is a delusionist. A man who doesn't make a just estimation of you is an ignorant and knows nothing, and a man who believes that you will turn back to someone else other than me is a dreamer.

- *Kheily Qshanq* ha ha ha...

C'est la Suzan!! Breakdowns, crashes, collapses that don't last for more than ten minutes followed by loud laughs. She started cooking a meal while asking me about recent developments with Assaf. I made the nature of my work and the must trips clear for her.

- So, you are going to London.

She wondered with a raising tone.

- It's not what you think. These are irregular monthly short trips; once or twice a month, each time I'll stay for three days, inspecting the restaurants and be cognizant of the latest procedures that need to be taken care of, in addition to meetings with area managers, then I return back.

- Meaning that you will be leaving for six days a month!

- At most, yes. Look, I am more than eager to stay beside you Suzan, I promised you, but this is the nature of the job.

- Alright then. Let me tell you what the women said about you last night, I was about to kill one of them; "Oh, have you heard his music? Even his voice was a crush! I was taken by his goatee dressed with white hair".

- Really? Which one of them?

- None of your business.

- Just kidding..

She finished cooking the meal and placed it on the small table.

- Yummy.., looks delicious. You are perfect. This perfection in you crushes me and makes my loss worse.
- Don't say this. With all the more reason, somebody else should have said this. Tell me Zeyad, is it possible that one doesn't fairly appreciate the precious things he/she has, just because the grass is always greener on the other side of the fence?

- If you are talking about the world of men and women, I guess so. Lots of men are driven towards the forbidden fruit, just because it's not theirs. It inflames the love, the instinct, and the desire which has been put out by time and routine. Men totally forget their women who probably would be more beautiful compared to the forbidden ones from inside and outside. Other men ask themselves in secret, what's wrong with this stupid man? His wife is more beautiful than the one he is stalking! And that's what he exactly says about them too.

- Derangement, thy name is man.

- It's very simple, let me explain it to you. You women keep trying to apply your data on different diagrams and schedules, this is the mere problem. Men are not women to dream of one partner who would love them and be loyal to them; men are of different natural disposition and makeup with different data and of different programs. They seek hunting all the time, and most likely get confused between liking someone and loving someone. They even don't bother to name this relationship. The more expert in hunting the man is, the more popular he becomes among his kind and the more flattered by lambs, too. This makes him feel satisfied and assures his potency which affects his behavior, too, as a man. When man becomes impotent his spirit dies, exactly like woman when experiencing menopause or female climacteric. Men like to test themselves by indulging in such relations to check their potency and how much they are desired and wanted. Regarding his wife on the other hand, she knows no one else and her husband has never been a subject to comparisons, in fact he is the only player in her playground, therefore she must accept some missing goals and sluggish acting of this player by the course of time.

- What about you? Am I going to be a run of the mill for you one day? Even if we had married?

At that moment, I put the knife and fork on the table, I knew where this conversation would lead to.

-Suzan, when I say men I mean the overwhelming majority of the men. This means that exceptional cases of the minority who are aware of this trick do exist. That's why such minority don't intermingle with foreign women to save themselves guilt and remain content with their kismet, and stay away from comparisons' traps. I myself don't belong to any of both categories. I knew that some sort of weird obsession affected me in my love to you that made me ascetic, fedayee, and intellectual. Your love rectified me, cultured me, and made me look better. I dwelled in you long enough to the limit I could introspect about you, know all your details, and be aware of all of your attributes; the strong points and the weak ones as well. I read your history, constructed bridges to your present time, and became a phantom that embraced you and comprehended your future too. I love the spirit, the mind, and the body of Suzan, I love her in her state of calmness, and in her state of storming. My love to Suzan is a faith that became firmly established in my heart and spirit, and also became a concrete knowledge that called for the reality of devotion to Suzan even when she is away. Your love made that man in me who follows the traces of your breath in the air for the chance of having them as his own too. I was created for you, and only for you.

She was looking at me with tears in her eyes while I was talking to her. I guess that Suzan started to complain, like the rest of women, from the languor feelings of Waleed towards her. I know she loves me and she loves hearing such words from me, still in point of fact, she is a married woman who cries the state of all-alike women. They cry all those vows of love, pledges, and promises of devotion made to them one day. They weep over rosette dreams which they told each other in secret, wrote on ornamented diaries left to toll the world of oblivion. They talked to each other about their princes of their dreams during school classes and breakouts. Despair and loud outcry they feel due to their disappointment of their husbands; who get enchanted by younger women with gracefulness and presentable attractions. She wiped her tears and faked a smile, then she said:

- I'll tell you what Waleed said about you. You won't believe it, he talked about you in good manners; he said that you are a great, educated, and social man, a man with a charisma. I think you'll be good friends.

- That's great!

She continued talking about Waleed, but I wasn't listening. I kept looking at her and smile back if she smiled. I was completely absentminded, praying to God that this beast wouldn't come close to her. Suzan also abhors it when he touches her, no doubt he is aware of that, that's why he treats her with men's continence as a punishment. Either he deliberately shows interest of other women before her to despise her, or he is tormenting her by neither holding on equitable term, nor separating with kindness. I don't know, she doesn't look alright, and I will not wait long if Suzan is the one being treated like this.

- Oh…, we ran out of time. I have to go now, Zeyad. By the way, I made a copy of the key for myself, this one is yours, and I'll keep mine in my medal. Come on, get up. I must go now, and you have to go back to the hotel. Assaf will take you tomorrow to your new place.

- Alright, let's go.

I took a taxi and drove Suzan back home first, and then went to the hotel. Before I started reading all the notes of Mr. Assaf , I called Mom, Sura, and the kids on the phone. We talked long; I told them about the great opportunity I won in a very short period of time. They were delighted at this news and wished me luck. After that I turned to Management Science according to the facts and information illustrated by Mr. Assaf to me. I surfed the internet and went over lots of websites to get comprehensive information about the places where the branches of the group dwell in. I also investigated about the economic situation in Britain to be familiar with any sign or indication that would foreshow how the coming days will be like.

*****

We seek knowledge to be intellectual and gain success in life, but we seek innocence through love to remain human beings. I've never heard of knowledgeable innocent man yet!

~17~

No doubt that an observer of the international policy can predict the economic conditions in different parts of the world, due to the development of audiovisual inventions; which made the whole world a small village. I have found through my readings and by surfing the net, that London for example - which Mr. Assaf called it the city of money - started to complain of millionaires emigration to countries with less taxes relatively speaking; like Australia, Spain, France, and America. When one hears a raise in the percentage of basic products theft in a country, one can predict how the economic conditions are deteriorating, and also can assume a wane in the middle class of that country, which we in restaurants business are concerned with. The retention of some branches, which have no future due to demographical reasons, like Golders Green branch, made the mission so challenging and next to impossible, especially when one also takes into consideration the competition with Lebanese, Indian, Italian restaurants and many others as well. Even the bastions which such millionaires went to, like France, don't escape the danger of railway stations strike, because the government there exceeded the proper bounds and damaged the peoples' money by the modification of retirement law; in an economic reformation plan. In Spain on the other hand, public activists organized a day of fury held by half a million due to deterioration in economic conditions, corruption, and unemployment. I have advised *Sheikh Mit'eb* to extend his business and invest in more stable countries like Europe, but it seems that this is a global economic crisis that no one can predict how long it would last. Does Mr. Assaf expect me to carry out miracles when he is aware of all these challenges? Does he want me to play the role of a peg, and be responsible of all coming and expected flaws? Wasn't it more appropriate for both *Sheikh Mit'eb* and Mr. Assaf to take the recommendations of all their economical consultants into consideration, rather than risking business during such an international crisis? Why didn't they think of getting rid of such wide branches, and gather up as much of the cash money as possible and invest them in ... buying shares in such huge companies which Mr. Assaf talked about? Would it be possible that this group of dining restaurants is no more than a cover of dirty business, for money laundry, or money washing? Is that what *Sheikh Mit'eb* admired me for? Is this what Mr. Assaf wanted me to know? What role has he prepared for me? What kind of illegal business is it? Weapons.., drugs.., prostitution...., or what? I kept working earnestly for a late hour, with a hundred questions in my mind, till I couldn't lift up my hand.. then.. then.. I heard Mr. Assaf coughing through the corridor, I went hurriedly and opened the door for him, he was heavily armed with files as usual.

- Good morning Zeyad. It's your leaving day..Are you ready? The men will take all your stuff and I will stay here with you till we finish our work, then the driver will take you to your new house. Did you have your coffee?

- Right away.

I called the room service to bring us coffee while I was detecting Mr. Assaf who was arranging the files and coughing.

- Zeyad.. today we will hasten the mode a bit discussing some financial issues and the banks we deal with, which eases the transfer of liquid capital between the branches, and then transfer the total amount to the main branch in different and various bank accounts.

- Mr. Assaf why don't you abridge the two weeks into a few moments and tell me, how are your deals and transactions made or carried out? Tell me about the real business you deal with?

Mr. Assaf pondered at me for a while and deduced the fact that I became aware of the crimes they commit in their business. I probably caused him confusion for a minute, yet my question eased down his fears and his hesitation.

- Don't worry Mr. Assaf the suite is not bugged, say whatever you want.

- Ha ha ha.. awesome! I had no doubts at all that you will get over all the obstacles in a very short period of time, and you will overcome the rest of the matches who tried hard to occupy this position. You didn't let me down Zeyad, I've never underestimated your insight, your cunning, and your ability of elusion, argumentation, and winning the competitions. Your mental propensity of justifying the irregularities and turning them into beliefs that urge you to wage and win wars like of Suzan, makes you an undefeated arm. Regarding bugging the place; don't worry, this is our job, and I strongly trust you.

- There are some questions that I need to know their answers. Why did you choose an inexpert like me? What is your mere business? What happened to all those who occupied this position before? Were they wiped out? What mistakes have they committed? Am I going to be wiped out as well? Do you have any warranty, or promises, or word of honor I can count on if something bad happened to me? Would you take care of the bereaved? Would you extort and blackmail me through my family and through Suzan?

- Why did I choose you? I was looking for a man with no experience at all in commerce and business and never been spotlighted in such domain, so that I teach him what I want and he becomes a turning point with our customers who will get confused, fear our intentions, and count hundreds of times before committing any foolish mistake. A highly educated academic man with a cloudy and an ambiguous reputation will urge the circles' anger, and everybody will wait for his responses. This silence and calmness of yours should be very breathtaking and make them fear for their lives. We will spread out rumors about your mystery as a trained killer with the concept of the psychopathic but highly educated *"Hannibal"* who no one wants to fuck with. What is our business? Every kind of job that brings forth lots of money in a short time is an illegal and internationally forbidden business that we are concerned with; arms, drugs, trafficking of migrants, women, children, trans-border, prostitution, alcohol, tobacco, medicine, buying offices and positions, bribery, hitting the economy of countries, pilfering, wiping away trouble makers.. this is a wide sea Zeyad, you have to throw away the trolling spoon and wait. What happened to previous matches who occupied this position before? Some of them still work for us, others rest in peace for committing fatal mistakes, and some others are still waiting.. we don't blackmail our officials, either they work for us or we leave them in peace! Regarding punishing their families, well we don't do such dirty jobs, and we don't have to. We own the money and we buy the authority, the one who works for us gains gifts and donations, but for the conscience, the ball is left in the chooser's ground, nothing is free of charge. Did I answer your questions?

- You have probed my spirit and explored my character and came to know me the way you know yourself. For once I wanted to believe that an opportunity like this was offered to me on a silver platter by life. I was mistaken by being optimistic, I should have leaned toward being pessimistic from the beginning and figure out that all this care and attention is in fact a focusing on your ego..; the ego of Lucifer.

- Dear Zeyad, don't deny the fever of Lucifer on you; he has all the good turns upon humanity. Wasn't he punished for bringing forth knowledge to you? Who made him speak out and be arrogant? Wasn't there a sense and an invitation in his argument, pride, and philosophy of democracy? You are acquainted with his beauty, with his smartness more than anyone else. Lucifer bestows you with money, glory, fame, and might. Think of what you might bring to your children.. to your Suzan.. Do you think that Suzan would have kept you a lover if the charm of Lucifer didn't leave an influence on her, by tempting with money, with gifts, with beauty, with fame, and with authority? Come on Zeyad.. she is an Eve, and this will make you strike the balance with the poor Waleed. This will make her forget everything but you.

I wasn't desperate for a temptation to seize this lifebuoy opportunity, for everything turned out to be a delusion. Virtue is a delusion, justice is a delusion, equity is a delusion, peace is a delusion, all the talks and promises are delusions, our history is fake, deception and delusion, our tales of heroism and bravery are delusions, our future is a mirage and a delusion, our freedom is a superstition of delusion, our reforms are fibs of delusions, our unity is a legend of delusion, the applied religion of the government is a deviation of law based on delusion, even our certainty and sureness became mere delusion, if one told me that the sun is in the sky I would say it's a delusion, for neither the sky likes the sun in our countries, nor the sun likes to rise on countries of worry, of grief, and of delusion. These are the days and the times of brokers, merchants, loan sharks, and dissolute. These are the times when rulers slay their nations, suck their blood, and announce all the resources, and their history of culture for sale, then they leave under the protection of an international initiative proposal to a refuge that would warmly welcome them and welcome their stolen things as well. These are the times when wars are possible to be waged only if the war bill payer is determined. Nizar is right: "*Our abstinence is adultery, our piety is dirt and filth",* and I say that our struggle is a lie and that politics and prostitution are synonymous.

I don't act as if I know what the future has in store for us, but no doubt that the future is inevitable; the seeds of evil are already sowed and fertilized in the land of aggression, killing, pilferage, displacement, rape, invasion, and solitude. We are away of censorship, of care, of ethics and morals, and of religion, so not to acquire any immunity to this decay, thus what generations and harvest do we expect of such seeds? What future but devastation and ravage? How am I supposed to raise my children? Must I teach them the virtues in times of vices and turn them into lambs in the valley of wolves? Or must I bring them up as wolves not to be eaten by dogs? The logic of evil wins, and Assaf is still waiting..

- I am not meek and broken, and I'll never be a sitting duck or an easy catch for money or glory, Sir. I am rather quenched with beliefs that I saw with my naked eye and understood with the logic of Lucifer. *"Corruption of the best is the worst"*, a hand of violence driven by the logic of evil. Neither have I an internal conflict of a conscience nor have I leftovers of human mercy. Pity the one who clashes with corrupted intellectual. Do you think that my reputation is clean enough and my hand has never been a wrongdoer before? How often my mind and my reason have committed crimes that never crossed the mind of evil itself! Don't deny me If you saw what might shock you of my deeds. Provide me with all means Mr.Assaf, make me read your teachings, leave your amulets on me, and let me think up all deals and transactions in the lands of stupid and stupidity..

I awoke of this confrontation on the shouts of Mr. Assaf calling my name and his knocking on the door. I went hurriedly to the door and opened it. Mr. Assaf looked suspiciously at me with his deep eyes, and then said:

- Don't tell me that you were asleep till nine o'clock!

He took a few steps inside and looked at the jumbled up papers on the table, then he sat and started arranging them.

- In fact I reviewed some files till midnight.., and after that I surfed a few websites to detect the factual economic status in London, then.. I guess.. I've fallen asleep!

That's good.. you are doing good son by dedicating yourself for work till midnight. Such drudgery work will tire you out at the beginning, but then things will be much easier. Don't misunderstand me, but the fact is that lots of people burnt the midnight oil working in this company in hope of occupying this position. We want the ambitious and high aiming people not greedy and avaricious. The wisdom which you gave to Sheikh *Mit'eb*, regardless of its spontaneity, indicates good knowledge, and intimate feelings for those whom you care about. When you give a piece of advice to your benefactor without waiting a reward in return you transcend from being an official to a truehearted platonic guardian friend, and this is exactly what I want, and that's precisely what *Sheikh Mit'eb* needs. I don't have enough time Zeyad, and this is something I didn't tell *Sheikh Mit'eb* about, and here I am.., telling you. According to recent medical tests and reports I have only a couple of months to live, and I don't want *Sheikh Mit'eb* to hold me back from working and take care of me. I want to die like a war veteran in a battle field. He is like a brother for me and I want to give back some of his grants and donations. I want you to be his sword that he fights with, his shield that protects him, his tongue that speaks his words, his master mind, and his friend that he seeks refuge to in need. All the people around us are dazzled by the money, the glory, and the influence. This is self-sacrifice Zeyad, this is what I want for *Sheikh Mit'eb*. Regarding taking the charge of the restaurants in London, that's easy, you can learn handling the group by time. To tell you the truth I was taken by your character in the conference first, but then when I knew about your Suzan, I was obsessed by feelings that I couldn't put in words by then. You are the mad man I was looking for. Keep this a secret and don't you ever dare telling *Sheikh Mit'eb* a word. Let us finish work first, you can move to your place of residence later.

Who would ever think that Mr. Assaf is dying? Even his lasting coughs, his emaciation of body, his set of teeth, and his grey hair are not warning enough to assume the coming death of this wholeheartedly devoted energetic man.

- I am so sorry to hear that Mr. Assaf. Is there anything we can do?

- Sorry! What are you sorry for Zeyad? You hardly know me.. there is nothing you can do.

- Don't judge my admiration by the period of time I knew you Mr. Assaf. I am not *Iago* to seek any opportunity so as I extrinsically declare my love and devotion to you when I hide my own desires and wishes. Verily, I saw a self-denying ideal in serving a master, like once you assimilated us to the knights of King Arthur. Not before long, I lost a king that I served for my whole life. I lost my father Mr. Assaf, and I am here today not to be bereaved of the last sublime; my baroness, my lady whom I burnt my ships, slain my horses, and left everything behind for. We are of the same nature Mr. Assaf. Each one of us dedicates himself to serve his master. As for *Sheikh Mit'eb*, heavens bestowed upon me a master to serve and be loyal for, and this will not clash with my love and devotion to Suzan. I promise you, by the oath of knights, to carry out all your wishes and meet all your expectations. Till then, this will not keep me from esteeming and glorifying a brother in arms even if we didn't know each other for a long time.

- All what I want from you is just to keep the group's business in the front. This group is like my own child.., that I took care of till it prospered, and now I am proud of my achievement.

- Be sure Mr. Assaf.

- Come on.., we don't want to waste more time. We both need to finish work as fast as possible, because we have other things waiting to be done, right?

- Right.

We exchanged views in most of the topics that had to do with business. Mr. Assaf never spared an effort providing me with all possible pieces of advice that could be of a good help for me to be aware of all the details at work. We finished as usual at three o'clock, and went down heading the hall's open space. There were two cars waiting for us, Mr. Assaf asked one of the drivers to take me to *Bastakiyah* villa and wished me luck. On my way to the villa I recalled my talk with Mr. Assaf, and kept thinking of his helpless health case. I was confused thinking of his end while being attracted by Dubai's districts which were made of modern and originality meshing. Again, *Bastakiyah* stands as another example on the determination of Dubai emirate governors on leaving over the ancient architectural style and fashion, by keeping the extrinsic shape as is without any reparations or pillaring. The car stopped by one of those mud-like houses, the whole district made me feel as if I was Sinbad in one of his tales in Baghdad. The driver got out of the car, unloaded it of my baggage, and then handed me the house keys. I thought it was a joke at first, I didn't complain, in fact I was taken by the charm of the orient and its mystery which preponderated over any question or doubt. I went toward the door, which was made of arabesque engraved wood, and widely opened it. The creaking torn sound of the door.. with the metallic tapping of the ornaments were musical instruments that allied to make me surf-ride the past. I took a few steps into the hall.. and stood still!! I couldn't believe what I saw.. it was an Arabic house with all the meanings of the word. One might think it one of those Damascus ancient houses we see in T.V. series; the roof was opened to the sky, and in its yard there was a big lemon tree with huge branches that lean like two wings cuddling the rooms on both sides. The small fountain in the middle, under the shadows of the lemon tree branches made the view glamorous. In front of it, there was a place for gathering and sitting made of arabesque wooden seats with a table in the center where a sieve, a *Mihbash,* and a *Mehmas* were left there. The rooms were lined up in a row surrounding the yard, sweet basil beds here and there...an old closet inlaid with shells in the corner. The driver dropped the baggage and handed me the car key, and asked if I needed anything else. I thanked him, walked him to the door, and slipped a handful of money bills in his pocket, then he went away. I pondered around checking the place.

Sitting in *Ard el-Diyar* as called by the Syrians, looking at the sunrays slipping away through the lemon tree branches, I felt so sad, wanted to hear Suzan's voice so bad, look at her eyes, hug her, and stay with her forever. I don't want from this life more than this modesty, what if life was fair and granted us this dream? Wouldn't we live happily? God.. I don't want any of these boons and blessings you bestow upon me, I don't want money, or glory, I don't want to travel around the world, and I don't want a longer life, I just want her.. with her hellfire and with her coldness.. nobody else.. Oh, please God..

I kept pondering till I went far..., very far..

- I thought you were busy.. I couldn't get to sleep last night.. the sun rose while I was awake thinking of you. I made up dialogues between us to relieve my worries and my grieves..
She sounded sad as if she was crying..

- *Turn down your awakening to naps, and forget your troubles..*
I will stay awake, instead and carry all your woes.
Leave the toil for me,

Accept drowsiness like a present,
Get to sleep in meekness of a child between my arms,
And feel the warmth of my lap in dreams..

She burst out crying.., for my words touched her nerve of grieves, I won't ask her what makes her cry her, I know exactly the enormity of the pain she suffers from, because it caused me damage already. She cried in appetite that agitated the saliva of my eyes, a chill flared up in my whole body that gave me rapture of emotions. Who is capable of doing this to me except you, brunette? Oh Suzan.. you are unique in everything.. even your crying is a temptation, a seduction, a bringing gradually, and a sin. What are you busy with? What are you thinking of? Why do you sit alone on the edge of the fountain? Why do you distort your image and reflection in water? Look at me sweet Suzan.. Suzan..

My loneliness with Suzan was interrupted by a phone call…

- Hello..

- Zeyad.. where are you? Is Assaf still around with you? Am I interrupting?

- No..I am by my own darling.. I was just talking to….. forget it.. I am in *Bastakiyah*. It seems that Mr. Assaf found out and deduced my taste; that's why he granted me an Arabic house.

- Really? *Bastakiyah* district? That's really strange!! I know you like this modesty and dislike towers and high buildings, but I didn't expect *Bastakiyah* to be your place of residence. As long as you are happy and you feel comfortable there, that's fine.

- I am happy here, love. What is your plan for this evening?

- Not much.. I want to see you.. My orphaned heart wishes to be warmly hugged and fall asleep in your lap, you spirit guardian. My body also needs a therapy with your touches, to calm down its cramps and get rid of loneliness and be saved of groans, but I don't know how. You were in our house last night, and I don't want Waleed to question or doubt any of the coincidences we make.

- You are right.. never mind.. but you need to know my address and see the place here to organize it, and set it up.

- Sure, I will not allow any slander, or treason, or mutiny, or existence of dissidents in my kingdom, I will interrogate the water and the stone and leave nothing unturned so as not to have a she snitch pauper manipulating in my possession, thus I set in fiasco and heartbreak crying over wasted property.

- Whooo.. hold your horses, what she snitch pauper are you talking about? What wasted property are you crying over? I am the hidden untrodden land between your two shell skies, if your sun sets, your moon does rise over my lands.. You're the ever eternity of love, when you are away from me.. my heart feels at ease with your effect left upon me, till passion springs up with your emergence. Don't make me hear such doubts from you as if you were like the rest of women, and I was like other lovers. No .., Suzan, my heart made every effort in your love and passed all levels of liking, of cordiality, of affection, and of love. It even left behind ardent love, abstinence, insanity, enthrallment, and distraction.

- I know how much you love me.. God be my witness, I know.. but women like to hear such a talk so as to live in comfort, in ease, and in peace.

- You are not like the others, and you will never be one, regardless of your claim, and please don't you ever compare me with the denier and ungrateful, or with a naïve who doesn't know what he is saying and doesn't appreciate what he has.

- I won't.. I promise you. Say.., how about if we, the three of us, had coffee in your place this time? First, I can see you and know where your house is, and secondly you can strengthen your relationship with Waleed, thus we clear the way for more frequent chances of meetings.

- No problem…I will call him now and insist on your coming; as a sign of befriending him, and drawing on an invitation for you and for your friends to have dinner in my place, to get to know you all more.

- That's great.. Don't invite Dilber.

- Love.., I don't know Dilber, I will assign Waleed to invite whoever he wants, let it be on Thursday.., two days from now, what do you think?

- Good. Now relax for a while, but don't forget to call Waleed.

- I won't forget, love. Bye, my brunette.

I called Waleed and informed him with the address of my new place and invited him over for a cup of coffee with Suzan on Wednesday, and over dinner with the rest of friends on Thursday to enjoy the night in this Arabic house. He apologized for not being able to come on Wednesday, claiming that he has an appointment with somebody, but he welcomed the idea of inviting the whole gang for dinner on Thursday. He also asked me to allow him to bring another two friends whom he wanted to introduce to me, I agreed of course, I was in a need to adapt, and this can't be done without having friends around.

Being alone in that Arabic house made me feel the separation from my native country more than the loneliness I felt in the hotel. Probably the open wide space and the many rooms made for a whole family was behind my feelings of estrangement. Arabs have always boasted and felt more secure having many sons around. People were even evaluated by the number of sons they have, regardless of the deterioration of their economic life and means of support, and even though the reasons behind the need of having many sons has nearly disappeared; such as helping hands in cultivation or to make up for fatalities in wars. The family through customs and traditions on one hand, and the religion on the other hand support any man whose wife is barren to get married to another. In their opinion this is a must for keeping progeny and assuring rights in inheritance. "*A house of men is better than a house of money*", "*He who has a successor behind shall never die*", "*Successors make a value for the cheap and mean*", "*A bundle of sticks is unbreakable*". And the authorization of Islamic law, as some assumed, supports this fact; the fact of increasing the numbers of sons after the prophet's *hadith* "Intermarry, propagate, and breed for I'll vie in glory with other nations in the day of resurrection" which people considered it an invitation to destroy the thought of birth control, thus we started to care for quantity over quality depending on God to vouch for food, education, health, housing, and work. This house fits for a whole Arab family and I will occupy it by my own self. I'll make use of one bedroom, one guestroom, and an office room only, I'll close the rest of the rooms doors till I see what am I going to do later.

Next morning Mr. Assaf arrived on his usual time, and we discussed some new issues for hours, he wreaked his wrath on China this time, explaining that due to cheap power hand there, lots of industries closed down in Europe causing inflation, unemployment, and recession. As usual his talk makes me aware of the mission impossible I am indulging myself in. Later he asked me to get prepared for having dinner with *Sheikh Mit'eb* in the Marina resort at eight o'clock. I got ready early after he left and went out promenading with no specific place in mind. I wanted to explore all districts of Dubai without a guide. It was still early to head for the dinner of *Sheikh Mit'eb*. I pottered among *Bastakiyah, Jidhaf, Sfough, Nahdha, Marqabat, Rashideyah*, and ended up in *Jumeirah*. I stopped there and wanted to have a cup of coffee while observing the blood of dusk and sunset glittering over the waves of the sea. Homesickness was about to sneak into my heart, but I hurriedly started to think of other things, so as to close the door in the face of such longings and never be torn again. I sat there listening to Triton's talk in agitation and in calmness; this kind of talk which its tone is associated with the mystery of the seabed, with the terror of waves, with riddles of the shores, and with the charm of bays. The nightfall was so sad.., the sun was being slain by the waves' blade and by the skyline's sword.., it died like a supplicant.., like a desirous.., like good people and servants of God.., in peace.

At eight o'clock I headed toward the resort of *Sheikh Mit'eb* in Marina, it was crowded there and lots of people had to leave their cars for the guards to park them somewhere else. I left mine on the gate and went inside the hall of the resort. Mr. Assaf saw me and waved a hand so that I join him. He welcomed me and started to introduce me to the guests there. I could hardly hear their names, the music distorted Mr. Assaf's feeble voice. There were about twenty men and women standing in separate groups talking to each other. I and Mr. Assaf walked around welcoming them, but their responses were not pleasing, they didn't like me at all. *Sheikh Mit'eb* entered the hall wearing *Bisht*, accompanied with two; a queen on each side; a blond and a brunette. The sound of music died down, everybody became silent and turned around to greet *Shiekh Mit'eb*. His Excellency "God grant him with long life" started to welcome the guests with a sentence or two for each one, while shaking hands with them till he reached me.

- Welcome.. Assaf's recruit.

- Thank you.., your Excellency..

- So.. are you going to be ready on time?

- I am ready to start right away, your Excellency.

- Great.. great.. I'm not surprised, for you are a student of the devil, come and sit next to me.

The man's admiration ran in my heart, and I was obsessed by altruism to his halo, as if I was touched by a wand. Everybody sat around the table with bootlicking smiles. I wanted Assaf to sit next to *Shiekh Mit'eb*, but he sat in front of me on the other side. Waitresses started serving food and drinks for everybody, while the two queens on both sides of *Sheikh Mit'eb* exclusively served his Excellency.

- Help yourself..

Sheikh Mit'eb spoke in a friendly tone, pointing to the table. At that time one of the waitresses drew near me and asked in English language about the kind of drink I prefer to have. I thanked her and said:

- Just water please.., thank you.

A woman, who was sitting in front of me and next to Mr. Assaf, burst out laughing in a dramatic way, to draw the attention of everyone. I wasn't aware of her existence until then, she was wearing a white formal shirt with fringed sleeves, long collars, and loose unbuttoned folds.. her boobs begged the careless eyes for attention, I pondered her for a while to see the one that I am going to make a scapegoat for other opponents. She was with sharp features, boney cheeks, wild eyes, short hair, and without earrings. I wondered if she was adopting masculine manners, or if she was a she-male that didn't gain any attention of a man. I took off the serviette in silence and with a smile, for I knew that *Shiekh Mit'eb* was waiting to hear my response. I spoke up saying:

- I don't know which thing of yours is more notorious and shamed! Is it your jealousy? Or your curiosity? Or your wish of drawing the attention to your deformation? Or probably your masculinity. Look at you, did you come out of a Spanish colonial era or dreamt of being Lolita Pulido of any of the Zorro's here? I wondered at first how must I address you, but then I thought that you are lucky, for I am speaking to you in English. In English, you know, the second person pronoun "you" is used for both man and woman. If I switch to Arabic I would have said "Anta"; the pronoun used for addressing male..! Must I proceed ? you can follow me if you didn't get tired.. I am just getting warmer…do you like sarcasm? I can repeat this joke again according to your request, let's do it again..

come on.. Water please! Water please... Why aren't you laughing anymore?

She was wonder-struck looking at me, others were waiting her reply too, but *Sheikh Mit'eb* interrupted with a modest comment to save her water and bridle my tongue.

- The Indian spicy dressing and pepper with hot sauce that is presented with fish and shrimps and served with Californian red wine make me feel young again. Did you know that Californian wine is the best in the whole world?

- May God grant you with good health.., no, your Excellency, I didn't know that. Can your Excellency explain to me the difference?

- Oh, you are a good student, alright let me explain this to you. In most occasions inexperienced ones believe that wine is chosen according to the color of the meat they are having; if they are eating lamb meat they choose red wine, and if they eat white meat like fish or chicken they choose white wine, but this is not a must. Experts prefer red wine for it is heavier and stronger, where as white wine is not clear of sweetness, but it has its occasions too. The amount of rainfall which is poured down during harvesting Zeyad, you are a farmer and you should know what I am referring to, manipulates the proportion of sweetness in grapes. That's why quality changes from a year to another. Age has nothing to do with taste as they claim. In fact the proportion of acidity, the proportion of sugar and sweetness, the proportion of alcohol, the amount of Tunic acidity, the kind of container, and the way of storing are the elements that play part in deciding the taste of wine you are having. Personally, I prefer the Californian wine. Regarding testing the wine, one has to run and employ all his/her senses in this experience. For example, you have to notice the clarity and purity of its color which must be void of impurities. The color must be deep glaring and not dim. The smell must be inviting, like the leftover of the vine on the thighs of Spanish brunette virgins after smashing the vine under their feet. The smell must be pure too. Regarding the taste, and this is the most important part, a sip that is not gulped, but instead kept behind the teeth gargling the lips, while inhaling and exhaling the smell of it, till the tip of the tongue feels the sweetness.., then you gulp it slowly and breath the pleasure.

I wasn't sure whether *Sheikh Mit'eb* deliberately drove the attention and changed the subject to stop that beast from replying, or he talked at great length when he shed the light on wine to boast among his experiences and knowledge. Whatever the reason was, I found myself obliged to show respect and salute this man who gave me the privilege to fire back and kept me from being under fire. I started acclaiming and clapping as a sign of respect and admiration to *Sheikh Mit'eb*, the puppets and parrots imitated me and did the same. We finished the dinner and I went to the terrace towards the sea, holding a cup of pineapple juice in my hand thinking of Suzan, and leaving behind the rest of the guests talking to each other on the sound of music..I wonder if Waleed told her about my phone call and that he turned down my invitation for coffee and he apologized! I think he did, and now she is disappointed, that's why she didn't call me the whole day. I don't want to cause her embarrassment, or put her in critical situations, or even draw the attention to our relationship.. Hmmm, I wonder who those people, Waleed wants to introduce me to, are.

- Hey.. Zeyad.. how was the wine lesson, ha? She was about to answer in kind.. her name is Toulin Moghraby, she is the chief accountant, a Harvard graduate. She has been working with us for five years.

- Accountant? Your Excellency! I guess she is a hobbyist of division, then.

- Really? Is it that clear? I thought she is a hobbyist of addition only.

We burst out laughing together, *Sheikh Mit'eb* patted on my shoulder.. I guess he understood my reference to Toulin's jealousy.. How great this man is..!

- Tell me Zeyad, what are you addicted to?

- Excuse me! Addicted?

- Yes addicted. Every one of us is addicted to something special.. something that we practice doing in exaggeration, and in secret. Usually it leads us to get mad and lose our minds, most of the times we die due to an overdose of this addiction. Some of us are addicted to alcohol, others to gambling, some others are more stupid to be addicted to drugs and heroin, lucky ones are addicted to women, or money, or even fame. Weird ones are hypochondriac. Helpless ones are addicted to T.V, or computer, or food, "you can follow me if you didn't get tired.. I am just getting warmer…ha ha ha", I liked your sarcasm.

- I don't know if it's right to tell your Excellency, but my addiction is named Suzan.. she was one of my students who graduated, got married, and lives in Dubai.

- Oh, this makes a multiaddict of you; love addict, gambling addict, and adventure addict at the same time. You are in a continuous and a constant rapture; this will wear you out and lead you to destruction. Love of a woman is like drug injection Zeyad, you know it will break you down; still you risk it for minutes, maybe moments, of ecstasy, or probably less than an hour. You bet on constant love, on constant gain without taking into consideration any chance of loss caused by vicissitudes of time. Do you think you will win this bet without paying a ransom in return?

- May God grant your Excellency with long life, I know how critical and risky the situation is, and I am not looking for winning or shutting my eyes to defeats and loss.. It's like what your Excellency said; it's an addiction that calls for an overdose every time.

- Relax, I understand. Your calmness, your smartness, and your quickness of intellect, are all privileges that are of good help in such a situation. Just don't let this act negatively upon work, other than that you can depend on me. Those stupid ones think that money is everything, but you and me know for sure that the addiction on surviving and enjoying the adventure is our sublime and utmost purpose.

- Don't worry, your Excellency, the job will get a glaring clear priority that is void of any impurities, with a taste of exquisite wine; good proportion of acidity, and stable proportion of sweetness.

- Ha ha ha.. you evil-minded!! Did Assaf tell you that you will start your shuttling next Sunday?

- Yes he did, I am ready your Excellency, I will ensure your favorable judgment. I am grateful and appreciative for the chance and the trust your Excellency granted me.

- Mark Salman will take you in a tour for all the branches of restaurants there, he will also inform you of the challenges we are facing in running the business.

\- It is all right.

* * * * *

I kept complaining of misfortunes, I got tired and sick of being stressed out, till I realized the fact that I was born gifted to handle such circumstances, and talented to survive such misery. God knows better.

~18~

I tried to stay late that night in the resort exchanging views in business with the attendants, when I left the place I roved deranged without having a destination in mind. I noticed the lights of a shopping center near, so I stopped and went to buy fruits, desserts, and juices, then I stopped over at a restaurant to concur with in getting the invitation dinner on time and deliver it to my address in *Bastakiyah*. It was almost one o'clock after midnight; I don't know how Suzan spread all over my mind at that moment. *Sheikh Mit'eb* was right; I was like an addict who is in a bad need for a shot. Is this why I am trying to distract myself with other issues till midnight? I bought a cup of coffee and went to her neighborhood, stopped the car where it was possible for me to see the lights of her apartment, and went considering what happened so far, and what would happen in days to come.

"..So, here I am love.., close to you and still feel the distance between us. My friends once told me that I am running after a phantom which will lead me to a waste land, where self deception and delusion are. They anticipated my death to be among reality thorns and disappointments. They were wrong.. the distance between us is just the jeopardy all around which we got used to. I didn't change, neither did your love. The three of us started to tighten our grips on each other. I am trying excessively to take you in; Waleed on the other hand is trying to keep me from you by standing between us, leaving his back towards you. You, as usual are trying to make approaches to me, keeping Waleed on a precise distance.."

Since the dawn of time and probably before the rise of religions, mankind found in sacrifices, scapegoats, giving up the ghosts, and bloodshed a salvation and an expiation of their mischievous doings. They convinced themselves that by doing this, heaven will forgive them, and mother earth will bridle its anger, that's how they justified the sublime of some races over the rest which indirectly rationalized committing massacres and blood baths in different parts of the world under the patronage of religions and terrestrial ideology. I don't want to be different from those waves of mankind, neither be a wiser one, but instead I will become content with the sacrifice concept as long as Suzan is not on the scapegoat list. Let the scapegoat and the whipping boy be led to the slaughterhouse. If Suzan was the reward for the first to be burnt my heart would hasten to be the one, and if my closeness to her is a wrongdoing as they claim, then absenting myself from her is a heinous sin.

Next day evening, two hours ahead from my guests' arrival, I shaved my beard and took a shower and put on my suit, confirmed to the restaurant the time of food delivery, and then called Waleed to fret Suzan a bit. I deliberately didn't call her the whole day long, to look as if I meet her for the first time that night once again. I've always been obsessed with the concept of stupor in "Sophie's World". Suzan meant to amaze me whenever and wherever I met her, so as not to be distracted or miss out her presence. She knew exactly the influence of repetition, routine, and weariness on the relationship between couples. That's why she was proficient, distinguished, and exceptional in amazing the attendants by keeping her aura and stamina at peak. Waleed told me that they will gather first, then they will come together. I sat in *Ard el-Dhyar* trying to clear my mind of all kinds of thoughts, awaiting the arrival of charm suzerainty, and the rise of wild eyes, in longing and in sighs.

A few minutes later, somebody knocked at the door; I jumped and went in haste to check, but then lagged a little at the door. Their voices behind the door whispering and laughing were naïve and hearable:

- What is this place?

- Why did he choose this place to live in?

I whispered from behind the door saying:

- Because it's a calm and quiet here and it helps in relaxing more than anywhere else.., it also has originality and tradition.

I opened the door slowly; the squeaking acclaimed my praise emphasizing its sense of honor. Everybody started to laugh; women who whispered were so embarrassed.

- Hi.. and welcome. Please come on in.

Waleed nosed his shoulder pushing all the friends in his way to play the part of an usher; introducing his friends and presenting a brief résumé of each. In short, he looked stupid.

- *Abdullah Tarawneh*.. an executive in the Jordanian Embassy, his wife Mrs. *Sana'a Shamayleh*.
Hussein el-Yaseen, the head of personnel in *Fujr* Publisher Press, his wife *Suheir Abbas*.
Nefeesah Fadl el- Mawlah, a bank teller.
Na'eem Selawi, you already met him before in my place, he is a contractor, his wife *Eidah Lidawi*.. she is a teacher in the National School. *Suzan el-Ahamad*, unemployed.

She looked like a goddess with two rosette blushed cheeks when Waleed presented her that way.

- Please come on in.

Waleed lagged behind and whispered in my ear saying:

- Dilber will come later.. say that you invited her when she gave you a ride the other night.

He spoke loudly after that saying:

- Welcome to everybody in Dr. Zeyad's house. We wish him a good staying and prosperity in Dubai among his friends. This is a beau geste as a sign of friendships that we pray God to make it last forever..

He thought for a while that he trapped me, but what I was really worried about and concerned of was whether Waleed was covering the ass of one of the attendants for having a relationship with Dilber, or whether he himself was flirting with this Assyrian, or probably he wanted to set me up and check out if I was going to tell Suzan about this collusion, blackening my image along the way. Any how I deliberately sat next to Na'eem el- Seelawi and whispered in his ear to have him talking to me in the same manner before Suzan, then I welcomed them all again and turned my eyes towards the ladies saying:

- Would you please feel at home and give me a helping hand in service?

They all headed towards the kitchen and started getting the kitchenware ready, while showing them the places of things I made a gesture to Suzan to check her mobile phone, then I sent her a message:

- "I don't know how dares a man, whom I only met twice, embarrass me and ask me to claim inviting Dilber on dinner to cover his ass in front of his wife!! What kind of friends are they, Suzan?".

She replied writing:

- "Dilber? Really? I noticed how he whispered in your ear.. That stupid low one..! I am sorry love if we caused you any disturbance".

I wonder what she would say if she knew that it was Waleed who was behind this. I will not embarrass her, and I will not cause a hurt to her pride.. I'll check out later and find out why Waleed asked me to say that. I returned back to sit in *Ard el-Dhyar* with the rest of the men. The first round was already started..; they were talking about the revolts in the streets of Arab countries during what was called "The Arab Spring", when Mohammad Bu Azeizy undertook the first move of refusal by burning himself in Tunisia. Some were supporters, others were opponents as usual..

- Yes, it's time for Arabs to be awakened and freed from this slavery which lasted for long.

- Don't hasten your judgment and take a stand in advance, "don't cross the bridge, till you come to it", who knows, we might regret doing this and weep over old days!

- You must be kidding me! Weep over old days? The revolt broke forth against all tyrants, spreading over *like fire in dry stubble,* we had enough of slavery, enough of despotism and enough subdual of nations by force, or would you say it's a collusion?

The manner of talk between Abdullah and Hussein went up irritably, it was hard to interfere, or claim to be moderate in the heart of such agitation. I preferred to remain silent and listen. Waleed tried to change the subject and calm them down a little by asking me about the business with *Sheikh Mit'eb*, women came out of the kitchen to *Ard el-Dhyar* holding the utensils filled with fruits and ushered by Suzan. They sat in silence listening to the argument and clamor. Hussein turned his eyes towards me and surprised me saying:

- Isn't it true, Doctor?

It wasn't right to ask him his question again, I was busy watching Suzan moving around, but I could deduce what the question was about according to his stand in the argument.

- Well.. actually, I try to avoid talking in politics because I ...

- ".. because I don't want to make enemies of the people whom I meet for the first time", you said this before.

Na'eem interrupted me satirically while the rest remained silent, looking at me suspiciously. Even Suzan looked at me in wonder, doubting the reason I accept the embarrassment which Na'eem brought forth to me for the second time. I didn't want the attendants to question my silence, but I had to know the level of such intellects first, and their acceptance of receiving opinions and concepts that sound uncommon like mine.

- We want to know what you think of the talk of the town, you represent the academics and the intellects here.

What's wrong with this jackass! He insists on provoking me, and indulging me with engagements that I am trying to clear myself of. Woe unto men!! They think that politics is exclusively monopolized by their voices virility, their rough thinking, and their totalitarian ideologies. They deny any opponent suggestions even if they were right, just to be spotlighted and in the center of attention. They claim that they are offspring of a nation of pride and honor, and descend from pioneering cultures! When shall Dilber come, so that I notice the influence of marshmallow on their rough masculine vocal cords? All right, you asked for it..

- I've accustomed myself to hush up and never talk about something I am not acquainted with its details. I used to analyze things from a historical approach first, then I compare it to other cultures to measure and evaluate our stand to a reference point, and finally I analyze it from a sociolinguistic and nations' psychology point of view, revealing this in translation if possible. Probably this distinguishes who studies English language and other languages in general from others, one becomes more enlightened with more developed and prosperous cultures who are more experienced of course.

I took a quick glance at the attendants by then, and realized that they were all ears, as if their breast expanded to hear the talk of an intellect, as Na'eem wanted, so they became inclined to my picking of words. I noticed a smile and an approval on Suzan's face, thus I proceeded dramatically; by taking a few steps to take a knife and an apple from the fruit bowl, and said:

- The whole issue bifurcates to a controller on one hand, and the controlled on the other hand. A sadist controller, or ruler if you want, married to a Marie Antoinette, who is aware or probably unaware of what is going around him, and sees himself as the center of the universe; believing that everybody and everything revolves around him, and is associated in a way or another with his Majesty. All princes, princess, retinue and dependant servants are beneficiaries who set his Majesty aside in an ivory tower from knowing what goes on in other orbits than his. They make him believe that he is the ruler of the Platonic City, the source of inspiration for his people, and the Savior. Statues are sculptured for his loftiness, he is a god whose words are made into islands and inscribed in towers with a "be" of his. His coughs are pressed and published in schoolbooks; seminars are held to translate the Majesty's vision which is financially supported by other dominant superpower budgets. Thus, they rule over for forty years, or probably for more than ninety years, believing that the royal and prophetic blood still runs in their veins. He has the scepter of reign, the scale of justice; he is the protector, the defender, and the guardian. He is the one who keeps the balance, ceases the fire, and maintains stability of having a multicultural clash, even if they vend the countries fortunes, the countries themselves, and even if they conspire with their enemies against their people, still they believe that they must be obeyed. I say his Majesty because Arab world has never experienced a serious republic system, all systems and regimes turn into hereditary monarchical systems brought and formed of the minorities, but supported from abroad. In case the mob revolt, they make the mob "an offer they can't refuse"; either corruption with stability, or reforms with instability. He claims applying democracy when he is vested with all powers. In his Majesty's country, there is no space for honest election; for the hand of security forces that interferes to maintain the outcomes that please his Majesty. We, the mobs, have never experienced the right of deposing the elected, or removing the president elected in a republic country - if found. Long time ago, Arab rulers were brought to Persia to die under elephants' feet, if once they declined obeying the insulting orders. In our times, leaders either die by the hands of enemies, if they happened to be good, or they die by the hands of their people if they were traitors. A ruler who rules over for a long time is a worldly-wise traitor who surf-rides both; the abroad demands and the inside popularity. If his Majesty inclines to the mobs' wish and think of making serious reforms, beneficiaries will lose their privileges, thus they will turn against him with lots of options in hand.

On the other hand, we have the controlled, the masochist, the subdued; who got used to hard and miserable life by the course of time, lived the disgrace and slavery, and deified the ruler willingly for the sake of the country's stability, and unwillingly for being helpless of making serious changes. The mob; who see the leftovers thrown to them as noble deeds and donations. The mobs, whom you should not feel sorry for, who become sadists on themselves, and divided into either opportunist seeking any chance of making approaches towards the ones in charge, turning his/her back for his/her people if ever was bestowed upon a duty-free car, or a chance of embezzling to live in Beverly Hills of his country, or choosing to go away from this pain at a blow, and look for a warmer country offered, among lines before embassies in *Deir Ghbaar*.

Some of the attendants started to nod their heads agreeing on what I said, asking me to proceed.

- I've never heard of a ruler, or a chief, or even a prophet who ruled over by his ideology, or applied the doctrines of sent down and revealed religions, and administered justice, and then preferred willingly to abandon the reins of power after his certitude of legitimate constitution completeness; which ensures everlasting justice, regardless of changeable circumstances, but our Prophet Mohammed peace be upon his soul. Alas, his recommendations are not practiced or applied anymore, and we do not adopt the concept of *Shura* in electing our rulers. Our method in electing our leaders and rulers was and still is, in one way or the other, based upon party and tribal spirit. You as a person have the choice to pick out the side of the story and the tendency of the historian to believe in one sect and take an attitude against the others. That's why the sword is put back to sheathe and will never be drawn except against each other till dooms day, regardless of the old glory of the past.

That's a prophecy, ladies and gentlemen..didn't you hear the *hadith*; that *one day the prophet, peace be upon his soul, came from the Alia, till he passed by Bani Mo'aawiyah mosque, so he entered it and prostrated twice and we prayed after him, then he supplicated for long ,and when he finished he turned to us, peace be upon his soul, and said: I've asked God for three things and He consented to two and denied me one; I've asked my God not to punish my people with drowning, with wind, with tremor, with thrown stones from the sky, and with punishment of this kind, God consented to this one, I've asked God not to destroy my people by an enemy that would proscribe their blood, God consented to this one too, I've asked my God that my people never become different or unlike or conflicting among themselves, God denied me this one".* Thus, we shall face the music which *Gibran* warned us about when he said, *"Pity the nation divided into fragments, each fragment deeming itself a nation".* In my opinion the whole problem lies in the Arab mind ladies and gentlemen.. are we capable of casting away all racial and tribal conflicts and disagreements, organizing ourselves, and bringing up the coming generations to accept their differences, doing what is good for our countries, and ensuring safety for all? I am neither with nor against such revolts.. in fact I am worried, George Orwell once said in his prophecy of 1984, that *"Until they become conscious they will never rebel, and until after they have rebelled they cannot become conscious",* a revolt with no awakening or carefulness will surely lead to chaos and disorder, and will cause the killing of its founders due to showdown, and this is exactly what is happening now. This convulsion will be of a good help for foreign agendas, but territorial this time. Once again you can't deny the conspiracy theory because foreign countries will interfere to lay hand on oil on one hand, and to keep away revolts from their borders, but preferring this revolt to carry on with all possible means to exhaust all opponents. The whole Mediterranean region has become a mined land that is ready to explode. Are we really aware enough to take all precautions to avoid such revolts of hunger rather than revolts of Enlightenment ideals? Don't you think that we still need to understand and practice the alphabets of the traffic lights first? How long can we stand? What is the price that we are going to pay, when we know that the prophecy I mentioned is something that you can't keep away from?

Believe me, I am not with the revolts, neither against them, but I know who will surf-ride these revolts at the end, I know that smarter pigs will win the rule and will feel obliged to flatter slavishly and row with the tides willingly or unwillingly. They will stand on two feet like bad forefathers and owners, and they will sell all the eggs, the fodder, and all the chickens too for the benefit of one sect. Such a sect has no experience at all in governing a country, thus they will commit the same mistakes ever again, and all dreams of rebellions will fade away, and will be in chaos again lagging behind hundreds of years from procession. We will be plunged in debts and in dependency till we become the way we were before the revolution. By the plans of the superior and by the deeds of our hands we will go back in time to Stone Age. He who doesn't incline by his own will, shall incline and be brought to knees by force.

I am really sorry for disappointing you this much, but I see the future in blues, and without any glimpse of hope. If you have ever reviewed the history and the past before, you would notice how we tried to ask for the world's sympathy over what happened to the Arabs by the Spanish Inquisition when Arab rule came to an end. Tell me for God's sake, how is *Abdullah al-Sagheer* different from our rulers of today? He impoverished the country for his own pleasures, and when payback time came, we started condemning the revenge of the Spanish people, but excusing the showdown among ourselves who share in race, in religion, in language, and in history, but divided into supporters and opponents. Slaying each other with electric and power saws, throwing corpses from above buildings, killing kids and raping women became easy and forgiven; as long as other foreign enemies are not involved!! Our rulers are tyrants for sure, but they are somehow secretions of our tyrant cultures. "*Rulers appointed on you, are people of your kind*", because *"Allah will never change the grace which He hath bestowed on a people until they change what is in their (own) souls: and verily Allah is He Who heareth and knoweth (all things)."*

- Wow!!

- You are right..

- Hufff..

The attendants' responses varied from one another; some were depressed, others were admiring, and some others were opponents. Waleed was busy all the time looking at his watch.. a few minutes later somebody knocked at the door. Everybody looked at me, wondering who that could be.., except Suzan, she knew who it was. I headed towards the door saying:

- It's food time..

What a meal it was!! I opened the door, Dilber was on the door standing between the two shutters, making one of them a rest for her arm, looking at me with her green eyes and protuberant curly hair like a Persian cat. She came to attack with her marble-like thighs unsheathed from a short skirt...

- I guess they forgot the appetizers, and went too far with flesh. Remind me of your name again, please?

- Won't you say welcome, Zeyad? Come in.. for example?

- Oh, please come in.

- *Kheily Mumnoon.*

Before reaching *Ard el-Dhiyar* Waleed called me pretending to be spontaneous:

- Any help Zeyad?

- *Kheily Mumnoon* Waleed.., it's just Dilber!!

- Oh, Dilber!

- Shub Bikheir..oh, hi..

- Welcome, please come in.

Everybody stood up to salute and shake hands with her, men started to do their ties foolishly and fix their shirts in stupid ways, some had to suck their stomach, pull up their trousers, and hold their breaths for a while. Jealousy flared up in women's eyes. Suzan kept observing the responses of the attendants on the revealed thighs of Dilber. A few minutes later, the door was knocked again.. Suzan called the women to help her in doing the table, but spared Dilber to let the legs' show resume before the drooling wolves. No sooner had the food been put on the table and the guests started sitting around, than I drew near Suzan while all women were busy and whispered saying:

- You look like a goddess tonight.

At that moment she smiled again, and the outburst of jealousy ceased and calmed down, then she took a seat with the rest of the guests around the table. I myself don't blame women for being jealous, because most of the men are subject to be trapped by legs show, in contrast with their women who are asked and ordered to be modest and descent. Even when women show their beauty to their men, men always complain of fraternity and apathy towards legal seduction after marriage! Sophie's World again; when you lose being amazed, you lose being alive, and you lose all kinds of interests. I sat near Mr. Hussein el-Yaseen, he looked exhausted.

- You look tired my friend.

- Hell.. you didn't suffer extremely the way we did, Zeyad. The high costs of living here, the rent, the tuition, the responsibilities towards the family back in Jordan. You had a fat chance for not being to hell and back. We work like animals here to buy an apartment or a piece of land when we return back home, every time we go to Jordan we find that the prices of apartments have doubled, thus we come back and work harder. We have become strangers in Jordan, we lost our friends there, and we are foreigners here too. We don't have social life. Oh, did you know that monthly money transfer is considered an income pillar in Jordan, friend?

- Ha ha ha.. you made me laugh. I know. Dear *Abu Odei*, I have written some symbolic stories, and recently I started writing a novel, but I didn't finish it yet. I want to have them pressed and published by your publishing house.

I talked with Mr. Hussein, for a couple of minutes, about the way and the conditions of having my writings published, then we finished eating and went to sit back in *Ard el-Dhiyar*. When all of them were seated, I hemmed addressing them all, saying:

- I'm so pleased to meet you, and to be introduced to you, and I hope that our relationships would last forever. Waleed I owe you and I owe your wife Suzan big time for your accommodation, creating this family like surroundings which saved me from homesickness and cultural shock. I also would like to tell you that *Sheikh Mit'eb* and Mr. Assaf, whom I work for, informed me that I will initiate my first shuttle to the United Kingdom on Sunday morning for a whole week, therefore if you want anything from London I will be more than glad to fulfill your requests and demands.. I'll leave my mobile phone number on these cards for you just in case, please don't be hesitant or shy, again welcome all of you.

Suzan kept looking at me with a smile, studying my glances and moves towards everybody. I wanted to relieve her worry and fear again saying that the daughter of the winged lion means nothing to me, and that I prefer being a prisoner of her Arab eyes than being Shahryar in Khosrau palace. I moved towards Mr. Abdullah el-Tarawneh welcoming and talking to him, when suddenly Suzan spoke loudly, addressing me:

- We all wish you a Bon Voyage and a safe arrival doctor. Don't forget to bring us presents from London; the city of fog, the proverb says "*Though rich, I receive presents in cordiality*", and commenting on what you said earlier doctor, I give credit to your viewing, and with respect, this brings to my mind that history repeats itself. Arabs long time ago were scattered tribes fighting each other, that's why they were a sitting duck for the wolves of Rome and Persia, till Islam came out and made of *Abdullah Bin Huthafah el- Sahmy;* the one with the thick cloak- a messenger scaring not only the mighty powerful of Khosrau, whom God disrupted his demesne and put out his fire, but also a source of disturbance for the great Cesar of Rome as well. The two camps are still around, though they changed, and Arabs are still bitten and torn in between without the shield of their religion which made them subjugate both camps before. Arabs are arrogant among themselves, but low and humble before their enemies.

I didn't know the precise reason for being sharp-tongued, talking about a historical and a religious fact in the way she did, was Suzan that jealous of Dilber? Was Suzan's talk a slap in the face for that Assyrian who was showing her semi-naked photos in *Sharm el-Sheikh* to boast among the women? Or was it a rebel against the exclusive right and role of men of talking about politics in the Arab world? Whatever the reason was, I couldn't deny supporting her view with a smile and a nod of my head. How weird to see such conversion between the active Suzan and the passive Waleed! God! What an ostrich are you Waleed before this peacock!

Some started to talk to Dilber indirectly including Waleed of course.. he tried not to draw Suzan's attention in doing that. The evening gathering was spent in a friendly atmosphere till midnight. Later on, my guests started to ask for permission to take leave bringing out different excuses for that. Suzan seized the opportunity to have a talk with me while collecting and picking up the cups. I've tried to help her brining things to the kitchen, at that moment she said to me:

- Saturday afternoon, five o'clock..in "Les Fleur Du Tulipe", I want to give you something on record before your leave to London.

- All right sweetheart..

Waleed dashed in at that moment and said:

- Well..it's midnight doctor, we've got to leave now, we wish you a pleasant trip, oh.., don't forget to call us when you come back to Dubai.

- Of course, and thanks for everything.

- Bye, Doctor.

- Bye, Waleed.

- Take care, Doctor.

- Thanks for everything Suzan, good night.

When everybody left the house, I sat by my own in *Ard el-Dhiyar* for a while, I found it appropriate to call my family in Jordan and tell them about my trip to London. First I talked to my mother and my sisters, and then I talked to Sura and informed her with the chance of dropping by in Jordan for two days a month after returning back from each trip to London. She was so happy when she heard that, I wanted to talk to my kids too, but unfortunately it was late and they were in bed. I went into the bedroom and lied on my side..I was still under Suzan's presence effect, lots of thoughts flared up in my mind, but finally I surrendered to sleep in peace and quiet.. then suddenly I heard a hoarse whispering voice reciting:
"Thy Lord does create and choose as He pleases: no choice have they (in the matter): Glory to Allah! and far is He above the partners they ascribe (to Him)!" *

I went slowly and opened the door of my bedroom which was fronting *Ard el-Dhiyar*, no sooner have I revealed that corner near the basil pot, than I stood frozen in shock.., shivering in fear.. I saw my father in his shroud reciting from holy Quran.. I stood still observing him reading in horror till he finished, then he stood and headed towards me. A strong odor diffused from him that made me feel exulted in loftiness and in peace.. he grabbed me by hand, and we went away together.

I narrated my dream to Suzan when we met in "Les Fleur Du Tulipe" on Saturday as we agreed on..

- Wish all the good of this sign, I hope.

She hugged me, seeing how deplorable I got while I told her about the dream. I proceeded saying:

- I was so happy seeing him again, though I got panicked by the way he looked. I awoke shivering in horror and cry, I didn't know where he took me to..

- It's OK love, it's just a dream. Come on! You spoiled my present to you.

- What is it?

- She looked at me in a smile that made me forget any interconnection with the spirits of the other world.

- I might cause you a severe pain, don't get mad at me, please.

- A severe pain! I don't get it.

- Would you please let me bite all your fingertips.., strongly, and this spot of your chest too?

I laughed while talking to her denouncing her request. At first, I thought she was kidding around, but when she didn't wink an eye while asking.., I asked her in return:
- Why?

- I want to leave you with pain that streams like an electric shock in all your body in every moment, I don't want it to be vanished, or last only for a short time like an orgasm.. it must last till you come back to me. I must not detach myself from your mind, or your soul, or your body even.

- Would you let me to harm?!

- Because I wouldn't, love!

I closed my eyes handing over my fingertips to her. She set about biting them mightily. My body started sweating and twisting in pain, till some drips of blood leaked from beneath my nails, and tears flew over my cheeks, then she leaped upon planting her bicuspids and canine teeth in my chest. I lost the sense of feelings and went into numbness, but felt the heat of my whole body. She embraced me strongly and whispered in my ear saying:

- I love you.. I love you, don't get mad at me, you are mine, I will never spare you a minute without me.

With one move of her, she set free her breasts from the shirt's slavery to make me taste the madness of pain and the numbness of happiness in an overdosed deathblow. She didn't refer to Dilber at all, but I knew it was the effect of Jealousy on Suzan, the blatant challenge that she could let down all other counterparts of females in my world. She hugged me for almost an hour, touched the ruin scar of her teeth on my chest, sobbed in tears and regret for what she did to me. I couldn't talk much; I just hugged her and smelled the scented breasts of her, and said in a tired voice:

- If pain granted me this ecstasy, I can't imagine how pleasing dying in your arms and lap could be!

How could risk be pleasure when accompanied with the intention of committing suicide? Isn't the search for pleasure a proof on persistence in life and its delights? Running after elongating the time of ecstasy in all domains of addiction is what makes one risk taking an overdose every time. Suzan -without recognizing this fact- started to make me convinced of taking this risk of having more pleasure every time. She spread out and magnified the handful of ecstasy and the dose of Testosterone of my body this time. Woe unto me... I don't even care if I die for her any more.

- I'll wait a daily phone call from you.

- If my fingertips could press the numbers, you insane!

- I've got to go now.

She stood up, thrusting her charms and beauties in between her shirt's folds, looking at me while setting her neatness with a smile... I said to her:

- How do you feel when you dump a fallen, a butted, and a prey behind which even a wolf would abhor?

- Not like the rest of your kind, you know how women feel! That's why I am crazy about you. Won't you say good bye to me?

She fell down again, hugging me, kissing me, and embracing me.., away from my fingertips. I got up to walk her to the door, pondering at her, kissing her, till she went out.., leaving me behind in confusion and in fatigue, but with utmost pleasure that can't be imagined.

*****

*Whenever diplomacy, media, and etiquette
are used, there is a hoax candied.*

~19~

The idea of going to the airport, leaving Dubai behind, was itself a disturbing one. I've tried that early morning to call Mr. Assaf, but he didn't answer my phone calls. I wasn't in a good mood that day, I was confused and in my worst conditions, until I got into the plane. I had only one suitcase with some stuff. My handbag which I took inside the cabin was so small, enough to keep a ticket, a passport, a novel, and some documents. When the hostess drew near asking for the boarding pass and the ticket, I had trouble opening the handbag because of my swollen fingertips. I've got so desperate that I started to laugh at the end. The hostess opened the bag for me and checked all my documents.

Most of the passengers in the first class cabin were of businessmen; who looked luxurious in appearance, and eager to arrive at Heathrow Airport, in the city of fog. God, how I hate businessmen, merchants, and ministers, because the whole world in their opinion is subject to profit and loss…everything is for sale and barter according to their perspective. They justify their dirty deals and transactions, even if they had to arrange a treaty with the devil himself, as long as such deals bring about benefits and interests for their own. Why I hate them most of all? Well, because they monopolize all the sources when the country is in peace, and when the country becomes in danger, they are the first ones to leave it torn, among the hyenas of foreign companies, which would rush madly upon its natural sources, with a free invitation within international contracts and agreements. I still remember how the Czech mass media broadcasted the scandal of Czech president Vaclav Klaus stealing a pen, when he was in a press conference alongside with his counterpart Chilean president Sebastian Pinera in an official visit. I don't understand how all our intelligence agencies, our mass media, our news agencies, and our cameras couldn't record any of those who stole the countries' reserves in our Arab World, those who robbed the people and left them pale in despair with no future of any kind? Look at them.. they have lots in common.. same beer bellies, same grey hair, same big noses, same arrogance and sniffy looks, same expensive suits, and same lingo. Yes, I had an experience once with one of those lofty eminent ministers, who came to inaugurate activities and ceremonies of a conference held under his patronage at Al al-Bayt University. As usual, modest people who are poor and needy seize such opportunities to have their demands carried out by a benefactor. A poor old Bedouin woman squeezed herself among the guards and the throngs, till she reached the minister and addressed him with one of the most common idiomatic expressions ever used in asking for a help in the region, saying:

- *Ilak walla lal-dheeb?*

She was simply saying "If it's not much of a trouble", but with a stronger linguistic stimulation to draw his attention; which was equivalent to "Are you up to it?". The minister looked around at the faces of the people finding the expression unusual to his Massachusetts and Michigan accent, and with an arrogant classy tone said:

- What does this woman mean?

They hardly understand our dialect, or know the meanings of the folkloric lyrics in our songs; they are incapable of joining us with any kind of folkloric dances named "*Dabkat*". The gap between those people and us is getting bigger and bigger. We don't trust them, and they don't trust us either. In respect of the warm intimate dialectal terms they use when they shuttle between the governorates like; "*deereh*", "*asheereh*", "*rabe'a* ", "*izwah*" the merits and credits are attributed to the star makers behind them. Who knows.. probably such terms are written in transcription too. If The Royal Military Academy Sandhurst has to graduate leaders of the future the way I see them doing, I guess they must understand the importance of teaching its students the folkloric dances of their countries and the various dialects too, so that they make firm their grips on the peoples' admiration as well, the way Lawrence of Arabia did long time ago.

I sat quiet and didn't talk to anybody, and started to read the third greatest novel of Dan Brown *Deception Point* to have the coming seven hours worn out in enjoyment. Howsoever I made a move I moaned, by reason of the pain Suzan caused me. The novel made my blues and depression even worse despite my awareness of global corruption. When we get trapped and become a prey of the western mass media over the years, we start to believe in a world governed by rules, by justice, and by equity. We started to believe in making serious changes in our customs and traditions, in our conceptions of things like reality and certitude as well, and in our political philosophy, moving away from religion; the source of legislation - which is one of the factors that played a significant role in weakening us, as theorists of materialism and communism deemed appropriate. Thus we melted our culture, our language, and our identity to comply with the procession. This big lie didn't last for long, when witnesses of their own party revealed this conspiracy and this corruption, uncovering the influence of the mass media on peoples' minds, and peoples' way of thinking, only then we became like the crow which wanted to imitate a dove in walking, thus became neither capable of doing that, nor able of recalling its own old way. When one sees Opera in her show crying with the attendants over her late cat, when Opera offers help through donations campaigns, and when she urges other rich people to do the same, while the U.S government applies suppression inside and outside the country without trials on prisoners in *Abu Ghreib*, and in Guantanamo, one realizes by then that governments and nations are two entirely different parties. The deception is played worldwide, and the freedom of the press is a lie. Michael Moore, John Perkins, Roger Garaudy, Edward Sa'eed, David Icke, Jon Stewart, and many others, are examples on those who resisted and challenged the influence of audiovisual mass media and press deception. They revealed how natural resources and fortunes of the third world were plundered, and pumped into the veins of Europe and America. Arabs intellects also shed the light on how the influence of the misleading mass media took the privilege of rhetoric in Arabic language in making their devilish aims candied. We were fought by our sword this time, thus euphemism and dysphemism were effective weapons in their hands. *Khamr* became *spirits ,Usury* became *benefits, depravity* became *freedom, imperialism* became *democracy and maintaining humans rights, Jihad and holy war* became *terrorism, religious referential* became *extremism, modesty* became *narrow-mindedness, telling the truth and demanding the rights* became *impudent , defamation, and crossing redlines.*

The seven hours passed while I was alert to the greatest degree, due to what I was reading, and due to the thoughts and questions that were crossing my mind. When the captain announced the arrival of the flight at Heathrow Airport, I finished the procedures so quick and went out of the customs hall to the arrival square, trying to find Salman by reading all names written on held nameplates. My name was on one of the plates held by a man who was fifty something years old; he was bald, wearing a black suit and a red tie. I took a few steps towards him introducing myself:

- Good evening.. Zeyad Al Juneidy.

- Good evening Mr. Zeyad. I am Mark Salman. How was your flight?

- Not bad.., things can't be without disturbance.

- I have made a reservation for you in Milestone Hotel, in Kensington county.. I hope you like the place there.

- I hope that too.

- After you, Mr. Zeyad. David.., the bag.

The three of us went out of the airport, the weather was cool out there, and the views were charming, slight breezes of fresh air gusted from time to time. We got in the car and went away. Salman started overdoing etiquettes, trying to break the ice with me.

- I wish you a good staying, Mr. Zeyad. I hope we cooperate with each other for the purpose of the job, so that we please both *Sheikh Mit'eb* and Mr. Assaf. I am more than happy for you, taking the charge of....

Probably Salamn was older than me, and I should have treated him better than I did, to make our talks friendlier later on, but the position obliges one to comply with the hierarchical order, so as everyone recognizes the ground he/she is standing on, and knows his/her rights and responsibilities. I drew an affected smile, interrupting him saying:

- In spite of the fact that you live up to the recommendations of Sheikh Mit'eb himself, and you are well-thought- of , which I take into consideration of course, still in our language we have lots of common expressions, which we are going to use between us, that have to do with welcoming and greetings. You see, "*Overstating of greetings and etiquettes dampen intimacy*", and we also have another saying Salman; "*Keep greeting guests and you'll have greedy ones at the doors*", we dislike exaggerated greetings Mr. Salman. Even the French have their own word regarding this issue; they say, "*Get together like brothers, and work together like strangers*". We have to agree on the basis, so that we understand each other at work. I am entitled to take all necessary measures according to the plenipotentiary attributed to me, Mr. Salman. I expect you to be of a good support in illustrating clearly all the things concerned with the job. Be sure that I'll not hesitate in calling a spade a spade in the eye, and that I'll not beat around the bush, as some linguists and orientalists accuse us of doing.. I hope I made myself clear.

- Yes Mr. Zeyad..

Salman sat up straight after he was leaning forward, and looked through the window on the other side. I probably made him downhearted and depressed at that moment, but in fact I wanted to pluck out any misunderstanding later on one hand, and make the concept of open communication between the board and the employees deeply-rooted. I know exactly how the middle management seal off the fact of what is going on from the board of direction. Does *Sheikh Mit'eb* really expect Salman to be my guide and illustrate all the challenges at work and play fair, without leaving surprises that would be evidence on my weakness before *Sheikh* Mit'eb? He is deprived of this position, and no doubt he feels so angry because of that. I know he will seize any opportunity to find mistakes, done in my "term of office", to inform *Sheik Mit'eb with*. We are talking about a group of five star restaurants, which their income is estimated in millions, any mistake would cost the work a fortune, and would cost me the golden opportunity that I've been given, which comes once in a life time.

The car stopped before the Milestone Hotel after a period of time we spent in silence, each one of us persisted in studying the other without causing hard times later on for one another. Salman in his turn tried hard to overcome the slump drawn at his face on one hand, and tried to talk to me on the other hand, wondering if, I am going to consider, walking me to the reception a kind of adulation or not. I didn't pay him any attention, instead I stopped pondering at this marvelous edifice baroque building, trying to hide my fondness of such originality which I have always been dreaming of standing on, I imagined the influence of Cathedral hymn on my hearings too. My imagination winged far in the sky due to this mingling of originality and modernity in such milestones! Salman gestured to me to walk into the reception hall before him, I finished all the necessary procedures within minutes, then a porter took the suite key from the receptionist, my case, and with a courteous expression of invitation to make me follow him, went ahead of me. At that time I looked at Salman and said:

- Never mind, I'll go up by my own, what's our program for tomorrow?

- We will head for the main office of the group at half past eight first, then we will shuttle between the branches.

- That' fine.. Oh, would you please keep my arrival a secret? I want to walk in before you.

- Of course, no problem, see you tomorrow morning Mr. Zeyad.

I went upstairs to the third floor examining the flight of stairs, the decorations, the aisles, and the oil paintings till I reached the suite. The porter opened the door, put the case inside, wrapped around the curtains, opened the balcony door which affords view of Kensington Park, and stood politely waiting for tips and orders. I tipped him good money, and asked him to come in person if I ordered anything. I started checking the charming classical furniture here and there, which was carefully selected, till I came to a wooden bookcase with glass display and some shelves. I picked out one of the books and started skimming it over, when suddenly I heard footfall behind me, I turned around unconsciously, ready to push back any threat, seeing that a brunette girl standing in the aisle, wearing a white short bathrobe, wrapping her hair up with a white towel. She looked charming with her Latin-American features, stood still there looking at me, breaking the dullness of the situation by rubbing her hair with the towel in a seductive way, that let some of her beauties appear.

- Who the hell are you? How did you get in here?

- Isabella.., Isabella Khmineiz.

She answered probably in a wild Mexican accent, remaining in her place. Damn you Salman! This is one of the oldest tricks of blackmail adopted by our intelligence agencies in the Arab countries. From now on, I should know that I am watched, and the suite is bugged.

- Come on.. get out right away.

She drew near and unwrapped the robe, saying:

- Why? Don't you like me? Let's talk a little..

- Stay away from me. Don't come closer.

- Are you afraid of me? I won't hurt you!

I shouted at her pointing at the door..

- I said get out!

- Calm down! Let's talk..

I stepped toward the phone to call the receptionist, at that time she knew how much serious I was, so she started shouting and jargonizing in her Anglo-Latin accent:

- All right.. all right I'll go, I'll go to face troubles out there! Puta madre, a que chirlo, vete ala puta verga!

She started putting on her clothes in a hurry, swearing and breaking everything around her. I have no idea what language she spoke in, but she looked wild and flared up. She went out heaping insults upon me, carrying some of her clothes with her, and whammed the door behind her. I sighed deeply for minute. I am not going to converse with Salman about what happened here. This is the least of what he needs to know about, if not already recorded, to give him the opportunity of adding insult to injury, which he himself probably planned for. I started unpacking my stuff, putting them in the closet. My fingertips were still in hurt, and standing in the way of having all my work done. I sat in the balcony looking at the park, the view was fascinating, but I was tired, depressed, and bereaved. I closed the balcony's door, unwrapped the curtains, turned the lights off, and lied down on the bed in my clothes. I went back to Dubai.. to Dubai... Dubai.... I started to get her prepared, murmuring and dismissing everything that could take me away from being in telepathy with the possible means.. I got myself used to strong meditations, to probations, to open-spirit and receptiveness, I had to master such means since I knew her..Suzan..Suzaaan.. Suuuzaaa…

*****

I had those moments when I wished that God would put an end to my father's sufferings, now I hate myself for once wishing that. He wouldn't have wished me the same for sure. Oh God, why do you answer our prayers when we wrongly supplicate?

~20~

I woke up at half past six next morning, had a shower, put my clothes on, and went out to have a walk in the nearest part of the Hyde Park in Kensington gardens. The nice twisting of the fence and the benches, the fine trimmed fence plants, the mowered lawns, the fountains, the colors of various roses here and there, the running squirrels on trees, the tweets of birds, and the jogging of men and women, all this made the place a paradise, a rest, and an assembly to the spirits. I sat on one of the benches to relax, and closed my eyes to eavesdrop to the birds' speech. The tweets of birds sounded different of what I am used to hear of birds in my country, could it be possible that birds have different dialects due to the different places too? Or is it the different species that make the tweets sound different? I opened my eyes towards the round pool.. Suzan was barefoot, walking in slow motion on waterside, wearing a short summer rosette dress, holding her sandals droopily by her fingertips. She looked at me and smiled, then she dropped the sandals that she was holding, and walked to the middle of the pool to melt little by little like a sugar lump, and turn into a flamingo.

I sat there till quarter to eight, then returned back to the hotel, deciding to call Suzan. The difference in timing makes the time eleven o'clock in the morning in Dubai. I closed the door behind me on the balcony to have some privacy, and called her mobile phone.

- I saw you minutes ago ascending your throne on the water..

- Good morning love.. how lovely your tired voice sounds. How was your flight?

She sounded sad.

- How much do you miss me?

- So desperately. I got used to your presence and being here.

- It won't take long. Holding my breath diving away from you can't be long without enough safe inhales of you, just like the ones that bleeded my fingertips and my chest.

- Ha ha ha… don't be mad at me.

- The greatest favor you have ever bestowed upon me when being away from you.

- I'll wait your phone call every morning.

- I'll be mad If you don't conjure me up in every minute.

- I do, that's why my life turned into hell.

- Pleased to hear that honey. I don't expect less than this love from you.

- I love you.

I got inside again, collecting some documents to take with me, having lots of questions on my mind regarding not being called by Mr. Assaf. Does he want me to work by my own to test me? I don't need help, and I don't need a reference, but I am a bit worried for his breakoff, I got used to his active presence in the morning. No sooner had Big Ben announced eight thirty by its sharp decisive strikes, than Salman called me on the suite phone informing me that he awaits me in the car, outside the hotel. I went out, and got in the car with him, and we both took off among the motions of active people with their optimistic smiles, heading towards their work.

Salman began directly talking about business while we were heading towards Kilburn district in Brondesbury Avenue, where the head office of the group is. He simply tried to make me understand that the costs and expenses which the board pays on chefs' salaries, in addition to the salaries of other employees, and their dues of social security, health insurance, along with the taxes, purchased goods, requirements, and bills of electricity, water, and gas, all these expenses are just about to go beyond the income of these branches. He made it clear for me that they can't increase or raise up fees of services due to the competition on one hand, and the stability of the middle class person's income or wage on the other, taking into consideration the existing deterioration of the global economic state. Salman also talked at great length about his fears of the peddlers spreading who sell hotdog, fried fish, and potatoes publically, before the very eyes of the Ministry of Public Health, who don't care about the concerns of five star restaurants' owners.

We arrived at the head office; I preceded him and asked him to lag behind for a while. Everyone was working, inclining their heads on documents, making phone calls, acting on their computers. I asked Salman to come in to his office. Salman started to illustrate the details of the challenges, I can't deny that I was frustrated, but I've found myself propelled with anger when commented on his discomfitures, saying:

- I think we should close down all these branches, dissolute them to stop losses, and get prepared to draw back from the market. We might also think of having some apology words written to our employees before terminating them, what do you think?

- I am sorry, Mr. Zeyad, I didn't mean to....

- You don't expect *Sheikh Mit'eb* to turn his business into charity, do you? Tell me Mr. Salman, how do other restaurants and other groups withstand the challenges you mentioned? Would you say they confer us the honor of drawing back from the market, yet they follow us one after the other? Tell me for God's sake, how does a director of such a big group like ours, consider peddlers a real threat to our business? Are you ready to look for a job, and a safe boat in such circumstances? Or would you prefer to play the part of a captain who cares about his ship and does everything before he submits to sinking? I've never heard of an everlasting economic crisis before. This crisis is a passing tornado, which we will bow before till it passes.

I drew near to Salman and fixed his tie, saying:

- Keep your head above water Salman, and let the waves take you wherever it may. Come on, stop complaining and let's work.

Later on, we planned out some lines of actions which would limit and reduce payments in branches of less challenges, and support branches of more difficult ones. We also postponed what is possible of payments till we find alternatives, meeting with the bank's representative to discuss the chances of scheduling the loans, in addition to meeting with the governmental institutions' representatives to discuss all possible compromises over the dues that the group must pay, were also on the suggestions. Finally, planning out the possibility of making a percentage of stocks and shares of the group to tender, trying to find partners in proportion to twenty five percent. These were the thoughts that crossed my mind; the most painful one was the idea of finding partners for the group, which required *Sheikh Mit'eb*'s approval and a legal opinion, that's why I postponed this decision till I meet Mr. Assaf. Things were more difficult than I expected, I had to convince Salman first that I am entitled, and up to the challenge of taking all necessary procedures, and secondly I had to make some formal changes to make Salman get back his self-confidence and be convinced of our ability of overcoming this crisis. He had to trust me as an area manager who is an expert in dealing with such hard times. I also had to convince myself that I am capable of looking after this business and anchoring this ship in peace by carrying out all these procedures, waiting for outcomes, and reducing as much of the losses as possible.

After that, we paid a visit to Kensington's branch till the evening, viewing everything in real, and meeting all employees there, discussing with them some of their suggestions to overcome certain problems. I was surprised when I looked at my watch and found that it was about eight o'clock, I asked Salman to take me back to the hotel, yet we meet in the same time next morning to drop by Chelsea branch.

I arrived at the hotel, took a shower after this long day, had a dinner, and sat in the balcony having a cup of coffee. I became way distracted, thinking about Suzan and some thoughts to write down; I went to my niche calling for the laptop, carrying on with my novel:

"...One day I read about the women of Indian Sati tribe culture, and how they get themselves burnt in a ceremony after their husbands' death, so that they don't become subdual, ignominious, and subject to profanity, by the men of the tribe after the decent life they had once with their husbands. Taking all the differences in mind, and the fact that religions do deny such customs into account, still, I think God prohibited the Prophet's women from getting married to other men after his death, for his sublimity, his highness, and the distinguished attributes he had, so it doesn't make sense for them to get married to normal men and be such normal women afterwards. Today, I find myself wondering..; if you had to leave me because you didn't want to live like a normal woman in this joint, and you didn't want to accept half of my presence, then you should have burnt yourself in being single forever, and stayed in an illegal relationship with me, rather than becoming subdual, ignominious, and subject to profanity by marrying Waleed, and yet remaining in an illegal relationship with me, accepting half of my presence! Because of religion you didn't want this physical contact to remain illegal, here you are love; passions have flowed over the dam of religion. What kind of loss have you come under now? What kind of conflict are you facing? I wish that you know how much I love you, and how much I am trying to stop the suffering of yours. What fate is surrounding us, and surrounding our moves? I wish that, for once, I can say "Checkfate" .. I wish that I can stop your pain without hurting you. If you are wondering whether Zeyad appreciates this sacrifice or not, I want you to know that I do appreciate your tragedy, but I will not accept from you less than that. Love is a criminal to its beholder, and crimes are of different sorts and concepts. Have you ever asked yourself, for instance if I wish you to live after me when I am gone? I have a different understanding of love, dear. Because fathers and mothers are more selfish, they prefer to die before their children do, so that not to suffer their leaving, and to avoid this everlasting daily grief. That's why they sacrifice everything for their children, and that's why God promised bereaved parents with a house in paradise, because he knows the void of a bereaved parent suffering his/her child's death. The one who dies inclines to different world, we don't know whether he or she is suffering or in real peace even. I don't want my beloved to suffer this everlasting pain since I know what I mean to her. I prefer to live the eternal hell, than to make you suffer one day of this void. I guess they call this "mercy killing", even if it varied in shape and form. Here I am crying over you, for death and farness are the same".

I continued shuttling between the seven branches of the group for five days with Salman, during which I formed a good material for the working paper to discuss with Mr. Assaf, which would probably leave a good impression. We also carried out some of the procedures we had in mind, such as meeting with representatives of both governmental institutions, and banks as well, to settle down all hanging in issues that would postpone bigger losses, and offer opportunities for more reasonable solutions. Those days were the hardest of my entire life; I had not time for my own, except when I fell asleep.

On Thursday evening, one night before coming back, I went shopping for more than three hours in Knightsbridge, Brompton Road for my two little kids. I also bought some expensive jewelry for *Sheikh Mit'eb*, Mr. Assaf, Mom, Sura, Waleed, and of course Suzan, from Bond Street. I didn't finish shopping till midnight, therefore I asked Salman to tell David to be at the hotel at eight o'clock to pick me up and give me a ride to the airport. Although I consider my first shuttle a successful one, to some extent, still, I was confused that Mr. Assaf hadn't called me for once till now. Was he confidentially in contact with Salman? I wasn't sure. I wrote a full paper about my visit to the seven branches, and my vision of the promising solutions as well. At two o'clock after midnight I finished my paper, packed my stuff, and got ready to leave and spend two days with my family before I return back to Dubai. Just two days my love.., two days and I'll be there with you.

I arrived at Amman next day at five o'clock afternoon. I headed directly to my city in the north..; to Irbid. My mom, my sisters, Sura, and my two little kids were awaiting me. I missed them a lot, though it wasn't long enough since I left them a month ago, but it was the first time I leave them this long. I sat with them and listened to their long talking.

- You are a pious son Zeyad, that's why God granted you with this opportunity in a short period of time. That means we can see you, and you can get together with your wife and kids for two days of each month. Your work conditions are still better than the conditions of your brothers.

I was about to say sarcastically, "what a pity"! In her opinion they are a cause of sadness, and deep sympathy since they work "day and night" to secure their "basic demands"! That's how mothers are like, either they become victims of the lies of their sons', who live away from their native country, due to their lasting complaining of their "miserable lives", so that mothers do not dare ask them for financial support from time to time; or they know the truth like Prophet Jacob, but don't prefer to let others know about, probably to keep the bond flexible.

- Mom, life is not that difficult in the other part of the world, and I don't have caviar on my breakfast every morning.

I kissed her, kissed my sisters too, and handed a present for each one of them, they looked happy when they saw their presents, actually I took into accounts their interests and likings, and brought them things they didn't expect. I went to my apartment upstairs with Sura and my two little kids. I talked to my kids for almost an hour and listened to their comments regarding keeping my promise in returning back within a short period of time. I was so delighted seeing them happy running to their room. I handed Sura her present and talked to her.

- Look Sura, I know how much you suffer alone with the kids.. and I know exactly the loneliness that bites you, don't you ever think that you and the kids don't occupy my first priority, even if I had to live away from home. I also know that I am a source of trouble, and that I don't perform what is expected from a man towards his wife, but you must be certain that I'll do everything to make you, and make the two kids happy. I want you to forgive me for the things I can't offer you.

- Don't worry.., mom used to say that bad husbands are like waste farms, you don't get benefit from, and you can't abandon them, but you are a pious person, I know how much tender your heart is, and I know the internal conflict inside you and how much you hate capture.

I kissed her for understanding what I wanted to say, and started to explain to her the nature of my work, and how much lucky I was to get this opportunity. I spoke at great length of what I dream of doing, and where my expectations conduct to. I also tried to make her understand that the financial returns of the job can be invested for the benefit of the children in the future, and that she herself must feel the difference in the standard of living. As usual, Sura didn't show any response towards what I said, thus my excitement cooled down, my dreams turned to rest, and silence overcame me.

I spent the two days with Sura and the kids. We went to the Dead Sea, Jerash, Ajloun, and Amman. We spent pleasant times in shopping, promenading, and at restaurants. I wanted to prove this presence of mine, though it was short, by all means. Sura's silence and deep looks confused me and troubled my desire and joy, as if she was complaining the presence of absence, and doesn't feel my presence at all. Why does her silence kill me this much? Why is she barren of feelings that way? What thirst rottened her femininity? Would that I could introspect your thoughts for a minute, I wonder what your thoughts would say! Am I the one to be blamed? Am I the troubled halo around you? I wish that you know how much I respect you, and how with the internal conflict of a criminal I ask for your forgiveness! But it's love Sura.. it penetrated through me like a light of thunder.., spreading its rays in my whole body. My fingertips are burnt by its molars; my chest is inflamed by its tattoo. Men think, or probably convince themselves, of mates that love has driven to them as their integrals, till they get struck by this thunder without warning, only then they recognize and distinguish love from liking. Don't you ever think that this slips by without a ransom to be paid. A one who is not satisfied with his fate or with his means of living, or with his destiny, and the limits of his knowledge, drives himself to destruction. I wish that I seek this jeopardy away from you, and away from her too..

I tried to remain stable in my endearment without exaggeration, because wives suspect such sudden alteration and smell treasons and presence of other females in their husbands' lives when doing so. I think the two days passed in peace, though I was about to be exposed, when I insisted on keeping what covers up Suzan's tattoo on my chest, in spite of the fact that I hope that the ruins of her tattoo would last forever. On Sunday evening I said farewell to everybody, and asked them to pray for me, I also told them that I'll call them when I arrive and will work on keeping my regular visits as promised.

I kept thinking of Suzan the whole way back, and how I am going to meet her, although I was confused of Mr. Assaf's breakoff, and the cessation with *Sheikh Mit'eb* as well, but my need to Suzan and moans of my ribs to hug her, prevented me from thinking of anybody else.

I arrived at Dubai at nine o'clock, and till that moment I expected Mr. Assaf to come and meet me at the airport, if not for my personal standing which he made me feel its importance, then for his curiosity in knowing the latest of my first visit to London. I was completely disappointed when I stood in the hall and didn't see him among other receptors of the arrivals. I pushed the baggage trolley forward, when a man interrupted my way.

- Good evening Mr. Zeyad. I am Pierre Shudyaq, the manager of Public Relations of the group, I came to meet you.

I've never met him before, but he looked polite, elegant, and expert in his work, which was plain and apparent in his self-confidence.

- Hi Mr. Pierre, and thank you for showing up.

We got into the car and went away from the airport. Pierre asked the driver to take us to Marina Resort. At that moment I lost my patience and couldn't help asking about Mr. Assaf, I didn't like the idea of passing a reference, or talking directly in business with *Sheikh Mit'eb*.

- Mr. Pierre..Where is Mr. Assaf?

Suddenly Pierre frowned after being asked, as if he was surprised, he looked at me and said:

- I know you have been waiting to hear from him lately, but the fact is that people around advised me not to tell you, or let you know till you come back and find out what happened. They didn't want you to be distracted from taking over all the hanging problems.

- Find out what, Pierre?

- Mr. Zeyad. I am so sorry to tell you this, but Mr. Assaf died six days ago. His state of health deteriorated recently, due to acute hemorrhage. They couldn't save him. We didn't know about his acute myeloid leukemia till he died. We are all shocked, *Sheikh Mit'eb*'s state is deplorable; he was a brother to him since the mid seventies. He was the mastermind behind most of the successes. He was my master in person. We didn't know whom to call of his family. He was closemouthed regarding his family, all what we know about is that he lost two sons during Lebanese civil war. Please try to help Sheikh Mit'eb, though he is in a bad condition, he remembered your arrival and ordered me to meet you.

I didn't talk at all. I felt a lump in the throat while listening to Pierre telling me the news of Assaf's death. I turned my face away and became absentminded, recalling that dream..; my father came to take Assaf. Why does fate insist on my orphanhood each and every time? I met him for two weeks only, but fate weaved a father-son relationship quickly and in secrecy.. that's why I missed him this much in London. I just wanted to hear his voice, seeking the confidence and trust which a son awaits from his father for support. He came from nowhere for two weeks to make me a favor that would last for a lifetime, and now he's gone. He dedicated himself to teach me the secrets of life, as if felt the oncoming of his death. He was playing against time, aiming at accomplishing his tasks.

Assaf was a noble man, self-denying, hid his wounds in pride of a knight, and refused to fall but from a horse's back.

The courtyard of the resort was crowded with people and cars.. I saw the manager of legal affair Mr. Yusri Yaseen talking to Toulin Moghraby at the doorway of the reception hall. I walked towards them, greeted them and said:

- How is the Sheikh now?

- Still refusing to talk to anybody.., secluded at his suite, drinking day and night.

- I want to talk to him.

- If you want to be thrown with a bottle of whisky, go ahead.

- Do you think he remembers who you are? How many times did you meet him, ha?

- In such hard times, one needs the close ones of his friends; those who spent their times together in thick and in thin, not an opportunist who wants to fish in troubled water.

I knew how much Toulin hates me, but it wasn't a right time for fights and clashes.

- Oh, yeah. Probably that's why he keeps you outside the door and throws you with bottles of whisky, but remembers my arrival time and sends me Pierre to meet me at the airport. Get the f…out of my face!

In fact I didn't blame Toulin for what she said, though she was rude again with me. How does *Sheikh Mit'eb* refuse those who went along with him through the years and remembers me in such a situation? I went inside his suite without permission, the place was swarming with chaos; bottles of whisky on the floor, leftovers of medication pills, bed sheets dropped here and there, broken glasses, torn curtains.. the *Sheikh* stretched out on the floor, keeping his back supported by the front of the bed, holding a bottle of whisky between his thighs, inclining his head downwards, his hair roots broke forth in white among dyed black ones, tearing in silence without wailing. I sat beside him, the same way he took form, and without looking at him I said:

- People outside think that I am wheedling now in such hard times. They don't know that my father died a few months ago, and I still, up to this moment, deny his death. I can still see him sitting in the balcony greeting our neighbors, and inviting them as usual over tea and coffee. He was hospitable. Once, while he was confined to bed due to his weakness, told me that he would rather be a healthy porter or a doorkeeper than a paralyzed prestigious academic professor. I lived with him for thirteen years, looked after him and watched over his most personal and private issues. When he died, all people told me that I was a lucky and a pious son for being offered the opportunity of helping and serving him till he emitted the last breath. They didn't know how much I cried, and how much weeping over him caused me sleep deprivation. Do you know why?

At that moment I burst into tears, as if I had just lost him..

- Because there were moments when I prayed to God to put an end to this suffering. I've tried hard to avoid facing myself with a question; which suffering was I referring to; his unbearable suffering from the incurable disease, or my suffering from the drudgery of looking after him, and the commitment towards a sick person for the whole thirteen years? Did I wish him death to make him rest in peace, or I wished him death so that I live in rest and peace? A man once said to *Caliph Omar*, may God be pleased with him, that he had a mother who grew old and couldn't relieve herself unless he carries her on his back to and fro; he also cleansed her, keeping his face away. He asked if he had, by this, fulfilled her rights. *Caliph Omar* said no. The man replied: Didn't I carry her on my back, dedicating myself to her? Caliph Omar said: "*She did you the same, praying to God to grant you with a long life, but you did her that wishing her to die*". That's right; we are impious and undutiful whatever we do.

I cried a lot till I got tired.

- Till this moment, I wish that he comes back to life again and that I remain at his service for the rest of my life without that devilish insinuation, but he will not come back..God sent me Assaf as a lifebuoy for two weeks. He chose me, refined my knowledge, and made me feel his love and trust. I was afraid of revealing my feelings towards him in return, so that he wouldn't see me emotional and then not consider me up to the mission, which needs reasonable prospects. I waited for his phone call when I was in London, but he didn't call me. I said to myself; he might surprise me and come to the airport to meet me there, but he didn't show up. Here I am, weeping over the loss of two.

- His very last words were "I strongly advise and recommend you Zeyad, take care of him, he is a noble and a trustee knight, take him on a son, so that no one dares to open his mouth too wide…forgive me if I ever failed.. I've tried my best..". I've never had a son, Zeyad.., and you'll never be convinced of their leaving.. from now on I'll be your father, don't be stupid and leave me. That's why I called for you.

- Would you let me shave your beard? You look like the backside of back weather; your queens will be scared away.

He found my offer pleasant, thus he nodded his head. I laid my arm on his shoulder and said to him:

- I will ask them to make you some coffee, while I myself shave your beard and bathe you, after that you will have dinner and get some sleep. We've got to start working tomorrow morning, may God grant you with long life, the group is facing a real hard time. We must stand together to manage passing this crisis for the sake of the hard work over the years. Tomorrow I'll call for a meeting, to view the faltering of this delay at work; we will also work on a ceremony of a funeral oration for Mr. Assaf next week.

Pierre was waiting outside, ready to carry out the orders. I called him and whispered in his ear to get some coffee made, and get the bath ready for *Sheikh Mit'eb*, I also asked him to inform everybody to attend the meeting at ten o'clock next morning, and to dismiss them, so that *Sheikh Mit'eb* gets some rest. The *Sheikh* submitted to all what I say like a meek baby. I shaved his beard, helped him in taking a bath, helped him eat some bites, and walked him to bed. I told him that I'll sleep in the next room of his private suite.

- Pierre. Whose room is this?

- It's Mr. Assaf's room. He used to sleep in, if he stayed late with *Sheikh Mit'eb*.

- Where does he stay permanently?
- In Bastakiyah.., same place of yours. He moved all his stuff lately, after meeting you at the hotel. He wanted to stay with you, but he told me that

you were a lover, and that your beloved might drop by for visits in anytime. Don't worry Mr. Zeyad… Mr. Assaf was my master, my benefactor, and a father for me..; he placed his confidence in me, and trusted me with all his secrets. When he recruited you, he told me that you reminded him of himself..; ambitious, with strong personality, smart, and most of all loyal and honest. He asked me to remember his words.

I deduced that Mr. Assaf was aware of his health deterioration lately, and wanted to stay close to Sheikh Mit'eb. I also think that Pierre is of the few who knows everything about Mr. Assaf, except of course his health state. That means neither Mr. Assaf, nor Pierre knew about the *Les Fleur Du Tulipe*.

- Thank you Pierre.

- Don't mention it, Mr. Zeyad. Here you are.., the key of his room and his drawers. All his stuff are inside, untouched. You might find or notice some beneficial things.

It was almost midnight, I thought it proper to inform Waleed with a message of my arrival, and of the death of Mr. Assaf, and that I'll be occupied and engaged with morning meetings, perchance he mentions this before Suzan. I called mom and Sura as promised when I arrive in Dubai. I wanted to give my entire attention to the documents and papers of Mr. Assaf before the meeting in the morning. I've done well by that!!. The documents were very important, and of great help to answer most of my questions, stress a great deal of my fears, my wariness, and my suspects towards some issues. The best part was that Mr. Assaf habituated taking records of everything that happens in the group, and noted down his personal opinion regarding any of the job affairs, and towards those who are on charge of the head office. A note written in red ink attracted my attention concerning the group in London," Something weird is going on there…, I can smell it.., see it coming.., but I don't know what it is; I must ascertain it". He didn't even forget writing about me in his notes, "Zeyad is a skeptic pessimist man, dashing by natural powers and special philosophy that justifies for him anything he pleases, adventurous.., loyal, honest, content with his goals.., heading for his bitter fate carelessly". Wow, was that a praise, or dispraise? It was so important to me to know what Mr. Assaf thought of me, and thought of my weak points. At three o'clock in the morning I was totally exhausted, therefore I went to sleep before I finish reading all Assaf's confidential papers. Next morning I awoke at Suzan's phone call, it was almost half past eight.

- Good morning love.. Welcome back home, and I am so sorry for Assaf.

- Good morning honey, and thank you my dear, God, how much I missed you my angel. Listen love, I'll be busy till afternoon, can I see you after that, there?

Assaf's words were still storming in my mind, he believes that there is something suspicious, I've got to be very careful and take all precautions.

- There? Oh.., sure.

- Good then..

- At five?

- That would be great love, bye.

- Bye.

I got out of my bed and went to the bathroom. At nine o'clock I was ready, and went to the suite of *Sheikh Mit'eb*, awakened him, and asked him to get dressed. Pierre had already ordered for the breakfast to be prepared, and for the Espresso to replace all liquors. *Sheikh* Mit'eb entered the divan, swollen eyed, and unsteady a bit. He took his breakfast, had his coffee in quietness. I worked over improving his look with all details. No sooner had everybody arrived at the meeting room, than *Sheikh Mit'eb* entered, looking as they are acquainted with his appearance in the usual days.

- Come on, let me know the brief about recent developments..

He spoke in equanimity and decisiveness, though his voice sounded tired. His words were a relief for me. The meeting started in calmness, then it went up intensifying, till Sheikh *Mit'eb* scolded some of the attendants for the bad decisions they made. I don't deny that I was more than happy seeing him come to sedateness and normality back again this fast. He deterred all sharks who wanted to fish in troubled water. The meeting lasted for almost three hours, in which Sheikh *Mit'eb* carried out some decisions and held back some others. He became strict with all details. Pierre was thrilled; he tried to hide his smiles and gloating over some attendants' grief, stealing looks at me from time to time. The meeting was adjourned later; everyone went, whispering, winking at one another, walking to the doorway, to their jobs. I stayed with *Sheikh Mit'eb* and Pierre for a couple of minutes longer, discussing some issues related to Assaf's balance in the bank, and his property. *Sheikh Mit'eb* ordered me to take care of this issue. Of course I needed legal referential from the group's legal consultant to help me in this. I referred indirectly to the importance of sending away all Assaf's money to almsgiving and charity.

- Do you have any idea the amount of money you are talking about, Zeyad?

- No your Excellency, but what's wrong with that.

- Do whatever you want.

- I think it's a good idea; he didn't leave us a will, as if he left all this money to us to do whatever we see it appropriate.

Pierre's interposition was spontaneous and supporting, I guess I like this man, no wonder he was trustworthy, reliable and the secrets' keeper of Mr. Assaf.

- Zeyad.., your presence around the clock is a must from now on. You must understand the oversize of responsibility burden in such given period of time.

I still believe that occupying the position of a third man in such a group in this short time was next to a wonder of the world. Even when I was introduced to *Sheikh Mit'eb*, I've never dreamt, or desired for once being the second man in this group. I don't want more responsibilities. Being a loyal pious son, and close to *Sheikh Mit'eb* is a thing, and accepting all what Assaf was taking care of is another thing. This was the last thing I wanted to hear from *Sheikh Mit'eb*. I might be lucky to be trusted by Mr. Assaf and *Sheikh Mit'eb*, but it seems that I'll be burnt as a result of this trust. I don't want anything to distract me from taking care of Suzan.

- Don't look at me like this! I know what disturbs you, and what you came to Dubai for. You have my word, I'll not keep you from her, in fact I might be of a good help for you later on, but I need you now, till I make sure that you are acquainted with all what Assaf was taking on, after that things will be more easy and simple. Go anytime you want, but you have to be aware of all details, and in control with me. You have to go to work hard when everyone goes back home to sleep. I only trust two; you and Pierre.., do you understand?

- I do, your Excellency.

- I will be very close to you, waiting for your orders Mr. Zeyad.

- Thank you Pierre.

- Don't mention it. You are up to the trust Mr. Zeyad. We will not let the grass grow under your feet, your Excellency. We will live up to your expectations.

At five o'clock in the afternoon, I headed towards Rashidiyah district waiting for Suzan. I sat in *Les Fleur Du Tulipe* confused, don't know how to play schizophrenic; between the reason, the awareness, and the wisdom *Sheikh Mit'eb* requires from me on one side, and straying in that dream of Suzan and becoming deranged. This took me back again to the onset of knowing Suzan, when she told me about the love of Napoleon to Josephine, and the love of Hitler to Eva Brown. I know that my love to Suzan is stormy and violent, and much stronger than keeping me on a fair distance from both sides; which would tear me into two parts. What kind of weakness that comes upon me when I meet her? How does she plunder myself and my will, and work on swaying me like the light of a candle before a gust of wind? I hear only her mumbles around me, and see her reflection on things. I can't sleep without her lull, and without her warm breath, I can't awake unless she awakens my spirit to meet her. She makes me feel my tender when she runs over me with her softness. I feel the beauty of things around me when she is around. She wipes away my inadvertence by her soft hand, and suddenly the whole world turns into a vivid one. She turns me into a prince with one clap of her hands. How can I serve two masters? How can I answer more than one call when fate and wills are against me? How can I …when fates conquer me and celebrate keeping me away from her?

I heard her footfall behind the door and the clicking of the key; she walked in slowly without talking to me, or looking at me. She just dropped her handbag down, walked towards me, and sat on the floor between my feet, resting her head on my thigh, looking at me and holding my hand in her two hands. Her eyes looked like two sad moons. She didn't talk; she rather turned her head down, kissed my hand, and became distracted. Once again, you are mistaken Dr. Gray, silence of women before men is not always an invitation to warm converse. This cat doesn't want to talk at all, she rather wants to relax and just purr. I rubbed her head gently trying to start a talk.

- This is a torture Suzan! I can't help staying away from you.

My voice was rattling, as if I didn't speak for days. Suzan started wiping away her tears in silence, then held my hand again and said:

- Every morning, with the wish and please of a paralyzed to turn his reality to dreams and his dreams to reality, I try getting up my determination and my wishes on foot, but this body falls down as soon as I open my eyes and see the one sleeping next to me. Why all my prayers are not answered? I abhor my body, and abhor the stink of my soul..

- Why did you choose us this agony?

- Because I don't want your love to me to go out one day! Look at you!! Though you love your father so much, and you miss him much more after his death, you can still put on a smile from time to time. I don't want you any kind of life with anyone if I am gone, I don't want you even to pretend one. I want the firebrand of my love to last forever in your heart. If we had married, you would have wanted to separate yourself from me at a moment of anger, this would have killed me twice. A girl lives a love story once in a life time.

I didn't ask her why she was so desperate to say this. She couldn't have put up with any longer conversation; she was like an abandoned shipwreck laid out on its side on a far-off shore. I carried her and we both lied down on lifebuoy bed, dressing the deep longing wounds in us.

Meetings with Waleed and the rest of the gang succeeded one another to strengthen the friendship ties between us. I made advances to Waleed in particular, and worked on his trust by tying Dilber (the carrot) to a swaying stick, in addition of being on the lookout with Suzan in his presence. I rendered many services to his friends due to my connections which spread out in Dubai. I made them members in clubs they never dreamt of parking their cars in. It was enough for them to bring into view my cards to make all their affairs agreed upon and approved. I became the Sesame password to their cave in Dubai. I dazzled them with precious gifts, and they competed among themselves who is a closer friend of mine. I knew most of their secrets, and their hidden affairs as well. After becoming the second man in the group company, I didn't hesitate in employing all means to seek my first and last purpose in life, which is being close to Suzan around the clock. I put myself under an obligation of making her forget who of us her husband is.

On regard of work, I visited all places where the group had branches in, and most of all London. So far I visited the group of restaurants seven times. Everyone got familiar with my position and relationship with *Sheikh Mit'eb*, and treated me accordingly; even those who took attitudes against me became helpless and declared loyalty. Me and Sheikh *Mit'eb* formed an integral entity, having our own language, concepts, and visions towards things. I remember a meeting once we held, when *Sheikh Mit'eb* informed us with the intention of a company to participate and share our group in gas prospecting project in Qatar. The development of discussion that took place in the meeting -which was attended by twelve managers- was a cause of sarcasm. In fact, decisions were restricted to *Sheikh Mit'eb* and me only, the rest were incapable of understanding what we were saying..

- What do you think about their offer of partnership in gas prospecting project?

- I beg your pardon! What do you think? Do we need to think about it? If we don't accept their partnership, others will do, and they will transfer the tender to others for sure, they are influential and powerful, and they have connections too, your Excellency.

- That's right.., but "those" might get angry because of this swindle of joining in the alliance with them, thus we lose what we have achieved there for years.

- Why should they get angry? The whole world knows the intimate feelings between both of them, why is it legal for them and illegal for us? Why should we seek working with them through "those"? They have stolen enough from us already.

- Zeyad, you know exactly that they want their share of the cake too.

- I'll fool them…I'll ask "those" to stress on her to take by force all approvals from them, formally speaking, in return for her share.

- That's dirty business, Zeyad!

- What's wrong with dirty business as long as the "dirty she" accepts this deal and spares lots of bribes here and there?

- You devil.

- What do you think, gentlemen?

All attendants were looking at us, without having any idea of what we were talking about. Then, they looked at each other in wonder, at that time I broke their silence and their stupid confusion and said:

- I can probe your agreement by common consent gentlemen.., with good fortune and prosperity, then.

Only two had plenipotentiary on making and carrying out the decisions; *Sheikh Mit'eb* and me. The manager of legal affairs department and the manager of accounts department in the main office were to follow. Their jobs were merely executive, though we counted on them a great deal at work. I've tried my best to adapt between the business on one side, and Suzan on the other side, and this blend made me work day and night because I didn't want to let *Sheikh Mit'eb* down. One day he pitied me, seeing me torn in between, so he courted asking me:

- Why didn't you marry her, Zeyad? You are neither the first nor the last to be in love with another woman..

- Be in love with another woman? I've never loved one before knowing her, and I'll never be in love with another except her. My marriage to Sura was of fate's arrangements, and please don't think I am turning my back towards my responsibilities in consequence of a wrong decision which I made once, as most men do when justifying their affairs with other women. It's just a matter of bad timing, nothing more. I was deceived by the fates. I was quite sure of her existence, and I kept dreaming of meeting her, and waited… I waited for a long time, that all people around convinced me that I was a sensitive lover, and a dreamer of a woman who doesn't exist. Eight years after my marriage, fates granted me this agony while I was walking in campus. She spoke to me to make me feel the bitterness of fate's victory upon me. She came to make my chronic defeat inflamed, she made my sorrows and heart break and bleed for the rest of my life.

- My question is why didn't you marry her?

- When we streamed like spirits in each other's body, and she had witnessed the real marriage life through the experiences of all the married couples around her, she decided to defend the survival of this love which she never experienced before, and will never experience its like again in her life. She imposed a commitment on keeping the torch of love lightened forever. She said that if we got married, and lived a life free of trouble at best, this torch of love will be blown out due to custom, fraternization and slackness of bodies towards each other, habituation of one's' presence, and exigency of closeness.

- Wow..!! You know what? You will meet thousands of women in your life Zeyad, but honestly a perfect woman like this one comes once in a life time. How about if we invite them.., I mean Waleed, Suzan, and the rest over dinner, cruising on the yacht.., in moonlight? I want to see you happy before we go to Geneva.

- We? Geneva? Why? I mean.., what business do we have in Geneva?

- A recreation trip, and a medical consultancy in General Paulino Clinic, nothing to worry about.. just checkups.. for five days.

- No problem. Good idea.., thanks for the invitation your Excellency.

Of course I had doubts of the Geneva thing which no one mentioned before in front of me, I didn't ask more questions about it, because I didn't want Sheikh Mit'eb to think that I don't want to go with him. No sooner had I been alone with Pierre, than I asked him about this visit to General Paulino Clinic in Geneva.

- Oh God, not again!! Don't worry, he is in good health, but he doesn't accept the fact that he is growing old, and of course the consequences of being advanced in years.

- Oh, really…is that why I don't see *Tatiyana* and *Rosaria* around anymore?

- I don't know when he is going to give in to the fact that he is over sixty five.

- Show some mercy, Pierre.. Isn't his loneliness, the bereavement and the barrenness are of enough misery? What do you want him to do? He is fighting the fates by approach.. he wants to survive.., to resist.., and to be happy.. He wants to run and never stop. Please don't underestimate what he sees it fateful.

- All right, but you will be responsible if he suffers a relapse after being informed of his impotency forever.

- Don't worry.. I'll let them fill him with confidence and relieve his worry by leading a life on hope. What is life to a man without hope, Pierre? Listen, you might not understand now how important this issue is, but you need to know that when a man loses his potency that means a declaration of his spiritual death, and his loss of the most enjoyments of life. He loses what makes him dignified and respected in the eye of his matches, he becomes imperfect and with less confidence… Why do you think they shoot the horses, then?

- Come on, for God's sake.., you are exaggerating.

- When I was a clerk at Queen Alia International Airport, there was an office boy whose name was Abu Ali. He used to work in the Royal Stables before, but then he was sent to work at the airport. He was proud of himself, confident, and lofty, I don't know.. probably due to watching over horses he became of the same qualities. One day I saw him standing, as usual, in the customs hall at work, he looked crushed and defeated in spite of his standing high and the intertwine of both hands behind his back. He was looking at a girl who was about seven years old running around her mother with her doll in her hand. I drew near and looked deeply at him, he was crying in silence, and his trembling lips tried hard to muffle his cry. I put my hand on his shoulder and asked:

- What is it, pal?

He tried to speak steadily, but the tone of his voice was troubled considerably as he talked..

- I have a little daughter of her age, who was born with a deformation in her two hands. She asked me last night; "Why can't I make tricks with the threads, or knit like the rest of the girls? When am I going to learn doing such things?", I wish that she died long ago, rather than dying every day because of sadness and comparisons.

When one becomes incapable and loses his/her confidence, knowing that he/she is not like the rest of the people around anymore, and when fates occupy what makes him/her distinguished of, he/she wishes by then that someone shoots them down and ends his/her misery. Some people who are lucky and of strong determination turn their points of weakness into a points of strength, adapting with their defects, and competing even with the normal people in all domains. Promise me to understand Pierre, and never become hard in judging Sheikh *Mit'eb* on this regard. You know what, this irritability of yours reminds me of my young sister's sparrow couple which was bestowed upon with a deformed fledging bird. The father sparrow kept heaping the young fledge with blows of both wings to oblige it to stand and fly. The father sparrow couldn't understand the helpless case of the screaming young fledge, having only one leg and a deformed wing, which shut it out from flying. Sparrow the father got angry and refused to eat or drink till it died. This anger and strictness is a sign of love, Pierre. Yes, we do become hard upon whom we love, sometimes. I understand you, you want him at his best, safe from all kinds of deadlocks, but he wants to defend his last pleasure.

- Got it.. I promise.., just like what you said.. I just want him safe, that's all.

After talking to Pierre, I withdrew to call Waleed and invite all the gang to have dinner on the yacht in the company of Sheikh *Mit'eb*.

- Good evening Waleed, how are you.., and how is Suzan? I hope you are doing great.

- Oh, hi traveler.. On what planet are you?

- Ha ha ha... still in Dubai. Listen I would like to invite you all on dinner, but this time we will enjoy the seafood and the moonlight, on the yacht of *Sheikh Mit'eb*, who will accompany us. Is the day after tomorrow good for you?

- How lovely! It would be a good opportunity to meet *Sheikh Mit'eb*. Would you please invite the rest of the gang yourself, Zeyad?

I guess Suzan was very close to him, and he was referring indirectly to invite Dilber over.

- Absolutely, I will..

I'll ask him for her phone number later and invite her to distract him from Suzan, who knows Dilber could be a good courtesan for Sheikh Mit'eb when due.

*****

Every time you say to yourself, "that's it, I can't take it anymore", learn better about your patience capacity, because when you get heartbroken once, you can take anything in the world"

~21~

I tried many times to call Suzan in the evening of that day, but she didn't answer my calls. I was haunted and confused by her absence. I thought of sending her a message, but I changed my mind at the last moment. I wonder what happened! If something bad occurred, Waleed wouldn't have answered my call in a friendly way, and he wouldn't have hinted at inviting Dilber and the rest of the friends. I waited long for a phone call from her, or even a message if it was difficult for her to call me, but she didn't do any. She has never been this late before. The scruple seized me by the neck, and I couldn't wait anymore. I burst out heading towards her dwelling, parked the car on the opposite pavement and waited. I went out of the car and walked to and fro on the sidewalk for over an hour, watching the balcony and the lights in..but she didn't show up. I went into the car again and waited for another hour till I felt a heavy burden on my chest and chocked with my breath. I lost control on my limbs, wanted to wreak my wrath and the fatigue of my patience with motion, I went crazy; punching the steering wheel at times, and kicking the pedals at others. The more I waited for her, the longer her absence stung me. I felt a bitter crush crooking my stomach.. I wanted to cry.. to shout..to kill myself…whatever..in order to stop this deterioration, this disturbance of my nerves, and this involuntary movement. I stayed like this till midnight, my strength weakened little by little, till I delivered my final helpless glance of consciousness to her balcony..

At four o'clock in the morning I awoke on the sound of a message tone of my mobile, I took a glance at the balcony before reading the message, and there she was, standing in worry. I picked up the phone in eagerness and read her message:

- "Go now, we will meet in *Les Fleur Du Tulipe* tomorrow at nine o'clock in the morning, I can't talk on the phone, and I can't explain everything in a message... I am sorry that I made you worried.. you'll forgive me when we meet and know what really happened".

My fingers went running on the keypad.

- "Not this time, I'll not leave till you tell me what happened.. I swear that if you don't tell me I'll come upstairs right now, whatever it takes"

I saw how she flounced her hand in anger, or probably in confusion of what to answer back.. I got scared again..; wondering, what would it be? Suzan has never been hesitant towards telling me anything before.. I received her message while I was still watching her disturbing movement..

- "In spite of the contraceptives, I am pregnant"

Her message hit me like a thunderbolt. My sight was wrapped up by a blur that made everything around me look cloudy. I still remember how the roaring of the fast cars whipped my ears. I tried to look at her, but my eyes sank in tears, touching the front of the car till I reached the side walk and then.. I sat.

Why has it never occurred to me that her pregnancy is a natural or a possible outcome of her marriage? Why has my mind kept denying any possibility that she could depart from me in such a situation, or distract herself with anyone else other than me? What partition did fates found between us this time? What cruel fate allowed this mean to insert bombs of busyness in the interior of her body? How can an innocent child, a fetus, threaten my entity?! How am I going to accept the idea that her hands will be occupied by another, and her fingertips will treat gently some other, and she will hug to her heart another? Am I going to die accepting one third of her time from now on, after going through the worst when accepted half of it? Am I going to suffer children' jealousy of their fathers for years to come when I show love or affection to Suzan? Does this mean that I should be careful with every word I say, two or three years from now, if children become aware of the world around them at this age? Am I going to occupy second position of your priorities in the future, Suzan? Fates.. distances... time.. are all kinds of waves that keep away a drowning lover from a beloved' lifebuoy. I also have children, Suzan, but left them back there to be here with you. We both know that seeking means of living here in Dubai is an unjustified and a weak excuse. Would you prefer hidden love to motherhood, or fates will enforce your motherhood to make a bigger loser of me? Who would draw your smile from now on, my touches on your neck, or the kicks in the interior of your body? Who would cause the shed of your tears in your eyes, my words of love, or his first tender talk? How did you replace me with the orgasm of your abhorred.. how? What have you done to me?

Suzan kept calling me over and over again, I know that she was risking the turn of her life upside down, not only by calling me, but also by standing on the balcony this late, but I couldn't answer her calls. The phone didn't stop ringing, and so was she walking to and fro. I went back into the car, and sat for a minute behind the steering wheel, and then I moved away without a final glance at her balcony.

I deranged aimlessly, not knowing where to go, but finally I found myself parking somewhere in Rashidiyah district. I went out of the car, walking on foot to *Les Fleur Du Tulipe*. I went in, and lied down on the bed, Suzan was still calling, the sound of the mobile drove me crazy, I stood up.. had a look at her name on the screen, then I threw it on the wall, till it scattered into pieces.. then I dropped dead in silence.

I don't know much time passed, but I was completely exhausted when I heard the door whamming. I opened my eyes, and there was Suzan, standing unveiled near the bed, her hair went wild, and her eyes were red and full of tears.

- Get up..!

Her voice was scarred with a beautiful husk, but ready and eager. I leaned droopily on the edge of the bed, pillaring my arms on my knees, and nodding my head downwards.

- Look at me!

Though she killed me with her message, still I honestly wanted to hug her when I saw her in this miserable outraged look..

- I said look at me, Zeyad..!

I had a look at her, and I wish I hadn't. She was shivering in anger, and her looks were full of blame, admonish, and scolding.

- You thought this will set you aside from me, and make me reconsider my relationship with you from now on, right? What a fool! I don't deny the fact that womanhood becomes complete, when women' last piece of jigsaw puzzle, which is motherhood, is set into place. We feel happy when we know that we are pregnant, and when we deliver as well. Kids are the source of all delights in this life..; without them life becomes barren, deserted, and boring regardless of all the suffering we pass through when looking after them. We have the right to run our hands over this innocence of childhood since we miss such a spontaneity in such a bad time, but I am not naïve or inexperienced to mingle this and that. This motherhood might bring us real burns and scars and we might not get the goods of it in return, we will go through the hell of their selfishness, of their impiety, and of their occupancy with the others later. Love, on the other hand is that thing which I depend on, and which makes me survive with hope. You want me to choose between my instinct as a mother, and my instinct as a female? No problem, I'll show you what I am going to do with it before your eyes…

She opened the window wide and drew a chair near, then she set her foot on the chair, and leaned forward towards the window, my mind was denying what I was seeing…No…she can't mean…I don't know how I jumped towards her shouting and grabbing her before she sets the other foot on, till we both fell down on the floor..

- You crazy..!

I am not quite sure if I uttered this word or not, but I know I stuttered with something similar. She was writhing on the floor, inhaling in quietness, till she burst into tears. I felt weakness in my knees and a shiver in my whole body. I've tried to breathe in, helping myself to speak, but I couldn't even hum..I felt as if my heart was snatched out of my chest. I rolled and went on all four towards her till I reached her head, and stuttered..

- Hush.. Hush..

I laid my arm under her head and folded her, till we exchanged the breaths..

- What have you done you crazy?

- At best I'll kill myself, at worst I'll kill you if you do this to me and turn your back again.

She was still gasping and shivering, her husk and the leftovers of her cries let some of letters' pronunciation down.

- You know what? Being this close of death, and feeling the pour out of life blood in our veins, I want you more than any time before!

She stood up unsteady for a while, and closed the window behind her, then she got herself unsheathed, and made me surf the Testosterone in my body. Every time she gives me much of a killing.. plunges the climax into a deeper me… causes me to bleed longer, she enjoys.. she overdoes… and she goes too far… surfing heavier and more abundant shudders of delight…what have you after that, Suzan? Where are you taking me? What terror and hell you want me to go through? Doesn't this spring of wonder of yours run out? Don't you have a wish to be at anchor, and stop sailing once and for all? Don't you get tired of running? I got tired.. for once be like the rest of the woman so that my spirit calms down for a while.. breath in from time to time.. consider things around me for a minute. I run away from your blaze in my awakening to seek refuge in dream, alas.. scorching heat remains my destiny though. I no longer recognize any of the colors, but that of your eyes, neither get my thirst quenched, but when your tears flow, my food sprout in your lips, my dormancy lies in the fluff of your eyelids, my pens, my papers, my thoughts, and all of my fingers became means of writing the story of my life by your hand.

- I thought that my femininity has become weak, and that my spirit got tired till you came over. You came over to tell me that I am the same brunette who revealed herself before you once, as if she was a wild mare with no stableman nor tamer, but rather she left the deserts, the plains, and the slopes of lands, and detested the mountains, the earth, the wasteland, and the wild lands as well, but drew near willingly strutting, and tempting you with the swaying wisps of her hair, flirting the palms of your hands by her sniffs of nose. You shouldn't have come over!! You shouldn't have re-awakened that female inside me again; however you did, and released your bridled lover, then relish the flavor of the woman you loved, and woe to both of us from an evil that is surely coming close..!

- I am not going to be worried about any of the consequences any more, he who loves a wild mare fears no falling downs, or wounds, or scars. Let alone the black and white areas, for knowledge awakens the roaring voice of conscience and sets on fire the internal conflict which distorts all kinds of rapture. Let us live in late afternoon, in the twilight, and in the afterglow of the times.

- Such times don't last long, Zeyad..

- Stop talking like this. What do you repent of? Do you repent being close to me? Hush.., the talk of conscience!

- Damn you! This is fear.., no more..! Wish that I get tongue-lashed by the conscience voice you are talking about. If it did, my repentance would be approved. The problem is that I don't feel the conscience-strikes, in other words; there is no way to turn from your sin, do you know the kind of punishment for that?

- Don't buy any of baby needs from here, I'll take care of it, and buy everything from London.

- No matter how much promises we make of not doing this again, I know such promises will not be kept.

- I think you should move to a bigger apartment now, you need a room for the baby.

- What weakness comes over me before you..!

- I'll take care of that too, the baby must have a well-prepared room.

- How long the twilight time will last before it gets folded by the darkness?

- What are you going to name it?

I looked at her and found her looking attentively at me, then she said:

- You have lost your mind, Zeyad… I swear to God that you have lost your mind. I have got to go now. When are we meeting in the resort tomorrow?

- I'll call you, and we'll come to an agreement, then I'll come to get you. Stay for a while till I fall asleep in your lap, then you can leave.

- Don't be greedy, love. You have to go to work too, come on.

I stood up, and tried to put the phone together again while Suzan was dressing up before the mirror.

- You.., men.., vent your anger breaking things, while women vent theirs fixing what you break!

I gave Suzan a ride to her house, then I headed towards the resort to start a day that wasn't like the normal days of my life. I felt the extremes of life and death, the restrain and the stretch in that day. It was a young day, a various day.. that is filled with grants of the skies. I started with the preparations and the requirements of the invitation first, then I buckled down to work with *Sheikh Mit'eb* and the rest of the managers of the group. It was one of those days which we attend meetings in, pursue the carrying out of some decisions, and make surprising field visits. I saw the mingling of beauty and duty in the performance of *Sheikh Mit'eb*. He was totally aware and acquainted of all details at work. I learned how he gets information from, how he becomes certain of the information credibility, and how he keeps his opponents and his enemies under his nose. I learned what it means to pursue the carrying out of your decisions without orders or interdiction, so that executors believe the orders to be of their own making. Urging this…, threatening that…, and bringing about alternative plans according to changes of facts. This kind of experience can't be gained but through trial and error, and time. When I finished the work for that day I took leave early to make sure that all requirements for the dinner next day are being prepared. *Sheikh Mit'eb* gave Pierre a wink while laughing.

- I saw that, father.

- Ha ha ha.. I was telling Pierre to have a look at you.., torn and dying between here and there.

- Dying!! My father used to say that, "*You can die in your free time, son*", but I am still busy for today. "*The woods are lovely dark and deep, but I have promises to keep, and miles to go before I sleep*". I want to die with dusty anklebones.

I turned my back and walked away waving to *Sheikh Mit'eb* and Pierre, their laughs and guffaws were easily heard from outside..

*****

I don't understand why people are asked about their age by "how old"? Probably that's why some take attitudes and consider it personal. We euphemized lots of terms, how about if we replace this question with: how many pleasant days have you had? Wouldn't we all seem younger?!"

~22~

On Thursday evening, Waleed called me at six o'clock to tell me that the rest of the friends are at his place, waiting for me. I headed towards his apartment in Nahda district and accompanied all of them to the Marina first to introduce them to Sheikh *Mit'eb*, after that we were put to sea by the yacht from there. Darkness was spread over by then, and we were unable to see anything except the reflection of the moon's sad face on the broken waves. The lights of the yacht mingled fear and beauty on the voyage at the time. Lights of far coasts of Dubai also loomed like hopes from its towers. Everybody was enjoying the mix of darkness, the roaring waves, the iodine smell of the sea, and the slight breezes among the awe of the place and the womb of nature which is full of mystery and surprises. The crew catered the food after a while, and all the attendants took their seats after choosing their participants on both sides. I sat next to Sheikh Mit'eb, who kept calling me "son" to back me and expose my position before the guests. Hussein sat on my left, Abdullah came next, and then Na'eem and the rest of the women till Dilber, whereas Waleed and Suzan sat in front of me, next to Pierre, on the right side of *Sheikh Mit'eb*.

- It honors me to give you the glad tidings, Zeyad!

Hussein spoke a bit louder than the rest of the attendants to hush them and to ask them politely to stop clicking the dishes with the forks and knives, drawing their attention to what he wanted to say.

- Glad tidings? Of what?

- No sooner the general manager of the publishing house read your first story of the stories you handed me, than he asked for me inquiring about the writer. He wants to meet you, so that you sign a contract, permitting the stories publication.

I can't deny how thrilled I was hearing such news from Hussein. I wanted to jump off the table, but I bridled my reaction for a minute or two, expecting Sheikh Mit'eb to take offense. He looked at me in surprise and said:

- Does my son write novels and stories? What is he good at besides?

- Oh, he is gifted by nature. I myself got surprised of his writing level, which bespeaks the proficiency of writing, rather than avocation. Ummm.., didn't he tell you that he plays lute too, and sings like a sparrow?

- Really?

Sheikh Mit'eb gradually brought Hussein to confession, every time he hears something new he peeps at me, and keeps step with flatteries around.

- Would you please tell me Mr. Hussein what the story, which was received with the manager's favor, was all about?

- Yes, your Excellency. . in fact it talks about a throng of apostate thieves, who come from faraway lands and break into a farm of a woman left alone with her kids and her suckling baby temporarily, till her husband finds a better place to change residence to. Those outlaw thieves plunder everything in the farm, make the woman and kids suffer the hell of torture. They take them all prisoners to their land and oblige the woman to suckle their kids leaving her own kids in hunger, they rape her before her kids' eyes, and then they enslave them all in their farms and in their houses too. One day, one of those ruthless apostate thieves asks the woman her name, she looks at him in the eye, then she looks down in shame and says " Decapolis"!

- "Decapolis"! Isn't that the Greek name of the ten cities in the Mediterranean region?

I kept looking at Suzan; she was hearkening to the narration in sadness. She looked pale and grief-stricken with tears in her eyes. I had to interfere and bring up another subject to find out why was she sad. I looked at her in a remarkable way before the others and said:

- I guess you are seasick, you don't look well. Is there anything wrong Suzan?

Waleed looked at me and said with a smile:

- You hit the needle on the head, Zeyad. She is definitely sick, but it's not the sea. She is lightheaded because of pregnancy, friend. Yes, Suzan is pregnant.

Everybody whooped in surprise, Suzan was heaped up with blessings and best wishes of everybody. I had to fake being surprised too, and invoke a blessing on her first pregnancy like the rest of the guests. I felt the lump and the heartbreak of Sheikh *Mit'eb*, but I was heartbroken too.

- Congratulations Suzan, wish you all the best and blessings.

- Thank you.

At that time Sheikh *Mit'eb* drew near and whispered in my ear:

- Did you know about it, or are you that much stonehearted and slow-going?

- I knew about it before your Excellency, I was about to die when I knew, but she told me that her pregnancy will not change anything at all.

- For God's sake, how does she accept such a man to be her husband!

- Please your Excellency.., we'll talk about this later.

I made a gesture for a member of the crew, and soon enough violin players and guitarists came out and started to play near the food table, the matter that added charm to the dim lights and calm wave roaring, mingled with the sound of music. After finishing food, the guests started having cold drinks and walk on the yacht, mumbling in side talks. I came close to Suzan, while everyone was busy with their concerns, and said to her:

- Imagine that if we were alone on the yacht Suzan, I would barter the rest of my life for this night.

The women suddenly yelled pointing at the sky, fireworks lightened the darkness in different colors and shapes from far away locale. I was looking at Suzan's eyes by then, and didn't turn away my face from her. Tears stood in her eyes for a while, but then ran on her silky cheek when couldn't be withheld. She looked at me and beckoned:

- I love you..

I had a look at Waleed and made sure that he was busy trying to get closer to Dilber in the darkness, I said to Suzan:

- Why are you so sad like this? Is it the pregnancy hormones, or is there another reason?

- Do you remember that Bedouin's expression Zeyad?

- What expression?

- "*Don't effeminate the talk*", don't even try of finding an equivalent translation for this expression, but you know what it means, right?

- Ha ha ha ha.., yeah yeah, never mix joking with seriousness in talk.

I laughed in bitterness when remembered those days..

- I am so happy for you, that you have achieved one of your most important dreams of your life, but I am worried; knowing that you are going to publish these stories on the other hand. Do you think that I didn't understand the intentions of that story? When are you going to let go the fates, the politicians, the corruption of work in London you told me about, the influential plutocrats, and the gangs? When are you going to understand that it is not of chivalry to fight the windmills, but it's rather stupidity?

- Love, I am not claiming any chivalric deeds or looking for fame or money or higher positions. I want to live happily and freely till the last spark of life, and I'll not permit anything -neither fates, nor men- to stand in my way.

- I'll always be worried about you, whom do you entrust me to? Without you, I am just a widow, an orphan, and a bereaved, don't you get it?

- Cool down baby, and don't you worry. Life is still going on, look at the sky..

The night passed away in peace without troubles, we stayed in the sea till midnight. Later on, we went back to the coast, anchored the yacht in the resort of Sheikh *Mit'eb*, and wished a good night for all. Everybody thanked Sheikh Mit'eb for the cruise and for the accommodation, and wished to join over again soon. Sheikh Mit'eb and I burnt the midnight oil talking about my relationship with Suzan and my writings. We ended up talking about work and our visit to Geneva as well.

*****

The closer you get to your homeland, to your beloved,
and to the shelters of comfort, the undesirable
stranger you become. Thus, keep sailing
and live the dream of anchoring
before receptors' waving

~23~

I met Suzan twice before my leave to Geneva with Sheikh *Mit'eb*, we talked about many things, but the most annoying subject we discussed was the change of the way Waleed treats her. She used to tell me that she doesn't blame him for the spiritless way he treats her in, as a sort of accepting the least of fates' punishment due to her relationship with me. I promised her once that I will not be a reason for her conscience conflict, and that I'll never put her in the place of a guilty; who seeks forgiveness from a master who rooted up her youth and would seize her sin, condemned religiously and customary, to throw her to the bottom of sins among the mischievous ones with a scarlet "A". Stupidly, I broke my promise to her, thus I became the fire that burns her. I wish I could put out her fire by telling her how Waleed flirts with Dilber. Once she told me that offenses, guilt, and sins shouldn't be returned in kind. She doesn't compare herself or sues herself to this or that, but she rather derives her retribution from religion and traditions, and by both references now, she is considered……

"What can I do to make your world fall like music upon your ears? Wish that sins are to sell and to buy, I would have bought all your mischievous deeds by all what I have of righteous ones. Even those who are of less education keep asking universal and philosophical questions in view of the fates' wisdom behind mining their passages in hide when the doorway of hopes are closed in their faces. Probably the most common and repeated question of them all, regardless of the variety of the situation, the reasons of pain, and timing, is "*Eli Lama*?", "*Oh, God..,* *why?*". May be the question has lost its theological sense and became more philosophical in view of wisdom and knowledge inquiring the happenings of fates upon us. Is it true that peace lies in inclining to the word of God, disavowing all lessons, wisdoms, experiences gained by time? Do we depart from God when we make decisions according to the circumstances we go through? Wasn't it fate itself behind our meeting? What can I do Suzan when I get burnt by your conscience fire due to your closeness on one side, and the fire that burns inside due to you farness? You saw our togetherness ending as dull, of dissonant rhythm, and boring due to your acquired experience, what end have you chosen to us, when fates turn against us and you anticipate the outcomes clearly this much?"

I called Suzan hours ahead of my leave, when Sheikh *Mit'eb* surprised me by our departure time in the evening of that day. I told her that I won't be late in my trip this time for more than a week, I explained to her that I'll stay in Geneva with Sheikh *Mit'eb* for two or three days, then I'll make a surprising visit to London for a day, and finally I'll spend a day or two in Jordan, then I'll return to Dubai. She asked me to call her every morning, and I, as usual, gave her my word.

No sooner had I finished packing my case at midday, than I received a phone call from Sheikh *Mit'eb*, telling me that he's going to meet me within a couple of minutes in the businessmen lounge at the airport. I rushed to the airport and called Pierre on my way to tell him that I am going to meet Sheikh *Mit'eb* at the neck of time, I asked him to make sure that all orders and procedures we've agreed upon are carried out. I arrived at Dubai airport at quarter past four, Dubai timing, and handed my passport and documents to the usher of businessmen lounge. Sheikh Mit'eb was watching carefully the latest news of the "Arab Spring" revolts on the giant screen. Shouts, and race of correspondents in streets; each one tries to come up with scoop coverage that serves the channel's intentions and policy. Distorted translation and stuttering of European leaders and American President during their interviews and their press conferences, photos of destructed cities, of dead bodies left in streets, screams of mothers crying the International Community for help. Threats bluntly announced, breaking news at the bottom of the screen, dispatching aids by United Nations Support Missions, camps for refugees on the borders, outcome of martyrs numbers, photos of kids torn in the pulling down, some are supporters others are opponents, live cock fighting on political programs, thousands of people spreading out in hard conditions.. I saluted Sheikh *Mit'eb* and sat near, he didn't salute me back, he was busy saying "There is no power or strength save in Allah", twisting and turning his hands over in worry, then he said:

- What is going on? What's happening?

- In brief your Excellency.., the end has already started, and these revolts are all introductions of ripping apart the countries into petty countries to reorganize the map of the region according to sectarianism. Sinking people in a blood bath, to guarantee that the duration of civil wars will make all parties exhausted, helpless, and left only with the outlet of imposed conditions upon them. Meanwhile, organized criminal countries will fish in troubled water, plundering all supplies and resources, even the water resource, and will market all arm industry products of giant factories to those stupid countries who will sink in debts forever, and who will also grant the building of the country once again to the organized criminal countries industry. The most important issues for these sharks are; the supplies and resources on one hand, and guaranteeing the safety of their spearhead in the region on the other. This time we are of a good help for them; hitting two birds with one stone. Do you remember your Excellency when you said to me that "you, the Jordanians, will never learn how to be opportunists and fish in troubled water?"

- I do.

- I bet that we have learned the lesson from our mistake when we backed up the Iraqi nation during its war in the nineties and were left to face the economic breakdown alone by then. This time we will gamble on the winning horse by taking advantage of our geographical spot, not to make up for the deficit of our indebtedness which was plundered by our sharks, but to bribe the sharks for their vision and stand this time with the wining horse.

- This is madness! Thousands are being killed in cold blood on hands of their leaders just because they are asking for reforms, and asking to obtain a piece of the cake after decades of tyranny. What do nations of first world think of us?

- Naïve ones see us as slaves; revolting for freedom and taking back the resources consumed by the one ruling family, but decision makers see us as stupid who get killed in thousands to step aside one man, or one regime, when on the other hand we will remain slaves for another ruler who is one of their traitors. No matter how the east and west clash defending their interests in the region, they will distribute the resources among themselves.

- How does your country face the emigration of refugees? Aren't you worried about what is going on there?

- Worried? Why should I be worried? Haven't you heard the saying "*Rob Peter to pay Paul*" before? In our country we live on other nations misfortunes, we trade in their national cases under the name of the aid and the contribution offered by International Community which will never be handed to the people in need. You just need to adopt a broadcasting voice that turns black into white and defeats into victories like Ahmad Sa'eed and Mohammad Sa'eed that sang Arabism outwardly to hide the inherent deep-seated and chronic corruption. Why should I be worried? The national anthem doesn't carry the name of my country at all, but instead it glorifies his Majesty! Our safety and stability is nonnegotiable since the establishment of the Emirate, and those who are cashed in millions to shove thousands of people in the country don't care if we become in need of a sip of water. If such crises takes place somewhere around, Jordanian citizens become the cheapest resource of the country, but when peace is spread over in the region, we become the richest resource of the country for paying the tax of the tax. Do you know your Excellency that we form the minority in our country, after the emigration of the Palestinians, the Iraqis, the Syrians, and some other nationalities as well? Our hospitals are filled with Libyans, when the Jordanians don't find empty beds in the hospitals for their patients. Iraqis don't allow Jordanians to rent an apartment in a building owned by an Iraqi in the center of Amman. Lots of Jordanians got shocked to hear rude responses like, "we don't rent out to Jordanians". That's how they wanted the country to be like, and that's how it is going to be like. It's the substitute homeland for the overwhelming majority, even without the need of announcing this publically. When the financer of the war and the payer of the direct costing is decided, the Armageddon will be waged.

- That's really woeful.

At that time, the final call for the departure of the flight heading to Switzerland was announced; ushers started walking us to the gates to get into the plane.

In the course of the flight, Sheikh *Mit'eb* looked worried, I ascribed his fear and worry to the medical test results - not to what was going on in the Arab world - for he was fighting the fates by playing against time with the last chance he had, whereas fates were fighting him and the likes of him with various choices and uncounted options, in calmness and with certainty of winning. He kept saying that we; the Arabs do inherit the worry and the feelings of guilt from the very beginning of our childhood, and that feelings of regret are transmitted by inheritance over the loss of our sacred and holy sites, in addition to the melting of honor elements, thus we don't enjoy times of happiness and the pleasure of real relief and ease. I guess he was justifying the reason behind this flight to Switzerland, in a try to recover his excitement by the search for the syrup of eternal potency. Most likely, he predicted that I would inquire some information for this medical trip from Pierre, because I didn't insist on knowing from him in person. I wanted to tell him that I do support him heart and soul in maintenance the machine that will make him survive, even on hope, for years to come, accepting the kind of life he is living, but I didn't want to embarrass him more.

After landing on Geneva International Airport, we headed towards Generale-Beaulieu Clinique in the capital city of peace and money, located between Lac Le'man and river Rhôn, and barricading among the old aged massif summits of Alp Mountains. Sheikh *Mit'eb* was tired, he didn't take an interest in all the spectacular views around, either he got used to it due to medical visits, or he is absentminded, and worried, thinking only about the reason of coming to Geneva.

We were lodged in the private suite assigned for Sheikh *Mit'eb*, the nurse concerned with receiving patients and accommodation told us that Dr. Philip Juliann will come to meet us in an hour from now. I took a leave of Sheikh *Mit'eb* in excuse of making an important phone call, but in fact I followed Nurse Eva to explain to her the necessity of meeting Dr. Julliann before he joins us in the suite of Sheikh *Mit'eb*.

I went back to the private suite and told Sheikh Mit'eb that Sura is at the hospital in Jordan, and an urgent operation of cholecystectomy was assigned for her, two days from now. I wanted him to understand the necessity of my leave after he finishes the medical tests and I make sure that he is going to be alright. He immediately asked me to go to Amman, as soon as he finishes the medical tests, and stay close to Sura, he also wanted me to wish her good health on his behalf. I didn't want to make Sheikh Mit'eb know about my intention of heading to London, so that to keep this visit a surprising one. The words of Assaf which I read months ago were still storming in my mind.. "Something weird is going on there,… I can smell it.. see it coming.. but don't know what is it, I must ascertain it". This maneuver must be quick, clean, and a surprising one.. without mistakes as well, so that Salman doesn't take precautions in advance, and I look stupid before Sheikh *Mit'eb* accordingly and lose his trust as a result of that. I formed one jaw of pincers, and I needed the other trusted jaw, that's why I called one of my retired relatives, who used to work in the secret service, his name was Mohammad Barakat. I asked Barakat to precede my arrival to London and try to associate with the branch managers of the bank we deal with, and try to bribe any of the officials, or the manager to get a genuine and original statement of account with account receivables and payables for months before. This surprising visit shouldn't be suspicious to any of the bank managers, because I am entitled and authorized to check the accounts in any time I want, without the reference to Salman, but if there was some kind of a conspiracy, a manger will supply me with a ready fake statement of account, which doesn't unveil such details. The reason why I chose this specific time was because the head office believes that I am busy with Sheikh *Mit'eb* in Geneva, considering that I didn't ask any of the public relations' officials to book me a ticket to London at all. When I checked Mr. Assaf's regular visits to London I noticed that he was accustomed to shuttle there in the first week of every month, I don't get what made him suspicious of the work in London, but I chose the third week of the month this time to surprise the fellows to see what changes would I find, after getting the statement account which reveals everything in details.

The time went so fast, while the nurses started drawing blood samples, probing his blood pressure, and investigating about his medical record. They got him dressed and ready after that for MRI. I stood outside and waited Dr. Juliann's emergence, thinking of what to say to him to get him convinced of the importance of not telling any bad or disturbing news to Sheikh *Mit'eb* to spare him further psychological relapses. Dr. Juliann arrived accompanied with three nurses to the ward that leads to Sheikh *Mit'eb*'s suite, I asked him if he allows me to speak to him in private before he gets in, he was a gentleman and didn't let me down.

- I don't know where to start from, but I find it so important to make you understand the sensitivity of Sheikh *Mit'eb*'s health state, you see.. this impotency which he suffers from is looked at as a deficiency in the manhood in the culture of the Arab world. He is growing old, he lost his best friend months ago, and he is still suffering the consequences of losing all sorts of joy in his life. So, he believes that this sexual capability is not only his lifebuoy, but it is also his hope in having an heir. In our culture if a man doesn't bring the good news of expecting the arrival of an heir within months of his marriage, he becomes the talk of the town and the center of sympathetic looks. Even the naïve starts giving him pieces of advice, such as knocking the door of fortune-tellers, or getting married to other women. You can't imagine the effect of telling him the catastrophe of his lasting impotency. Please, I know that you tell the truth to your patients here, but not in this case, he is so arrogant, confident, and proud of himself, you must tell him that the tests' results are so promising, and that his health state is showing progress. Tell him that he must get rid of his gloomy and his melancholic mood, and that he will pass this relapse with medications and instructions.

- Got it.., don't worry.. I have lots of friends in the Arab world and I know exactly what successors mean to you. You simply don't see it an illness to accept the idea of living with it, and I also know that adoption is looked at as an abhorrent issue from your view.

- Great.., that's all.. I have to leave within two days. Sheikh Mit'eb will remain in your care till he finishes all medical tests.

- Don't worry we will do our best to make him feel comfortable.

- Thank you doctor.

I went out of the hospital dashing towards the nearest telephone booth, and called Barakat.

- Hi, it's me…what happened?

- Hi Zeyad, I was waiting your call on tenterhooks, the choice has landed on Golders Green branch manager, Jerald Ranan.

- Golders Green? Interesting…it makes sense.

- Listen carefully, he wants five million English pounds in exchange for the statement account, he also insists on your presence, to claim that he was surprised by your demand of the documents for months ago, when he didn't have enough time to call them back, and didn't take orders from them to supply you with fake statement in case. You were right, brother. This is a conspiracy of money laundering in collision of several parts. He says that they transfer millions of pounds outwardly to banks in Switzerland. What do you want me to do now?

- Five millions? Of course.., he is checkmated, he is losing anyways, he must think of indemnifying his losses as much as possible. All right, tell him that he will get the five million pounds on delivery, just give me two days.

- I'll tell him that, by the way who is Toulin Moghraby?

- Toulin? She is the chief accountant of the group in Dubai? Why?

- When I told him that you can simply fire them without the need of paying five million pounds he became lightheaded and said "You do that, and you won't be able to snatch the rats involved". I told him that it won't be a big deal, they can make reforms and dust off the rag from all the moths, but he said "They? Who are they? The wrongdoer hand is pure and clean, I fool you twice, shame on you!".

- Oh, great then.., he decided to bring the temple down on everybody before he turns his back. Don't worry, I'll be in London within two days, just tell him that he will get the money when he delivers the documents.

- Ok. I've got to go now. See you.

- Take care, see you.

Assaf sensed the conspiracy for some reason, but it seems that he was satisfied with hundreds of thousands a month as gross profit from the restaurants in London, due to being busy with Sheikh *Mit'eb*, and due to his sickness as well. After making the phone call with Barakat, I sat in the English Park for almost two hours to clear my mind and think carefully of what to do next. I returned afterwards to the hospital, when all of a sudden Sheikh Mit'eb looked dispelled and excited.

- Zeyad.., come here boy.

His arms were wide open; I drew near and faked a surprise. He hugged me for a while and then walked me a few steps away..

- Dr. Juliann said that the medical tests are normal and that the results show progress and must be translated to reality in the near future.

- Oh, that's great! I beg your pardon! Translated in the near future? What is that supposed to mean?

He cleared his throat, set right his talk, and said:

- Did you call your wife? You should be going now; you must stay with her when she needs you.

- I won't go now, not before I make sure that you are going to be alright.

- I am alright, I'll amuse myself for a couple of days, and then I'll return to Dubai, don't worry. I called Pierre and told him that you are going to Amman. He wanted to come and join me instead, but I refused and told him that I am going to be fine, and will return at the weekend.

- Really, did you tell Pierre that I am going to Amman?

I wish that you didn't, I don't know whom to trust now. Pierre kept the diaries of Mr. Assaf untouched; if he was involved he would have got rid of such a hint. No.. he is faithful to Sheikh Mit'eb, I sensed that too.

- Yes. Come on, get yourself ready and buy a ticket to Amman right away.

This is what I am going to do..I'll buy a ticket to Amman, and keep the return ticket to Dubai to fool them all. I hugged Sheikh Mit'eb as a sign of gratitude and understanding, and asked him to take care of himself.

I betook myself to TGV high-speed Rail Europe, by which I can go from Geneva to London passing by Gare de Leyon station in Paris, on board of Euro star train, which takes me to London within five hours and a half. In the meantime I called Barakat and informed him of my arrival to London of the same day. I asked him to work on arranging a meeting with Ranan in the evening of next day if possible. Meanwhile, I jotted down in brief all the notes on a diary just like Mr. Assaf used to do. I had enough time to proceed in my novel, at least to ease my stress and calm down. I was definite that the novel was not meant only for publishing, in fact the novel was long and flowing, just like the everlasting of "One Thousand And One Nights", I wanted it to expand to generations to come and cover the stories in spans of time, which might end only when the ink of my pen runs away, and when my leaf attached by an umbilical cord to the age tree of mankind falls down.

".. It seems to me that real love emerges oddly, and later on, retraces its steps to oddity again.. translated into innocent feelings, eager looks, and satisfied hand touches. In first dates, one imprisons the wild id of himself deep inside, and keeps busy thinking of how to crush the other with tender words, and feelings of pure love, without sexual images of any kind. The same goes to last dates and gatherings, when youth and strength set in the decline, feebleness, hoariness, and worst part of life rise, only then real love remains in a kindhearted grip of an old man's hand to his old wife's.. in a waiting room for a medical appointment in a clinic. How many love stories have succumbed under hard and miserable life, and remained like hidden treasure, figured out by signs of this kindhearted grip? Why has love become a sort of grief, this much of depression, and of such satisfaction? I wish that you know Suzan, how much I am willing to barter all joys in life for the sake of sitting with you.. holding your delicate hand to calm you down.. and we wait together".

I arrived in London at half past three in the evening.., six o'clock in Dubai timing of the same day. Barakat confirmed me -with another phone call- the meeting with Ranan arranged at nine o'clock next day in Sheraton Park Tower, Knightsbridge district. It was one hour ahead of banks closing, I headed directly to the bank and informed the manager there of my will of withdrawing Five million pounds next day morning. After exactly half an hour, Sheikh *Mit'eb* called me, inquiring the reason behind the will of withdrawing the five million pounds in cash.

- I guess Harvard's graduate dropped you a line by now, to inform you with what the bank manager in London told her.

- That's right, what do you need the five million pounds for, Zeyad? Why didn't you tell me that you are heading to London? Why did you lie to me, son? I had to tell them that I am the one who asked you to do that in order not to look like a fool before them.

- You did well, your Excellency, by doing that. I can't tell you anything now. Do you remember our first dinner, and the wine lesson?

- Yes, what about it?

- Do you still remember when I told you that the mouther looks like a fan of portion and division, not an addition fan?

- Yes, I remember.

- I can't tell you more than that now, if you ever trusted Assaf and me your Excellency, please confirm the cash check.

- Don't make me the talk of the town, Zeyad. Don't let me down.

- That will never happen, I just want you to tell everybody including the mouther that you and I have some sort of understanding, and there is nothing to worry about.

- All right, Zeyad.

When I finished the phone call with Sheikh *Mit'eb*, I immediately called Barakat back and told him that the news came to main office ears in Dubai, and that Ranan must print out the account statement now before they take necessary procedures from their side. A few minutes later, Barakat called me back and told me that Ranan has indeed printed out the genuine certified account statement earlier that day. At that moment I went to a travelling agent office and bought a ticket to Amman, booked and confirmed it for the day after tomorrow to mislead any expected tails, I planned with Barakat to spend the night in his bachelor apartment in London.

The very next morning I and Barakat got ready for the long day, we agreed upon the things that must be done, such as; drawing the cash money and sending it to QNB safe deposit lockers in Grosvenor street, entitling Barakat to draw the money in exchange of the account statement after I make an agreement with Ranan, then taking these documents directly to Geneva by trains, and finally heading towards the final station in Dubai.., and waiting for me there. It looked like an American gangs film due to all these precautions, but we had to be cautious, especially when keeping in mind that Sheikh *Mit'eb* is in a difficult position before those exposed bastards, who made use of the restaurants in laundering money. Though Barakat was an expert in such hard times and situations, I found myself obliged to tell him this..

- Barakat.. you must understand how important the issue is to me, and my stand in front of ....

- Stop it, Zeyad..please. I owe your father for standing beside me in the past, and for supporting me in when the going got tough. Give me a chance, for once, to express my gratitude and show how thankful I am. You are like your father Zeyad, loyal and faithful.

- Forgive me Barakat. I didn't mean..

- Don't worry, I understand. Let's go.

We have tried to delay drawing the cash money as much as possible till the evening, and when it was time, we drew it and headed towards Grosvenor street to deposit the total amount of it in the safe deposit locker by Barakat's name. Ranan sent his representative to the same street without telling us of course who he was, till the minute of meeting him in Sheraton Park Tower.

At nine o'clock I arrived at Knightsbridge district, aiming at the hotel, and asking about Mr. Ranan suite. I tried to remain calm and quiet to deal with Ranan in proficiency. I got to his private suite, the door was open, and a man welcomed me and asked me to come in. Ranan was standing in confidence and elegance, putting one hand in pocket and twisting a Cuban cigar in the other.

- Hi Mr. Zeyad.

- Hi..

- Cigar?

- I don't smoke, and I don't drink .

- Please have a seat, you don't drink.., you don't smoke!! Is it due to some sort of a religious doctrine, or an extremist sect?

- How about if we start talking business, Ranan?

- All right.

He exhaled clouds of smoke of his cigar, and leaned it on the ashtray, then he reclined his back, intertwisted his hands, and crossed his legs.

- Mr. Zeyad.., after years of working in banks, and getting slipped disks in the back and in the neck, man has the right to retire and enjoy what is left of his years of life in a small farm for instance, and have a decent amount of money which offers him a decent life in case hardships of life emerge. He who thinks that the gratuity, and bank facilities for its employees are enough for a decent life of a family man in such economic crisis is no doubt mistaken. I will lose my job, and I will leave this country, that's why I demanded a guaranty.

- A guaranty? Ranan.., why do you bother convincing me by your excuses of accepting this deal? I am not really interested of your affairs and how things are going to be like for you; the minute I get out of this place. I offered you a deal, and you accepted it, end of the story. We have the right to defend our business and protect it from any prosecutes, and you have the right to seize this opportunity and demand a bribe... sorry, what did you call it? A guaranty for this favor and service. If your man arrived at QNB let's do this, so that each one goes in his way.

- You are right.

At that time Ranan dropped a line to his representative to meet Barakat inside QNB safe deposit lockers, and deliver him the account statement, after receiving the agreed upon amount of money. Ranan talked about Mr. Assaf, and mentioned the many times he met him before in the last years, he also offered his condolences to me for his death, bringing to mind his virtues. Of course we were not interested in listening to each other's bullshit, but the meeting was charged with worry and disturbance, that's why Ranan tried his best to calm himself till Barakat and his man finish barter. Half an hour later, Ranan's representative called and told him that everything went so fine, at that moment I called Barakat and he also told me that he got the documents and he was on his way to Waterloo station, and that he will call me back when he arrives Gar du nord station in Paris. We both got up at that moment, and Ranan laid a hand in happiness, believing that I will shake hands with him..

- Wish you all the best.

- You said that you wanted to live a decent life! You might think that you earned a great amount of money overnight Ranan, and that is genius, but believe me.., he who puts his conscience to sale dies low at a later time. Look at our Arab leaders and how much money they piled up, and the way they groveled before..

I left him behind to take in his hand with a smile and in irony, and went out. I don't know why I doubted the ease of the interplay this much. It was confusing, terrifying, and fatal for some, why didn't Toulin stop this step, even by force if she had to? Was it only because she was a partner in this conspiracy? Not anymore, Ranan scapegoated her, and the only thing she did was informing Sheikh *Mit'eb* of my intention of drawing the five million pounds! I don't get it, calm water runs deep, I must take care, and I must remain among people till I get back to Dubai. I went to Barakat's place and remained there the whole night, watching the streets through the window, till finally I dropped dead sleep for almost fifteen minutes, before I got shuddered by Barakat's phone call to tell me that he arrived in Paris.

- I know how much worried you are, relax, everything went so fine..I have the documents now, don't worry. The documents reveal money laundry in terrifying amounts, Zeyad.

- I know, but I was about to collapse waiting your phone call.

- Sorry for being late, that representative sent his greetings to you, Zeyad.

- What? Greetings? Does he know me?

- You won't believe it, Zeyad, it was Salamn! The one whom you told me is in charge of the restaurants in London.

- What? Salaman?!

I fell down on the floor …shocked. My nerves relaxed and all my fears faded away, I started to laugh hearing Barakat's voice calling on the phone "hello, Zeyad…what happened.. talk to me , Zeyad". That son of a bitch was aware of everything; he shunned Toulin to spare her share for himself and for Ranan after all what she did for them - of transferring money to Switzerland. He knew that I will fire him soon, and that I will prosecute him if ever found any thread that would lead to him. Ironically, I paid him a severance pay for all his thefts to get the account statements that incriminate others.

Next morning I woke up at nine o'clock by Suzan's phone call, London timing..

- Is this the way you keep your promises, Zeyad? Didn't you promise to call me every evening, to relieve my worry and fear?

- Take it easy, love. I am not one of those who break their promises, and you know that. Unexpected things came about, thus I had to leave Sheikh *Mit'eb* in Geneva and shuttle to London..I'll explain to you everything when I get back. Tell me now, how are you doing?

- Oh, that means you are in London now!

- Yes, love.

- Oh, I see.., except the morning sickness every day, and missing you around the clock…nothing new under the sun.

- Do you know what I am going to do now?

- What?

- I am going shopping for your baby from the most famous stores, I'll buy all the requisite from here.

- Don't bother yourself, love. We still have time.

- Don't worry.. I am coming tomorrow.., wait for me.

- I am sick of this life, how many times am I supposed to wait?

- Don't rush, baby

- Yes, easy to say..

- Tomorrow morning, love. Wait for me.

- Beggars can't be choosers, take care of yourself, honey. Bye.

- Bye, love.

When I ended the phone call, I immediately called Sheikh *Mit'eb* and told him everything in details, I also asked him to pass his commands for his trusted guards to keep their eyes on Toulin and the rest of accounting department, in addition to the manager of legal affairs. I've never heard flattery like the one I heard from Sheikh Mit'eb on the phone, thanking me for unmasking this conspiracy, and for saving his face from any prosecution. He promised me to take revenge for himself on them all. I was so thrilled knowing that I gained his trust, and didn't let him, or even Assaf down. Later on, I had to go shopping and solve all problems left on this visit. So, first I went to the head office of the group in Kilburn, Brondesbury avenue, and appointed the Indian Abhay Malak, an area manager till I get back, after I informed him of what happened to Salman. I told him that there is a good chance for him to be the permanent area manager if he shows dedication and devotion at work. Finally, I headed to the market to buy the baby's stuff. The stores of babies' requirements were charming, with the very meaning of the word. I dropped by three famous stores; "*Carry Me Home*", "*Felix & Lilly*", and "*Mammas & Pappas*" and shipped all the stuff to Waleed's address in Dubai. In the evening I had dinner in Barakat's place while talking to mom, and Sura, then I went to sleep, looking forward for a day full of events and turning points.

*****

"Forgive us.. forgive us..
Forgive us if we rejected everything,
Forgive us if we broke everything,
Forgive us if we plucked out everything,
Forgive us if we threw you our names,
For the desert spat out us,
The harbors spat out us,
The airports that receive and meet birds
day and night also spat out us,
The sun of repression..
that rises everywhere.. burnt us,
Forgive us if we spat on an age
that has no name,
Forgive us even if we disbelieved.."

Nizar Qabani

~24~

That day was not overloaded with fears and worry the way I thought it to be like two nights ago, it rather was a calm beautiful day, till I reached the airport.. the airport; that border which isolates the nations and the conditions. The T.V screens were broadcasting the news of the Mediterranean region; the revolts close to us, and the concentration of eastern and western camps over that cake. The whole region was ready by now for a regional war, expecting a new imposed map and demarcating for centuries to come. Damn! Where are we supposed to go this time? We have never ever had a peaceful day since we were born Arabs and Muslims in this spot. What kind of fates that don't play the nations by turns, so that we hold the breath for a decade of time? We are fed up with wars, with killings and with homelessness, we are sick of thefts, and high treasons. We became tired of insolvency, and the economic difficulty that will never be driven away. We became bored of the promising future for generations to come. When shall blessed and endowed humankind understand that the blood which runs in their veins is our blood, and our kids' blood? When shall humankind take into consideration that we are human beings the same as them, and we have the right to live, to dream, and to hope? We became tired of carrying other people burdens, we became exhausted of slavery, don't they consider it carefully and think of such consequences? When a slave gets hopeless of his master's mercy, and payback time becomes due, this very slave turns against his master and becomes a source of threat to his life, even if the slave had to bring the roof of the temple down on everybody. If this is the democracy of the west, and the equity of the east, then "forgive us if we disbelieved..".

I know how other nations complain of unemployment, of homeless people who lie down on the ground in thousands, of gangs, of drugs, of illegal immigrations, of taxes, and many others which make life so difficult, but lots of emigrants work day and night and manage to live a decent life at the end. This is all what we want! We are ready to work day and night to live and let our children live decently. We became weary of the thrown leftover from the tables of thieves, war opportunists, and pimps of countries. I was so miserable when I got on the plane, due to the scenes I saw on T.V.

I arrived at Dubai at three o'clock in the evening. Barakat was waiting for me in the arrivals hall. I handed him his fees and thanked him a great deal, he handed me the documents and farewelled me before going to Amman. Pierre called me and informed me that Sheikh *Mit'eb* will arrive in Dubai tomorrow, coming from Geneva. He asked me of what happened in London, but he sounded admonished for being in the dark side, and not being trusted at that time. I apologized to him and made him understand that I didn't know by then whom to trust. I made it clear for him that my greater concern was revealing the conspiracy, for securing the company of Sheikh Mit'eb, and keeping his name away from any prosecutions. Pierre thought highly of my efforts, and understood. I promised him to drop by in the evening, and talk to him in person. First, I thought of going to Le Fleure de Tulip to have a hot shower, and then copy all the notes and documents on a flash memory, after that I must have them printed out and attach them with the account statement in one file. When I did all this and found out that I still have enough time before meeting Suzan, I printed out my uncompleted novel to bring it before Mr. Hussein, and put it on the desk. I noticed that Suzan put a bunch of flowers in a vase, and filled in the fridge with fruits of all kinds. I put on my suit and found it appropriate to have a meal with her in a romantic place after causing her all this abrupt turning overs, thus I took the documents with me and went out.

I headed towards Festival City in Khour Dubai, and sat in the Italian "Macaroni Grill" restaurant, ordered an espresso and called Suzan..

- Hi love, your coffee is getting cold; I give you only fifteen minutes to show up, otherwise…

- You hold the time the way you hold a rein in your hand, you extend it and roll it up whenever you want.. last night you asked me to wait for you, and now you are rushing me.

- You have fourteen minutes and thirty seconds left. I am in the "Macaroni restaurant", in festival city, come on.

- Do you remember what you answered me back when you waited for me in our first date, and I asked you if I was late?

- "Wait for her".. I will, even if the seconds turned into firebrands that run in my blood and veins.

- What kind of man are you?

- The most loving one, the most patient, the most to sacrifice himself, the best of talking, and the greatest of length when it comes to living your dream.

- Definitely, that's why you are the most fatal, the most abundant in agony, and the richest of hurt. Be a normal man and let me hate you a bit, so that I can live with a neutral one normally.

- That can't do, love. Come on, your surprise is getting cold.

- Coming.., coming.

I sat there pondering at the file in my hand, investigating the dates of money transfer on one hand, and the dates of Mr. Assaf in which he was in London coming back to Dubai, as recorded in his notes on the other hand. Sheikh *Mit'eb* was disturbed by this conspiracy, he didn't have the time to celebrate his "health improvement"; I hope that he never finds out the way I conspired with Dr. Julianne on him. I started to feel sorry for all the misfortunes he is going through.

Almost half an hour passed, turning the pages, observing the notes, jotting my own marks by hand till Suzan arrived. She was wearing beautiful loose clothes to hide her pregnancy. I stood for her in respect, kissed her hand, and seated her, then I said:

- Don't even try.. "love, pregnancy, and riding a camel can't be hidden".

- So, I am exposed with two out of three. I give up.

- You are transforming into perfection in everything.

We talked about lots of things for an hour and a half while having a meal, and the most important thing we talked about was what happened in London, the way Waleed started to treat her like after pregnancy, and the dangerous revolts in the Arab countries, especially the closest to our homeland. I had a suggestion for Suzan, I explained to her that it's very important nowadays according to the present situation to think of moving to a safer place, like Canada or America. I wanted her to live in peace away from any danger or risk. While I was talking to her, I handed her the receipt of the shipping and the manifest, she took it and wanted to put it in her purse, along with her keychain which she kept flipping while talking to me, when she suddenly had a look at the keys.. and turned pale.. she started to bring out all the stuff from her purse.. then shuddered..

- What is it Suzan?

- The key!!

- What key? What are you talking about?!

- The key of your place in Rashidyah. It's missing!

- May be you put it in another key holder, or slipped it somewhere by mistake.

- No I didn't place it elsewhere, it didn't slip either, look, the rest of the keys are all here!

- When did you use it last time?

- Yesterday evening.. I went there.. put some flowers in a vase and bought some fruits too.

- Yeah, right…I noticed that.

- God! Could it be Waleed? Is it possible that he found out and knew about our affair, Zeyad? Now I get it…he got confused yesterday morning when he was looking for something in the drawers and I dashed in the room. When I asked him what was he looking for, he told me that he was looking for his old watch there. The key holder was in the same drawer. Why did he doubt me? Did he follow me? What should I do, Zeyad?

- Nothing. Calm down. Even if that was true, love I am not going to let him lay a hand on you!

Suzan was tensed and terrified like never before..

- Is there anything that leads to me, Zeyad?

- No, not really. Just your photos, your messages, and the novel that uncovers everything!

- What? God..! What should I do? Fate has dismounted its curse on us.

- Suzan!

I shouted in her face, so that she awakes from this heavy blow that came over her. The people around started looking at us, I held her hand and we both stood up while she was still under the influence of the shock. We went down to the garage and I seated her near me and said:

- Listen…we will go together now and find out whether he knew anything or not. In the worst case scenario, I know how to make him shut his mouth. I am not going to let him lay a hand on you. I swear to God if he does, I'll kill him. Now, calm down.

- What if he divorces me?

- You are pregnant, he can't divorce you. Even if he does, that will be much better, and the best thing he probably would do. Don't worry, I am here.. with you.

No sooner had we parked the car in the edifice garage of the Rashidiyah, than Suzan shouted:

- Look!! It's Waleed's car!!

I wanted to go and kill him so that she stops being terrified like this.

- Suzan.. I'll go to the apartment by my own. I've never seen you this terrified. Are you really that scared of him? Didn't you see this coming? It was just a matter of time. Go home now, and let me handle this. I swear to God I am not going to let anything bad happen to you, no matter what happens.

- You don't understand, I am not afraid of him. I just didn't want this future to my baby, and I didn't want my family to think of me as a recalcitrant woman.

I stopped a cab and asked him to take her to the address I mentioned to him, she was unaware of what she was doing. I left the file of the document in the car and went to the edifice. A big man entered the elevator with me, I didn't pay attention to his features.. I was busy thinking about Suzan and her unexpected reaction..then suddenly, I was pushed roughly to the wall, and the man pressed the button to stop its ascending. He kept pushing me with his other hand, dropping his heavy weight on me, firming my head against the reflecting metallic wall so that I don't see him clearly. I've tried to reform the enlarged vertical deformed image, looked at him in the eye, and said:

- Which of my enemies are you?

I hardly managed to utter the sentence

- Why? Are they so many? Tell me you bastard, how many times did we warn you from having the audacity to your masters? How many times did we warn you from speaking ill of them?

- Men like me have no masters, you raged bull.

He started punching me hard on my kidneys, and pushed me again to the wall.

- Who gave you the permission to write again and to criticize your lords, you idiot? Looking for money, or fame?

- Oh, you belong to those bitches. Listen you son of a bitch! I don't get paid from anybody to claim patriotism like you and the likes of you, you hear me! Tell the dogs that sent you that I will write about them and unmask their conspiracies whenever I can.

- You had your last chance, idiot. Taste what you have been promised.

He pushed me hard again to the opposite wall, then released the door and went out. I kept trying to put myself together again after all the hurting blows I had on my kidneys and my head, till I reached the floor of my suite. I walked the corridor unsteadily, the door was opened a bit, I entered…Waleed was sitting on my bed, holding the printed papers of my novel in his hands, and reading it without haste. I didn't speak to him, I stood in silence for a while, pondering at the mess he made while searching my stuff and the whole place too, then I sat.

- As usual, your novels and writings are outstanding.

- Really? I was really eager to know the selfsame perspective of yours, regarding this novel.

- We have to make certain modifications and changes first, if you want it to be a masterpiece and a best seller.

- Oh.., yeah? What modifications?

- Well, for example you can adjust the names; Rosan instead of Suzan, Jawad in place of Zeyad, and you can give the name Sa'eed in exchange for the idiot Waleed.. Why did you do this to me Jawad? I received you as a guest, and gave hospitality to you, I introduced you to my….

- Hey.., hey.. hey!!

I interrupted him with a louder voice, I was still feeling the pain all over my body..

- Don't think for a second that I feel sorry for what I did to you, don't sing the cheating friend song, because I will not deplore or mourn for you. Look at you! You should have burst forth, swooping down with punches on me, or pulled out your rifle to shoot down the one who brought you about the oppress loss, instead of making me feel sorry for you. Is this the way you defend Suzan?

- Rosan, you Judas! Rosan not Suzan.

He kept interrupting me every now and then, minding names!

- She deserves better than that, a war of attrition with knives that only takes place among real men, whom you don't belong to of course Waleed.

- Sa'eed, my name is Sa'eed you villain. Are you this much out of your mind? Why did you make me a joke between you and her? Why didn't you both get married and save us suffering? Why did you insist on slaying me like this?

- First of all, stupid and shallow men like you won't understand, and I am not in the mood to make a prolonged speech, therefore I'll condense my thoughts in the least possible words, but you need to read between the lines and catch up with me. Suzan didn't want to..

- Rosan..!

- Shut the fuck up..!! She didn't want to marry me because she didn't want us to end in a routine-like, spiritless, boring, and tepid marriage just like your own, and the rest of marriages as well. Secondly, some of freeborn sensitive and understanding women don't accept being a reason of family breakup, and they don't accept at the same time a half timed man; of half presence for a half life, therefore she kept me a husband spiritually speaking, and accepted what fates have brought her forth to fill the rest of the physical demand, assumingly. Now comes the turn of the stupid Waleed...Oh, I mean Sa'eed. Sa'eed was looking forward to get married to a beautiful graduate girl coming from a decent background and of good reputation; he wanted her to be smart, adaptable, and a follower. Su..I mean, Rosan could have forgotten me if that stupid had intimated himself with her properly. Fortunately from my perspective, and unfortunately from yours; you failed and lost ground to absorb her, faster than ever expected. Yes, you ran after that Assyrian leaving behind that angel whom you didn't estimate justly, integrating my victory by giving me the floor to obtain her love for ever. Thirdly, tell me for God's sake.. didn't you notice, or sense any of the signs or marks of such deterioration or loss? Haven't you ever asked yourself why you don't know what she likes and what she dislikes? What color does she prefer? What fruit she picks up first? Which of the names she wants for her baby? Who is her favorite poet? Which poetry she keeps reciting? Have you ever asked yourself about her dreams and ambitions, you stupid? Have you ever brought her something that impressed her? Have you asked her who of her brothers or sisters she likes best? Tell me, have you, out of curiosity or love, asked about her childhood, or requested her photos? Say something, don't remain silent like this you son of a bitch, have you or have you not asked her before to tell you what memories pleased her and what memories annoyed her of her past? Do you know what perfumes she wears? Which side of her body she likes to lie on? Do you recall her birthmarks, or her moles, or the wound on her left eyelid? Have you got any idea which of her hands she eats with and which hand she writes with? Do you know that she dreams of performing the ceremonies of Hajj, and she also wishes to attend a live concert of Fairouz? You don't even deserve to have a look at her, so don't chop logic over what things winded up with!

- What about her pregnancy, Zeyad? Is it …

I was shocked by his question and his doubt of the pregnancy, before even he finishes his talk. Why can't a man feel or sense the conception when it takes place the way a woman feels it? Why does the one who feel the pleasure of the sexual intercourse hardly pays attention to other senses?. Woman; that weird creature is led by her GPS senses that never misses a mark. Suz..an would do anything, except begetting a bastard. I still remember how I flung off my seat, grabbed his neck and pushed him hard to the wall..

- How dare you doubt her abstinence and purity, you son of a bitch! Can't you even sense whether the child is your son or not? Wish that I didn't feel her worry on her child's father if he was driven by madness and decided to leave her, I would have snatched your heart out of your chest to see if it beats like a normal one!

His face turned blue, I pushed him hard to the floor..

- Before you leave, read my lips.. I swear to God if you touch her, or hurt her, I will make you an unforgettable masterpiece in crime victims' records. Now, get the fuck out of my face…

- It's not over yet! We'll meet again Jawad.

He went out coughing and groaning like a beaten dog, I went to the bathroom and had a shower full dressed, to revive after this pile of troubles. I can't believe that our concealed secret has become exposed this fast in Dubai, after years of having it out of sight in Jordan. I can't imagine that Rosan is sitting terrified now, fearing that fool's reaction, after taking into her account a calculation of a new variable in her life. I must meet Sheikh *Mit'eb* first and sweep the leftovers of London's problem, and then I'll give all my time to that son of a bitch. Troubles always come in threes. Heaven must be laughing by now, come what may.

It was almost eight o'clock in the evening, I didn't want to stay by my own, thus I thought it proper to call Rozan and find out if she is all right before I go to meet Pierre, I promised to meet him this evening.

- Hello.., Rose, you can turn the speaker on darling, I know that the dog is standing by your side now. Listen to me love, tomorrow I will bring the problem of the work I told you about to an end, and then I'll come to dot the i's and cross the t's with that vile. I swear if he hurts you I am going to kill him.

- Please, Jawad, for God's sake calm down and stop provoking and inflaming him. He didn't hurt me, he didn't even talk to me, you are right, he is standing next to me, and he is listening to what you are saying, but I swear to you he didn't hurt me.

- Then, why do you cry? He doesn't deserve your tears. He asked me about your baby, if it's his or mine…can you believe this? Tell him in the eye that you don't accept a low father for your kid, tell him that his silence is neither a virtue of a man, nor a wisdom.

Rosan was crying her heart out, yelling on the phone, "Stop it!! Both of you". I ended the call upon her request, and sat to calm down, in spite of my wish of going to her. I started to think of what to do, Sa'eed's calmness worries me more. Is he really shocked this much? Or is he thinking carefully of what to do next? Is he trying to think of a way to cause us real and sever hurt, or is he thinking of a way to keep his face and pride before his family and his friends? Why does he make me feel that the ball is in his court now, despite of his distraction which I feel from a far distance. I've tried to turn the leaves which he had in his hands to figure out what he is acquainted with so far. I am the one who is distracted. Everything is mentioned in details..no benefit of doubts are available, nor a place for pun, or justification, or pragmatics of any kind. The pain of punches on my kidneys tolled the emergence of a new threat that messed my concentration. After the sudden leave of Mr. Assaf, I must take all the probabilities seriously into accounts, regardless of being worried thinking about Rosan, the intentions of Sa'eed, and the threat of that bull in the lift, I must write down and document everything.

.

.

.

.

Jawad met Pierre for a couple of minutes, Pierre asked about his miserable look, and the reason behind being worried, but he didn't tell him anything. He only handed him the file and headed towards my residence in Al-Nahdha. He stopped on the opposite pavement, for more than an hour, but he didn't notice anything abnormal, I saw him through the bedroom window, but I didn't let him notice me.

Later on, almost before midnight, Sa'eed dropped him a line.

- Do you know the "The Desert Addax" on the high way, between Dubai and Ein?

- I know it.

- Meet me there, one hour from now..I don't want anybody to hear what we are going to say.

- You got it.

*****

He shall be honored;
the one who dies with life scars,
He shall be freed;
the one who escapes from body's bars

~25~

Sa'eed kept crying in silence the whole way. I've tried to talk to him many times to figure out why he chose that place to meet Jawad in, but he didn't answer me. My whole body shivered of fear; I didn't know where the two maniacs are leading themselves to. Something was weird, the inversion of their parts confused me; Sa'eed, who has the right to flare up, is silent and cries in pain; Jawad, who had to absorb Sa'eed's rage and give vent to his congestion, is flared up and has turned into a tiger. The silence and darkness of the desert highway was scary with obscurity. We stopped on the roadside; Sa'eed turned the front of the car backward and let the lights on. A few minutes later, Jawad arrived and stopped his car in front of Sa'eed's and also let the lights on. Sa'eed told me to stay in the car, when both of them got out and stood in front of each other, keeping a few meters to separate them aside, they started talking:

- Then what, Jawad? What do you want now? If you think that, I'll divorce her and give her to you on a golden plate, you are wrong. I'll burn your hearts.

- It's low one's custom, I know you will not do so willingly, but for God's sake tell me something, how do you become content with marriage, knowing that your wife loves someone else? She will not accept keeping this marriage anymore under any circumstances, or staying as your slave after what happened now, she is a woman of honor, but you are tractable, timeserver and a yes-man. I'll not let you imprison her in your profane.

- What are you going to do?
- Nothing, I'll kill you if I had to.

I was listening to them talking, while breaking into tears inside the car. The sound of cars on the highway passing through so fast distorted my hearing a bit. Thus, I went out of the car and drew near to hear what they were saying..

- Jawad, I can hurt you, I can sue you in court, and put you in prison. Sheikh *Mit'eb* will not accept this black reputation for his assistant.

- Black reputation? What about your scandal you son of a bitch? What about Rosan's reputation, who is pregnant with your child, come on be wiser than that?

- That's my concern; it's none of your business.

- No Sa'eed.., you will divorce her.

- This I will not do.

- Thus, she will become a widow; I am not going to let anything put us apart from now on.

- Would you accept the same to your wife and your household?

- You really make me laugh, God how desperate you are. Aren't you ashamed of yourself, using the most common saying of yellow people with the man who won the love of your wife? Does your oriental ideology allow you of being a two timing man, craving after that Assyrian love? God, how an oriental man lives the double standards! You should have felt that you were engaged to a body of a woman, who was fond of someone else. Were you blind to be content with "Eleven Minutes" Sa'eed? Go on. Get the fuck out of my sight. You should have declared the shortcoming of your manliness, to spare me the effort of this fracas. Look down whenever you see me before you..

- You will see what wrath this frailty will bring forth upon you.

Suddenly.., a fast car passed rattling on the high way, when a buzzing sound of an explosion echoed in the desert coming from its part. I trembled and looked around me, but I couldn't see anything. I looked back again at Jawad and Sa'eed, they were not standing in their places, but instead they were lying down on the ground. I ran towards them, Sa'eed shuddered and started crawling, looking around in fear, when

Jawad remained on the ground without moving, I passed Sa'eed and ran to check Jawad, shouting his name:

- Jawad, oh no.., no..!

He was bloodstained under the beams of car lights trying to uplift his head to see me. I hugged him in shiver, belying what is happening. I laid my hand on his chest and shouted, when I saw his blood on my hand.

- Jawad.. I am here, love.. stay with me.. keep your eyes open, please stay with me.

Then I shouted at Sa'eed.

- Sa'eed please call an ambulance.. call for help.. Jawad is dying! Please..

I lifted up his head and laid it in my lap, touched his face and the tearing eyes. I was shivering and acting unconsciously..

- Please Jawad.. look at me.. don't leave me..

With great difficulty he tried to pull something out of his pocket. I helped him taking out his mobile phone and a flash memory drive. He wanted me to keep them. He grabbed my hand with a smile, shed tears that ran on his cheeks, and tried to speak.. but he couldn't, his grab loosened gradually..

- Jawad..Jawad..!!

I set about hitting his chest with my hand, shouting... I lost my mind, slapped my face and jumped in madness. I couldn't breathe, I felt that my lungs were about to explode due to inhaling in silence, before the burst of my crying in the open desert reechoed.

- Jawad..

Sa'eed tried to carry me away from him, but he couldn't. I stayed in this state, till I felt the numbness of my whole body, and was about to faint. I picked his mobile phone up.. tried to call Sheikh *Mit'eb,* my fingers let me down several times before I found his name and dialed the number. Nobody picked up the phone on the other side of the line. The last dialed call on the logs was with Pierre.

- Hello.. Jawad, hello..

I wanted to speak.. to shout.. it was as if a hand seized me by the neck, I couldn't breathe or speak out, I tried hard, till some stutter gushed forth first, then my voice became louder.

- Killed… Jawad is killed..!

- What? Who is speaking? Hello..

- Rosan.. I am Rosan.. Jawad is killed.. he is shot.. somebody shot him.

- Jawad!! Oh God, no.. Where are you?

- Somebody shot him..

I don't know what happened next.

*****

Thank you God for making his last wish come true, thank you for saving me from being dull and boring; for I had no more rabbits to pull out of my hat for him. Thank you for making me the smartest, the kindest, and the most beautiful woman in his eyes. Thank you for giving me the chance of loving him. Thank you for the good times I had with him, thank you for the difficult times I had without him. Thank you for making me live this void after him. Last but not least, thank you for the hope you bestowed upon us of being reunited in the eternal life.

~26~

I awoke from my blackout in a place I was not acquainted with. I tried to convince myself that I was asleep, and that was just a dream..no, it was a nightmare. A woman - whom I had no idea who she was - was sitting near me, and when she saw me awake, she went hurriedly shouting:

- Your Excellency.., your Excellency.., she awoke.

No sooner had Sheikh *Mit'eb* entered the suite, than I began to recall what happened, and realized that it wasn't a nightmare, but rather real. He took a few heavy steps towards me trying to put himself together, I shrank in my bed and shouted..

- Jawad..

I recalled all the details by then, and set to slap my face again. Sheikh Mit'eb cried his heart out like a baby stuttering "Oh, Jawad, my son". He hugged me, trying to stop me from hurting myself, saying:
- Calm down, my daughter.. please calm down.

- I want to see him.. I want to see him.. Please Sheikh, I want to see him. Is he dead? Is he dead tell me!!

- You will see him.. you will.. Pierre..

- Yes, your Excellency.

- Is he dead?

- Take her to see him. I also want you to send our lawyer to stand by Sa'eed, I don't want Rosan's name to be mentioned in the investigation. Don't also forget to call his brothers and inform them of what happened. They must come tomorrow as fast as possible. If they couldn't for a reason or another, I want you to take care of all necessary arrangements. Do you get it?

- Yes, your Excellency. Rosan, listen to me.. you must calm down if you want to see him.

- God!! Jawad is dead and you want me to calm down. I want to go now Pierre!

- Just calm down Rose.. I'll take you right away.

Pierre wanted to give me a shot of some kind of medication.. I snatched the injection out of his hand, threw it on the floor and smashed it under my foot until it started bleeding.

- I don't want to get a sleep..! I said I want to see him now.

- Damn it. It wasn't meant to make you asleep, but to make you calm. Listen! I swear I'll take you to see him if you calm down.

I started faking calming down, wailing in silence, till Pierre got ready after making some phone calls. Sheikh Mit'eb went out crying and closed the door behind him. I didn't believe what happened, I got myself prepared to go, straightening my clothes and adorning myself to look stunning in his eyes, the way I used to do before seeing him. I lost my mind trying to deny such tinges of flashback of what really happened. The woman I saw in the mirror wasn't me, it was someone else.. older in age, with swollen, flabby, and withered features. I went out with Pierre towards Oud Mith'a street heading for The American Hospital, Pierre was talking on the phone with some people, informing them of what happened last night, and telling them that Sheikh Mit'eb arrived in the morning and heard what happened to Jawad, and was about to collapse. I understood by then that I was unconscious for more than eighteen hours. At that time I asked Pierre:

- How did you consent to keep me away from him since yesterday? How did I arrive at Marina Resort without feeling that?

- When Sa'eed told me what happened I called the police, specified them your location, and went directly to meet them there. I arrived a few minutes ahead of them, and found you fainted near Jawad. So, when the police arrived Sa'eed narrated what exactly happened, thus they took him to the police station to give his testimony there, but later they found it proper to reserve him in custody for interrogation, that's why I brought you Marina resort to make sure that you are safe. The minute Sheikh *Mit'eb* arrived this morning and knew of what happened, he put himself together for your sake, and as a special favor to Jawad. He immediately started calling his acquaintances to stop any further investigations, so that your name won't be mentioned and the whole story is not stated. Here you are..

He handed me Jawad's mobile and his USB flash memory which Jawad gave me before he died, then Pierre said to me:

- I didn't deliver his stuff to the police, though I know such things could be of a good help in solving the crime case. I know Jawad wouldn't want me to indulge you in this bullshit even if he wanted us to find out who his killer is. Please tell me, who killed him?

He is asking me who killed Jawad..! I wish I know. I cried and shuddered every time I heard the word "killing".

- The shooters are many, but the bullet is one..Oh God, Jawad, how does a man like you have enemies?

We arrived at the hospital, I hastened my walk. At times he follows me and at other times he guides me to the morgue till we got to the ward. He asked me to wait for a minute so that he works out with the keeper to allow me seeing him. A minute later, Pierre returned back and told me:
- You've got only five minutes.

- Please, Pierre.., give us a minute, we would like to stay alone.., please.

- We? Don't scare me Rosan, please. Are you sure you want to go inside alone?

- Yes.

    Pierre stayed outside, and I entered alone that ward in silence. He was asleep on high bed, covered with a dangling white sheet that wrapped him up to his chest. He looked like an angel with two white wings under that light. I took a few steps in quietness, looking at him.

- Are you afraid of getting closer?

- Shshshsh.. don't speak my love, they say you are dead?

- What say you?

- I know you can hear me, and you can talk to me.

- For once, I guess fates treated me squarely. Our story was a maze, and phases of preposterous. Forgive me for I went away before you, and left you behind suffering alone. I wished you this peace in fact, leaving behind the hell of missing, the flame of loneliness, and the blaze of longing for me, but..

- Shshshsh.., don't feel sorry, for you are the one who chose to leave. I told you before, stop fighting the windmills, don't dare pulling out your sword before the face of the sky, don't compete with villains and wicked ones, leave alone the thieves, the politicians, and the bawds, keep away from sly and foxy ones, but you didn't listen. You insisted on being checkfated, ousted, and obliged to leave the lifeboard. You had lost rounds with fates, love. At the same time, I can't deny feeling responsible and plead guilty for your loss, for I am your "fatal woman". I wonder if that girl didn't introduce herself to you years ago, and infatuated you, like you said, would you have remained that unbelonging teacher in that miserable spot, satisfied and content with what wills may bring forth to you? Or have you been waiting for me to break away from your orbits, causing all this pandemonium? Now, I feel guilty and bereaved for your loss before your family, traitor in the eyes of Sa'eed... fatal and recalcitrant in the eyes of Sheikh Mit'b and Pierre. In spite of this, have a look at yourself Jawad.. look at this smile of yours, and the apparent peace on your face. I've never experienced you this calm except when you awake and sit firmly on, after every time your body and soul overflow cuddling and hugging me. What is death like, love? Does it look like me this much? Does it have the same tenderness of mine? Does it lengthen the time of your rapture more than I used to do? Are you safer and more comfortable in deaths' hand now? I used to tell myself, since I got to know you, that his soul is too big to be imprisoned in this body! Is it why they say *"Fadhat Al-Rou'h"*, to mean the spirit flowed over the body? Can't the storming spirit of yours be handled by the boat of your flesh? Verily, I envy death for having you for good.. I rather envy death as it stole you from me, in fact I consider it a fellow wife. You have to treat us both with justice, love. I don't know how, but you were capable of running away from your commitments and orbits when I needed you before.. Look! Even the fellow wife couldn't erase me off your chest! Those remains and scars of my bites insist on your association. Oh, Jawad God how I love you.. God, how I hate you. Can't you see that you have taken me to faraway lands, to heaven, and to fairy tales on clouds, and prohibited me this bliss by your sudden leave? You have planted me in the comfort of passionate love till I got quenched, sowed me in the heaven of dreams till I got budded, cropped me in the immortal devotion till I brought about violet pledges. You sheltered me from the fangs of life and made me experience the peace in a safe place, moreover you drew off the magic carpet from beneath by your leave, and made me fall in the sea of oaths, the nights of loyalty, and the traps of comparisons that don't show mercy, but rather flashback and restores memories in bitterness. Look at me Jawad.. look at me.. I've grown old, withered, and all the leaves of my life dried up and fell down after only one night of your leave. Get up and shake the death off.. look what happened to the woman you love..!

- That's enough Rosan..

- Leave me alone, I want to know who gave him the right to leave me behind like this and go away? He turned me into an orphan… he made me a widow.. he caused me to lose everything… he disregarded me… I became a leaf in windward…

- Come on, I said enough.

- No.. I don't want to go.. I don't want this life anymore. I want to stay with him, I want him to wake up. Let me slap him..he will speak, please

Pierre.. I can hear him.. I am the one who can hear him when he doesn't even speak.. please leave me alone..!

It was the disastrous moment that I will never forget in my life, Pierre pulled me out with the help of the guard; they took me to the emergency room where nurses rushed madly upon me. Some grabbed me while one worked on giving me an injection. I weltered among their hands as if I was haunted with a devil, till they offered me a chance of meeting him.. there..

He was with huge wings flying up and swimming in the sky.. smiling in happiness.. looking at me.. coming towards me ..till he got nearer and took me by hand. Suddenly I felt I could fly and turned into a creature of lights with wonderful wings too.. the gusts of winds bantered with me and lifted me up like a tremendous wave.. taking me faraway.

*****

"Under the wide and starry sky,
Dig the grave and let me lie.
Glad did I live and gladly die,
And I laid me down with a will.
This be the verse you grave for me:
Here he lies where he longed to be;
Home is the sailor, home from sea.
And the hunter home from the hill."

Robert Louis Stevenson

~27~

I awoke next day morning, finding myself in the resort. Shiekh *Mit'eb*, Pierre and a woman were sitting around the bed.

- Thank God, you are back again.. we've been sick worried the whole night about you, daughter. Would you please eat something, you must keep your strength. Tomorrow we are all flying to Jordan, and you are pregnant, so you must take care of yourself. Jawad's brothers arrived and we've got everything prepared to take him back home. May be it's not the right time to talk to you about this, but because you are getting back to Jordan, and I am not sure what do you intend to do later on, I have to inform you with something.. Pierre..

Pierre handed Sheikh Mit'eb a file. I hardly could open my swollen eyes..

- One day Jawad and I exchanged and discussed our wills, so that we leave no confusion to the ones who come after us, like the confusion we experienced when Assaf passed away..

Sheikh Mit'eb kept his eyes down, trying to hide his tears..
- In this file, you will find Jawad's will with regard to you. It has an apartment title deed by your name in Irbid. He told me that it is well equipped and supplied with everything so that you need no help what so

267

ever, if ever something happened to him. As if he felt that his journey came to its end. He also left you a teaching and educational center title deed, so that you be in charge of. He was so worried about you all the time. I've never seen a decent man like him before. He opened a bank account for you and left you a fair amount of money. When I asked him about his will to his kids and wife, he told me that, "They will become your family and your kids by then, I trust you..".

I cried in silence after hearing that will of Jawad. My eyes burnt with every tear that slipped out on my cheeks. This is Jawad.. he claimed that I was the one who kept surprising him.. when in fact, he was the one who surprised my life, even after his leave. He did that three times till the now moment; when his last wish came true and died smiling in my lap, when he left me this will, which saves my face in this ordeal, and when I read his novel, where he gave lasting fame and immortalized me with golden lines.

Sheikh *Mit'eb* and Pierre spent the whole night talking before me, trying to solve the puzzle and figure out who the criminal would be. When Pierre read all the memos, which Jawad wrote on the file he handed to him, Sheikh Mit'eb and Pierre placed their doubts in three suspects; Salman and Ranan on one side, after revealing their conspiracy. Security force agent, or a mercenary on the other side; after publishing his writings. Sa'eed; as a third suspect, when he chose that place in specific. Yes, they were right. All of them had their motives to get rid of Jawad. Sheikh Mit'eb told me that the police will release Sa'eed for not having enough evidence to convict him of, after all the efforts the lawyers spent, by the instruction and insinuation of Sheikh *Mit'eb* himself. I asked Pierre to do everything he could, so that I don't see Sa'eed from now on; a decision which he warmly welcomed. After that Sheikh Mit'eb and Pierre headed to see Jawads' brothers to back them up and lift up their spirits. Sheikh Mit'eb wanted them to understand that he will keep his promise and will never abandon his liability towards his wife and kids.

I sat in the back terrace of the resort; the one with the sea view, hearing Jawad's voice roaring through the sea waves, calling me:

- "It's not death that subdues us most, it's rather the parting and the separation. The late conjuration and resurrecting, is possible if we overcome life partition".

"I don't believe in the severance between the two worlds, each one sends messages to the other. We only need to decode the cipher telegram and get over the bordered senses to become aware of".

"I don't want you to live after me, just hold your breath and swim towards me".

"Recite me day and night like your prayers, put me on like your elegant shawl, embrace me like your favorite perfume.. or as your childish memories and properties under your pillow. I will always be there for you.. you will see me in sunshine guts…in moonlight grief.. in love popple.. in slight breeze of love around you..I am the summer in your awakening and winter in your sleep, vivacious April runs in my blood, Oh Suzan, my soul flies all around you, I can see you, hear you, and speak to you if you listen carefully, call me anytime you wish, I don't become weary of you, or become bored of listening to you, or even tire of talking to you. I promised you to be conjured up before you, till we meet again.. I promised you Suzan, and my promise is a decision that will be carried out".

- Rosan.. Rosan.. come on, get up my child.. you need to get some sleep before sunlight.

I went to his private suite, delving into his stuff.. blankets, bed sheets, clothes, looking for leftover threads of his smell, the last of his touching, and the remaining reflection of his face in the mirrors.. wish that everything can be brought to life and speak out, so as to inquire about missing moments too..

Next morning everybody headed towards the airport when it was time, they all gathered in the business pavilion by orders of Sheikh Mit'eb, and then boarded in first class cabinet. His brothers were still shocked, and in utmost grief. They didn't even talk to each other throughout the whole flight. They were introduced to Sheikh Mit'eb, Pierre, and the rest of the men before, that's why they didn't pay attention to them at the time, but they looked skeptic when they saw me pale in black with swollen eyes and talking to Pierre from time to time. Sheikh *Mit'eb* wore his black big sunglasses and became completely absentminded, trying to hide his tears. Pierre was heartbroken, but kept checking out Sheikh Mit'eb every now and then. No sooner had we arrived and started getting off, than his family ran to carry the casket. It looked like a parade of love, welcoming him back. There were large gathering of people and cars out, diadems of flowers, men wearing black suits. When the cars arrived in Irbid and parked near the house after an hour and a half to see him for the last time, the men stood in line and started entering gradually. Twenty minute later, they carried him on shoulders to the mosque near. When they finished the prayer after that, they went back again to their cars and followed the "last ride" car to *Bushrah*, where his final resting place is. After that I went to my family house and spent the night there, waiting for the morning to visit him with the eagerness of a lover in her first date.

Here we are, love, alone like you always wanted and wished. You asked me to be the last one to see you, and it's done. You wanted me to be the last one to leave you, and it will be. You wished that my staying wouldn't take that long after your leave, and here I am praying to God that you won't wait for long again... I don't know if my writing ribbed the shoulder with your style of writing, but I just wanted to finish up what you started. Some sorrows and grieves can't be put into words. When one starts with the best, one surely lives shorter. I started my life with you, and it won't take long..

- May he rest in peace, madam. Stop crying, please. You have been here since the morning.

- I want you to take care of the grave. Please plant some flowers too, I will make regular visits..

- All people say that, but no one comes back. Life is cruel..

- I said, I will make regular visits... just take care of the grave.

- Anything you say, lady.

I wanted someone to embrace me without asking me about anything. My appetite to cry the rest of my life out was voracious. I wanted to disappear from the sight, wait for the will of the heaven to release me from the colorless waste world. I went back to my mother's lap.. shrunk like a baby. She hugged me long, without asking me what has happened unless I talk to her. I stayed there for almost a month, never went out.. except when I visited Jawad every Friday. I informed my family that I am getting a divorce the minute I deliver the baby. The political situation was intensifying to the worse in the country, and in the whole region as well. Everything around was warning of serious corruption, sectarian and civil war, and a beginning of the end, especially after indulging the country deliberately in a regional war. Clashes and fighting on the borders were already taking place. We could see plane lands of *Houran* burning in the skyline. The sounds of the bombs were so close, and the noise of the fighting planes breaking the sound barrier every now and then kept us on the alert for the worst. All this didn't stop the people from living and doing their usual stuff, at least to supply their kids and families with the basic demands. I didn't find anything to do, by the time, for the circumstances taking place, thus I stayed at home and postponed checking out the teaching center which Jawad left me. One day a thought of checking out the apartment crossed my mind. Jawad chose it to be in the *Naseem* district; overlooking *Al- Rabiyah* café where we dated tens of times. I went there, in the back of the religious courts, in *Secrets* building, second floor. His picky touches were waiting for me even before getting in. The outside door was made of antiquated wood, and grafted with captivating ancient antique ornaments. No sooner had I entered the apartment than I burst out crying, as if I have just lost him. He left me all his belongings and possessions there. His cup of coffee, his clothes, his bottles of perfume, his writings, his laptop, and of course his lute. Who brought all these things here? Is it Pierre, or Sheikh Mit'eb? Why did they bring forth his possessions to me, not to his family? Did he write this in his will too, or they want me to remember him forever? Are these things what will make me remember such a lover? Do they think that by the course of time I will forget the one whom my womanhood blossomed and brightened by his hands? Decent women do disdain love and lovers, but live bereaved the missing love they had once. I will burn my soul as once Jawad wrote about *Sati* tribe women, and remain a loose mare in the wild till I die.., and meet you to run together for ever after.

I inspected his clothes and things carefully, and folded them in his wardrobe. I remembered what he wrote about emptying his father's closet after passing away, as if the bereaved want to get rid of everything that would remind them of the dead. Your closet will never be emptied, Jawad.

I felt so much comfort crying alone in that apartment, I lied down on the sofa in the living room hugging Jawad's jacket, becoming absentminded.., when suddenly I felt the first kicks of the baby growing inside of me....

*****

The End